SISTERS

OF THE

PERILOUS HEART

MAP OF KEPLER
THE ATLANTIS OCEAN
NEW PARIS
WEST COAST SHORES
FORMER WESTERN REPUBLIC
MORKUM
GALILEO FIELDS
IMMORTAL EMPIRE
SOUTHERN KINGDOM
N
W
E
S
THE MEDICI OCEAN

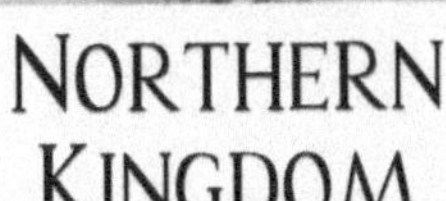

THE ASIMOV STRAITS
NORTHERN KINGDOM
CERULEAN
SILVER ORCHID
MOUNTAIN OF PERIL
SEA OF DAO
SLED LODGE
NEW AMERICA
WATERTON
EASTERN RIDGE TRAIL
GREAT CRATER LAKE
SHADOW OF THE MOUNTAINS
BUS STOP
EASTERN DESERT
GANDHI
X
FIRST MEETING
CLEMSON
GUARNERI
NATIVE VALLEY
FORMER EASTERN CONFEDERATION
SECOND ATTACK
NOVI DUPREE
ALIGHIERI
CAPE GREGORY
JOURNEYS TAKEN BY CARINA AND QUEEN VIVIAN
THE AURELIAN GULF

SISTERS

OF THE

PERILOUS

HEART

SANDRA L. VASHER

MORTAL
INK PRESS

Library of Congress Control Number: 2019919924

ISBN 978-1-950989-01-0 (paperback)

ISBN 978-1-393850-79-3 (ebook)

Cover design copyright © 2019 by Jennifer Zemanek / Seedlings Design Studio.

To my parents, who read this cover-to-cover at least twice, and to my husband, who probably won't ever read it cover-to-cover because he had to listen to every scene at least four times.

M. KAYES FINAL MISSION LOG

The worst part of the trip was the last five minutes before Earth disappeared. I watched it become smaller than the pinprick on my finger, where a needle had tacked through my skin that morning before launch for a blood sample. I was scheduled to give another in ten days. The ship would have 109,378 samples in its database before I arrived at my destination: the planet Kepler.

As home faded, I indulged one more time—and I told myself it would be the last—in imagining *her* on that pinprick of a planet. It was her birthday. Perhaps she was wearing my last gift right then—a delicate, rose gold, self-winding perpetual watch with a leather band she might have to replace once or twice in her lifetime.

She was twenty-six that day. I was twenty-seven. But I didn't wear a watch. I was Immortal. Unless I managed to die of an unnatural cause, I would maintain something close to my current physical state forever.

If she had gone through with her promise, forever would

have been with her. Now, she would be dead before I was even a tenth of the way into my journey.

The betrayal *still* stings.

"Myles Alexander, stop! You can't dwell on the past. It's already gone."

I looked away from the speck of Earth to see Lizzy Dupree behind my shoulder, smiling at me with bright, optimistic eyes that I'd never seen turn red. Immortality was possible thanks to the Immortality Virus, an engineered strain of influenza. No one could be cured, but the upside of survival was attractive and the fatality rate low. A stress reaction that increased blood flow to the retina, rapidly blew out your pupils, and made your eyes change color was a minor downside.

"Please, Myles. Your eyes are red."

I was alone on this mission. Lizzy was not. She was here with her sister, Anna, who had already told me—bluntly and without solicitation—that the two timelessly beautiful women had sworn off love for good. "Because it ruined our parents," is what Anna said, a day into our training program. Lizzy found me later, though, told me she thought it was too soon in our Immortal lives to swear off any vice, and kissed me to prove the point.

I told her I was in love with someone else. I never wanted to hurt anyone the way *she* had hurt me. Lizzy only said, "But this isn't love, Myles. This is distraction."

Then she kissed me again.

I suspected that day—and I still believe—that if I ever fell for Lizzy, it would be in an excruciatingly damaging way. Thankfully, she had good intuition for when I might not be up for distraction. She did not kiss me as I stared back at Earth.

"I came to tell you the meeting's going to start

soon." She leaned casually against the wall of the ship.

"They want to start planning."

"Seems early for that," I said.

"Right?!" she exclaimed. "We have three-thousand years to figure out how to take over the planet. I voted to start the meeting with a hundred-year ice breaker."

I wondered what Lizzy Dupree's idea of an ice breaker might be.

"Oh good, your eyes are blue again." She looped her arm around mine and pulled me away from the window. "You're much cuter this way.

"How's your sister?" I asked.

"Do you have siblings?"

I shook my head.

She laughed heartily and patted my arm. "Let's just say she's hard to explain."

This is the story of what happened 4,194 Earth Years later, on the planet Kepler. It is not my story, though I was more tangled up in it than I wanted to be before I returned to Earth, in a ship packed with several crates of sassafras beer and a note from a very old queen that said, "Thank you for your service. Farewell until we meet again."

Mortals.

~Myles Alexander Kayes

A POEM FROM *THE COLLECTED WORKS OF ANNA DUPREE*

We do not speak
—anymore—
of the dreams and schemes we planned
before we knew
trouble.

(And our troubles are not the same.)

We digressed idly in guileless youth;
now we diverge on separate paths,
believing in struggle, waving our flags
—alone! I am alone! do not come to help!—
as proof of our bravery.

(You are not she who needs a friend.
I am not her, the indebted one.)

But I knew you when you were
a spark of magic,
a wisp of light,
an endless possibility,
when you wanted everything for me
and I asked you to be wise,
when I wanted everything for you
and you asked me to be free.

(We trusted each other.)

Now we sail our ships
in the currents of a stranger's whim.
I see your banner,
you see mine.
We are in the same treacherous depths,
the same boiling sea.

(We cannot speak across the waters, dear,
nor scream against the wind.)

Yet you are there,
I am here, and
—somehow—
that is enough, together.

When distance keeps us apart,
we remain sisters of the perilous heart.

THE FRONT PAGE OF
THE ALIGHIERI POST

THE ALIGHIERI POST

Wednesday, August 6, 881 AAH

CORONATION ANNOUNCEMENT

Hear all you Mortal citizens of Kepler: let it be known that on this, the sixth morning in the eighth month of the eight-hundred-and-eighty-first year After Arrival of Humans,

PRINCESS VIVIAN ELIZA ANDREA WELLINGTON

Heir to the Throne of the Southern Kingdom of Kepler shall be crowned the fifteenth

QUEEN OF THE SOUTHERN KINGDOM OF KEPLER,

which Kingdom extends from the West Coast to the Eastern Ridge Trail, North to the icecaps, and South from the Galileo Fields to Cape Gregory at the furthest reaches of the Aurelian Gulf.

The coronation ceremony, scheduled to take place, as per custom, immediately after the Dawn Prayers, shall precede the Parade of the Red Leopard. All citizens are invited to greet the newly ascended monarch as she takes her first steps as Queen through Alighieri, Capital City of South Kepler.

God save the Crown.

CHAPTER ONE
THE ASSASSINATION

The queen of South Kepler was dying, and not in a metaphorical way. Queen Vivian could feel blood seeping through her silk corset. A long arrow stuck out from her chest. She watched it wobble from the place where it'd pierced her heart.

Queen for two minutes. That's how long she'd lasted. Two minutes ago, she'd been dripping sweat in the stifling summer heat of the Royal Cathedral of Alighieri, wondering if she could ask someone to open a window before she recited the Coronation Oath. She'd sipped water from the Cup of Truth, and the officiant had given her the words she needed to dizzily promise her life for her kingdom as she focused on Not Passing Out. Then came the arrow.

It didn't matter now what she'd promised.

Vivian pitched sideways. The trumpeters, celebrating the end of an early morning ceremony, didn't notice. Her mother, standing next to her, failed to reach out. Vivian could only hear a single yell above the jubilant march.

Bastian.

She'd never heard him yell like that.

From where she landed on the elevated dais of the cathedral's apse, she could see Bast leap forward, leaving Nate behind in the front row of the nave, standing uncharacteristically still. The guests in the second row had caught on, and their screams were contagious, spreading terror while the royal guards sprang into action.

"Viv."

She opened her eyes. She hadn't known they were shut. The voice had sounded distant, but Bast and Nate were both crouched right beside her. She feebly grasped the air above her, found the wood arrow and followed it down to wet fabric. Her lungs felt like they were being torn from the inside walls of her chest. Needles stabbed through her hands and feet. Her brothers were saying things she couldn't hear. She coughed, splattering bright blood across their faces and into their dark blond hair.

More arrows whizzed above them, and Vivian wondered why time had decided to slow now, as the agony of death seized her. Someone tumbled down, landing with a hard thud, but Vivian couldn't see who it was. The officiant maybe? A guard sweeping in belatedly to protect the new queen? Her mother, the queen consort?

"Immortal assassins! Guards, capture them!"

Not her mother, then.

Queen Constance's powerful voice echoed through the cathedral. She was untouchable. While Bast and Nate tried to help Vivian, Mom stood with deadly poise commanding the royal guards to eliminate the Immortals responsible for Vivian's near-complete assassination. Too bad Dad hadn't had the same talent for self-preservation, but King Herschel had been dead for three years and sick for much longer.

Queen Constance turned her head briefly toward her children and caught her daughter's eye. A fresh chill crawled through Vivian. Mom had worn her thin-lipped smile, stained with red contempt, to the coronation ceremony. Vivian couldn't tell if she had taken it off yet; that smile wasn't all that different from a frown.

Mom shifted her gaze to the boys. She loved Bast as much as a woman like Constance could love anyone, but Mom had always regarded Vivian with suffering indifference at best and jealousy at worst. She barely acknowledged Nate as her son at all.

Poor Nate. He'd have it rough now that his turn was up. It was a curse that sixteen-year-old Nate was a year older than Bast. Nate was hot-headed, clumsy, impulsive, dull. A general disappointment. Bast took after Mom. He was brilliant, calculating, confident, cruel at times—the family prodigy without any doubt.

The boys looked a lot alike, though.

Before her father died, King Herschel had confessed to Vivian that he was glad she was born first. He thought it was a blessing for the kingdom that she would be queen. "The pressure wouldn't have gotten to Bastian either. But Nate ..." He didn't have to finish for Vivian to know what he meant.

Vivian favored Bast to Nate for company herself— she couldn't have an in-depth conversation about anything important with Nate—but she, at least, cared about them both. There was only a year and a half to go before Nate would be old enough for a coronation ceremony, and from the look on his face now, she thought he might already know he was in trouble. She wondered if Bast would try to help him.

If Vivian had been capable of more than a tormented,

shallow breath, she would have sighed. She had a complicated family.

"I told you to put pressure on it!" Bast yelled, pushing
Nate aside completely and pressing his hands down on
Vivian's chest. Bast's voice shook her from her haze. "Put
your hands there … no, Nate, *there*, and do what you would
do if you were warming something up."

Nate followed instructions, and Vivian had the strange
sensation of warm, magical energy flowing over her skin
from Nate at the same time she felt Bast's cool energy circu-
lating through her blood. Bast cursed and began a soft chant.
Nate's eyes shifted nervously, but he joined in. Though their
voices were low and muted by the chaos, she recognized
the prayer. Maybe she was already gone. Praying was not on
Vivian's list of things she thought her brothers would try
together to save her life.

"It's 'Holy Spirit peaceful *be*' not 'Holy Spirit peace to
me,' you moron!" Bast yelped. "You're not asking for peace
for *yourself*!"

Or maybe she was still alive. Though she did feel
nauseous and sort of light. Bitter saliva was pooling in her
throat. It seemed unlikely that either magic or prayer could
save her. Mom would be pleased to have her title back, but
what a lousy eighteenth birthday. Vivian had preferred being
seventeen and a princess. She'd also preferred having a father
who was living. You didn't always get what you wanted. Her
mother gave her a single, last, nearly emotionless glance as
Vivian shut her eyes and slipped into the darkness again.

Something her dad told her before he died came
back to her. She'd complained that it wasn't fair he
was dying. He'd said: *"Life is a death sentence for all of
us, Vivian. The only question is how long your sentence is."*

So. Her sentence had been precisely eighteen years.

"NO!" Bast roared.

Vivian's world blackened …

… and then brightened. She opened her eyes.

Something was wrong.

Her head felt fuller and heavier than she thought it should for a dead person. The arrow was gone, but her chest still throbbed with pain. She was breathing. Her brothers were lifting her up between them, her arms draped over their shoulders.

"We have to get out of here," Nate was saying.

"You think I don't *know* that?" Bast answered. "Viv, can you walk?"

She nodded weakly and started moving forward, trying to ignore their painful grips. They passed the officiant lying by the altar. Dead, probably.

"Where are we going?" Nate asked. Clueless as always. How did he know so little? Vivian knew where they were going as they moved swiftly from the dais to the prayer chapel at the side of the apse. Bast opened the door to the chapel and shut it hard once they were inside. Filtered light from a stained-glass window illuminated an ancient tapestry hanging behind a prayer rug on the back wall.

"Don't you know *anything*?" Bast pointed at the tapestry. "There's a door there."

"A door?"

"*Yes*, stupid, a door."

"Why?"

Bast flicked his hand, and the tapestry rolled neatly up, revealing the hidden door. "This is the *Royal* Cathedral, Nate. It's there in case the royal family—that's us if you didn't know—needs to get out fast."

"I *know* we're the royal family!"

They squeezed through the door together. Vivian was having trouble finding her feet, and she thought she was about to collapse or vomit. She wondered if the boys would be strong enough to keep her upright.

"I cannot believe you are in line before I am," Bast muttered, closing the hidden door behind them. As it shut, they were consumed by a light-less void.

"Whoa," Nate said. "It's really dark."

"Yeah, *fire*, Nate," Bast ordered. "This would be a good time for you to be useful."

"Oh." A splash of flames rose in the dark from Nate's hand. The fire seemed like it could dance off his fingertips and out of control any second. Vivian wanted to tell him to stop and say she could do it instead, but she didn't think she could.

"Light switch," Bast said, nodding to the wall and flipping the switch telekinetically. Dim overhead lights crackled to life and Vivian was relieved when Nate doused the flames.

"There will be royal guards on the other side," Bast told them.

"How do you know that?" Nate asked.

"I just do."

"Why do *you* know everything? No one tells *me* anything."

"Viv doesn't need to be told anything."

That was true. She'd had a foreboding sense of doom about the coronation for weeks now, and given what had happened, she wouldn't have been surprised if Mom had somehow had a hand in allowing Immortals to infiltrate the crowd at the coronation ceremony. Mom might even have had a conversation with Bast about the possibility beforehand. She'd have done it casually. Something like: "Oh, Bast, dear, don't forget about the escape tunnels. This is a high-profile event. You never know what might happen. I'll put guards at all the exits."

Bast wouldn't have thought twice about why she was reminding him. He'd have taken for granted that those were standard precautions. It would never have occurred to him that Mom had come up with a way to get her favorite child out of a bloodbath she was orchestrating.

A muffled crash alerted them to someone entering the chapel behind them. Several someones, from what they could hear. Probably the assassins. It sounded like they were tearing up the chapel trying to figure out where she, Bast, and Nate had gone. It would only be a matter of seconds before the hidden door was found.

Bast frowned. "We need to seal that thing up."

Vivian tried to step away from her brothers. Bast was right. They needed to close off that part of the tunnel. She would have to do it. Nate couldn't be trusted with magic like that. He'd accidentally kill them all trying to do it.

Her brothers held her back. "Not *you*, Viv," Bast said.

"I can do it," Nate offered.

Vivian tensed up. "I can," she tried to say, but there was phlegm in her throat that still tasted like blood, and her voice would only come out as a choked rasp.

Bast waved his hand impatiently. "No, you *can't*." He looked sternly at Nate. "And we need to seal it anyway, not blow it up, or we could risk damage to the Royal Cathedral. I'll handle this."

He let go of Vivian and went back a few steps. They heard someone say: "found it," but Bast had already gone to work jamming the door with ice. Vivian could feel the cold on her skin even with Nate right next to her. When whoever was behind the door tried to open it, it wouldn't budge.

Bast jogged back to her and Nate while the assassins began pounding the door. "There." He picked up Vivian's arm again, now with cold hands.

"Doesn't sound very sealed," Nate said as they all flinched at a loud yell on the other side.

Vivian agreed. "Bast, you should let me—"

Bast growled in frustration and yanked her and Nate forward. "What part of 'no' don't you understand?"

Vivian struggled against him. "The part where *I'm* the queen!"

He dropped her arm again, turned to face her, and jabbed his finger toward her heart.

"What do you think happened there?" Bast demanded.

Vivian stood still. "I was shot," she said slowly.

"Correct. And why did you almost die?"

She was confused. "I was *shot*. But you healed it, and—"

"*In*correct." He rubbed the vein that stuck out by his left temple when he was upset.

The word made her feel unsteady. "Meaning I *wasn't* shot? But I thought ..."

"No, you were shot for sure," Nate said. "But that's not why you almost died. Bast thinks the water in the Cup of Truth was poisoned."

Bast rubbed the vein harder. "Not poisoned. *Infected.* With some strain of the Immortality Virus. And I *don't* think it was in the water. The Immortality Virus usually spreads through blood. It was probably on the arrow."

Vivian put her hand on her chest. Her heart was beating, wasn't it? But Immortals had beating hearts, too. "Am I ...?"

"Your body isn't compatible with the virus, Viv. It's not going to make you Immortal." Bast stuck his hands in his pockets and shook his head at the ground. "It's faster than any strain of the Immortality Virus I'm familiar with. It infected your entire system in a few minutes. That's why you were coughing up so much blood. You should be dead. You *would* be dead except for magic. It's the only thing keeping whatever's in you now from destroying you. And even with magic from all three of us, I can only slow the virus down."

She stared at him, trying to understand.

He ran the back of his hand over his forehead and closed his eyes for a second before he opened them and looked fiercely at her. "Look, we'll figure out what to do. We'll get help. We'll find more magic. But we're barely keeping you alive. If you try to use magic—*any* magic, Viv—it might kill you. Understand?"

Someone was still trying to break down the door. Bast went back to add another layer of ice. Vivian hoped he was creating a secure enough seal. She couldn't really think any more about that, though. To tell the truth, she had other things to worry about.

The queen of South Kepler was dying after all.

EXCERPT FROM *THE GANDHI MEDICAL CENTER DISEASE TREATISE, 2ND ED.*

Section III, Viruses.

Chapter 5, The Immortality Virus.

General.

Discovered on Earth by cancer researchers in the 21st century, the Immortality Virus (IV-933) is a highly engineered hybrid virus combining elements of human immunodeficiency virus with influenza. IV-933 is transmitted sexually and via blood. A child born from an Immortal mother has a forty percent chance of being infected with IV-933 from birth and will otherwise be Mortal. It is possible for IV-933 to pass via contact with respiratory droplets, but such transmission is rare for anyone who has already been exposed to another strain of influenza.

Symptoms of IV-933 typically begin five days after exposure and commonly include congestion, coughing, body aches, nausea, and fatigue. In advanced cases, difficulty breathing, fever, confusion, and hallucination are sometimes reported.

Assuming a baseline level of resistance to influenza,

IV-933 has a fatality rate of 1 in 10000. Without such baseline resistance, IV-933 has a fatality rate of 1 in 5. Survivors experience various changes to their physiology, including most dramatically a decline in the natural aging process such as to make them effectively "immortal." Additionally, IV-933 remains in the body and has both immediate and delayed impacts, including:

- Structural alteration of the anterior insular cortex, resulting in heightened self-awareness, increased ability to sense temperature, decreased ability to regulate blood pressure and heart rate, and high sensitivity to emotion (i.e., emotional experiences may seem painfully intense);
- Broken blood vessels in the sclera, accompanied by eye itching and irritability, sensitivity to light, vision loss, headaches, and dizziness;
- Hormonal changes that may result in episodes of mania, anxiety, and depression, and are also responsible for drastic changes in eye pigmentation, which, in combination with the above, frequently make the eyes appear red or pink; and
- Gradual frontal lobe atrophy commonly resulting in an inability to express appropriate emotional responses to a situation, as well as decreased executive functioning, such as long-term planning, judgment, decision-making skills, attention span, and inhibition.

As no other influenza virus exists on Kepler, IV-933 is highly dangerous for Keplerian Mortals. The GMC highly recommends vaccination treatment for Mortal infants, followed by booster shots for teenagers and the elderly. Vaccination will not prevent transmission of IV-933 via blood or sexual contact but will normally provide enough exposure/

resistance to the virus to prevent transmission by contact with respiratory droplets and may reduce the likeliness of a fatal outcome. Mortals with magic are particularly susceptible to IV-933 and should receive booster shots every ten years. Mortals born from Immortal parents are not less susceptible to IV-933 and should also be vaccinated.

CHAPTER TWO
THE GIFTS OF MAGIC

Vivian was well-suited for royalty. She had high-end tastes, but she was willing to get her hands dirty when necessary. She had a healthy complexion and thick golden hair that her attendants could blow into loose curls or twist up into structured designs. She was beautiful, but not precious. She looked fit in well-cut jeans and powerful in expensive designer gowns.

She was intelligent, fair, and not too kind. She thrived at the center of attention, and she thirsted for control. She didn't want power necessarily—she really wouldn't have chosen to be queen—but she craved order. She was making plans for her kingdom.

And she was *not* well-suited to lay control of her own physical well-being at the feet of her younger brothers.

She tripped over a place where the packed dirt of the escape tunnel floor dipped. Bast and Nate steadied her with fast, tight grips. They were "letting" her walk between them with "minimal" assistance because she'd ordered them to.

They'd wanted to carry her through the tunnels telekinetically.

"I feel like a prisoner," she complained.

"You look like a zombie queen," Nate said.

"Little early for that, Nate." Bast shook his head with disapproval. "I think we're almost directly under the castle now. This tunnel can't be much longer."

Nate craned his neck to look around as they walked. "I can't tell any difference. What makes you think that?"

"I'm observant," Bast said arrogantly. "And it smells like mold and excrement here. We have to be near the castle dungeons."

Nate sniffed the air and made a retching noise. "Why do we have something in the castle that smells like that?"

"To give you incentive to stay on Viv's good side."

"Viv's not going to throw me into the dungeons."

"She could."

"She won't."

"But she could."

"Maybe she'll throw you in instead."

They were fifteen and sixteen. Did your brothers *ever* get old enough not to sound like squabbling toddlers all the time? Vivian stopped to catch her breath again. "That's enough." She gasped for air. "I'm not throwing anyone into the dungeons."

"Take it easy," Bast said. "We can slow down if you want."

"Yeah," Nate scoffed. "Except we could easily be ambushed down here, so we can't slow down too much."

Bast scowled at Nate. "You. Are. A. Complete. Idiot."

Nate scowled back at Bast. "At least. I'm not. A liar."

"*I'm* not a liar!" Bast shouted.

Vivian still hadn't caught her breath. "Let's just keep going." She could smell the stench of the dungeons, too.

She forced herself forward.

A few minutes later, the tunnel opened directly into a large shelter area with poured concrete walls, iron support beams, and a high ceiling. A company of what looked like twenty or so royal guards was already there waiting.

Vivian didn't recognize any of them. Her gut clenched.

South Kepler's military was formally called the Southern Kingdom of Kepler Armed Guard Forces, but it was referred to casually as "the Southern Guard." The Royal Guard of South Kepler was a special branch, selected by the reigning South Kepler monarch to guard the royal family.

When her father had been alive, Vivian had known and was even friends with most of the royal guards, along with most of the castle staff and attendants. But the king's death was caused by a slow-moving strain of the Immortality Virus, and no one knew how he'd been infected. After he died and Vivian's mother took over as queen consort, nearly all the royal guards and the entire staff that had served the royal family were dismissed overnight. Presumably, the Immortal Empire was behind the king's death, but Queen Constance said no one could be trusted. Only her own inner circle of guards and attendants—those that she knew were loyal to her—stayed.

The person Vivian didn't trust was Queen Constance. She had seen the connection between her mother and her father change. It was one of her gifts. She could physically see connections between people in colors that gave her an intuitive sense of their relationship. The connection between her parents had been a dirty-dishwater gray before, no love or hate or really *any* emotion but ill-tolerance for each other for years. The year her father got sick, the connection turned the thrashing red of rage and violence.

She couldn't prove anything—her gift wasn't precise enough for that—and it would have been impossible to make the accusation anyway. But Vivian *knew* her mother was somehow behind her father's death. She knew it as sure as she'd known she was in trouble herself when the last wisp of orange—the color of the bond between family—burned out between her and Mom. After that, all Vivian could ever see between them was neon green jealousy crawling around a blood-red line that grew thicker over time.

Maybe Mom had invited the Immortal assassins to the coronation.

Maybe Mom was experimenting with the Immortality Virus.

"Your Highness." One of the unfamiliar guards approached and bowed his head briefly to Vivian. "I'm Captain Brandon Thurlow. We received a message. The assassins were apprehended and contained, and the Royal Guard is performing a sweep to determine where Alighieri's security was breached. Your mother recommends that we escort you out of the capital to the borderlands until we have more information."

Vivian was distracted by the crest on his uniform. It should have been her family's crest, a red leopard clutching a golden scepter in its paw. Instead, it was her mother's personal insignia: a C painted to look like a thorny vine and adorned with red roses.

"Your Majesty?"

Could she trust the captain? She looked past his shoulder at the company waiting behind. They were suited up like they'd prepared for this. She couldn't see a connection between her and the captain. She searched for it. Usually, the magic she needed to see a connection came as easy as pulling in air to breathe. Now she felt like she was pulling taffy.

"Stop that," Bast hissed. "I told you, you can't do magic right now."

Vivian's family was the Cardinal Family of the South, the last remaining of the four most powerful magical families that ever existed on Kepler. All First Degree Cardinals—members of the Cardinal families in the direct line of succession—were gifted with telekinesis, thermodynamics, and telesthesia. The telesthesia was where the gifts varied the most. While Vivian perceived connections, Bast perceived lies. Vivian truly was well-suited for royalty—she could be a very good liar—but she could never lie to Bast.

That seemed inconvenient to her for the moment.

"I was barely doing anything," she complained, and she was going to try again despite Bast's orders, but then her knees gave out.

Bast and Nate reached simultaneously to catch her by her armpits. Vivian thought of fairy tales about damsels in distress (normally princesses) being saved by handsome heroes (normally knights or princes). What rubbish. She couldn't imagine a situation in which being caught by the armpits would be anything but awkward and painful. She was glad it was her brothers doing it.

"My apologies, Your Highness," the captain said. He seemed a little older than her, but she noticed his eyes roving over the blood stains on her dress. Bast had helped her loosen the laces in the back so she could breathe better. Now she felt uncomfortably like the captain had caught her only half-dressed. "I'm being insensitive. You're injured. We are blessed it was not fatal. Do you need time to rest before we can move?"

"Blessed," Vivian repeated absently. Did it count as

a blessing if it had been her mother trying to kill her and her brothers trying to save her? She'd grown up in the Royal Church of South Kepler. The royal family was supposed to model piety for the whole kingdom, but Vivian's feelings about God weren't especially positive today.

"No, we'll move on now," Bast said. He never thirsted for control. When he wanted it, he took it. "The queen will recover, but we need to hurry. There could be more Immortal assassins nearby, planning a second coup."

The captain turned his attention to Bast, responding to the compelling authority in Vivian's youngest brother's voice.

"Yes, Your Highness," the captain said smartly. He turned to signal a few of the guards, who immediately rushed off. "There's an underground path leading from here all the way out of the capital. It will take us several hours on foot, but it's the safest way. We've had guards at all the entrance points." He glanced hesitantly at her. "A caravan will meet us at the end of the tunnels with supplies. Will the queen be able to walk until then?"

Vivian's vision wasn't very focused, and her body felt like it weighed twice as much as normal, but Bast answered for her again. "She'll be fine with our assistance."

The captain nodded. "If you need help, I would be happy to—"

"We won't need help," Bast snapped.

The captain had the good sense to look chagrined, but Nate spoke up. "Actually, I should go with the guards to get the horses."

Bast looked skeptically at Nate. "Why? Do we keep sick horses at the castle?" He lowered his voice. "Do you need to give them a pep talk before they hit the road?"

Nate tapped his foot. His telesthesia gift was an ability to communicate telepathically with animals. He was particularly good with horses and dogs. It was practically a family joke. He spent more time in the stables than he did in the castle, and he had a loyal following if you counted the family canines as subjects.

But Nate didn't look like he appreciated Bast's humor right now, and he seemed to be trying to decide how to respond. He finally said: "I don't recognize any of these guards." Then he lowered his voice so the captain couldn't hear. "And these are *Mom's* guards."

Bast's eyes narrowed. "What does *that* mean?"

Nate fidgeted at Vivian's side. Bast never saw fault in Mom, and Vivian had never discussed her suspicions about Mom with Bast. She hadn't talked to Nate about it either, though. She hadn't expected him to have suspicions of his own.

"They don't know the horses like Nate does," she said, plastering a wry smile on her face. "They might forget to bring his favorite."

Bast looked critically at her. He knew she wasn't saying exactly what she meant. She stubbornly returned his gaze. "Fine," he grumbled, and he waved his hand. "Go get your stupid horse, Nate."

They watched him run off toward a tunnel the captain said would lead straight to the stables. Bast shifted to allow Vivian to lean more into him as they followed the captain and his guards in a different direction. It was a relief for Vivian not to have to listen to her brothers bickering anymore, but somehow the quiet only made everything sink in:

She'd just become the queen of South Kepler, she'd almost died less than an hour ago, and she was already fleeing her kingdom.

"Viv, you're going to give yourself an aneurysm. Relax.

I have this under control." Bast squeezed his arm around her lightly.

She tried to straighten up. "I'm queen. *I* should be the one controlling things."

He laughed. She wondered if he ever laughed genuinely with anyone but her. "In case you haven't noticed, you're in a situation."

Vivian fingered the ripped fabric where the arrow had pierced her. She could feel the scar. But something she hadn't felt at all was killing her.

Bast followed the action of her hand with his eyes. "Don't do that."

"How long do you think I have?" she asked.

"I can't answer that, Viv. I'm good, but I'm not God. We're going to use all the resources we have to get help, and you're going to be grateful that your brother is such a phenomenal healer, and you *have* to stop worrying. It's a waste of energy."

Vivian didn't respond. A tremble was building inside her.

Bast stopped them and turned to look seriously at her. Vivian's own eyes were brown like Mom's, and Nate's were a cloudy hazel, but Bast's eyes were clear blue like Dad's had been. Light flickered off them like they'd flickered from Dad's as well. "Look Viv … you might die tomorrow. So might Nate. So might I. So what? You can't spend your time wondering when you might die."

"My probabilities are worse than either of yours," she said.

His upper lip curled. "Nate just went off alone into the supposedly secure tunnels."

She smirked despite herself. "Well, *you're* likely to outlive me."

Bast picked up his chin. "*I* am the family prodigy, magical genius extraordinaire. I was always going to outlive you."

"I was hoping it wouldn't be by quite so long."

"The queen is supposed to be a light of hope for the entire kingdom, Viv," he admonished. "Where's your faith?"

"Completely in you for the moment," she admitted.

"That's a start," Bast said, and they continued through the tunnels.

CHAPTER THREE
THE SECOND MORTAL COMMITMENT

South Kepler took the Kepler Declaration of Mortal Commitments seriously. The Second Mortal Commitment—to be stewards of Kepler's natural resources—was not a guideline, but a duty to be upheld. Horse-drawn carriages, wagons pulled by ox beasts, bicycles, and solar-powered scooters were allowed. Dirty, fuel-guzzling vehicles were banned.

Just in case the Southerners were ever tempted to get lazy about the Second Commitment, the Royal Church liked to preach about the fall of the Western Republic and the Cardinal Family of the West. The Westerners had interpreted the Commitments far more loosely than the Southerners, and then they had perished. Lesson learned.

Vivian didn't want God to punish her kingdom or wipe out her family, but she was going to have more roads paved after all this was over. Presently, she was curled on the thinly cushioned bench of a rickety coach, and the difference between a royal carriage and a common coach was at least five inches of bench cushion greater than she had expected.

Her teeth chattered and her head throbbed as the coach traversed the rough road.

Captain Thurlow had apologized several times. He said it would draw too much attention to travel in royal carriages. It would have been better if her brothers had decided to ride with Vivian in the coach because at least then she wouldn't be spending every other minute worried about her own impending doom, but Nate wanted to ride his horse and Bast didn't seem to want Nate by himself with the guards.

Without them, she was alone. She drifted to sleep.

Vivian was young the year her dad took her to Alighieri's summer festival and allowed her to play with children her own age. She hardly ever played with other children, and she was delighted by her new friends, who all acted like she was very important indeed. By evening, she was high on sugar and fun. Then the real excitement began: fireworks.

Awesome, bright, booming balls of fire lit up the sky. Vivian loved them, so when the show was over, she decided to create her own. It took a few tries—she had only recently learned to make fire with magic—but soon colorful explosions were bursting out around her. She didn't understand why the other children started running and screaming. Her fireworks were beautiful.

Then her dad came back. He walked through the fireworks, took her firmly by the arm, and stopped the magic. He was silent the whole way back to the castle, and once they were home, he took her to his library and sternly told her she must not play with *fire* around other children. Vivian was stung by the unexpected discipline. She began to cry.

King Herschel immediately softened up. "Other children

29

aren't born with magic like yours, Vivi," he said, pulling her onto his lap. "You're special."

She snuggled firmly into him for comfort. "But why?"

"Because you're royal." He tickled her sides, and she giggled. "And a Cardinal. Our family has more magic than anyone else in South Kepler. That's why we're the rulers."

She tugged on his beard. It was a good beard, golden like the rest of his hair and the right length for little fingers to grip, but not long enough to make her dad look very old.

"What about the rest of Kepler?"

Her father tickled her again. "Why do you care? Are you planning to move?"

"No!" she squealed. "I want someone to play with!"

"The boys have magic," he said. "You can play with them."

"But they're *babies*," she complained.

He kissed her cheek. "They won't be forever, Princess."

The coach came to a stop. The door opened, and Bast popped his head in.

"Viv, you awake?"

"Yeah." She tried to sit up, but a wave of pain stopped her.

"What's wrong?" Bast asked as he and Nate climbed into the coach. They sat on the bench across from her.

"You mean other than the obvious?" Nate said.

Vivian closed her eyes. "Headache. Keeps getting worse." She opened her eyes and gave Bast her most pathetic look. "Help?"

He reached across the bench, touched her forehead, and hummed unhappily. "You're probably dehydrated. We'll have someone bring you water. But I can't do anything with magic. Too risky when we need all your magical energy to fight off the virus."

Vivian buried her head in the bench cushion. "Why are we stopping? What's the plan?"

When Bast didn't answer, Nate snorted. "He doesn't have one yet. He wants your blood."

She eyed Bast. "Why?"

He pulled a thin envelope from his front pocket. A blood sample kit. "I only need a couple of drops. We're going to send it to all the major research labs. I've never seen this version of the Immortality Virus, but there might be a researcher that has."

"He's even sending a sample to New Paris Medical School in the North," Nate said. "And he thinks they're crazy heretics."

Bast agreed. "All Northerners are crazy. That's why we were at war with them."

That was *not* precisely why South Kepler and North Kepler had engaged in various unpleasant border disputes before the Immortal Empire took out the Cardinal Family of the North. If Vivian had had more energy, she would have called Bast on it.

Someone knocked on the door to the coach, and Bast swished his hand to open it telekinetically. Captain Thurlow was outside. He looked in at her, then shifted his eyes quickly to the boys like he was embarrassed, probably to have caught her looking like she'd just woken. Vivian pushed herself up and tried to smooth her hair. Someone had retrieved fresh clothes for her, so she was at least out of her bloody coronation gown.

Bast leaned back with a huff. "What is it, Captain?"

Captain Thurlow lowered his head. "Sorry, sir. The scouts think we're being followed." He glanced at Vivian again.

"Have you had a chance to …?"

Nate snickered. "We haven't told her yet."

"Told me what?"

"We can't stop at any of the public rest areas." Nate's eyes flashed with mirth. "If you need to pee, you have to do it outside. Now."

Great. And she did have to pee. She tried to stand, but her head swam. She fell back onto the bench.

Captain Thurlow took a quick step toward her. "We have a medic—"

"No." Bast stopped the captain from progressing farther with a harsh telekinetic shove. "The medic won't know how to handle Vivian's physiology. We'll have one of your attendants help you outside, Viv. Then you can sleep off your headache while we head north. We're meeting Mom in Gandhi."

"Gandhi?" Vivian asked. Gandhi was the only surviving original Mortal city—one of the three places where humans first settled Kepler and also the place where the Mortal Commitments were penned and signed. The original document was still preserved in Gandhi's Museum of Science and History.

But …

"Why there? That place is overrun by Immortals, isn't it?" Vivian said. She did not add that she also wanted to know why they were meeting Mom *anywhere*. That was an awful idea.

"That's exactly what I said," Nate said.

"And how much do *you* know about the Immortality Virus?" Bast asked Nate before directing the conversation back at Vivian. "We're going to Gandhi because that's where Gandhi Medical Centre is. The vaccination that keeps us from catching the Immortality Virus like a cold was developed there. Those doctors know more about the Immortality

Virus than anyone else."

"Yeah, but don't they employ *Immortal* doctors?" Nate said. "I thought we were trying to get *away* from the Immortals."

"We're trying to get away from the Immortal assassins that tried to kill Vivian," Bast said. "And they were almost for sure Empire Immortals, not some stray Immortals hiding in Gandhi."

Nate made a face that Vivian thought almost made him seem like he was thinking hard. He must have been. She agreed with him on this point.

"The assassins could have come from Gandhi. Maybe they were only hired by the Immortal Empire," she argued.

"The assassins *could* have come from *anywhere* outside Alighieri, Viv," Bast said. "There are Immortals all over Kepler. It's just most likely that the ones that tried to kill you were Empire Immortals."

"*That's* a comforting thought," Nate said morosely.

To Vivian, it was about as comforting as the thought of meeting Mom in Gandhi, where there would be a surplus of Immortals of all kinds hanging around, waiting to be paid to do whatever Mom wanted them to do. She grasped for a reason to change plans.

"Don't the Gandhians still blame us for the problems between North and South Kepler?" she tried. "Unrest is high in Gandhi. They hate being under South Kepler's rule. Why would anyone at Gandhi Medical Centre help me? If we're looking for a cure, maybe we should ask some other medical center for help."

"We're sending your blood to several places. But the Gandhi Medical Centre is the place to go if we want help with the Immortality Virus. Anyway, the Gandhians hate the Immortal Empire a lot more than they hate us," Bast reasoned. "They know we're the only thing left standing between them and the Immortal Empire."

"It's risky," Vivian complained.

Bast got up. "It's the best option we have if you don't want to be the next dead Cardinal," he said, and with that he stepped swiftly out of the coach, pushing the captain out of the way and dragging Nate along before she could ask any more questions.

She was alone again.

Vivian grew up understanding that a Mortal that wasn't with South Kepler was as much a threat as any Immortal. That was why South Kepler was in an undeclared war with North Kepler. The North had refused to ally with the South to face the Immortal Empire directly, forcing the South to expend all their resources fighting the Immortals. Vivian's kingdom had no choice but to take control of Northern territory where necessary to gain strategic advantages. It was this or let Empress Hildebrand take over.

Vivian was eleven-going-on-twelve when the news came that the Cardinal Family of the North had fallen. In the capital city of Alighieri, there were fireworks. Mom took Vivian, Bast, and Nate to see them, and she laughed with delight at the celebrations. This was a turning point, she said. Now they could expand into the North. Now they would have every-thing they needed. The Mortals finally had a chance.

At first, Vivian was excited, too. But King Herschel refused to join the party. She found her father in his library after the fireworks ended. He saw her come into the room, raised a glass of rich, amber-colored liquor to his mouth, and took a long drink as she sat down in a chair next to him by the library's fireplace.

"What's wrong?" she asked.

He sipped his alcohol silently. He didn't seem well.

"Didn't you want to see the fireworks?" she tried.

He snorted out a harsh chortle that made bumps rise on her skin along with the flames in the fireplace. "We're celebrating because a few days ago, a whole family like ours was wiped out. They were the only other Cardinal Family left, and their place was razed to the ground." He lowered his glass. "They had children, Viv. Two girls and a boy."

She squirmed. "Weren't the children taken somewhere else?"

King Herschel took another drink. "We don't think so. There was a massive explosion. We can't even recover the bodies."

Vivian didn't know what to think about that. "But aren't the Northerners a threat?" She tried to remember what she'd been taught about why the North was so bad. "They don't help us with the Immortals, do they? They make it hard for us to win."

Her father sighed. "The Northerners have different ideas about the right way to stop the Immortals. They never attacked us. We occupied their land. And we haven't always been kind to Northerners who make their way to South Kepler, especially when they speak against the Royal Church."

Vivian was stunned by his words. "You think what we're doing is wrong?"

"I think our fight with the North was never about just the Immortals and that things are never black and white. A lot of Mortals have died already. We shouldn't celebrate more death."

The fire was crackling now because Vivian was so upset. "But didn't we need control of the borders? Do you think we should have let the Immortals take over?"

"I didn't say that. Look, Vivian, as a leader, sometimes you have to do things you don't want to do to protect your own people. But you also need to know your greatest threats. We had bigger problems than the king of North Kepler. He never wanted a war."

Vivian's eyes bulged out. "Have you met him?"

King Herschel laughed. "Kings have to meet up now and then to try to end wars." He drained the last of his alcohol and threw down his glass. "He was a good man."

Vivian didn't know what to say as her dad stared into the fire looking like he'd lost a good friend instead of an arch rival.

"Maybe he's still alive," she said after a while. "Maybe the reason you can't recover the bodies is that they weren't in the explosion."

He rubbed his eyes. "We have reports from survivors. The whole family was there."

Vivian thought about a whole family with children dying all at once, and she felt smaller than normal. Her dad looked sympathetically at her. He opened his arms for a hug that she went gratefully to him for. "It's not going to happen to us, Viv."

She sniffed into his shoulder. "Do you think I would have been friends with the girls?"

King Herschel kissed the back of her head. "I don't know. But I do know the king of North Kepler tended hot like you and me. If you were friends with the princesses and one of them tended hot, too, we could have made some pretty spectacular fireworks."

CHAPTER FOUR
THE WHITE BRIDGE

A ruckus woke Vivian as her coach veered suddenly left. She toppled to the floor, then slammed into the door as the coach crashed. She could hear a fight going on outside.

She climbed from the coach with a new gash on her arm dripping blood onto her clothes. The horses were injured, and her coachman was stuck in the wreck. Someone was lying on the ground nearby. A horse reared up as three Immortal assassins lunged at its rider with swords. Or at least she thought they were Immortals. It was hard to see in the dark if they had red eyes.

Vivian did recognize Captain Thurlow as the rider, though. He took a broad swing with his own sword. Someone howled in pain.

Vivian looked away down the path, then looked the other way. This was clearly an organized attack, and Vivian's guards were outnumbered. She wondered again if her mother had been behind the attack at the coronation ceremony. Had she tipped the assassins off about where to go to finish the job and how many people they would need to get it done?

The captain took off someone's head, and it rolled away as the body fell. Vivian thought somewhat reluctantly that she probably could trust the captain if her mother disliked him enough to send him out with *this* caravan.

A female guard dropped right in front of Vivian, and an assassin pulled a sword out of the guard's stomach. The coachman called for help, but not in time to avoid his own death by the same brute. Vivian stepped back toward the coach. She'd made a mistake climbing out. Two more assassins stalked toward her. This close she could confirm that they were Immortals.

She was going to have to use magic.

"No magic!" Bast hurtled toward her out of nowhere on a horse that bucked wildly as he tried to stop it nearby. He waved his hand at the Immortals approaching her. Their red eyes turned gray as deadly frost immobilized them. Vivian shivered. Blood she could handle. Freezing to death was not high on her list of ways to go. Bast reached down for her hand, and she reached up, but his fingers were ice cold, and she pulled back. His thermodynamic magic was hard to take in full force.

He growled in frustration, and his horse reared up again.

"Come on." Captain Thurlow grabbed her arm and helped pull her up onto the horse he was riding. "Are you okay?"

Vivian breathed heavily from the effort it had taken simply to mount the horse. The captain's eyes were a warm brown color, like her own. She shouldn't have wasted time noticing, but he was looking so sincerely at her.

"Queen Vivian?"

"I'm okay. Where did they come from? We have to do something."

Bast, who was continuing to struggle with his spooked horse, managed to glare at her. "*We're* not doing anything." He nodded at Captain Thurlow. "Get her out of here. *I* will figure out what to do."

"No!" Vivian protested while the poor captain looked back and forth between her and Bast like he wasn't sure which of them he should be listening to. "We're outnumbered!"

"I know that! It doesn't matter! You can't use your magic—" Bast stopped abruptly and looked past her. "Oh, Sam Kepler, what is he doing?"

Vivian followed Bast's line of sight to a horse and rider galloping through the battle with a blaze of fire following in their wake.

"Is that *Nate*?" Vivian shrieked.

"What *is* he doing?" the captain asked.

Bast fought harder with his horse. "Telling absolutely every tracker in the area exactly where we are, that's what."

Vivian could use fire like a knife. She was so precise, she could have branded someone with her initials from twenty feet away, and she had small handwriting. Nate had never mastered his thermodynamic gift. He was too impulsive to control it. When he really tried to use the gift, it was like someone setting fire to a pool of petroleum.

The fire sparked dangerously toward the trees. They were going through a forested area. Bast yelled to Nate to stop.

"I can't hear you! I'm rounding the Immortals up!" Nate yelled back. He rotated his hand in a circle. "In fire! And you're making that horse panic! Calm down, or it'll throw you off!"

"Calm down?! You're telling *me* to calm down!" Bast screamed while his horse went crazy. "Stop setting things on *fire*! You're making everything worse!"

"We're losing too many people!"

"You idiot! We'll lose even more if ..."

A spark caught a dry branch, and Vivian saw the branch glow. Then another caught, and smoke began curling into the sky. They would have no chance to hide. No chance to get far enough away not to be so easily hunted down next time.

Nate stopped his horse near Bast's and reached out to grab the reins. The horse stilled, and Nate tossed the reins back to Bast, who looked angry enough that Vivian wouldn't have been surprised if steam started pouring out of his ears, regardless of what he tended.

"What's wrong with you!?" Nate asked, apparently oblivious to the problem he was causing. "Those red-eyed freaks are killing our guards!"

"Who's guarding who? It's their job to protect us!" Bast pointed to the sky. "And look at what you're doing, dumb-ass!"

The connection between Bast and Nate always carried a lot of static. Vivian thought she could see it crackling in the smoke without even trying. The colors were hard to distinguish.

"He's going to burn down the whole forest," the captain said. Vivian agreed. Nate didn't have control, and Bast was too busy arguing with him to fix it.

"It's not their job to get killed while we run away!"

"Who said anything about running away?!"

Smoke and fire. Fire and smoke. Brittle, cracked connections. Vivian gripped Captain Thurlow's shoulder and rose in the saddle.

"Queen Vivian?"

Someone had to stop it. Someone had to be focused. She couldn't help that it had to be her. She couldn't let everyone die. She called up heat from inside her.

"Queen Vivian, please—"

"What is she doing?!"

"Viv! Stop!"

But how could she stop? The magic ran thick through her veins, and she could feel it warming her, temporarily easing all her pain and bringing with it the most delicious feeling of power and a spiritual connection to the elements around her. She loved magic. She *was* magic.

"VIV! NO!"

"VIV!"

"Queen Vivian!"

"NO!!!!"

The magic exploded out of her, and she directed it to do exactly what she needed. She gathered all the smoke, flames, and heat from the air, rolled it into a single scorching ball …

"VIVIAN!"

… and sent the ball on a path right through the bodies of the Immortals attacking them.

She wasn't like Nate. She was controlled. She went one-by-one, weaving around her own guards and burning fiery holes through the Immortal assassins so quickly they probably never even felt it. It was strange how an aggressor could become a victim so easily. But she was the queen, and the guards and attendants in the caravan were her subjects, and she was protecting her subjects because wasn't that the whole point of Keplerian magic?

When she was done, she buried the fire in the dirt. Then she began to fall off the horse. She thought Captain Thurlow might have tried to catch her. She closed her eyes.

Vivian was riding an alabaster horse. King Herschel was riding next to her. They were trotting around a mountain near the castle. They reached a glimmering lake, and a bridge materialized from the shore, extending up over the lake. Vivian couldn't see the other side.

The king rode forward but turned to her before the bridge.

"Are you coming with me, Vivian?"

Vivian admired her father's eyes gleaming with the sunlight shining into them, almost the same as the sunlight shining on the perfect blue waters of their lake.

King Herschel held a strong hand out to her. He didn't look right. His beard had been graying and his hair thinning the last time she'd seen him. Now his hair was thick and golden under his jewel-encrusted crown, which also glistened in the sun. He didn't look younger exactly, more like healthier and like a man marked with experience.

She wanted to take his hand so they could ride over the lake together. The bridge was pretty: marbled white with perfect, clean lines. She breathed in the sweet pine in the warm breeze sweeping through her hair and listened to water lapping against the lakeshore. She started to ride forward. Then she stopped.

"Is something wrong?" King Herschel smiled like he was teasing.

"I … don't remember this," she said. "I don't think there are mountains so close to the castle. I don't remember a lake."

"This is a different place. You've never been here before."

Vivian let the warmth of the sun soak through to her bones.

"Am I dead?"

Her father's smile turned wistful. "Not yet. But you are crossing into death."

She looked over the lake. "Will the bridge take me all the way there?"

He nodded.

"Will you stay with me?"

"Yes, Vivian."

She thought about it. "I don't really want to die yet."

"I know. I had more planned for you, too, but it turns out this isn't one of those things you plan." He looked around with shiny eyes. "This is beautiful, though, isn't it?"

Vivian looked with him. "Yes."

"Imagine what it could look like on the other side," he said gently.

She imagined. "And you'll come with me?"

"I came here just for you."

She hesitated.

He faded out of sight.

She was in darkness, lying on a cold, hard, uneven surface. Her body felt heavy.

"Viv? Can you hear me?"

Bast.

"If you can hear me, please come back."

Bast didn't use words like "please."

"Please, Viv."

Vivian was in her room in the highest tower of the castle. She got up from her bed, with its silky sheets and fluffy pillows, and stepped into the flat shoes she'd left by her nightstand. There was a squashy, worn chair with a pile of books next to it that she'd been meaning to read. Her window looked out over Alighieri. She went to it. From here, she could see all the vineyards stretching past the castle grounds.

"This isn't how it was," she said to herself.

"You're wearing your favorite shoes." Her father was standing in the doorway to her room, leaning against the frame. "Are you ready?"

She thought about taking a book from the top of the pile but decided instead to go to the wardrobe on the other side of the room. She had a green sweater in there that she loved, though she was hardly ever cold enough to need a sweater. She took it from a drawer and felt it in her hands. It was impossibly soft.

"Imagine what you might be dressed like there," her father said.

She looked at the books.

He chuckled. "Imagine what you could learn there."

"But not by reading, I bet."

"Maybe there's something so much better you won't want to read."

"Maybe there's not." She touched the green sweater. "Do I have to go?"

There were tears in the corners of his eyes.

"You don't have to go."

She was lying on something padded this time, but she still couldn't make her eyes open.

"I can fix it. I only need a little more magic and a little more time, and I need you to help, Viv, because I need your magic, too. You have to *fight*."

She wanted to go back to her room in the castle.

A cold hand gripped hers. "Viv, if you die, it'll just be Nate and me. *Please*."

His hand felt like it was turning to ice around hers. She

wanted him to let go.

"She doesn't have to listen to you." A different voice.

"What are you talking about, she *doesn't have to listen*? If she doesn't listen, she'll *die.*"

"Maybe she doesn't want to live."

"Who doesn't want to *live*?"

"I'm just saying maybe you're hanging on too tight."

"Says the person who has the most to gain from her dying!"

"That's not true, and you know it."

They were making her tired. She let go of their voices.

There were fireworks above. Vivian would always love fireworks. She loved the colors, the surprise, the magnificence. She loved the explosion of power.

Her dad was standing next to her, and they were watching from the castle grounds.

"There are worse things than death, Vivian," he said.

She wasn't sure about that.

She felt cold again.

"Viv, Nate thinks I'm hurting you."

She thought Bast might love her too much. He needed other people to love. It would have helped if he and Nate had gotten along better.

"And I don't want to hurt you. So, if he's right … if this really is hurting you … you don't have to … you can stop trying if you want. I'll understand. No. That's a lie. I won't understand, but I'll try."

There was a pause.

"But if you go, you know what will happen to Nate."

Another pause.

"You know he doesn't stand a chance."

Was Bast right about that? Maybe Nate was more stubborn than she'd thought. Maybe he wouldn't be such an easy target. But she had thought the same about herself.

She could hear Bast breathing.

"If you can't try to live for yourself, and you can't do it for me … do you think you could at least do it for him?"

She floated away and dreamed while voices spoke to her.

"Don't leave us alone."

"You don't have to stay."

"You know they'll kill him."

"There are worse things than death."

"Please."

Vivian woke on a bed in a dimly lit room. She tried to sit up but failed and collapsed.

"You used magic."

Bast was standing in the corner of the room. She hadn't seen him there. She tried to sit again and made it to her elbows. "I know, but—"

He cut her off. "Save it, Viv. You knew what using magic could do to you. I told you not to use it. You did it anyway."

Bast wasn't the kind of person who raised his voice when he got angry. His voice became smoother and lower instead. Right now, Vivian wasn't sure she would have been able to hear him if it hadn't been completely silent in the room.

"It's not … that big … of a deal," she managed to say.

"Not. That. Big. Of. A. Deal?"

He crossed his arms and looked murderously at her.

"We would probably all be dead now if—" She started to explain, but it was hard to speak, and she gave up as a chill in the air made her shiver.

Bast spoke again. "I had it under control. I was going to stop Nate, and even if I couldn't have contained the fire, I could have gotten the three of us out without you doing anything."

Maybe she'd only been dreaming of him pleading with her to live.

"But—"

"*No.* I am *trying* to save your life. The least you can do is treat that like it means something and avoid doing rash, stupid things that might kill you. I'd expect that stuff from Nate. Not you."

He dropped his arms and left the room.

The cold lingered for a long time.

LABEL FROM A BOTTLE
OF SASSAFRAS BEER

CHAPTER FIVE
THE SASSAFRAS INCIDENT

Carina Garcia's butter knife wasn't anywhere near her hands when she impaled an enormous Kepler beetle with it. The knife shot through the air, nailing the bug into the thick oakory wood of the dining room table before she could think. It was an instinctive telekinetic throw. Absolutely not her fault. Giant Kepler beetles were constantly invading Novi Dupree Sanctuary. That one had been trying to attack.

Yet …

Two minutes into lunch. That's how long it had taken her to get in trouble today. Two minutes ago, she'd been enjoying a hot breeze wisping through doors that were all propped open. She'd nodded at the right pauses in the mealtime chatter while she daydreamed about Stealing a Bottle of Sassafras. Then came the beetle.

Who'd have thought a butter knife could be so lethal?

"Uncontrolled magic is dangerous," Sister Rachel hissed to Sister Agda, who stared at the knife standing at attention in front of her salad plate. The beetle's legs were still twitching.

Three more Sisters of Novi Dupree, sitting in a row between Rachel and Agda, frowned sternly in sync.

"No. I'd call that deadly accurate," said young Sister Elizabeth, and far-more-weathered Sister Raji lifted her glass of frothy caramel ale for a toast.

"To the demise of a bad bug!"

Raji took a giant swig of ale, and Elizabeth joined with a sip of paleberry lager and a wink that made guilt tingle up Carina's spine. If she had more control over her magic, no one would be watching a Kepler beetle the size of Sister Raji's thumb ooze green blood onto the table.

Then again, if Sister Agda would get her a *teacher*, she would have more control.

The beetle finally died as one more Sister entered from the kitchen with a tray of fresh ginger snaps. Sister Lindy. As soon as she caught sight of the carnage, she shrieked and dropped the tray. A dozen cookies tumbled to the knotted hardwood floor.

At that, Carina's little sister, Miguela—who was not a Sister—stood up like a perfect martyr and said, "I'll get the broom."

Carina threw her head down on the table.

"That will be unnecessary."

Carina picked her head back up.

Sister Agda's black pebble eyes were fixed on her. Carina had been at Novi Dupree for six years, and the prioress could still make her toes feel cold with a stare. She lowered her gaze meekly. "Sorry, Sister Agda."

Sister Agda yanked the butter knife out of the table with the beetle still speared at the end and set it on her salad plate with a clang. "We'll discuss this when *you're* finished cleaning."

Carina swept up quickly after lunch. There were worse ways she could have ruffled Sister Agda's feathers. At least this gave her an excuse to go to the kitchen, where Sister Lindy was stalking from cupboard to cupboard with a chef's knife gripped tightly in her hand.

"Any more beetles?" Carina asked, opening a drawer near the pantry and snagging a bottle opener while Sister Lindy stuck her head below the sink. The Sisters of Novi Dupree Sanctuary made their living via an impressive brewery. There were at least ten bottle openers in that drawer. One was not going to be missed.

Sister Lindy emitted a brief howl, presumably to show any remaining beetles she meant business, and Carina heard one of the chef's knives thwack into something.

Lindy held up her knife and beamed at another dying Kepler beetle with the glee she normally reserved for things like flawlessly baked cheese soufflé. She kicked the cupboard shut with a stout leg. "All clear! And if you're done, there's a fresh batch of cookies on the counter."

No Mortal on planet Kepler had evolved a magic baking ability, but Sister Lindy's warm ginger snaps, with their gooey, buttery insides, were magically appealing.

"Thanks, Sister Lindy," Carina said, taking a ginger snap. "Sorry about the first batch."

"Apology accepted," Lindy said, and as Carina left the kitchen, the good Sister added a dark twist: "Worth it to destroy the beast."

After that, Carina slipped quietly down the hall, hoping to reach the back door of the sanctuary's main house without running into any other Sisters. She certainly wasn't going to

Sister Agda's room before she proceeded. She didn't need anyone to scold her about her inability to control her own magic. She was well aware of the problem already and the danger it put her in.

Unfortunately, she was not *quite* to the door before she heard Sister Rachel calling. Rachel had a book that looked older than the time humans had been on Kepler, and she was waving it with her spindly arm.

At least four Sisters had lectured Carina individually about magic this week, but Sister Rachel's lectures were always the worst. She taught Carina's school lessons; she could add homework to scolding.

"I want you to read this by Friday," Sister Rachel said, handing the book over. It was titled *The Evolution of Keplerian Extrasensory Abilities.* "Agda told me I could give it to you. You need to understand your abilities better, because if you can't control them …"

"Yes, I know," Carina said, failing to mask her annoyance while she flipped carelessly through the book. "If I can't stop performing random acts of magic, then I can never leave Novi Dupree, because we're protected on our grounds by ancient wards no one understands or whatever, and if I do magic outside the sanctuary, the Red-Eyed Ones will sense it and I'm doomed."

She made a hand motion to illustrate "doomed" just so Sister Rachel would know she got the point.

Rachel looked over the readers she always wore. "You *know* it's more complicated than that. It's not just any Red-Eyed Ones that would be after you. You'd have Empire Immortals hunting you down. The Empress is *eliminating* Mortal magicians, Carina." She straightened up her gaze. "Did you read that article I gave you comparing the Immortal Empire to ancient Earthian empires?"

Carina continued paging through the book. It did not appear to have a single illustration. "Miguela read it. Who cares if the Red-Eyed Ones who kill me are Empire Immortals or not? Either way, I'm dead." She recoiled from a horrifically dense page. "Does this have any practical instruction?"

Sister Rachel pushed those glasses up her nose and tried to replicate Sister Agda's signature *look*. Carina didn't understand why Rachel chose Agda as a role model. Elizabeth was decades closer to Rachel in age, they were roommates, and Rachel would have been prettier practicing Elizabeth's glowing positivity.

"You are highly literate and extremely imaginative," Rachel said dryly. "Read between the lines and maybe you'll find something useful."

"I'll start it tomorrow."

"Start it this afternoon. After you help Raji in the brewery."

Carina shut the book, and dust puffed out. "But I finished my chores this morning! I'm supposed to have the afternoon free!"

"And since then, you've killed a helpless bug, and there's been an accident in the brewery and some big spill. Now, helping Raji is part of your chores. Agda's decree. Make the best of it."

Carina trudged away from the main house of the sanctuary ruminating on the irony of being stopped from achieving her goal by the *brewery*. If the Sisters of Novi Dupree had one outstanding quality, it was their commitment to damn good beer. Sister Raji was especially proud of their production. In fact, when Carina reached the brewery, Sister Raji was already there with Sister Elizabeth, standing in the brewing room between two enormous, shiny metal vats of beer.

There was not a spill to be seen, but Raji was talking animatedly and drinking something thick that looked like chocolate stout.

"He said the pilsner was like watery piss!" Raji took a vindictive drink of stout. "*Piss*, Lizzy! *Harry!* And then he *relieved* himself. Right there! In the alley! He nearly got my shoes!"

Elizabeth cussed, a skill she liked to attribute to her late, good-for-nothing parents. Incidentally, Carina, whose own dead parents had left her nothing, thought a colorful vocabulary was good for all kinds of things. She couldn't help but appreciate the high proficiency Elizabeth had with those words and the way she smiled cheerfully at Carina while she continued the conversation with Raji.

"It's too bad. Harry would be dashing if he weren't drunk all the time. What did you tell him?"

Raji bristled indignantly. "I told him he could be sure he wouldn't be drinking any more of our *piss!* The nerve! Our beer could compete on an intergalactic level!"

"That would be ambitious," Elizabeth noted. "Since Kepler doesn't have contact with other planets anymore."

"It doesn't matter. Heaven knows Harry repented after that!"

"But you're a Northerner, Sister Raji," Carina said. "I thought you didn't believe in heaven."

Raji crossed her eyes, stuck out her tongue, and made the kind of undignified noise only a woman of substance can make. Then she said, "You're completely missing the point."

"So, where's the spill?" Carina asked. "I came here to help."

Elizabeth smiled indulgently while Raji gave Carina a

naughty smirk.

"There *isn't* one. I told Rachel that to get Agda off your back. And by the way, that was some telekinetic throw this afternoon. Have you been practicing?"

"No," Carina lied, but when Elizabeth raised an eyebrow, she admitted: "I don't see how I can learn *not* to move stuff with my mind if I don't know *how* I do it in the first place. I didn't kill that beetle on purpose."

"Not consciously on purpose," Elizabeth corrected, but she was one of the few Sisters who was not terrified of magic, and as Raji nodded approvingly, a spark of hope ignited in Carina. Maybe she could get this day back on track.

"Actually," she said, "I was planning to practice today. Out by the stream in the back."

Raji guzzled the rest of her stout. "Don't let us stop you!" She pointed her empty glass at the door. "Go on. We'll tell Rachel it took hours to clean up the brewery."

"Are you sure?" Carina said.

Elizabeth twirled a lock of Carina's hair affectionately and let it go. "We're sure."

This was why Raji and Elizabeth were Carina's favorite Sisters. Though, even *they* probably wouldn't have approved of what she was about to do (or attempt to do). They wouldn't have crossed Sister Agda on the line she held between Carina and Novi Dupree's beverage production.

That was a hard line.

And yes, that's right. Despite the fact that the Sisters of Novi Dupree made supposedly exceptional beer—and although Carina and Miguela were nearly old enough (sixteen and thirteen, respectively)—the Sisters never allowed them to *drink* any of the beer. Not even the sweet stuff, like the sassafras, which was only 1.8% alcohol. Sister Agda said it was "too rich" for "young girls like Carina and Miguela" and treated that rule like it was one of the Mortal Commitments.

If Carina hadn't once tried a sip of sassafras beer from a glass Sister Agda (of all people) failed to finish, she wouldn't have known what any of the beer tasted like. Sassafras—that sweet-sting-on-your-tongue, bubbles-fizzing-in-your-nose, sugar-sticky-on-your-lips deliciousness—would have been entirely missing from her life.

But ... now it was not. Now she craved it *constantly.* Which is why Carina was on a mission today to steal a bottle.

The target bottle was ideal for magic practice. It had appeared just a few days ago on the windowsill of an abandoned shack sitting on the other side of a nearby stream that marked the sanctuary's northern boundary.

The shack itself had been there, empty, sullen, and existing with no consequence, for longer than Carina had been at Novi Dupree. As for the bottle, it was probably left behind by some hikers having a picnic. That was fortuitous for Carina *if* she could figure out how to get it across the stream.

But the thing is: she couldn't physically cross that stream. She could wade in halfway, something she had already attempted yesterday with much misery in the ice-cold spring water. Going all the way was out of the question, though. Too risky. The Red-Eyed Ones could sense her if she accidentally did magic while she was outside the boundary lines. Carina couldn't take that chance.

Miguela didn't have any magic, so, theoretically, Carina could have asked her to help. But Miguela would never have approved. And that left Carina with only one option: telekinesis. If she stayed on the Novi Dupree side of the boundary line and used her mind to magic the sassafras across the stream, that bottle could be hers without any risk at all.

Perfectly safe. Totally doable. No problem at all.

Or at least it shouldn't have been a problem.

But late afternoon found Carina alone, perched high on a tree branch that stretched over the stream, feeling like a stray rattycat and cussing like Sister Elizabeth. She'd started out today standing on the edge of the stream and trying to magic the bottle from there, but when that hadn't been enough, she knew she had to get closer for her magic to cooperate.

Thus the tree. But so far, no luck. How was she ever going to leave Novi Dupree if she couldn't do something this easy?

Perhaps she needed to get even closer. She wormed her way along the branch and felt the cotton of her dress snag. She winced. Elizabeth had only made this dress for her in the spring. Still, she continued, sliding out until she was *almost*, but not quite halfway over the stream. Then she screwed up her face, held up her hand, concentrated, and tried to move the bottle.

Nothing happened.

Her stomach gurgled as she hugged the thick tree branch. Honestly, who left a perfectly good bottle of sassafras in a dilapidated shack anyway? She gritted her teeth and held the tree with one arm. With her free arm, she reached as far as she could toward the shack, picturing the bottle lifting from the windowsill at her command.

"Come on, sassafras," she whispered to coax the bottle forward. She tried to imagine a line stretching between herself and it. "Come closer, sassafras … come to Carina …"

Truthfully, she hadn't expected that line to work—she'd been trying for nearly an hour—but right then the bottle connected to her mind.

The surprise nearly made her fall. She lost the connection immediately as the bottle opener fell out of her pocket and plunked into the stream. A harsh sting of pain told her she'd also torn a hole in her dress.

"Shoot!" she said (or something like that). Her hands burned, and she held one up to assess the damage. Her palm was scratched and starting to bleed.

It made her feel sorry for herself. She *needed* to learn how to use her magic, and not just to steal a stupid bottle of sassafras. If she couldn't do this, how could she ever hope to defend herself against the Red-Eyed Ones? Her skills were pathetic. A telekinetic master probably could have moved a whole case of sassafras across the sanctuary grounds. All *she* could do was sweat over a single bottle sitting in a shack across the stream.

She glared at the bottle and reached out.

"Come on, come on, come on," she chanted.

Somehow, she picked up the connection again. The bottle lifted from the windowsill.

"Ha," she murmured. The bottle hovered. Carina held her breath. The bottle tilted and dragged into the air. She was shaking from the effort, but there it was: a bottle of sassafras taking orders *from her mind*. Buzzing triumph swept through her. This was *success*. Soon she would be sipping sweet sassafras, the bubbles fizzing in her nose, and Sister Agda and all her pointless rules could go to—

"Carina!"

Oh no.

"Carina! Carina? Where are you?"

Carina cringed. Miguela was not going to screw this up. She was *not*. Carina tried to speed up the bottle. It wavered in the air.

"This isn't funny, Carina! I know you're out here. Answer me! The Sisters are looking for you!"

Miguela could have made worrying an extreme sport. Carina ignored her. The sassafras was hanging over the far side of the stream … Miguela's yells got louder …

Carina threw all her energy into the bottle.

It *sped* toward her.

She stretched out her arm …

Miguela appeared out of the corner of her eye.

"Are you using *magic*?!" she shrieked.

Carina looked down for a second … and looked back just in time to see the bottle veer away. She swung wildly for it, caught it in her hand (victory!), and lost her balance on the tree branch. She scrambled to regain her grip, but then she was tumbling down out of the tree, grabbing futilely with one hand for something to break her fall.

Nothing did. She splashed flailing into the stream, landing sprawled and twisted with all her wind knocked out.

Miguela was screaming: "You crossed the boundary!"

Carina thought she should be screaming: "Are you okay?"

She was lying in cold, shallow water, between several large rocks. She rolled her head toward her sister to respond with *very* colorful words, but something caught her eye:

One jagged, broken half of the bottle of sassafras was still in her hand. It had smashed on a rock when she landed. Carina lifted her hand and held it in front of her face. Blood and sassafras trickled down her palm. She licked a drop of sassafras …

… and promptly passed out.

EXCERPT FROM *THE EVOLUTION OF
KEPLERIAN EXTRASENSORY ABILITIES*

Though colloquially referred to as "magic," the extrasensory abilities expressed in human Mortals on Kepler are, in fact, rare, scientifically explainable traits caused by genetic mutation. Similar mutations are responsible for cases of enhanced vision and auditory capabilities, increased receptiveness to smell and taste, and certain skin sensitivities common to Keplerians. It is estimated that over half of all human Mortals on Kepler have one or more genetic mutation, though only a small percentage of those mutations are responsible for "magic" as it is now known.

Scientists currently theorize that some of these mutations are caused by radiation from the Kepler sun, which penetrates the Kepler ozone at a slightly higher rate than the last known rates of radiation on Earth. Scientists have also theorized that certain chemicals in the Kepler soil composition may influence gene expression in humans. While there are many other plausible theories, most of which are expertly discussed in later chapters of this book, some people do attribute Keplerian "magic" to divine origin. Most notably, the Royal Church of South Kepler refuses to acknowledge any scientific explanation for Keplerian extrasensory abilities. Children in South Kepler are taught that Keplerian "magic" is mystical, God-granted power.

The authors of this book neither deny nor accept the role of a divine creator in evolution on Kepler, but their excellent research and detailed explanation of the hereditary nature of Keplerian magic sheds new light on this development in human evolution. I caution against the practice of removing these theories of genetic mutation from textbooks and school lessons. Such a dangerous practice may well prevent bright minds from the opportunity to contribute scientific advances to humanity.

~Foreword by Dr. Oliver McRaffy
New Paris Medical School

CHAPTER SIX
A STRANGER AT NOVI DUPREE

Carina and her sister hadn't come to Novi Dupree by choice. They were smuggled there by a stranger, who rescued them from the ruins of their childhood home. He never gave them his name. He had a long purple scar that ran from his left ear to the right corner of his mouth. He said: "Be quiet. Come with me. Hurry, they're still looking for you." Then he hauled them into his wagon and took them away.

They traveled with the man for three weeks. Carina knew they were going into the mountains, but the man talked minimally and drove his wagon hard, making strange turns sometimes to retrace routes they'd only just passed. He rarely stopped. They slept in the wagon. He shared food, but there wasn't much.

One day, he drove them up a steep road, through an iron gate, to a stone-bricked complex high in the mountains. There he paraded Carina and Miguela out, hungry and dirty, to stand in front of doors that looked too tall and heavy to move.

The man with the scar knocked hard on one of the doors.

A woman with razor-sharp features answered. She was wearing a white blouse and a long brown skirt, both heavy and stiff like they'd been dunked in starch and left for days. Her dark hair was punctuated with gray and twisted into a low, tight bun. The top of her right ear was pierced with something that looked like a claw.

She didn't introduce herself. She didn't look at Carina and Miguela at all. She gripped the doorknob and said: "Why are you here?" like knocking on the door was a crime.

The man pointed at Carina and her sister, drawing the woman's attention down toward them. "Their parents are dead," he said, and the woman, who Carina later came to know as Sister Agda, towered over them without responding, her face stern and unforgiving.

Carina shrank, and Miguela cowered, her small hand shaking in Carina's as Sister Agda assessed the orphans below her.

"This is the only place they'll be safe. Everyone else will think they're dead." The man sounded grim and desperate. "I have to go back. If there was any other choice …"

Carina didn't like the way Sister Agda's eyes shot through them like she could kill with a single glance. She drew back, pulling Miguela behind her, and looked nervously at the man, whose silence had at least felt warm.

"Leave us on our own," Carina begged, though at barely ten years old, and with her seven-year-old sister to look after, she hadn't known what that would mean. "We'll take care of ourselves. You don't have to do anything for us. We'll be fine."

The man failed to acknowledge her, and if Sister Agda raised even a hair of an eyebrow, Carina didn't see it. A long time passed during which the only sound that could be heard was a rasp in Miguela's throat—a giveaway that at least one of them was sick.

At last, Sister Agda spoke. "They can sleep here tonight," she said, in a crisp, clipped tone. Fear of being left with her, even for a night, overwhelmed Carina. The man thanked Sister Agda, got in his wagon, and was gone before Carina could recover enough to protest.

It wasn't because of Carina that Sister Agda decided to keep them after that. Miguela won the Sisters over. She embodied their orderly, minimalist, grateful-to-a-fault philosophy. She (and the deaths of Sisters Faye and Gracie, longtime roommates who expired within three days of each other) was the reason the girls were eventually upgraded from wool blankets and hay in the barn loft to a room with a bed that smelled like old person. Miguela wanted to stay at Novi Dupree forever and become a Sister one day herself.

Carina would never have made it as a Sister, and the sassafras incident should have set her back with everyone. But the terrible thing about it was that Sister Agda barely punished her. At first, Carina was only sentenced to a couple weeks of bed rest for a broken ankle and several cracked ribs. When it turned out her injuries weren't as bad as they'd initially seemed—she could walk the next day—Sister Agda decreed that Carina should load all the beer into the wagons before the Sisters' next trip into town.

"By yourself," she said.

And nothing else.

The other Sisters were more lenient than they should have been, too. Sister Lindy didn't give Carina any extra cleaning duties, but she grumbled about how there was nothing nutritious at all in sassafras beer and how not even someone as picky as Carina was going to go hungry on her watch. Then she started whipping up new recipes to disguise foods Carina didn't like.

Sister Rachel said, "I don't understand how someone who can ace a physics exam would think it was a good idea to climb three meters up a tree for some stunt. And by the way, I want you to start reading *A History of Human Power and Politics*." That book was 625 pages of small print, and it began all the way back with *Earth* history. Still, it was a mild assignment, given the circumstances.

It would have been easier if someone had been nasty about the whole thing. At least then Carina might have had something to do with all the guilt and fear swimming through her at the thought of Red-Eyed Ones descending on them soon. But no one would whisper a word about what they were doing to prepare for that possibility. Sister Raji and Sister Elizabeth would have told her what was going on, but they left together on brewery business the day after the incident. Until they returned, all Carina could do was hope the Red-Eyed Ones had missed her magic.

Carina dutifully loaded crate after crate of thick yarn, wool blankets, cheese, jerky, and lots and lots of beer into the Sisters' creaky old wagons before their next trip into town. Then the morning after, as the sun began sifting through the trees, she hitched up the ox beasts and heaved three extra crates of sassafras that she'd forgotten onto the wagons. She watched the Sisters go, tracing the fading lines on her hand from where broken glass had cut her and wondering how the Sisters could all act so *normal*. All she could think about was what would happen if the Red-Eyed Ones came today.

"Oh, get over it, Carina," Miguela said after the wagons were out of sight. "It's nice outside, and Sister Agda didn't leave us any work. I'm going to read."

Miguela was reading *The Collected Works of Anna Dupree*, the founder of Novi Dupree. That probably *would* have served as punishment for Carina, but …

"Reading isn't going to stop the Red-Eyed Ones from finding us," she said drearily.

Miguela had mastered Sister Agda's "how many damns do you think I give?" face. She gave it to Carina now. "Fine, then. Take a walk. Circle the perimeter or something." She moved her fingers in an imaginary circle. "But it's not going to do you any good. They're either coming, or they aren't. The best thing you can do is stay out of trouble." She narrowed her eyes viciously. "And *don't* do any more magic."

At least Miguela was appropriately angry.

Carina did decide to "circle the perimeter"—mostly because she couldn't shake the feeling that the Red-Eyed Ones were going to show up exactly when she started thinking maybe they wouldn't—but walking under a rich blue sky in the quiet of the sanctuary grounds lifted her mood. It was difficult in that context to imagine a Red-Eyed One (or any other threat) showing up. So as Carina neared the tree she'd fallen from by the stream, and a bright red butterbird chirped abruptly at her, the scolding didn't even startle her.

Then the angry butterbird swooped down to a flat-topped rock that jutted out of the stream and hopped savagely around something.

Carina walked closer.

The butterbird was stomping around a single, brown

glass bottle. It was unbroken. And empty.

Prickles rippled over Carina's skin. Is this why the Sisters had been so nice to her? Had they decided to teach her a lesson by putting an empty bottle of sassafras here? Somehow, she couldn't even see Sister Agda doing something that passive aggressive.

When she realized it must have been Miguela—she had suggested this walk, hadn't she?—it made Carina queasy. Tears glazed over her eyes, the beautiful weather became instantly insulting, and if that was all that had happened, Carina's self-pity would probably have prompted a real cry.

It was not all that happened. Instead, someone coughed.

Carina stood dead still.

Whoever it was coughed again, then stopped, then started up again, worse the second time, with splashing, like they were choking in the stream. She looked over the water for a victim and spotted one lying facedown on the other side. Some guy was trying to lift himself out of the water while he coughed.

"Hey!" she shouted. "Do you need help?" She shuffled from foot-to-foot. She wasn't supposed to cross the stream— today especially—but leaving someone to choke like that didn't seem like an ethical choice. She remembered Sister Raji saying once that if it was coughing, it was probably breathing.

He kept coughing

She called out a second time. "Hey! Are you okay?"

His head and shoulders dipped back into the shallow water.

The coughing stopped entirely.

Carina stared for one moment, then kicked off her shoes and waded into the water, sloshing through the stream and all the time yelling, intelligently: "Are you okay? Are you dead?"

He wasn't moving when she got to him, but as soon as she knelt down, he picked up his head and started coughing violently again. She grabbed him by the shoulders and helped him roll over out of the water, and the next thing she knew he was sitting on his knees, she was whacking him on the back, he was coughing dirty water up, and it was *not* attractive.

"Are you okay?" she asked (even more intelligently), patting his back softer as his coughing died down. He looked about her age, but he was dressed strangely. His gray-blue trousers seemed stretchier than ordinary cotton, and his navy-blue sweater was too thin to be made from anything that would keep you warm. His shoes were too smooth for cloth or leather.

He turned toward her. His cheeks were plastered with mud, and he'd gotten it in his hair, which was thick, wavy, and so dark it was almost black. It was even in his eyebrows, which already seemed heavy on his face. His eyes popped as he noticed her helping him. They were a startlingly dark blue with almost purple edges.

She fell back and landed hard in the mud.

He stood and reached for her arm. "Are *you* okay?" he asked, lifting her out of the mud as if she was the one who needed help. He did it like she was featherlight, not like he had just been choking in a river, and it all made her feel uncomfortably disgruntled.

"You were the one passed out," she said.

He wiped dirt from his face. "Oh, no. I wasn't passed out. Just got a gulp of river muck and accidentally breathed some of it in. Anyway, you're the one who fell on her ass."

She thought he was blunt, but it didn't seem like he meant to insult her. "Where are you from? You don't look like anyone I've ever met."

He ran his hand through his hair, then held it in front of his face and frowned mightily at the dirt. "You mean you've never seen a guy this good-looking?"

It had been a while since she'd seen any guy at all, and her frame of reference for what she thought was good-looking was mostly derived from romance novels Sister Elizabeth read. She started to laugh but stopped quickly. It wasn't nice to laugh at a guy for thinking he was good-looking coated in river muck. What if he was being serious?

"I, uh, meant I've never seen anyone dressed like that. Though maybe I have. You have some mud—" she looked him up and down "—everywhere."

He eyed himself, then brushed his hand over the front of his clothes. The mud rolled off and splashed into the stream at their feet.

She was awed by the trick. "You have magic."

He magicked more dirt off his sleeves. "I thought *you* had magic."

She took a step back, trod on a sharp rock, nearly fell again, and then blushed from the amusement that appeared on his face. "How can you tell?"

"Where I come from, we usually start our introductions with names." He stuck his dirty hand out like she was supposed to do something with it. "I'm Max."

She stood awkwardly and unsure of what he wanted from her. He wiped his hand on his pants, reached out again, took her hand from her side, and squeezed it. As he did, his eyes locked on hers and she found herself staring at those purple rings. "God, you're … gorgeous," he said, still holding her hand. "If you can't remember your name, maybe I'll just call you that."

She pulled her hand back fast. "It's Carina."

"Great, Gorgeous. Now we know each other better."

"How do you know I can do magic?" she repeated.

"You ask a lot of questions for a girl trying to help a guy she met facedown in a river," he noted. "Also, you have some mud—" his eyes flashed over her "—well, it's not everywhere I guess, but it's mostly everywhere. Can't *you* use magic for that?"

She wiped at the mud on her dress with her hands, but there was only so much dignity Carina was willing to lose in a situation like this. No, she did not have the skill necessary to make mud roll off her clothes, but it wasn't safe to try anyway. It dawned on her that they were on the wrong side of the stream. She looked anxiously around, then started heading back across. "It's not safe to do magic here. You should come with me."

Max waded into the stream behind her. "To where?"

"To the other side. The Red-Eyed Ones won't be able to find us as easily there."

"How could they find us at all?"

The water was much colder now that she was in less of a rush. She was going to be freezing on the walk back to the house. "Don't you know? They can sense people with magic. But Novi Dupree is protected, and ..."

She stopped in the middle of the stream. He'd stopped behind her and was now crouched down by a boulder and nose-to-nose with a tiny frog.

"What are you doing?" she asked.

His eyes were glued to the frog. "I was trying to get a better look at those lizard fish things in the stream earlier, but this little guy is amazing. Those colors are so *vivid*."

What Carina thought was "amazing" was that Max was still standing in the middle of the stream. She peered into the distance behind him. She didn't see anyone else, but still ...

"They're on the other side, too. Come on," she urged.

"The Red-Eyed Ones could be coming for us."

He stood back up. "The Red-Eyed Who's again?"

"The Red-Eyed Ones. You know, the Immortals? It's what we call them here because they have red eyes."

"You call the Immortal humans Red-Eyed Ones?"

"Yes." She tried not to sound impatient as she started moving forward again without him. "And we are not safe from them because you did magic and Sister Agda says they can sense magic like a light in the dark."

"Huh." She heard Max wading behind her. "You don't have to be in such a rush then."

"Why not?"

"Because I didn't do any real magic. My clothes are made of a material that's designed to repel dirt."

She stopped at the other side and watched him splash the rest of the way in his apparently dirt-repelling clothing. "I don't think Sister Elizabeth knows there's fabric that can do that."

He brushed his slacks with his hands and the additional muck he'd accumulated slid off. Then he smiled pleasantly again. "Maybe you should introduce me to Sister Elizabeth."

She couldn't decide if she was impressed by his pants or jealous. "Maybe you should tell me how you know I can do magic."

His stomach growled so loud she heard it. *That* was impressive. He put his hand to it. "You don't happen to know a place I can get lunch?"

Sister Agda would never have allowed someone to bring a strange guy back to the sanctuary for lunch. Sister Rachel and Sister Lindy would have agreed it was too dangerous. Miguela would have left him on the other side of the stream.

But Max had a charming sheepish look, and Sister Agda

wasn't a good role model.

"If I find you lunch, will you tell me how you know I can do magic?"

His face lit up. "That would be a great deal!"

"Okay." She started trudging in her wet dress toward the house. "Follow me."

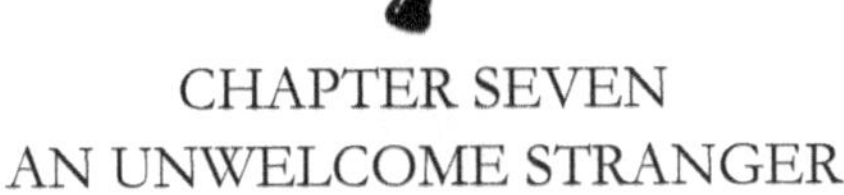

CHAPTER SEVEN
AN UNWELCOME STRANGER

Max ate like he was starving, though Carina was sure he wasn't. He had a solid build. He rolled up the sleeves of his sweater, and she noticed that his forearms were muscular and sort of hairy. Sister Raji had similarly muscular, hairy forearms, but Max made it look good.

She'd led him into the kitchen through the back door, hoping to avoid Miguela. Then she got out crusty bread and soft cheese, pointed Max to a stool by the old butcher's block, and told him to dig in. He did not need to be told twice.

"This is the best bread I've ever eaten," he said, tearing off another piece. "I haven't had anything so fresh in years. The mushy cheese is good, too. Did it come from a cow yesterday?"

Carina rifled through the pantry for meat. The only meat she ever ate was fish, but she didn't think Max was a vegetarian. "It didn't come from any cow. That's goat cheese, and we age it for months. But the bread was made this morning."

"You *made* this?" Max asked, his mouth so full of cheese

and bread that it came out something like: "Ew *ad* thes?" He swallowed and continued: "With your hands?"

She found the smoked wild pork and set it out. "Not me personally, but yeah, Sister Lindy makes fresh bread every other day."

Max speared a slice of pork. "Sister Lindy is talented." He licked his lips, and Carina realized she hadn't gotten him anything to drink. She opened the icebox to look for milk while he went on. "How many Sisters live here?"

"About thirty." There were several bottles of chilled ginger apple ale sitting on a shelf in the icebox. Carina considered the normally forbidden bottles. The Sisters were proud of their beer. It was only *friendly* to serve your best stuff to a guest.

"And Sister Agda's the head nun?"

Carina snatched two bottles from the shelf, retrieved a bottle opener from a drawer, shut the drawer with her hip, and levered the top off the first bottle. It made a satisfying hissing sound. She handed the bottle to Max.

"She's the prioress. Here, the Sisters make this, too."

Max took an enthusiastic swig and wiped his mouth with the back of his hand. "This is the best soda I've ever had. What kind of nuns make their own soda?"

Carina picked up the other bottle, opened the top, and tried not to make it obvious to Max that she'd never tried the ale. "It's light beer, and they aren't nuns. It's a solidarity thing, not a religious thing."

"Oh, this is a sorority," Max said, nodding like he completely understood now, even though Carina didn't know what a sorority was herself. "And is Sister Elizabeth, like, Sister Agda's second-in-command?"

"Not really. That would be Sister Raji," Carina said, lifting her bottle toward her mouth. The fizz in the air was sweet on her lips. The ginger tickled her nose. She could practically taste the ale, but it wasn't meant to be. A cry from the doorway leading into the kitchen startled her before she could take a sip. The bottle slipped from her fingers and smashed to the floor.

Miguela had found them.

Standing in the doorway and wearing an ugly brown dress that Sister Elizabeth had only made because Miguela said it was what she liked best, Carina's little sister looked like a miniature Sister Agda. The severe way she knotted up her hair with the same thin brown scarf every day contributed to the image. Carina didn't know how Miguela could stand it. Unless it was in a messy ponytail, her own hair nearly always hung down in curly, loose tangles. Also, dresses were easier than pants for Sister Elizabeth to make, but a girl could at least opt for some color. Carina's still-damp and muddy dress was bright green-apple cotton with dainty white accent stripes.

But Miguela probably didn't even notice the mud on Carina's dress. She was too busy gripping the door frame like this was her worst nightmare come to life. That was a clear misunderstanding of the situation. Obviously, this was *Carina's* worst nightmare. What did she have to do to get a tiny sip of beer?

"Carina! Who. Is. HE?"

Max gulped down the last chunk of bread he'd bitten off. "Uh, hey," he said brightly to Miguela. "I'm Max. Do you live here too?"

Miguela ignored him and trained her eyes on Carina. The girls had the same big, brown, upturned eyes with long arched eyebrows that (Carina thought) were feminine on her and evil on her sister. "*What* do you think you're doing?" Miguela gestured disdainfully toward Max. "Where did you find *him*?"

Carina tried to stay calm. "By the stream while I was out. He needed help."

Red hot circles glowed on Miguela's cheeks. "You *crossed* the border *again*?"

Carina lost her calm. "I wasn't doing magic when I did it!" She clenched her fists. "And I had to! He looked like he was drowning!"

Max lifted his bottle up toward them before taking another drink. "And probably like I'd passed out," he said, presumably trying to be helpful.

Miguela watched him nurse his bottle of beer.

"Which he *wasn't*," Carina clarified. "But I thought he was, and then I thought he'd done magic, so I had to bring him back here, and—"

"You crossed the boundary line again." Miguela's nose seemed very snout-like when she was this disgusted. "Do you *want* the Red-Eyed Ones to find us?"

Max tilted his stool back on two legs. "What's so special about this border?" He looked curiously at Carina. "And if the border is such a big deal, why didn't you use magic to lift me across? That way you wouldn't have had to cross yourself. Or is it the magic that can't cross?"

Carina's fingertips were cold now, and the feeling was spreading as she became more defensive. She didn't know how to explain Novi Dupree's special powers to protect them from the Red-Eyed Ones. She didn't know how the ancient wards worked. She opened her mouth to try to explain anyway, but Miguela cut her off with a cry:

"*You* were practicing magic, too?!"

"I was not!" Carina cried back.

"If you weren't practicing magic, then how does *he* know

you can do it?"

Carina didn't have an answer to that yet. Max had only been in the kitchen a few minutes. They hadn't gotten to talking about magic again. Still, she trusted her own instincts, and she didn't think she should have to explain herself to Miguela. Other than the apple ale, she hadn't done anything wrong.

"I don't know how he knows, but I wasn't doing magic!" she insisted. "And if you're so smart, why don't *you* tell me what I was supposed to do? Should I have left him by the stream to die, coughing up sludge?"

Max shuddered. "That would have been a nasty way to go."

"You could have come and gotten me," Miguela said sharply.

"I didn't have *time* for that," Carina retorted.

Miguela shifted her narrowed eyes to the ground and crossed her arms protectively over her chest. It was something she did when she didn't feel safe, and it always put a gnawing pain in Carina's own chest. It wasn't okay that they had to be so worried all the time about the Red-Eyed Ones. Carina hated that Miguela felt that way, but Max wasn't dangerous. She was *sure* of it.

"He needed help," she repeated.

"I thought you said he didn't. And you don't know who *he* is." Miguela pointed at Max. "He looks weird. He could be a spy for the Red-Eyed Ones."

Max was now rocking back and forth on the two back legs of the stool. "I'm not!" he said quickly, putting his hands in the air and nearly tipping the stool over. He grabbed fast for the edge of the butcher's block to catch himself. "Really. You can trust me. I'm not here to hurt anyone."

Miguela gave him one long, unimpressed look, then

turned back to Carina. "What are you going to tell the Sisters when they get back?"

Carina glanced at the broken glass and the ale seeping through the floorboards.

Miguela let out a short, nasty chortle. "You better clean that up before they get back … *if* you want them to wait until tomorrow to kick you out." Then she turned up her snout, pivoted on her heel, went out the door, and muttered something offensive about Carina on her way.

"I heard that!" Carina shouted.

"I didn't say anything!" Miguela shouted back.

Max took another slice of wild pork and wolfed it down like he thought maybe Carina wouldn't want him to eat more now. "That girl doesn't like you much, does she?" he said when Miguela was gone.

Carina laughed bitterly. "Not much. That was my sister, by the way. Miguela."

"I don't have any siblings. Are you going to be in big trouble for bringing me back here?"

She half-smiled at him. "I've been in trouble for worse."

He scratched the side of his face. "Like for floating that bottle across the stream?"

"You know about that?"

Max ducked his head apologetically. "I've been hiding in that shack for a few weeks. I'm kind of on the road, but I got lost, and it seemed like a safe place to stay while I tried to figure out what to do. There were a dozen cases of soda in there and all these jars of stuff to eat—" He blushed. "Though I finished those off fast."

If there had been anything exciting left about the bottle of sassafras Carina had attempted to steal, it was that she didn't know where it came from. Now she felt disappointed for unknown reasons. "You were the one who put the sassa-fras on the windowsill? Did you put that one on my side of the stream, too?"

"Uh, yeah." Max blushed. "I'd seen you out there, and I was trying to come up with a way to say hello, and … uh … sorry if I got you in trouble."

Max had a cute guilty puppy dog look. It was hard to be irritated with a boy who looked that way telling you he was sorry for getting you in trouble. Carina sighed. "Do you have anywhere else to stay for now?"

Max shook his head.

"Then I guess it doesn't matter if they're mad, does it? They aren't going to turn you out on your own without even giving you shelter for the night. It's too dangerous."

"And tomorrow?"

Carina didn't want to think about that. "Is another day. We can worry about it later. Maybe we can convince the Sisters to let you stay a while."

"Do you think that's possible?" Max asked eagerly.

Carina looked around the kitchen at the mess she'd made. "It's not *im*possible." She grabbed a rag from the counter. Only highly *improbable*, she thought.

She asked *really* nicely.

"Absolutely not," Sister Agda said, peering down at Carina like she was trying to decide if there was any prey worth being hunted where Carina stood. They were in Sister Agda's room. She and Sister Raji were the only Sisters that had their own rooms, Sister Agda because she was the prioress and Sister Raji because she handled all the finances and operations for the brewery. While Sister Raji's room was overflowing with paperwork and *stuff*, Sister Agda's room contained only a narrow cot shoved into a corner, a single wardrobe dresser that held her personal things, and a wide, sturdy desk. Not a pen was out of place on that desk, and Sister Agda was sitting behind it with her hands folded neatly over a closed ledger.

Carina sat in an uncomfortable wooden chair on the other side.

"But Sister Agda," she pleaded, "he's lost. He doesn't have anywhere else to go, and he was practically starving when I found him."

Sister Agda barked out a laugh. "He was hungry, not starving. And he's availed himself of our services already, tearing through our emergency supplies." She rolled her eyes. "He's a runaway, Carina, and he wandered into the wrong place. He can be on his way."

"You're going to make him leave?" Carina's spine straightened at the thought of the Sisters kicking Max out today. "There are Red-Eyed Ones out there!"

"He survived this long."

Carina leaned forward and gripped the edge of the desk. "Barely!"

Sister Agda opened a drawer and took out a pen and a piece of paper. "I'll give him directions to the monastery in Clemson. The monks will take him in if he really needs help."

Carina was horrified. "Isn't Clemson a two-day trip? With wagons!? He's on foot!"

Sister Agda waved her hand dismissively. "It's not that far. I'm sure Lindy will pack him a lunch. He has to go. He's the last thing we need right now."

"Sister Raji wouldn't have turned him out," Carina tried as a last resort.

"Sister Raji isn't here, and she doesn't make these

decisions," Sister Agda replied icily.

It was the cold shoulder that had always been hardest for Carina to bear with Sister Agda. She fought the tears now welling angrily in her eyes. "This isn't fair."

Sister Agda was unfazed. "Nothing is fair. Go tell Sister Lindy to pack him some food. He should get started if he wants to find shelter before the dusk moon goes down."

Usually, Carina tried to keep her temper with the Sisters—even Sister Agda—for Miguela's sake. But as Sister Agda wrote out directions for Max with short scratches of her pen, all Carina's feelings spilled out. "I hate you," she heard herself say. "And you probably think we're lucky you let us stay, but we would have been better on our own."

That last part wasn't true, but Carina did not care.

Sister Agda set down her pen and leaned back silently.

"If he can't stay, I'm leaving with him," Carina threatened.

"Go then," Sister Agda said, picking back up the pen. "No one's holding you here."

Carina stormed out of the room with tears streaked down her face. She'd left Max in the kitchen, and she needed to pack her meager belongings before she told him what had happened. But she didn't get more than a few steps out the door before she smacked into Miguela.

Her sister's face was pale, and her arms were crossed again. "You're *leaving?*" she asked in the brutally even tone she'd learned from Sister Agda and only used when she was furious.

Carina pointed at the door to Sister Agda's room. "What would I have to stay for? Strangers treat me better than she does!"

"She keeps us safe." Miguela's face was set, but there was a hint of panic in her eyes.

Carina's heart sank. "I know you don't remember as much as I do, Miguela, but this isn't what Mom and Dad would have wanted for us. It wasn't like this. They never would have locked us up like the Sisters do. There's no way they would have wanted—"

"They wouldn't have wanted us to be *safe*?"

"What's going on?" Max was walking down the hall toward them. He looked at Carina. "Hey, I know you said to stay in the kitchen, but it's been a while, and that woman in there— was she Sister Lindy?—says I ask too many questions."

Miguela spun toward him. "Good news, then. You don't have to talk to her anymore. Sister Agda's kicking you out, and Carina's going with you." She did not give him time to respond before she stomped away.

Carina swallowed hard while Max chewed on his lower lip, watching Miguela go. "What does she mean by that? I guess … if I can't stay here and you want to leave with me, that would be … it would be awesome to have someone to travel with, but …"

He paused for a long breath.

The rage Carina had felt before was deflating inside her, leaving a vast space for regret instead. "I'm sorry, Max. It's supposed to be a sanctuary for women, and Sister Agda doesn't know you, so you can't stay, and even if it *would* be amazing for me to get away, I can't leave Miguela."

He held up his hands. "It's okay. I get it. I wasn't here for … I mean, I wasn't looking for a place to stay long, and I didn't mean to get you into a fight with your sister. I'll go. We'll probably run into each other another time."

There was no way they would run into each other

another time.

"I'm sorry," Carina repeated.

Max winked at her. "It's no problem, Gorgeous. Family comes first, right?"

She didn't have it in her to say "yes."

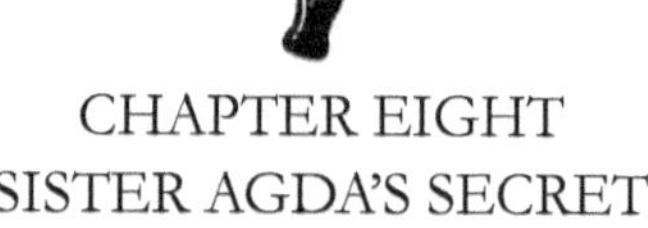

CHAPTER EIGHT
SISTER AGDA'S SECRET

Shadows darkened the corners of Sisters Faye and Gracie's room the night of Max's departure. He had been sent out weighed down by a backpack full of food and other supplies. The Sisters even gave him one of the wool blankets they made. ("Because we don't want him coming back," is what Sister Lindy said of the hospitality.)

Now Carina lay next to Miguela in bed, wondering how far Max had gotten already. They'd barely had the chance to talk. She didn't even know where he was trying to go. He'd said he was lost. Carina *wished* she had enough freedom to get lost.

"Why would anyone want to stay here?" she grumbled to the ceiling.

Miguela shifted on her pillow. "The Red-Eyed Ones can't find us here."

"Maybe the Red-Eyed Ones don't care about us anymore. There are tons of people with magic. Maybe that's why they haven't come yet. Maybe we would be fine if we left."

"Maybe we wouldn't."

"I guess we'll never know." Carina yanked the covers her way. "We'll probably die here like Sisters Faye and Gracie."

Miguela rolled toward Carina. "It doesn't have to be forever. If you could learn how to stop using your magic—"

"How's that going to happen if I never have a teacher?" Carina snapped.

Miguela lay quiet for a while. Then she said softly: "You don't ever have to leave. You could stay and become a Sister if you wanted. With me."

"As if Sister Agda would let that happen." Carina turned her back to Miguela. She wouldn't leave Miguela alone, but that didn't stop her from feeling angry about it now.

Miguela turned the other way. "Good night," she said.

Carina didn't say a word.

It was pitch black in the room when Carina opened her eyes. Miguela was shifting around under the blankets like she was having a bad dream.

Carina closed her eyes again.

And opened them.

Something was wrong. She felt … distressed. She could hear noises coming from outside the room. She listened more carefully. People were bustling around. She hoped something hadn't happened to one of the Sisters. Some of them were very old. She sat up, thinking someone might need help, and the door to the room swung open.

Sister Elizabeth was standing there. She was wearing the skimpy nightgown she usually wore to bed because she said it got too hot with Sister Rachel sleeping next to her in flannel. Sister Elizabeth had a lovely silk kimono that she wore if she was going to be running around outside her room in her nightgown.

She was not wearing the kimono now.

"Good, you're up." Sister Elizabeth flipped on the lights.

Miguela moaned in her sleep. Carina got up on her side of the bed. "What's wrong?" she asked as she searched for her robe. "I didn't know you were back."

"You need to go," Sister Elizabeth said, coming in and throwing a satchel toward Carina. "Get your things. Miguela's too."

Carina went to the drawers she and Miguela shared and started stuffing the satchel with clothes. "Why?"

Sister Elizabeth shook Miguela. "Wake up, Miguela," she said loudly. "You need to wake up, now."

Miguela stirred and sat up, rubbing her eyes.

Sister Elizabeth crouched by the bed. She stood up and handed Miguela her shoes. "Put these on." She looked at Carina. "Where are yours?"

"Desk," Carina said, shoving pairs of socks into the satchel more quickly.

"What's going on?" Miguela asked. "Why are we up?"

Sister Elizabeth tossed Carina her shoes from under the desk. "Quick. Get your coat, too. They're coming. You have to get out."

Carina tasted acid in her mouth and couldn't swallow. "The Red-Eyed Ones? How do you know? How close are they?"

Sister Elizabeth pulled Miguela from the bed, threw her coat around her shoulders, and pushed her toward the door. "Raji said—"

"Elizabeth! Are they up?" Sister Raji appeared in the doorway. Her cheeks, which were normally rosy and puffed into a smile, were drawn. She hustled in like she wasn't pushing seventy and grabbed Carina's wrist. "Come on, girl, we need to move."

Carina snagged her coat from a hook by the door and let herself be dragged out of the room by Sister Raji. "I thought you were still gone. When did you guys get back?"

"Late last night. We've been racing them here. Don't know how they found us. Someone must have figured out the connection."

Carina would have stopped at that if Sister Raji hadn't had such a tight grip on her wrist. "Wait, I thought—"

"Hurry!" Sister Lindy was sprinting toward them. Carina hadn't thought she was capable of sprinting. She was packing a lot of pastry on those hips, and right now she was holding another satchel, too. She thrust it into Miguela's hands. "It's packed with dried meats, bread, and enough cheese to last for two weeks. Then you'll have to find more."

"How did you pack this so fast?" Miguela asked.

Carina had far more questions than that. "How long do you expect us to be gone? How are we supposed to find food after two weeks? *When* did you pack these bags?" It had not occurred to her until just then that they were really leaving Novi Dupree, but now that reality was setting in, so was terror.

Sister Elizabeth laughed, rubbed her glassy eyes, and grabbed Carina's hands. "We've had those bags packed forever. You have everything you need, and you will be fine."

"*That's* how sure you were the Red-Eyed Ones would find us?" Carina said.

"Then this is all Carina's fault!" Miguela barked.

Sister Raji's face wrinkled. She turned unexpectedly on Miguela, clamping her hands down tight on Miguela's shoulders. "You listen. They've been looking for you all along, and they're going to keep looking, so don't blame this on your sister. The last thing you need is to make enemies of each other. You have to learn to trust each other again."

Miguela pulled back with a pale face. "We do trust each other."

"You love each other," Sister Elizabeth corrected more gently. "You haven't trusted each other in a long time."

Sister Lindy made a choked noise.

"Pull it together, Lindy!" Sister Raji ordered. They had reached the back door, where Sister Rachel was waiting with two backpacks.

She helped Carina put one on. "Agda made a map for you. It's in the front pocket. But tonight, don't stop to worry about that in the dark. Cross the stream out back, then follow it up the mountain as far as you can. Don't rest until you can't walk any further. The first town you'll come to is Clemson, but—"

Sister Rachel paused. She had the same expression on her face that she got whenever she was sure Carina wasn't getting something in their lessons. She swooped in and hugged Carina. "Tonight, all you have to do is get away from this place. And don't stop in Clemson later. That's where *they'll* expect you to go. There will be other towns on your way."

Carina was dumbfounded while Sister Rachel hugged Miguela next. "I'm so sorry," was all she could think to say as the dread inside her began to feel heavier than the backpack.

Sister Raji blew through her lips like a frustrated horse. "I *said* this wasn't your fault. I knew we should have told you more." She tightened a strap on Carina's backpack for her. "And there's no time now. But we were only trying to protect you. Even Agda. Especially Agda."

Miguela was crying. Carina was too shocked to cry.

Sister Lindy wiped her eyes while Sister Rachel wrung her

hands anxiously.

"Stop that!" Sister Raji ordered.

The back door opened. Sister Agda was behind it. Carina had never, ever seen Sister Agda in a nightgown. The one she was wearing now was black and silky, and her hair was down and blowing in the wind. For a wild second, Carina thought Sister Agda looked almost pretty—in a warrior kind of way—and that she was looking at her with a lot less fury than she should have been.

"The map will take you to the Eastern Ridge Trail. Follow it north to Cerulean. You'll find help there," she said.

Miguela flew at Sister Agda and hugged her tightly. "Will we ever see you again?"

Sister Agda patted Miguela's back, but ignored her question, speaking to Carina instead over her head. "A wagon would slow you down. You'll have to go by foot tonight. But there's money in the packs. You'll have enough to buy whatever supplies you need later."

Sister Elizabeth put her arm around Miguela and drew her away from Sister Agda. "We'll go with you to the stream."

Miguela moved forward with the other Sisters following. Carina started after them, but at the last second, Sister Agda caught her arm.

Carina was confused as to what Sister Agda might want, but she also still felt bad about what was happening. When Sister Agda didn't speak, Carina said: "I'm sorry. I didn't mean to put you or anyone else in danger."

Sister Agda made a cross noise. "As if the whole world revolves around you."

The regret Carina had felt momentarily transformed to rage, and she faced Sister Agda straight on for what she hoped would be the last time. "What are you talking about? I never thought I was important to anyone around here. You treated me like an ethical obligation from the very beginning."

Sister Agda seemed to consider the weight of Carina's words. "You are right about that," she said slowly.

Carina frowned. "Why do you think that's okay?"

The others had gone forward, but Sister Agda looked back. The south gate was visible in the distance, lit by the front lights that were always on at Novi Dupree at night. The gate was hanging open. Sister Agda pointed at it.

"See that?"

It was the gate Carina had passed through only once. She nodded. Sister Agda lifted her hand just barely, and the gate closed. Then she waved her hand again, and the gate opened.

She could do magic.

Carina didn't know what to say.

Sister Agda touched the claw piercing her ear. "There are things you need to know, and it's not my place to tell you. My responsibility was only to keep you safe until …" She stopped like she didn't know how to complete that. "For as long as I could."

"For as long as you …" Carina started to repeat as anger began to chill her. "But … you can do magic. Why didn't you help me? If you could do it … why didn't you teach me?"

Sister Agda rubbed the claw again. "Not everything is as simple as you think. Magic can be dangerous. I fled from mine years ago when it put my family in danger."

"Like mine put Miguela in danger?"

Sister Agda seemed almost contrite. "No. You've been in danger since you got here. I thought it would be better if you didn't know the truth. Your sister was always so afraid of magic, and—"

A noise that sounded like horses cut her off and made

them both look at the gate. Someone really *was* coming, and they were coming fast.

Sister Agda grumbled something Carina didn't understand, shaking her head while she did it, then nodded in the direction Miguela and the other Sisters had gone. "You need to go, Carina Garcia. You're not safe here anymore."

Carina couldn't make her feet move. "Then I'm not safe anywhere."

"*Go,*" Sister Agda ordered, and Carina felt like she'd been pushed physically back. She took the cue, though, and ran to meet Miguela, who was waiting for her by the stream.

Sister Elizabeth gave Carina a quick hug and a shove toward the water. The other Sisters shouted things like "Be careful!" and "Good luck!" And as Carina and Miguela waded across the stream, Carina thought she heard Sister Raji's strong voice last.

It sounded like she was saying: "Head to the North!"

EXCERPT FROM *FALLING FAST FROM EAST TO WEST*

The first record of magic on Kepler dates to the year 76 AAH (After Arrival of Humans), when Birch Talon fell while climbing the ridges of the Eastern Plateaus and avoided injury by controlling the air to slow her fall. The aerodynamic tendency was later exercised by both Talon's son and daughter. Although other Easterners began displaying magic traits, the Talon family became widely regarded as the most powerful in the East. A similar incident occurred on the West Coast in 85 AAH, when Solomon Fordham was observed flying a hang glider for over twenty-four hours. The Fordham family pioneered aviation in the West until their tragic demise.

In the meanwhile, two families from North and South Kepler, respectively, also acquired powerful elemental gifts, theirs associated with thermodynamics. Thus, in each of the four corners of the mainland continent, one family line was gifted with more magic than any others. These "Cardinal Families"—as we call them today—served naturally as regional leaders, displacing the need for central leadership from the original Mortal City of Gandhi as the Keplerian population increased in size.

In the year 276 AAH, Kepler officially divided into four nations: The Western Republic, The Eastern Confederation, the Northern Kingdom, and the Southern Kingdom. The event is known as The Cardinal Split.

Over the years, it was widely accepted that the Cardinal Families of the East and West were more magically gifted than the Cardinal Families of the North and South, but the latter proved to have more longevity. Though no one knows whether the Cardinal Family of the West would have maintained either its magic or its power if not for the arrival of the Immortality Virus along with the Immortal Ships in 492 AAH, it was only two decades after the last member of the Fordham family died that the Cardinal Family of the East renounced its leadership claim to the Eastern Confederation, conceding control to the Confederation's several clan leaders.

Kepler at large was shocked to discover that the reason for this shift was the decline of magic in the Talon family, which had failed to produce any members with First Degree magical capabilities in over three generations.

CHAPTER NINE
TOGGLEBALL

Vivian's new coach had bench cushions that were about a fingernail's length thicker than the last, if you were a nail-biter. The curtains were drawn to shade her from the sun, but the windows were stuck closed, and Vivian didn't know how to fix that without telekinesis. Her clothes were moist with sweat. She wished she could take off her socks, but she couldn't let her attendants see her like that. Queens didn't go barefoot.

She'd thought about asking Bast to sit with her—that would have cooled things down—but she didn't feel like asking for more help. He had siphoned more magic from himself and Nate before they'd gotten back on the road, and they weren't the kind of family that was good at sharing.

When the coach slowed in the afternoon for a stop, Vivian climbed out on her own. There were three steps to the ground, and she was so dizzy by the time she got there, she had to sit.

One of the attendants hurried over. "Queen Vivian, are

you okay?"

"I want to get up and walk," she said.

The attendant looked young. Vivian didn't know her name. "But Prince Bastian said—"

Vivian summoned the strength she needed to stand and put on her "I'm in charge here" look. She knew it was intimidating. She'd learned it from her mother.

The sound coming out of the girl's lips dropped off. Nausea rolled through Vivian's gut, but she drawled: "Is Prince Bastian the queen?"

"No, Your Highness," the girl said meekly.

"That's right," Vivian said haughtily. "He is not. *I* am the queen. Do you understand?"

"Yes, Your Highness." The girl appeared to be properly admonished. "May I assist you?"

This helped repair Vivian's pride, but her legs still felt gelatinous. Her mouth was also repulsively dry. She needed the girl to go away before any of that showed through. "You may bring me water and a meal, along with fresh clothes." Vivian waved her hand through the air to signal that the girl should leave, and she scurried away. As soon as she was gone, Vivian stumbled back onto the steps of the coach again. She shut her eyes.

When she opened them, Bast was standing in front of her. He was holding a bowl of soup; it sloshed over her fingers as he handed it to her. Bast never sloshed anything accidentally. He did not apologize.

She took a slow sip and said "thanks."

"You're supposed to be resting," he responded curtly.

She took another sip. "I rested all day."

Her brother's mouth closed in a thin seam while Vivian thought about how she couldn't eat any more soup. It was going to make her sick. She let the bowl hang in her hands instead. He watched her intently, and she wondered how she was going to retreat to the coach without letting him know how bad she felt.

Bast took the bowl back before she could figure out how to disguise the sickness. "The virus is going to make you feel worse as it spreads. If you need something, send for an attendant. If you think they can't manage, send an attendant for me." He nodded at the steps. "Do you need help getting back up there?"

Vivian looked past Bast. They were traveling on a dusty road through fields of sour corn and Kepler long grains. She tried to remember what else she knew about this area. There had been a briefing on the state of the kingdom before the coronation. She thought maybe there had been a drought in this area recently, but her brain was muddled.

"Viv? Do you need help?"

"No," she lied.

Bast set the bowl down and leaned in. She begrudgingly let him help her up three steps.

"Your telepathy gift is an unfair advantage," she complained. "And my coach is stuffy."

He barely fluttered his fingers, and the window opened easily for him. "Speaking of unfair advantages, Nate's thermodynamic magic is atrocious. We're going to travel through the night to put more distance between us and any Immortals, but tomorrow evening we'll stop in Guarneri, and I'm going to make Nate train with me. If you rest today and you feel up to it tomorrow, you can watch."

Vivian liked the Bast that bribed her with time out of her rolling jail better than the one that sloshed soup over her fingers.

"Maybe I can give tips from the sidelines?" she suggested.

"Yeah. I knew you'd want to help Nate," Bast said bitterly.

"It was *your* idea," she said, but he was already out the door.

Vivian lay back down and wanted to cry. But crying was not a queenly thing to do. Instead, she began composing a mental list of items she needed her advisers to brief her on when she returned to the castle. She fell asleep thinking about the drought she knew nothing about.

The next evening, they stopped in Guarneri, which was small enough that the guards could sweep it for Immortals in an hour. Then Bast commandeered a toggleball field for his training session with Nate and had Captain Thurlow set up a security perimeter so they could practice magic there.

Vivian had never been to a toggleball game, and she didn't know much about the sport, except that it involved a bunch of people running three balls back and forth across a field. In Alighieri, toggleball was considered a plebeian sport, but the field here was perfect for magic training and it was nice to be outside. Vivian sat in the field's bleachers behind chain link panels, savoring the fresh air while the sun began to sink and the dusk moon peeked out over the horizon. She felt better than she'd felt all day.

Nate, on the other hand …

"Oof."

She grimaced on his behalf as Bast slammed him against the chain links. It was already the fourth time that had happened, and they hadn't even started in on thermodynamics yet. This was a telekinetic warm-up.

"Viv, remind me to add basic language lessons after this," Bast called to her as Nate let loose a lexicon inappropriate for a prince. "Nate's limited to four-letter words."

Nate got up and dusted himself off. "How is this supposed to help? *When* is this supposed to help? What's the likeliness that I'll ever have to fight someone with as much power as *Bast?*"

He was probably right. Standing on his own, Nate could do real damage. His problem, as their early teachers had learned, was control, not raw strength. Nate had run through several teachers before he finally burned one. Bast healed the poor woman, but she refused to continue working with Nate.

King Herschel had not been happy with his eldest son over that. Vivian remembered herself and Bast eavesdropping from the hallway outside their dad's library that evening while Dad shouted things at Nate. Harsh phrases the king never used with Vivian, like "lazy," "stupid," and even "God damned stubborn" reverberated off the walls in their father's deep voice until the library doors swung open and Nate stormed out of the castle.

He was missing for five days. The third day, Vivian appealed to her parents on behalf of Nate and asked for a search party. He was only eleven. She was sure he was going to die out there alone. Dad said nothing, though, and Mom said Nate would come back when he got hungry.

Bast didn't question the judgment. Vivian, however, had a few sleepless nights after that. The paternal connection was supposed to be orange-gold. That's how it was between Vivian and her father. But with Herschel and the boys, it was always a more tarnished color. Bast at least had an orange-blue connection with Mom, who probably wasn't capable of an orange-gold relationship with anyone. Nate's connection to Mom was piss-gray. The only way she could have cared less about him is if she had never met him.

Eventually, it was another family member—their dad's cousin, Franklin—who returned Nate to the castle. The two showed up together at the gates on a rainy night, soaked and looking like wild animals. Franklin had a grip like their father's, and it was placed firmly on Nate's shoulder. Vivian and Bast followed as Franklin marched Nate through the castle to King Herschel's library, for what she and Bast both expected to be another fight.

Despite his strong hand, though, Franklin had a soft way of communicating, and Dad had also calmed down. Vivian and Bast couldn't hear anything going on behind the closed library door, and Nate refused to talk about it later. But Franklin moved into the castle the next week and took over all of Nate's lessons himself, in private.

Vivian never understood what Nate could be learning from Franklin, whose only gift was a weak telesthesia ability. She'd asked her father about it once, but King Herschel had dismissed the concern.

"Just because you have power, doesn't mean you should use it," he'd said. "Franklin is a skilled swordsman. If Nate can learn that, maybe he'll be useful in the Guard."

But as Vivian watched Nate on the toggleball field now, she bet Nate wasn't thinking about how skilled he was as a swordsman.

"Try to think of me as ten men," Bast told Nate.

Nate glared at Bast. "I don't *want* to imagine a world where there are ten of you."

Bast tossed his head back. "I can't imagine why not. Again?"

Nate grunted something that seemed like an affirmative, and they continued while Vivian daydreamed about how much fun she'd be having if she could play, too. She was so deep in the daydream that she assumed Captain Thurlow was part of it when he appeared at the bottom of the bleachers. She'd fainted right into the captain's arms. He probably thought she was *delicate* now. Vivian hated that, but she liked the way his uniform stretched across his shoulders.

"Your Highness?" He'd taken a step up. "Your Highness?" Another two steps, then he was in her row. She also liked how he kept his hair short and trimmed, and that he had small ears that lay flat against his head like good ears should.

"Queen Vivian?"

That last one startled her. It seemed he was not a daydream. "Captain Thurlow?"

He smiled, and she noticed his dimples. "Yes, Your Highness. I wasn't sure I was going to be able to get your attention." He gestured toward Bast and Nate on the field. Nate had fallen again. "This seems like an intense practice session."

Nate's face was flushed. Fire sprang up all around him, making him look like a cartoon devil. Bast smiled angelically, and the ground froze and fractured. Within seconds the freeze had overtaken the flames, and steam was rising all over the field. Nate hadn't thought that out at all. He had to stop with the low, direct attacks. Bast could counter those easily.

The captain watched her watch them.

"I'm better than my brothers," she told him. "When I'm not sick."

"Yes, Queen Vivian. I know. I've seen you."

"When?"

He pointed to her bench. "May I sit?" She didn't nod, but he acted like she'd said yes anyway and sat down. It confused her. What exactly was he doing up here?

"Do you need to speak with me, Captain?" she asked defensively.

He shook his head and held up an envelope. "Letter came for Prince Bastian. But since he's busy and you're here, I thought maybe you'd like company while we both waited. I haven't seen you since …"

"Oh." Right. He was checking on her. Like she was an invalid.

"I'm sorry, Queen Vivian. That was disrespectful. You didn't summon me. I'll go."

She turned quickly in surprise. He was already standing. "No!" she exclaimed, and heat spread up her neck as he looked at her with what she hoped was not fright. She wasn't used to being kept company by anyone outside her family. She softened her tone. "I'd like you to stay."

He sank back down. "Okay." She spotted a faint dimple again, and it made her want to stare, so she tried to focus on her brothers. Nate was stalking toward Bast with his fists clenched and a new trail of fire on his heels while Bast stood calmly watching.

Bast flicked his wrist and Nate flew back in the air until he hit the chain links. The metal jangled in a way that must have felt very satisfying to Bast.

"Is this safe?" Captain Thurlow asked.

"Not at all." Vivian watched them wistfully. "I wish I was out there."

He laughed again. He had an infectious laugh, not too low and not too high, and without the strict seriousness she associated with most members of the Southern Guard. She laughed too, and it caught her off guard.

Captain Thurlow was angled forward with his elbows resting on his knees. The Southern Guard's regulation uniform included black cargo pants and a fitted, deep red shirt. The captain ranked high enough for a leather military jacket, but it was too warm for jackets, and his sleeves were rolled up. Still, he was dressed for work.

He made a sympathetic noise as Nate went down yet again.

"I need to ask you a question, Captain," she said.

"Your Highness?"

She toyed with a loose thread at the end of her blouse. All her clothes were tailored specifically for her by South Kepler's most revered designers. She needed to find out who the designer was for this shirt. The quality was unacceptable.

"Queen Vivian? You wanted to ask me something?"

She really had to. If she wanted to continue to allow him to keep her company. She tried to sound regal as she asked: "How well do you know my mother?"

Captain Thurlow looked regretful. "Not at all, I'm afraid."

Vivian relaxed. He didn't have an "in" with Mom. Or he was a good actor. She thought it was the former, but either way, she respected him more. They watched Nate land hard another time and throw up his arms like he was frustrated with the universe.

"That's enough already!" Nate shouted. "I'm done!"

"So soon?" Bast called sweetly.

Nate stood. "I'm going to be so sore tomorrow I'll barely be able to ride. Unless you want to heal the *bruises* on my buttocks—"

Bast held his hands up. "We're done." He strode happily behind as Nate trudged to the bleachers where Vivian and Captain Thurlow were sitting.

Captain Thurlow stood and handed the letter he was carrying to Bast. "One of our runners brought this in today, sir."

Bast opened it, and as he read, the cheerful smirk that had

been on his face fell. He handed the letter silently to Nate.

Vivian watched warily. "What is it?"

Nate glanced hesitantly at Bast and returned the letter to him.

"Nothing," Bast said, folding it up. "Letter from a university down in Cape Gregory."

"And …?" Vivian held her hand out for the letter.

Bast gave it to her. It was printed on cheap paper. "They've never seen your strain of the Immortality Virus. They don't know how to treat it."

"You sent the blood samples to a bunch of places, didn't you?" she asked. "This is just one, right?"

"Yeah, Viv," Bast said. Still, he didn't sound very convincing, and he turned almost immediately to head back down the bleachers. Nate followed hastily.

"I'll accompany you back, Your Highness," Captain Thurlow said, though the uneasy tone of his voice made Vivian think he knew more than she knew right now, too.

She stayed seated and thought about ordering him to tell her what was going on. She decided against an order, choosing only to ask: "Do you know what they're not telling me?"

The captain stared off across the toggleball field at nothing. Was he trying to avoid answering? Had Bast ordered him not to tell her things? She reconsidered demanding an answer, but before she could do it, he gestured toward the letter and said: "That wasn't the first one to come back."

"How many have come back?" she asked.

"Seven."

That sounded bad. "And how many are left?"

It took him a long time to answer, "five."

CHAPTER TEN
BISHOP AND KNIGHT

The bed Vivian slept in that night was lumpy, and the sheets made harsh swishing sounds that made her cringe whenever she turned. She was not happy. Why had they stopped in a town that was too small to have an adequate inn?

The owners of the house Bast had appropriated were miserly, too. They didn't offer extra linens or toiletries. If they had been kinder about abandoning their home for the night, Vivian would have made sure they were compensated generously. As it was, her party might forget to pay the couple.

But in any case, Vivian only had to tolerate a few short hours of substandard accommodations. The attendant she'd scared yesterday woke her up before dawn.

"I'm sorry, Your Majesty," she whispered. "Prince Bastian was afraid you'd miss the sunrise prayers."

The girl looked terrified of Vivian, but this time she wasn't in danger of being scolded. There was hardly anything Vivian could say. She couldn't refuse to participate in the prayers. She was above Bast, not God. Still, it was Bast she was irritated with as she joined him and Nate outside, already kneeling on mats along with the guards and attendants.

South Kepler had a lot of things going for it. The farmers in this area had three growing seasons, and the wine that came from the steeps near the South Coast was the best produced anywhere on Kepler. The ox calves on the ranches to the west of Alighieri were fatter than the ranchers, and the lambies there had thick, shiny coats.

Historians said art and culture flourished in South Kepler because the land was so bountiful, and Vivian certainly would not have wanted to live in the North, where the economy ran on industry and trade. Whenever Vivian pictured a Northerner, all she could see was a dirty face and leathery hands. But the Royal Church of South Kepler was always there to prevent the Southerners from getting cocky about their blessings.

Vivian tried to be diligent about following the rules of the Church. She worshiped at the Feast of Plenty, participated in Evenings of Communion, and normally never skipped the prayers. That was saying something, too, because the Royal Church of South Kepler required followers to pray on their knees, twice a day, at dawn and dusk, always facing the sun. Vivian prayed. She did not, however, take it personally when God did not answer her prayers.

Bast did.

"Good morning," she said as she knelt on the mat reserved for her between Nate and Bast. Nate yawned out "morning," but Bast didn't answer. Presumably, he was too busy conversing with a higher power.

The royal family was expected to obey the tenets of the church, and they had to be better than the commoners, but they did not have to be as pious as clergy members.

Truthfully, Vivian thought maybe the Royal Church liked it when members of the royal family messed up. It gave the church elders an opportunity to show that no Mortal was above sin.

Nevertheless, Bast was obsessed with the Royal Church. Vivian would have liked to know why. Her family had always been dutiful, but neither of Vivian's parents was ever especially devout. The last deeply religious member of the royal family had been Vivian's grandmother. She was still alive; she'd outlived King Cassius by a solid sixteen years and counting. Bast couldn't have been influenced by her, though. Grandma Liza had suffered from dementia most of his life.

The origin of Bast's fervency was a subject that was off-limits with him, too. Vivian had a theory as to where it had all come from, but it wasn't well-developed. The summer Bast turned ten, he made friends with a boy his age whose parents were both ordained vicars. Vivian was jealous, so she was mean to Bast about his friend.

She needn't have been. The friendship didn't last long. The boy's parents were arrested for unauthorized use of magic, convicted of treason, and executed shortly after Bast met him. The boy was sent away to a boarding school for orphans. She'd asked Bast once if he'd ever heard from his friend again, and the room they were in turned so cold icicles formed on the ceiling. She had not asked again, but Bast's intolerance for religious deviation increased after that.

Typically, Vivian could handle Bast's religious requirements. Today she wished he could relax a little. She hadn't participated in the prayers since the coronation. She'd been too fatigued. Bast must have decided that if she was well enough to watch him and Nate train, she was well enough to pray, but as the morning prayers started, she thought that was very unfair. Sitting on the bleachers was a heads-up activity. She wasn't sure she could take kneeling in prayer for a quarter of an hour without blacking out.

"Do we need to pray formally while we're traveling?" Nate asked after they got up. "Viv was dying over there."

"Do you have *any* tact?" Bast muttered.

But Vivian was surprised at Nate. "How did you know?"

"You were twitchy the whole time," he explained. "Usually that's just me. So, Bast, do we really have to do it?"

Bast, who was leading the way toward the table that had been set out for breakfast, turned on them like he was utterly exasperated. "Yes, we really have to do it."

"But does Viv? Don't you think God—" Nate pointed to the clouds "—would make an exception for her for a while? Shouldn't He already know we need help?"

"Obviously, He—" Bast glanced at Vivian "—or She knows. But prayer is about staying connected to a greater power. Stop praying, and it's like you've chosen to withdraw from that power, and that is not what Viv needs right now."

"Are those waffles?" Nate asked, watching as one of the attendants approached carrying a plate stacked high with one of Vivian's favorite breakfast foods. "Man, that's what *I* need."

"You're a pig," Bast said.

"I am duly appreciative of God's gift to us of waffles, especially since we're on the road," Nate said, licking his lips. He took three waffles, then snatched Vivian's plate and loaded just as many waffles on it. She opened her mouth to tell him she couldn't possibly eat that much, but he said: "Consider it a challenge, Viv. You've barely eaten anything in days. Maybe you won't feel so bad at the dusk prayers if you're not so weak."

Bast frowned. "I don't think God wants you to pass out

during prayer. If you feel that bad later, you can sit up. At least then you're still participating."

Nate laughed. "And if Bishop Bast says it's okay, you probably won't rot in hell for doing it. Hey, Bast, do you think God would grant us more waffles tomorrow if that's what I pray for tonight?"

But they didn't get the chance to find out whether God would approve of Nate's prayer because Captain Thurlow walked up to them then. He had several letters in his hand.

"Oh no," Nate said.

Bast took the letters and flipped through them. "Only two are from research labs. The third is a message from Mom."

"Oh, hell no," Nate said.

Vivian watched anxiously as Bast started opening the letters. He threw the first two on the table scornfully but read the letter from Mom carefully. "She's already in Gandhi. When we get there, she can brief Vivian on the state of the kingdom, and we can decide if it's safe to return to Alighieri yet."

"Wonderful," Nate said darkly. "Let's make that decision with Mom. Great idea."

Bast glared at him. "We'll move out immediately after breakfast. If we ride through the night, we can probably make it to Gandhi tomorrow."

Vivian's waffles tasted like cardboard. She pushed her plate away. "Do we have to rush? I don't think I can spend twenty-four hours straight in that coach."

"You'll survive it," Bast said.

Captain Thurlow spoke up. She'd been mildly annoyed about Bast ordering everyone around, but as the light in the captain's eyes caught her attention, she forgot about that. "If you'd like, you can ride with me for part of the trip, Queen Vivian."

"That's ridiculous," Bast said savagely. "We all know what happened the last time she rode with you."

"I'm sorry, Your Highness—" Captain Thurlow started, but Vivian interrupted him:

"Bast! That wasn't his fault!"

Bast ignored her and waved his hand at the captain. "You're dismissed, Thurlow. We'll let you know if we need anything."

The captain glanced briefly at her, but then nodded at Bast. "Very well, Your Highness."

As he walked away, Bast pointed his fork at Captain Thurlow's back. "I don't like that guy. I don't think we can trust him."

"*Viv* trusts him," Nate said.

Vivian thought maybe the virus was making her thermodynamics go crazy. She was feeling unnaturally warm. "I don't see why I shouldn't."

"I don't ever remember seeing him around Mom," Bast said.

"That's probably a good thing," Nate said. He reached over to steal a forkful of Vivian's leftover waffles. "But if you want fresh air, you can ride with me, Viv."

Since a ride with Captain Thurlow wasn't on Bast's list of approved activities for her, Vivian took Nate up on his offer that afternoon. "Pepper doesn't mind," he said, "and he's glad you're feeling better."

Pepper was Nate's horse. He had been born in the Royal stables when Nate was eleven. Pepper's parents were beautiful, white Galilean horses. There must have been a dud somewhere in the family tree, though, because Pepper's coat was white spotted with uneven gray marks, and he had a mane that couldn't decide if it was black, white, or gray. Since he couldn't be bred that way, the Royal Stables had no use for him.

Nate decided the horse was his when he learned it was going to be sold, and he demanded that he be allowed to buy the horse himself. Out of his allowance. Even on a royal child's allowance, and even though the horse Nate wanted couldn't be bred, it would have taken Nate years to pay for him. Luckily, King Herschel thought the episode was funny. He told Nate the horse could be his "free of charge" if Nate agreed to work in the stables in his free time. Nate was pleased, and the deal was made. He named the horse Pepper himself.

Bast—who went into sneezing fits whenever he spent too much time in the stables—thought Nate should be prohibited from ever naming any of the horses again. He was also fond of reminding Nate that "stable master" was a downgrade from "prince." None of this bothered Nate, who was convinced that Pepper was the most impressive horse in the royal collection.

And *no one* rode Pepper without Nate's permission. Vivian thought that was probably the only offense someone could commit that Nate would have been willing to send anyone to the dungeons for. Kill your neighbor? Community service. Touch the horse? Lethal injection.

So, Vivian felt special being allowed to ride Pepper with Nate. It wasn't thrilling like riding with Captain Thurlow would have been, but Vivian thought it was probably easier for her to sit with Nate behind her on a horse with his arms held loosely around hers. She might not have known how to handle that with Captain Thurlow.

Also, Pepper had a smooth gait, it felt good to be out in

the open, and Nate didn't talk much while he rode. Or maybe he talked telepathically to the horse. She wasn't sure. All she knew was that for a little while, she could escape the stale coach in peace.

They'd been riding for almost an hour before Nate broke the silence and said: "Did you know Bast is sending daily reports back to Mom?"

She hadn't known that, but she wasn't exactly shocked. Mom was sending messages to them. Bast wouldn't have thought not to keep her updated in return. And Vivian hadn't told him she thought Mom might have organized the Immortal assassins in the first place. Bast would never have believed it.

"I don't get it," Nate continued. "Wasn't the whole point of getting out of Alighieri to hide while you recover? Someone's *after* you. We're not safe sending scouts back all the time. What if one gets intercepted? And why do we need to meet with Mom? You're the queen. We can make decisions without her."

Vivian laughed heartlessly. "You think we could have declined Mom's summons?"

"If we're already exchanging letters, I don't understand why she needs to see us at all." There was poison in Nate's voice. "What for? To give us hugs and say she loves us? We don't need her."

"It's not impossible that she's worried about us," Vivian suggested.

Nate duplicated her heartless laugh. "Yes, it is, Viv. It's possible that she's worried about Bast. Franklin is probably the only one worried about you and me."

"Did you send back word to Franklin?"

"Of course not. I don't need someone blaming *me* for

an intercepted message. Anyway, Franklin's smart enough to track us on his own if he needs to."

The respect Nate put into everything he said about Franklin made Vivian miss her father. Nate's connection with Franklin was orange-gold wrapped with vines of leafy green. It was almost as nice as the connection Vivian herself had had with King Herschel.

"Are you sure we should be meeting up with Mom at all?" Nate asked after a few more moments of silence. "If I were you, I wouldn't want her anywhere near me." He snorted. "I don't want her anywhere near me as *me*."

"Don't say stuff like that," Vivian admonished.

"Why? It's what you're thinking, too."

"Don't say it out loud. It's dangerous."

"What's dangerous is meeting up with Mom." Nate rested his chin on her shoulder. "Hey, Vivian, do you think you could talk me through what I did wrong in that training with Bast last night? It hurts my pride to ask, but for the sake of my ass, I'd like losing to Bast to take longer."

CHAPTER ELEVEN
CONSTANCE OF GALILEO

Gandhi's skyline rose over the south shores of Great Crater Lake, a large freshwater lake in the center of the mainland. Vivian could see the silhouette of the city long before they reached it the next morning. In South Kepler, cities sprawled, and the tallest structures were the cathedrals. Even along the Aurelian Coast, where many of the kingdom's wealthiest patrons lived, homes were built to span ground, not pierce the sky. Gandhi, however, had Earthian-style skyscrapers. It rubbed the Royal Church of South Kepler all wrong.

Vivian thought the skyscrapers were gaudy herself, and it went along with her perception that most of Gandhi's wealth was dirty. South Kepler's official position was that Gandhi was under royal rule. The truth was, these days the whole place was run by an Immortal mob, which had infiltrated Gandhi's city council, and there were nests of Immortals throughout the city.

She added this to her list of problems she needed to fix as queen. Her favorite shoes came from an upscale boutique in Gandhi. She didn't want them tarnished by corruption. But today, Gandhi was an unsafe place for her to be recognized. Vivian's caravan stopped at a dock on Crater River outside Gandhi and boarded plain, solar-powered commuter boats to travel the rest of the way to the hotel where they were meeting Mom.

The hotel had its own private dock, and Captain Thurlow, who had been in another boat, met Vivian there. He offered a hand as she disembarked and said: "My apologies, Your Highness."

"Why are you apologizing?" she asked.

Captain Thurlow had a sturdy grip. "You were stuck in the coach all morning again. I offered to let you ride with me."

"That was yesterday, though, and I didn't think Bast approved."

"He didn't." That spark Vivian thought she'd seen in the captain's eyes was there again. "But I take my orders from you, Your Highness."

Vivian was aware of the concept of being "hit on." She was unfamiliar with it happening to her. The prospect of dating Queen Constance's daughter terrified most men. Captain Thurlow must have been brave. He didn't seem deterred by Bast either, who was marching angrily up the dock. Bast had been in the very first boat, and, it seemed, had already gone into the hotel.

"Mom's in the penthouse suite. She wants to see you, Vivian." He regarded Captain Thurlow coolly. "*Alone.*"

Nate, who had just joined from the last boat, shot a look at Vivian. "Wouldn't do it if I were you," he said under his breath.

Vivian's stomach felt sick. "Now? I haven't had a chance to clean up."

"Now," Bast confirmed. "You can clean up later. Mom won't care."

Clearly, there were things Bast did not understand about their mother, but Vivian was distracted when Captain Thurlow asked: "May I escort you, Queen Vivian?"

At that, Nate shot her a different kind of *look* while Bast narrowed his eyes at the captain. "That won't be—"

"I'd appreciate that," Vivian said, and she pretended Bast was not seething and Nate was not snickering while she walked into the hotel with the captain.

The hotel reflected the kind of money that rolled into Gandhi. It had smart-suited doormen, a glass-domed ceiling, and a light-reflecting marble floor. Vivian thought the lobby smelled like green tea. She was wearing dirty jeans, and she thought *she* might smell like her stuffy coach. Hardly anyone looked her way. No one would expect the queen of South Kepler to look like she belonged at a motel with cheap linens and suspicious carpet stains.

The captain was quiet until they were inside the elevators alone. Then he said: "Your brothers really look out for you."

"Yeah. Too much sometimes." There were mirrors on all sides of the elevator. Her face was greasy and splotchy. She patted down a bump in her hair. "I'm a wreck."

Captain Thurlow glanced sideways at her. "You are? I hadn't noticed."

"My mother will notice." The door dinged, and the elevator opened on the top floor. "She should have let me settle into my room first."

They walked to the door of the penthouse suite. "You're the queen," the captain said as she hesitated before ringing the bell. "Can you tell her you're not ready yet?"

She was never ready to meet with her mother, and now was especially not a good time, though Vivian was pretty sure there was no real danger in her speaking with Queen Constance. Maybe Mom wanted to get rid of her, but she would never do the dirty work herself.

Captain Thurlow was waiting for an answer.

"Can *you* order *your* mom around, just because you're a captain in the Guard?"

He chuckled. "I guess not. Good luck then. I'll wait."

"Thanks," she said, and the door swung open.

Constance Davis of the Galileo Fields was born beautiful, intelligent, ambitious, and telekinetic to an ordinary and non-magical family of farmers, but she rarely talked about her past. When Vivian added up what else she knew about her mother based on only what her mother had actually told her, the sum total was trivial.

Her mother was accepted to the University of Alighieri on a full scholarship at seventeen. The day after she left home, a band of Immortals wearing the Empress's insignia raided the Galileo Fields. The major who gave Constance the news told her it was a blessing that only one of her siblings was younger than twelve. Everyone else was killed right away, while Constance's eleven-year-old brother was abducted. If she ever saw him again, he would be Immortal. So, Constance graduated from university four years later with high honors and one goal:

To destroy the Immortal Empire.

But that version left out critical details Vivian had to piece together herself about how Constance schemed to harness the power she needed to accomplish her goal. A tabloid Vivian found in her dad's library once spelled out what she suspected was the true story.

PLAYBOY PRINCE TO WED GALILEO FARM GIRL SHOTGUN STYLE

Is a royal baby on the way? Rumors are flying that local farm girl, Constance Davis, currently attending the University of Alighieri with Prince Herschel, is pregnant with the prince's baby.

The royal family has denied the rumors, stating only that they "couldn't be happier" with Prince Herschel's engagement to Ms. Davis and that King Cassius "encouraged" the two "love-birds" to wed because: "No Mortal has time to waste when it comes to love." However, close friends of Ms. Davis claim that the stunning beauty is already eight weeks pregnant.

"They met at a party," a source confirmed. "Herschel was trashed."

It would not have surprised Vivian to learn that her mother had purposely gone to that party to enter Prince Herschel's orbit and give him a reason to marry her. What better position to fight the Immortal Empire from than the royal castle? What better way to get there than an unplanned pregnancy? The Royal Church disapproved of children born out of wedlock, and Vivian's parents were married a few weeks after the tabloid story was published. She was born about thirty weeks after that. Constance got what she wanted.

Vivian had no illusion about her parents' lack of affection for each other, either. Theirs was not a marriage of love.

But she had once asked her father what attracted him to her mother at that first fateful encounter, and he said: "She was beautiful, and she walked like she owned the place. No one had ever made me feel less in control."

She supposed that explained a lot about herself.

When Vivian stepped into the penthouse suite, her mother was sitting at a writing desk, wearing a deep blue gown with a low-cut neckline that showed off her décolletage and one of her more extravagant pieces of jewelry. She was reading a letter, and she did not stand up as Vivian entered the suite, but she did close the door behind Vivian with a casual bit of magic.

The suite was opulent and enormous. Vivian felt like a fraud.

"Mother," she said.

"Queen Vivian," her mother said back, and then Vivian had to wait while Constance finished her letter. The room smelled like more green tea. Vivian wavered on her feet.

Finally, her mother set down the letter and looked at Vivian. "For heaven's sake, child, sit down. I can't speak with you passed out."

There had been times when Vivian had wished her mother was some other woman. Her father, she knew, had loved someone else. Vivian had heard another woman's name screamed during fights between her parents.

But Vivian really couldn't be anyone but Constance's daughter. She had her mother's straight-backed posture, her forehead wrinkle, her eyes that always made it look like she knew something you didn't. And she was nearly as stubborn as her mother.

Vivian did not sit down.

Queen Constance stood and came close. Vivian tried not to move as her mother stroked her cheek with the back of her hand, then tipped her chin up. "I'm very proud of you, Vivian. This is all such a pity."

Vivian resisted the urge to turn her cheek. "You wanted to speak with me alone?"

Constance's gaze moved slowly from the crown of Vivian's head, down toward her heart, where the arrow had pierced her.

"Bast is trying to find a cure," Vivian said.

Her mother smiled like she pitied Vivian. "Yes, he is." She walked back to her desk, put on her glasses and picked up the letter she had been reading. "Are you aware he believes you have only a few weeks left if a cure is not found? And he told me earlier he's heard back from all but three of the labs."

Now Vivian wanted something to lean on. A few weeks? That was … short.

"I know, dear. That must have been difficult to hear. But there's no reason not to tell you the rest, I suppose." Constance picked up a second letter and held it out with the first for Vivian. "Two of the labs returned their responses directly to me instead of to your brother. I'm afraid it isn't good news."

Vivian didn't take the letters. "Who's left to respond?"

"New Paris Medical School."

Vivian grasped for hope. "But there's still the Gandhi Medical Centre—"

Her mother sighed. "I'm afraid they've refused to see you. I've been in communication with them all week, but they've been in communication with several of the other labs. They say there is no way to help you, and they refuse to risk having you make an appearance at the Centre. They think it puts the other patients in too much danger." Constance sneered. "It's probably their donors they're afraid of alienating. Bastards. We'll withdraw all our funding, naturally."

So, that was it, then. A few weeks. That was all she had left.

"I didn't tell Bastian. It's going to crush him to learn there's so little left he can do. It would have been easier if this hadn't turned into such an extensive affair."

Vivian was breathing heavily now, and it occurred to her that she should have a turn in this cruel conversation. "Are you saying you wish I'd died during the coronation?"

Her mother took off her readers and tossed them on the desk. "Vivian, what I'm saying—and the reason I wanted to talk to you alone—is that you must think of Bastian now, rather than yourself. And the kingdom."

"And Nate?" Vivian asked glibly.

Her mother sat back disdainfully in her chair. "Nate would be looking for a way out of South Kepler if he had any intelligence whatsoever. Bast will succeed you, Viv. And if you care about him, you'll make the next few weeks pleasant and you won't make dying a long production."

Vivian hated when her mother called her Viv. "No one *chooses* a slow death."

Queen Constance bothered a nick in her nail polish, and Vivian heard slime in her voice when she said: "But if you could choose to make this easier for Bast, you would, correct?"

She wondered if the cold feeling inside her was what Bast carried with him all the time.

"That's what I thought." Her mother got up again and walked to an ornate chest of drawers, where a small, silk jewelry pouch was sitting. She picked it up, brought it to Vivian, and placed it in her hand. It hardly weighed anything.

"You must keep this a secret. Bastian must believe in the possibility of success until the very end, or he may do something desperate. We cannot have that. The kingdom of South Kepler needs him too much."

"But how?" Vivian asked, clutching the silk pouch. "How do we lie to *Bast*?"

Constance didn't flinch. "I have a dinner engagement tonight, and tomorrow I'll leave before breakfast and send word that an emergency came up. That will limit my time with him. It won't occur to him to ask you if you've heard from any of the labs, and he can't read a lie in a letter." She looked hard at Vivian. "I'm doing you a favor. You understand that, don't you? I didn't have to tell you any of this. You could have spent the last few weeks of your life waiting for a cure that was never going to come. Don't you think this is better? For everyone?"

Was it better? Vivian tried to imagine telling Bast and Nate what she had just learned. She found she could not.

"I knew you would see reason." Her mother looked at the door.

"Is that it?" Vivian said. "Is that how you wanted to say goodbye?"

Constance reached out with both arms and set her hands upon Vivian's shoulders. "Take some advice from your mother for once, Vivian. Long goodbyes are a waste of time for both parties. Check in to your hotel room—you're in a very nice dignitary suite—have your attendants run some water for you, soak in the tub, and think about what you want to do with your final days. Then do it. Persuade your brothers to take you wherever you want to go. Have a little fling with that handsome man outside the door. Live as much as you can in your borrowed days."

"Did you do it?" Vivian whispered. "Were the assassins working for you?"

Her mother burst into laughter. "You're so much like your father," she said like the accusation didn't even bother her. "Why can't you ever see the best in me, as Bastian does?"

Vivian hated her mother. "Why aren't *you* trying to help me?"

The laughter faded. "But I *am* helping, Vivian. I'm giving you much more than the last meal we give prisoners we execute."

Life is a death sentence. Vivian was clutching the jewelry pouch. The silk would be crinkled later. "What's in here?"

Her mother dropped her hands from Vivian's shoulders and raised an eyebrow. "It's cyanide. I told you. I'm doing you a favor."

"You're giving me something to end my own life?"

"I'm giving you control over something hardly anyone controls: your own death."

Vivian should have expected something like this, but what kind of woman gives her dying daughter cyanide and thinks of it as comfort? Queen Constance lowered her voice after that, though, and for the first time in years, Vivian thought she could see something genuine in her mother's eyes.

"I thought you would want that power. That's what I would have wanted."

There was no one who could make Vivian feel less like she had any say over her own life.

"Vivian?"

Vivian turned and left the room.

M. KAYES MISSION LOG #219389

Two kings dead in a single decade, and the Immortal Empire continues to rise in opposition against these pathetic, idealistic Mortals. I am disturbed at the developments, and I confess, I have lost hope. I fear I am not the only one. None of my associates attended the last funeral, which may explain the intensity of my current melancholy.

Foster Hinks failed to attend. It was probably for the best. I haven't seen Hinks in over a hundred years. He involves himself too much in the business of Mortals, while I have not yet forgiven them for what they did to us. It is no loss to me that another Mortal king is dead, but Hinks and I both see red whenever the matter of what we owe to the Keplerian Mortals comes up in our conversations.

I suppose it is different for Hinks. He still diligently maintains that database of Immortal blood samples, in some secret vault in Gandhi, though his progress on his disease research is stalled. It wouldn't surprise me if he blames himself for Herschel's death. Maybe for Reginald's as well. Perhaps this is why he didn't attend the most recent funeral. Foster thinks of himself as a Keplerian who was born on Earth, while I am an Earthian stuck on a foreign planet. I imagine the old doc is drowning in grief.

Lizzy Dupree didn't show up, either. I haven't seen her since the last time I saw Foster Hinks. I wonder if she's still in touch with the Immortal Empire and how she feels about this business with the dead kings. She writes and says I have become a recluse. She has no room to talk. I suppose I could visit her at Novi Dupree sometime, though.

I do miss Lizzy.

~Myles Alexander Kayes

CHAPTER TWELVE
THE RED-EYED ONES

Miguela kept looking back while she ran.

"Hurry," Carina told her. "I'm right behind you."

"I know *you're* there." Miguela panted. "I'm trying to see if anyone is following us. Do you hear anything?"

Carina couldn't see more than a few steps behind her. "No. But that doesn't mean they aren't there." Miguela stopped without warning. Carina slammed into her, and they both fell.

"What are you doing?!" Carina shrieked, scrambling to get back up. She grabbed Miguela's arm to help her. "Come on! We have to keep going!"

Miguela yanked herself away. "I can't! My backpack is too heavy."

Carina had been too terrified to notice how heavy her backpack was. "You have to," she urged. "Let me take your satchel."

Miguela dodged Carina's reach and threw her satchel to the ground. "I can't run anymore, Carina!" She shrugged her backpack off and wriggled furiously out of her coat. Carina couldn't make out her sister's facial features, but she could see that Miguela's hair had come out of the braid she usually wore it in to bed. Her sister stood gulping in air, a breeze tangling her fallen hair, and at that moment her silhouette was an exact replica of how Carina remembered their mom the last time they'd seen her.

"Whoa," Carina whispered.

"I'm sorry." Miguela's shoulders fell. "You're a lot taller than me, and I can't run as fast. I need a break."

Carina took her own backpack off. "A fast break."

Miguela knelt by the stream.

Carina cringed. "Don't drink that. It could be—"

"I'm not *drinking* it. I'm hot. I'm using it to cool off." Miguela splashed water onto her face. "I can't hear anyone chasing us. Can you?"

Even when she listened hard, Carina couldn't hear anyone nearby. She did not, however, see that as a good reason to stop. "Maybe they're waiting until morning."

Miguela unzipped her backpack and crammed her coat inside. "Maybe they decided they made a mistake." She stood up and heaved her backpack onto her shoulders again. "Or maybe Sister Agda convinced them they had the wrong place. It doesn't matter. I can't keep running. Can we walk for a while?"

Carina didn't have the impression from the Sisters that the Red-Eyed Ones would be easily stopped. Also, she and Miguela had hardly made any progress. Whoever had come to Novi Dupree had been on horses, and they probably had flashlights. If the Sisters hadn't been able to hold them off, she and Miguela would be easy to find.

"We *can't* run the whole way," Miguela said. "It would be

smart to save our energy."

It would be smarter not to be found, Carina thought. But what was she going to do? If Miguela couldn't run anymore, she couldn't run. They walked.

And Miguela turned out to be right. Carina thought she was in good shape from all the work she'd done around Novi Dupree, but four hours after they'd crossed the sanctuary borders, her hamstrings burned.

Miguela hadn't complained since their break. She had gone back to barely talking, though. Carina told herself it was because they were both tired and scared. Still, in the light of the dawn moon that had started to rise, it was hard to miss the clench in Miguela's jaw.

It made her ache in a worse way. There had been a time when Carina was close to her sister. The Miguela of their childhood had been playful and outgoing, not rigid and reticent. But that was before the Red-Eyed Ones killed the rest of their family.

That was a night Carina hadn't thought about in a long time.

Carina was ten years old when the Red-Eyed Ones came for her family. It was late, and she woke to the smell of trees and rotted fruit burning. Her family lived on an orchard. She and Miguela shared a room at the top of a big farmhouse.

The nanny was in their room. She was carrying five-year-old Eugene. He was crying. Eugene never cried. He wiped his eyes with his fists and said: "Rina, I wanna go with you!"

The nanny wouldn't let him. "Hold your sister's hand, and follow me, Carina," she ordered. "We're playing a hiding game."

"Are we going to the secret room in the basement?" Miguela asked. She was too young to know the special room she liked to play in with the cold metal walls and the strange narrow bunks was a panic room installed in their family home. Carina barely understood herself.

"Yes," the nanny told Miguela. "And we have to be very quiet, okay?"

Eugene sobbed.

"Okay, Eugie? You can't cry. This is a game. We need to hide."

There were voices and slams coming from the rest of the house, and Eugene couldn't be consoled. He cried all the way down two flights of stairs and into the back hall. Still, they had almost reached the door to the basement stairs before the intruders found them. The nanny ran for the door and called for Carina and Miguela to follow, but a woman took hold of Carina's wrists, and a man picked up Miguela. Carina saw the expression on their nanny's face go from fear to desperation. She opened the basement door—Eugene cried so loud it made Carina's ears ring—and the nanny took him down the stairs and slammed the door behind them.

Carina heard the lock click, but she didn't have time to feel betrayed. She barely had time to feel anything as she was dragged through the house. Outside, two boxy trucks were waiting. Carina tried to look back and see Miguela, but her sister was still inside when an explosion blew out the front windows of the house. Carina screamed for Miguela. The woman holding Carina screamed almost as loud, and she suddenly let go.

Carina sprinted for the house, and by the time she got there, Miguela had popped miraculously onto the porch, alive and unscathed. They ran together through the orchard to a decaying barn that had been their playhouse that summer. Then they huddled together behind a broken-down tractor.

"What's happening?" Miguela asked as another explosion shook the ground. She hid her face against Carina's shoulder.

Carina stroked Miguela's sweat-dampened back. "It's okay. Mom and Dad will be back soon. They'll come get us." Another blast sounded outside, though, and they could hear horses panicking in the new stables, not far from the old barn. Carina tried to control the way that made her shake. Her parents were at a party, and she didn't know when they would be back. "Soon," she whispered anyway.

Their dad's voice boomed outside. "Girls!? Girls!"

"Daddy!" Miguela cried, her head shooting up.

Someone entered the barn with a crying child. "Miguela? Carina!"

"Mom!" Miguela dashed out from behind the tractor. Carina's heart slowed down. She hadn't lied. Mom and Dad were back. They had Eugene. Everything would be okay.

Except it wouldn't.

Carina's memories of what happened next weren't complete. The shock made some things hazy, but what stood out was there in vivid detail. She could still remember how stiff her legs were, unmoving as she peeked out from behind the tractor. She could still recall the outline of the pretty party dress Mom was wearing. Mom was barefoot in the barn, and her hair had come loose. She was holding Eugene in one arm and a garden rake in the other and looking around like she was trying to find something.

Metal clanked against metal outside the barn. Carina heard her dad yell frantically: "Lucia? Is Carina in there too?" It occurred to Carina that she was what her mom was looking for, but her voice stuck in her throat as she saw a man and two women at the barn doors. The man came in holding a thick sword with two hands. One of the women pulled the chain by the entrance and a dagger in her left hand flashed as a light bulb flickered on. The other woman was carrying a shorter sword of her own. Their eyes all glistened red.

Miguela stopped halfway between Carina and their mom.

Mom gripped Eugene and the garden rake and said: "Miguela, stay back."

The man laughed: "Is that what you have to defend yourself and your children, Lucia?" He swung his sword at his hip and stalked forward.

"Careful," one of the women warned. "Remember what happened with the girls."

The man didn't heed the warning. Miguela shouted "Mom!" as he drew the sword back in the air and brought it down diagonally toward Mom and Eugene. Carina had never thought of her mother as someone who could wield a garden rake one-handed like a ninja, but while Eugene cowered, Mom fought against the man's sword, forcing him back with the garden rake, then swinging the rake up to gouge the man's face with its rusty rungs.

He put his hand to his face and wiped blood redder than his eyes across his cheek. Then he struck another blow at Mom and Eugene that broke the garden rake.

Dad finally rushed in, carrying a broadsword of his own. Carina had seen her father practice with that sword for fun with his friends. He'd said it was a sport they all enjoyed. Now there was blood on the sword, and the Red-Eyed women that had come into the barn were laughing. The man grinned wolfishly back at Carina's dad. "Too late, Reggie." He raised his sword one last time while Mom turned her shoulder to protect Eugene.

And Dad didn't charge forward as the Red-Eyed One swung the weapon down. Instead, his gaze flew back to Carina, now standing next to Miguela, though she couldn't remember her feet moving her there. She didn't understand why her dad dropped his sword. She didn't know what he was doing when he raised his hands. Over Miguela's piercing scream and Eugene's terrified shrieks, Carina heard her dad's voice reverberating clearly through her head:

Stay with your sister.

A flash of bright, blue-gold light blinded Carina …

and the barn exploded.

There was nothing after that but blackness for Carina until the man with the purple scar found her. She didn't know how she or Miguela had survived. Her sister was unconscious until morning. Then Miguela woke up and sunlight filtered in through the wagon cover, but Miguela turned into the shade.

The man with the scar never asked them to talk about what happened, and at first, Carina hadn't wanted to talk to anyone about it at Novi Dupree. Sister Raji coaxed her into it soon enough, though, using a litter of barn kittens to earn her trust.

Miguela was not so easily bribed. She'd never talked about what happened. Not then. Not now. Carina understood. It was hard enough to think about it without having to say anything. Still, she wished Miguela could find a way to be happy again.

Carina wondered just how deep Miguela had buried her memories. There was so much they didn't know. Maybe they needed to talk. Maybe if they compared what they knew, they'd understand better what had happened. Maybe they'd have some idea of what they should do if they managed to escape the Red-Eyed Ones coming for them now.

A man entered her vision and lunged at Miguela.

Miguela cried out in surprise.

Carina thought of putting something between her sister and the man, and a tree slammed down into him. He didn't yell. He only made a fast whooshing sound as his breath left his body. He hadn't seen it coming. Neither had Carina.

Miguela spun around. "Did *you* do that?"

"I don't know." Carina did not look at the man as they climbed over the tree. Now was the time to run, not to slow down and ask questions.

Miguela ran after her. "You don't *know*? Have you done that before?"

"*No.*" Carina's nightgown snagged on something, and she heard the fabric rip. "When would I have done that before? I've never practiced on anything that big!"

"Why would you need to practice if you can bring down a whole tre-ah!" Another man ran out at them and had Miguela in a tight body lock before Carina could blink. The Red-Eyed Ones had finally found them.

"Got this one!" the man holding Miguela shouted.

"Bind her wrists!" another man, somewhere behind Carina, shouted back.

Carina hurled the pack she'd been carrying at the man who had Miguela, but the other man grabbed her by the hair before she could get any farther. Over the years, she had worked hard to forget how it felt to be handled by a Red-Eyed One. As this one tried to pin her arms behind her back, she could hear his breath in her ear. That was the thing that had haunted her the most: Red-Eyed Ones weren't made of anything different anatomically than other humans were made of. Their lungs expanded, their hearts beat, their blood flowed. They were super-human, not sub-human.

Miguela was kicking and thrashing, but her attacker had tied her hands behind her back and was tightening a thick strap efficiently around her torso. He was dark-haired and had a misshapen nose.

"Carina!" Miguela yelled frantically.

"I don't think this is one of them," the man said.

Carina stomped on the foot of the Red-Eyed One that had grabbed her and jabbed back with her elbows. He grunted and pulled her arms so painfully she cried out. Unexpectedly, he also cried out, and threw her forward, away from him. She fell, scuffing her hands on the ground, and got up as fast as she could. But the man had gotten up too. He had a jaw too wide for his neck and an ugly yellow knit hat. He looked warily at her.

"*This* one is," he said

And then he pulled a *gun* on her.

Carina lost all the feeling in her fingers.

"What are you waiting for?" the other said.

Could she somehow take the gun away telekinetically? How fast would a bullet go? Why did her feet feel numb? The man didn't give her enough time to react. A flicker ignited at the end of the gun, and a blast rang through the air. She waited dumbly for a wound to make itself apparent on her, while the man with the gun looked dumbly back. Then his grip loosened, the gun fell out of his hand, and a thick line of blood dripped from behind his ear down his neck.

As he dropped to the ground, Carina heard Miguela screaming and realized Miguela must have been screaming the entire time. She took a step toward her sister that felt nightmare-slow, then saw the Red-Eyed One that had attacked Miguela slouched dead at her sister's feet. It didn't make any sense. What had killed the two men?

Miguela quieted as Carina came closer. She hadn't been hurt, but her face was gray, and her forehead was slick with sweat. There was blood gushing from the Red-Eyed One's head, down over the bridge of his nose. Miguela's nightgown was splattered.

The noise of someone walking toward them jolted Carina. She had thought these two men were the most dangerous things in the mountains tonight, but apparently, someone even more dangerous was approaching. She started to undo the straps around Miguela, aware that they needed to run, though unsure what instinct was guiding her hands.

Miguela screamed again. Carina turned.

Max was standing there.

"Relax, it's just me," he said.

The tension in Carina vanished. She breathed and finished freeing Miguela. It was *Max*. They were safe. She started to walk to him, but Miguela clutched her arm, stopping her, and pointed to something Max was carrying that Carina had not noticed herself.

"Where did you get a *gun*?"

CHAPTER THIRTEEN
THE FIFTH MORTAL COMMITMENT

Carina didn't know exactly how many years there were between when the first humans arrived on Kepler in the Nanny Ships and when the second batch arrived in the Immortal Ships. She did not know the nuanced differences in political ideology between the Cardinal Families. She had never memorized the Kepler Declaration of Mortal Commitments.

Miguela had.

"It's the gun that was issued to me." Max holstered it in a belt Carina hadn't seen him wearing before. "Lucky I picked it back up from that shack."

"What Mortal is issuing *guns*? Under the Fifth Mortal Commitment, firearms are weapons of extreme violence. Did you buy that on the black market?"

Max nodded at the Red-Eyed One lying dead at Miguela's feet. "That man was using extreme violence to try to kill you. I was defending you."

Miguela made a face. "You didn't answer my question.

Where did you get the gun? Who sold it to you? And why didn't we hear it?"

"Silencer. And plenty of Mortals have guns where I'm from. But no one sold me this. Like I said, it's the gun the Academy issued to me." He smiled warmly at Carina. "Didn't expect to see you again so soon." Carina was still looking at the guy with the misshapen nose. She had never realized how mortal the immortal Red-Eyed Ones were.

"It only took one bullet for each," she observed.

Max rubbed his neck. "I'm a good shot."

The sun was coming up behind the dawn moon now. Carina began looking for her backpack. "We have to start moving again," she said.

Max picked up her pack and handed it to her. "Are you going back to the sorority?"

"No. There might be more Red-Eyed Ones. We're heading toward Clemson."

Max's face lit up. "Me too. Now we can go together."

Carina glanced at the gun. She'd felt so helpless a few minutes ago. "Okay," she said, ignoring the look on Miguela's face that said *she* wanted Max in their party as much as she wanted a few Red-Eyed Ones. Carina found Miguela's satchel and tossed it to her. "Cheer up, Miguela. We don't have to be afraid if Max is with us."

Her sister shouldered the satchel. "Maybe *you* don't."

Over the next several hours, Max told them about himself. He was a scientist.

"Just finished my program at the Academy, and I'm specializing in the phylogenetics of Earth life on Kepler," he said. "I've been doing research on the adaptation of Earth amphibians to this environment, but long-term I want to be the first scientist to prove the existence of hybridization between Kepler and Earth life."

"Wow." Carina was enthralled.

"Don't 'wow' him like he's some god of science." Miguela cocked her chin up toward Max. "Sister Rachel's been ordering university-level textbooks for Carina for all her science lessons for two years. She probably knows more than you do."

"Maybe about chemistry," Carina admitted. Sister Rachel had taught chemistry in South Kepler before she fled to Novi Dupree, and she always gave Carina tough assignments. "But not genetics."

She stopped to pick up a pine cone on the ground. Kepler had been a good place for interplanetary human migration. Its day was supposedly only three minutes shorter than an Earth day. Its climate was human-friendly. Its dirt supported Earth trees and plants so well that half of the greenery on the planet was now Earthian. Its animals were mostly nonthreatening. It had an aboriginal species of intelligent life, but the Kepler natives never interacted with humans and were nearly impossible to see, except in Native Valley.

"Is there evidence that Earth species can breed with non-Earth species? How many planets are there that can even support Earth life?" she asked, examining the pine cone.

Max plucked it from her hand. "You're asking the wrong question. There is an infinite number of planets capable of sustaining Earth life. The right question is what gives us the right to colonize those planets? And there *is* evidence of hybridization. Some scientists believe the Kepler natives can form a symbiotic relationship with other life forms and transmit genetic signals that alter the other species' DNA codes. That could be how humans acquired the adaptations for magic." He tapped her shoulder with the pine cone. "You're probably a hybrid."

"But that's not hybridization, is it? Isn't it just …" She tried to remember the term. "Mutation of some kind?"

Max tossed the pine cone into the air and caught it while they walked. "How lucky am I to have run into a pretty girl who geeks about mutation?"

On his next throw, Miguela snatched the pine cone away from Max mid-flight. She chucked it to the ground. "How *unlucky* are we to have run into a misogynist scientist?"

"I'm here to find a colleague," Max said, shifting his attention smoothly from nature to Miguela. "The Academy sent him to the mountains for a study ages ago, but lately he hasn't been communicating with us."

"And they sent *you* to come get him?"

"I was the best choice. The guy's my, uh—oops, watch your step over that branch—uncle, and I have the right training for this."

"Fantastic," Miguela said sardonically. "Some crazy academics are sending armed scientists out into the wilderness on search-rescue-and-study-the-frogs missions."

"Armed Scientist," Max repeated. "That sounds awesome."

It was evening before they started looking for a place to rest. It took over an hour to find a cavern. Then Carina finally dug through her bags to see what was in them.

Packing must have been a collaborative effort. The ample supply of food, canteens of water, and light wool blankets had to be from Sister Lindy. The compass and compact survival guide were from Sister Rachel. Purse of money: Sister Raji. Extra balls of underwear tucked into the small spaces: Sister

Elizabeth for sure.

One of the balls escaped from Carina's bag as she was repacking and rolled to Max, where a scrap of paper fell out. He picked it up (the note, not the garment), read it, and started laughing while Carina whisked up the clothing and snatched the note back.

It read: "always wear clean underwear."

"It's important advice," she said with as much poise as she could muster. "And it's from Sister Elizabeth. Who is very …" She struggled for the right word; had Elizabeth *needed* to put the note in one of the cute pairs? "Wise and enlightened," she finished.

Max laughed harder. "I'm sure she is."

They agreed to take turns sleeping and keeping watch, and Max said he'd be on watch first because he was used to being up for extended periods of time.

"You'd be surprised the things they train you to do to become an Armed Scientist," he bragged.

Miguela grumbled something that sounded like "Armed Idiot," but she wrapped herself up in one of the light wool blankets and fell asleep immediately.

Carina settled down next to her to do the same, and she woke a few hours later feeling scuzzy and sleep deprived. Miguela was curled on her side with her back to Carina. She'd kicked her blanket off. Carina lifted it over her again.

"Good morning." Max had a map unfolded on the ground in front of him.

She wrapped her blanket around her shoulders, crawled over, and sat down by him. Yesterday he'd talked a lot, but he was quiet now scanning his map.

"Did you have a good night?" Her question came out sounding stiffer than Sister Agda's blouses. "I mean, do you want to sleep? I could take watch.”

He eyed her slyly. “What I want is to know how *you* slept at all. There’s no way I could have. All that noise sounded like a pack of wounded monkeys.”

“Monkeys? Do you know what they sound like?” Carina had read about monkeys, but there was only one monkey shelter on Kepler, and it was somewhere in South Kepler.

Max wrinkled his nose. “I’m just saying something was having a weird party.”

“Probably the owlets,” Carina suggested. “Miguela and I are used to it.” She leaned over his map curiously. It wasn’t like any she had ever seen. “Nothing is marked on this. Where did you get it?”

“It’s what they gave me to find my uncle. And it is marked. With important things.” He pointed to a dot in the mountains. “Here. This is where he’s supposed to be.”

“I don’t think this has been updated in a while.” She pointed to an area in the North. “I think that’s where Miguela and I lived when we were kids. Our family had an apple orchard.” She moved her finger up on the map. “But this makes it look like there’s still a forest there. That forest was destroyed in a big fire before I was born.”

“Figures he’d have a bad map.”

Carina and Max looked up together. Miguela was awake. Carina sat back on her heels and crossed her arms. “His map isn’t bad! It has the important things marked!”

“Like what?”

“Like the place where his uncle lives.”

Miguela came over to see. “That’s a satellite image, not a map,” she said scornfully to Max. “Your Academy must not like you much. This is a terrible substitute for a real map.”

Carina got up and went for the map Sister Agda had given

them. She unfolded it and set it next to Max's. Sister Agda's map was marked up with quickly scrawled handwriting. She'd drawn a path from Novi Dupree in the Red Ridge Mountains to the plateaus that divided the mountains from the Eastern Desert. The Eastern Ridge Trail ran along those plateaus, and the path went all the way up to Cerulean in the far North.

Max pointed to a place on Carina's map. "That's where my uncle would be on yours."

Miguela laughed out loud. "You're joking, right?"

"No, it's clear that this mountain on mine is the one on yours marked Mountain of Peril." He leaned back. "That doesn't sound very welcoming."

Carina looked at the maps with alarm.

"What?"

She hesitated before she tried to explain. "The Mountain of Peril is practically suicidal to climb. They say the natives have done something to make it unsafe for Mortals. Hardly anyone returns from trying to climb it, and the people that do have spotty memories and think they've seen this legendary magician they call the Guru. He's a myth, though. Saying you've seen the Guru is like saying you've seen Big Foot."

"Big Foot's an Earth legend," Max said. "There's no Big Foot on Kepler."

"Exactly. There's no Guru either."

"And if your uncle is missing, it's probably because he decided to do his research on the Mountain of Peril," Miguela said.

Max was undeterred. "Maybe he discovered something about the natives, and he's just immersed in his studies. Whatever. That's where I'm going. I have to try to find him. Too bad we're going separate ways, though."

Carina agreed. She and Miguela were ill-equipped for a

trek through the mountains to Cerulean, no matter how well they were provisioned. If Max hadn't found her and Miguela, they would probably be dead already.

"Too bad for you, maybe," Miguela said. "You're more likely to find the Guru than your uncle. And I take back what I said about the Academy not liking you. If they sent you alone to the Mountain of Peril, they must hate you."

"It *would* be dangerous," Carina said, "but maybe we should go with you."

"Really?" Max said.

"What?!" Miguela said.

Carina appealed to Miguela. "The trip to Cerulean is going to take weeks anyway. We'd all be safer traveling together. If we find Max's uncle, he can help us figure out an easier way to Cerulean than to walk the whole Eastern Ridge Trail. If we don't find him, Max can come the rest of the way with us, and we're probably still better off. And who knows? Maybe the Guru is real. If we find him, maybe he'll help me with magic."

Miguela shook her head vigorously. "We're supposed to follow Sister Agda's map."

"Sister Agda was crazy to think we could make it to Cerulean alone."

"She *didn't* think we could make it! That's why she was working so hard to keep you from doing something stupid to attract the Red-Eyed Ones! But that doesn't mean we should go instead with a stranger on a hike up the most dangerous mountain on Kepler!"

"We'll go with Max to the foot of the mountain, then," Carina said. "It's still safer."

"Sister Agda gave us explicit directions!"

Carina stood up. "Sister Agda sent us away from Novi Dupree by ourselves! She cares more about the Sisters than she does about us!"

Miguela stared at Carina for a few seconds. Then she got up and started stalking away.

"Hey! Where are you going?" Carina yelped.

Miguela grunted. "To wash up in the stream. Obviously, I don't have a choice here."

Max folded up his map while Miguela stormed away. He wasn't making eye contact with Carina, and she was instantly mortified. This was much worse than having a ball of underwear roll out at his feet. "Sorry about that," she said.

Max put his map in his bag. "You better wash up, too, if you want to before we leave. She's right. We should head out."

While they walked that day, Miguela dug relentlessly for information from Max that she seemed to think might discredit him, and she didn't let up the next day either. He seemed relieved when they finally came to a clearing that gave them a view of Clemson that afternoon. "Finally, we're getting somewhere," he said. "But why are they called the Red Ridge Mountains? All I can see is green anywhere. Blurry shades of green. And blue. And gray in the distance. Nothing red."

"We're not at the ridge," Miguela said. "But out to the east, near where we were supposed to be going, the mountains cut off along the fault line, and the ridge is red clay. Didn't you study this stuff in school?"

"Sure. But I've never seen it like this."

"Where are you from again?"

He shaded his eyes to look over the valley. "A long way away. You wouldn't know it."

Miguela persisted. "I'm good with geography. Try me."

"I bet you still don't know where I'm from."

"Why? Do you live somewhere secret?"

"As a matter of fact, yes. I could tell you where it is, but then I'd have to kill you." He winked playfully at Miguela. "Your choice."

Miguela opened her mouth to continue the interrogation.

Carina cut her off. "Give it a rest, Miguela. Where he's from is his business." She pointed toward the village in the valley. "That's Clemson, Max. Sister Rachel thought the Red-Eyed Ones would look for us there, but it's probably safe for you."

"I'll go down to the monastery and see if they can tell me how to get to the Mountain of Peril," he offered. "How long do you think that will take me?"

"An hour or so?" Carina guessed. "Miguela and I shouldn't get too close."

Max grimaced. "I don't suppose your Sisters packed mobile coms for you, did they?" He picked up his backpack again and swung it over his shoulder. "My feet are sore."

"Oh. Because where you're from people carry guns *and* phones," Miguela said sarcastically. "You're unbelievable. I bet you don't know Commitment Nine either, do you?"

Max hiked his backpack up. "Nope," he said as he started walking away. "You can teach me when I get back."

Miguela turned on Carina as soon as Max was out of earshot and said: "He's lying to us."

"What are you talking about?" Carina said.

Miguela's hair was frizzing at the edges. It made her look wild as she sliced her arms through the air and talked. "We can't trust him. We should leave now and go out on our own."

Carina sat down on a stump and dug through her

backpack for her canteen. "Why do you hate him so much?"

"He's a stranger! He's carrying a *gun*. Why do you like him so much?"

Carina took a drink from her canteen. She needed to find a place to refill it.

"He's not attractive," Miguela added. "He's whiny, stupid, and he laughs too loud."

"I like him," Carina said, and she got up to search for fresh spring water, leaving Miguela glowering at the mountains.

CHAPTER FOURTEEN
THE DELIVERY VAN

Max returned with fresh bread, cheese, salami, and a better map. Miguela didn't refuse to eat what he'd brought back while he spread the map out.

"The monks told me to go here first." Max traced a river on the map northwest to a place called Shadow of the Mountains. "It's where the climbers go before they head on to the big peaks. It's a three-week hike. Or there's a woman in Clemson with a delivery van who can get us there in two days. For a price."

"No," Miguela said. "Sister Rachel specifically told us *not* to go into Clemson."

"How much?" Carina asked.

"Forty dollars a person," Max answered. "The monks called while I was there—glad you at least have local phones. She was going to leave with three passengers tonight after dark. She has three spots left."

Miguela, who had just picked up her canteen to take a drink, slammed it down so hard water splashed out. "You *told* the monks about us!?"

"No. I didn't tell her I needed three seats. She just told me she had that many left." Max put more salami in front of Miguela. "There's a meeting place for passengers. We can go most of the way together but get on the van separately. That way you can act like you don't know me when you buy your tickets. But only if you have the money. The monks said they'd pay for me."

Carina thought of the purse of money. "We have enough."

"Perfect," Max said.

Miguela was jittery in Clemson. "Stop looking around," she told Carina. "You look like you don't know where you are."

"But we have a map," Max said.

"Having a *map* doesn't make us look like locals."

"Who's going to see us?" Carina said. "We're walking the alleys." Anyway, she couldn't stop looking. She hadn't been in a village in six years. Even the alleys fascinated her. They smelled like ripe compost and weren't paved, but there were rusty vehicles plugged into walls and parked next to ox beasts eating feed from troughs. A woman opened a back door and dumped a bucket of water onto the street. She held the bucket to her chest as they passed.

"Do you think she thought we were Red-Eyed Ones?" Carina whispered.

"I think Sister Rachel told us not to come here for a reason," Miguela said.

The meeting place was a street corner where an electric van with dirty solar panels duct-taped over the windows and dull camouflage-colored paint was parked in front of "Hiller's Quick Stop." Max went first, then Carina and Miguela walked up to the van. There were two men smoking nearby and laughing like someone had told a crude joke. Carina hoped they weren't the drivers.

Miguela coughed and waved smoke out of her face. "That's disgusting."

"That's my husband and my son," a rough voice said.

Carina and Miguela turned around. A woman with enormous shoulders and scraggly hair was leering at them. She was wearing a heavyweight, multi-pocketed jacket, and a jagged knife was strapped to her arm.

"You two here for the shuttle?"

Carina took a deep breath, then wished she hadn't. The woman smelled like dead fish. "Yes, please," she said, trying not to gag.

The woman put her fists on her hips and made a "humph" noise. "It's sixty dollars a person," she announced.

Miguela, who had covered her nose, dropped her hand. "Sixty?!"

The woman leaned ominously over Miguela. "You got a problem?"

Carina counted the money out of the purse and handed it over. "Nope."

The woman stuffed their money into her jacket and pointed to Hiller's Quick Stop. "I'm Mrs. Hiller. Toilet's in the back. Twenty-five cents a flush. Next stop's six hours away."

Miguela opened her mouth, but Carina pushed her toward the shop. "You never talked back to Sister Agda!" she hissed when they were inside. Miguela stomped through the store in front of Carina. The place wasn't well stocked, and the toilet looked like no one had paid for a flush in a while. Miguela came out of the bathroom with a green face. "I had respect for Sister Agda," she said, "And I hate you."

The 'seats' were two benches facing each other in the back of the van, and four passengers were already seated. A boy with glasses was near the front, clutching a small green backpack and staring warily at the guy across from him, who was asleep and had his legs stretched out so far the younger boy was forced to tuck in his feet. The guy looked like he might be in his twenties, and he was wearing black jeans, a crisp black shirt, and a black vest.

Max was already in the van, sitting on the same side as Vest Guy, and a teenage girl was sitting between them. She had shiny, caramel-colored hair that fell over her shoulders like she never had to do anything to tame it and a cute, curvy shape. Max was chatting with her, and he didn't even make eye contact with Carina as she and Miguela got in the van. Carina's stomach churned with jealousy as she sat next to Glasses Boy, whose eyes traveled nervously toward her.

The teenage girl looked curiously at Carina and Miguela. "Poor things. Who sent you out in handmade dresses? You look like orphaned urchins."

Carina blushed, while Miguela stiffened.

"What are your names? We're going to be together for two days; we might as well be friends." She put her fingers delicately toward herself. "I'm Reed."

Carina thought Reed's voice made her sound like a high-pitched goat. Vest Guy shifted. Miguela leaned back and shut her eyes like she'd rather sleep than make friends with Reed. Max finally made eye contact with Carina. "I'm Max. Who are you, stranger?"

Reed giggled obnoxiously and put her hand on Max's knee. "You are so funny!"

Carina thought maybe she'd rather sleep than make friends with Reed, too.

Mrs. Hiller appeared at the back of the van. "These roads aren't safe. There are Red-Eyed bounty hunters crawlin' all over. I drive fast. If you get carsick, throw up in your own bag. If you have to go, hold it. We don't have heat. The windows don't open."

"Brilliant," Vest Guy said without opening his eyes.

Mrs. Hiller slammed the doors shut.

Reed inched closer to Max. "I hope it's a fast two days."

Carina hoped so too, but hours later the back of the van was freezing and dark, and Reed was still talking. Carina couldn't decide if she was more motion sick or sick of Reed, nor could she see how far Reed had scooted into Max's personal space.

And Reed was telekinetic.

She hadn't stopped talking about it for at least an hour of the miserable ride.

"I can only lift little things, like spoons and bottles and stuff, but my mom says we can't take any chances. That's why I'm going to Shadow of the Mountains. To stay with my grandma for a while. There's been even more bounty hunters in Clemson lately. And you never know who they'll turn you over to. They say Hildebrand just kills Mortals with magic—"

Max interrupted. "*Hildebrand?*"

"Yep. Empress Hildebrand," Reed said. "But she's only controlling one faction of the Immortal Empire. There's a whole faction of Immortals under Lord Godric, and he's *experimenting* with the Mortals *he* captures. Some people think he's trying to create a superior race."

Vest Guy muttered something that sounded like "vapid witch."

"If you have something to say, say it out loud," Reed snapped.

Carina felt a thrill as Vest Guy sat up.

"Fine," he said. "You're a brainless twit. If you have any telekinetic powers at all—which I doubt—you should know better than to brag to everyone about them. Any one of us could be working for a bounty hunter. As for Godric: the Immortals are already superior. Godric isn't experimenting because he has an inferiority complex. He's doing it because he's bored."

Reed tutted snootily. "You don't know what you're talking about. I bet you're in this van for the same reason I am. All dressed up and taking *this* ride to Shadow of the Mountains? What are *you* hiding?"

The van veered to the right and came to a stop. The lights in the back blinked on, and Glasses Boy gasped. Carina clutched Miguela's arm. Vest Guy looked toward Reed. He smiled. He had perfectly straight teeth. And bright red eyes.

Reed shrieked.

"Now you know," he said, and he climbed over all of them, opened the door to the back of the van, and jumped out.

Mrs. Hiller's idea of a pit stop was an isolated area with a lot of trees. Carina was standing on the side of the road, rubbing sanitizer (thank you Sister Lindy) all over her hands and trying to come up with a plan that would get her, Miguela, and Max away from their red-eyed companion, when he sauntered out of the woods and came right over to her.

"Not every Immortal is out there to hurt you," he said, pulling his own bottle of sanitizer out of his vest pocket.

She looked ahead and didn't answer.

"Some of us enjoy civility. I'm Ivan."

He stood next to her while they waited for the rest of the group. Reed was with Max again. She had apparently been too spooked to go into the woods alone. They weren't far from the rest of the group, though. Carina could still hear Reed talking about how the Red-Eyed One was going to kill them all and *what* were they going to *do*?

"That voice would carry over a riot, wouldn't it?" Ivan said.

Carina had been thinking something like that herself.

"Ahh … there's a smile. I knew you could do it."

She peeked sideways at Ivan. He had a long profile with gaunt features. She wondered what his natural eye color was.

"Are you thinking of asking who I am? Or what a lone Immortal is doing out here?"

"That's probably what I should be thinking," she admitted.

"But it's not?" He sounded like he was genuinely curious. "Then what were you thinking, standing there in your worn dress, looking like you're not afraid of me at all?"

"I don't look like I'm afraid of you?"

Ivan laughed. "No. You don't."

She finally looked long enough to see that he had thin, elegant hands, confident body posture, and a charming smile. She was weirdly flattered that he didn't think she was afraid. Maybe that was why she found the nerve to ask: "What's your natural eye color?"

He seemed puzzled. "I don't think any Mortal has ever asked me that."

She heard footsteps behind her.

"Back off, you creep." It was Max. Carina looked to see if Reed had followed him and saw her getting into the van behind Miguela.

"Oh, look who's here! The oaf that saves all the damsels in distress." Ivan shaded his eyes and rotated his head like he was searching for land. "Too bad. No one here needs saving."

Max's hand hovered near his gun.

Carina thought of the Red-Eyed Ones Max had shot. "I'm fine," she said, and she realized she was. She *wasn't* afraid, and she *was* annoyed with Max. "I don't need help."

His hand dropped loosely to his side. "You don't?"

She turned and walked toward the van without answering. No one was supposed to know they knew each other anyway, and it didn't make her feel bad when she heard Ivan laugh again.

Miguela was sitting in the same seat she'd been in before, and so was Reed. Carina got in and sat down by Miguela. Ivan got in after her and sat in the same seat he'd been in, too, diagonally across from Carina and with his legs stretched out.

Max got in next. Reed patted the seat by her, but Max was too busy glaring at Ivan to notice. He climbed to the front of the van and sat down next to Carina, across from Ivan. Then he slouched, crossed his arms over his chest and stretched his legs out right next to Ivan's like he was daring Ivan to do something about the proximity. Ivan snorted, and Reed said: "Max, don't you want to sit by me? You'll have so much more room!"

Max shut his eyes and leaned his head back. "Yeah, but I'll sleep so much better here, without you talking to me."

Mrs. Hiller appeared at the back of the van. "Where's the boy?" She looked suspiciously at Ivan. "I told you there better be no—"

But Glasses Boy slid in under her arm and sat down in the last empty seat before she could finish. Mrs. Hiller slammed the doors shut. The lights went out, and a minute later the engine started up.

The van was still cold, but after they started moving again, Carina felt Max reach for her hand. "You're freezing," he whispered, and he let go.

"Sorry," she whispered back. The rejection stung, even though she was still annoyed, but only until he stretched his arm around her shoulders instead.

"Is that better?"

It was incredible how fast Carina's heart could go from being squeezed tight inside her to beating so fast Max could probably feel it.

"Aww … nothing like young love in the back of a smelly van," Ivan quipped.

Carina thought she heard Reed sniff.

The rest of the trip was far more enjoyable for Carina, though the van was still a little cold. At one of their breaks, she retrieved their wool blankets from their backpacks. Miguela said she was warm enough and told Carina to give hers to the boy with the glasses, who still hadn't spoken to anyone. Reed refused to accept when Carina offered the one she'd been carrying, so she gave it to Ivan instead. He took the blanket like he didn't understand what was happening and said "thank you" several minutes later with a sincerity she'd never heard in a thank you before.

Max grunted but didn't say anything. After all, that only left one blanket to go around, and he seemed happy to share it with Carina.

Ivan pulled Carina aside when they finally arrived at Shadow of the Mountains. He handed back the blanket she'd given him—neatly folded—and said: "You should be careful."

Carina glanced at Max, who was stuck trying to peel himself away from what looked like an overly clingy goodbye with a teary-eyed Reed. Ivan had made such a sport of harassing Max during the trip that Carina had even caught Miguela snickering.

Ivan swished his hand through the air. "No, no. I'm not talking about your boyfriend." He leaned closer and lowered his voice. "I mean about the magic. No one's going to care about the village idiot's pathetic telekinesis, but anyone in the know is going to pick up on what *you* can do immediately."

"What are you talking about?" She hadn't done any magic during the trip.

Ivan moved in even closer. "You know what I mean," he whispered. Then he kissed her cheek so lightly she hardly felt it, straightened up, and added: "The answer to your question is dark brown."

Max and Miguela were waiting for her with their bags after Ivan walked away.

"What was that all about?" Max asked suspiciously.

Carina thought of telling him, but what came out of her mouth was: "Nothing important."

"Mrs. Hiller says there's a youth hostel a few blocks that way." Miguela gestured in the opposite direction to the way Ivan had gone. "She says it's safe and cheap. Let's go."

CHAPTER FIFTEEN
THE HIRED JOB

The hostel was nestled between a dingy pub with a "help wanted" sign and a heavily graffitied building with boarded-up windows. When Carina, Miguela, and Max walked in, Glasses Boy was checking in at the front desk.

"But I don't have fifty extra dollars," they heard him say to the clerk.

Miguela took an immediate interest. "What's going on?"

The boy pushed his glasses up. "They only have quads, and they won't rent a single bunk without an extra charge."

The clerk leaned with his elbows on the desk. "Sorry, kid. Quads are harder to sell if one bunk is already taken."

Miguela grabbed Carina's satchel, eyed the receptionist crossly, and took out the purse. "There are three of us, and we have room for one more. You can be our fourth."

The boy glanced cautiously at Carina and Max. "Are you sure?"

This was the first time in a long time Carina had agreed with Miguela about something. "It's fine," she said quickly, and so, the four of them checked in together. The clerk gave them each a key, a set of sheets, and a lumpy pillow, and said: "The showers are communal. If you need soap, you can buy it here for a dollar a bar."

"A dollar a bar for soap!" Miguela said.

"Yeah, that seems cheap," Max said.

Miguela's eyebrows stretched across her face. "That seems *cheap* to you?"

"There's a supply store all the climbers go to," the clerk said. "Walking will take you half an hour, but it has better prices."

"Thanks," Miguela told him sourly. "We'll buy our soap there."

They went to their room and found two sets of bunk beds, some lockers that didn't look secure, and a small table with three chairs, none of which would sit evenly on the floor. Glasses Boy climbed into a lower bunk and curled up with his green backpack, which seemed to be the only thing he was traveling with. Miguela asked him if he wanted to come with them to the supply store, but he only responded, "No, thanks," so they went without him.

Carina didn't think there was any risk that someone in Shadow of the Mountains would be looking for her or Miguela, and she reasoned that there were probably so many people in Shadow of the Mountains with magic that the Red-Eyed Ones wouldn't be able to tell where any particular magic was coming from. That was helpful for her since she didn't know what she'd done in the van to make Ivan think she had magic. She would be safer in a crowd.

Since Miguela didn't disagree, they decided to take what

looked like the easiest route to get to the store instead of walking the alleys, but it was still a half-hour walk. On their way to the supply store, they passed a drug store, several more pubs, a bank, a bookstore that stayed open all night, two run-down inns, and several advertisements for a fancy-looking hotel for rich tourists vacationing on the other side of town.

The supply store was an enormous warehouse. A sign at the entrance said it carried everything the aspiring mountain climber could possibly want, but the store was so large Carina thought it probably carried a whole lot the climber wouldn't want either. Anyway, she was thrilled to find a clothes section with an entire wall of jeans. She hadn't worn jeans in years. Sister Elizabeth always said they were impossible to make, and Sister Agda frowned on commercially manufactured clothing. Carina tried on ten pairs before picking one.

Max tried on at least twenty.

"I've never worn jeans," he told her while he checked himself out in a mirror. "No one wears them where I'm from." He pointed to the tag on the pair he was currently modeling. It said LEVI 501 STYLE. "I can't believe I'm wearing a pair of Levi's. Sort of."

Miguela hated her jeans and complained that the fabric was too thick, but they purchased three pairs anyway, plus three pairs of sturdy hiking boots, three thermal shirts, three insulated sleeping rolls made from a featherlight material, three pairs of sunglasses, a deck of cards, and a pop-up tent Max swore he could put together in a snap.

And three bars of soap.

It cost them half the rest of their money.

Miguela bit her lip as Carina doled the cash out and Max turned guiltily away.

"What do you want me to do about it?" Carina asked

Miguela on the way back to the hostel. "We can't hike the Mountain of Peril in the stuff we've been wearing."

"It would have been fine for two people on the Eastern Ridge Trail." Miguela stuck her thumb at Max. "Which is where we would have been now if it hadn't been for him. Now we don't know if we'll have enough money to get to Cerulean."

Carina opened her mouth to protest, but Max cut her off.

"She's right," he said. "That was a lot of money. And I don't want to be a burden. Maybe that pub will hire me for a few days while we acclimate to the altitude."

"Carina and I live in the mountains," Miguela said. "We don't need to acclimate."

"But maybe the pub will hire all of us," Carina said. "We don't know when we might need money again. We should accumulate as much as we can as a group. And maybe they serve sassafras."

The owner of the pub was an old man with wrinkles that had probably come from years of scolding young people who came in and drank too much. Carina decided they would do better talking with a frazzled-but-friendly looking waitress.

"We're hoping to meet up with a group later in the week," Carina lied to the woman. "They're climbing Little Mount Everest. We just need more money so all three of us can go."

The waitress wiped her forehead with a rag. "You look too scrawny to be climbers. You're going to need more than money if you're planning to climb Little Everest." She glanced at the owner. "Tell you what. If you three want to be our help for the week, I can convince the old man to hire you. We'll pay you wages and make sure you get a hot meal every night this week. That way you'll have more meat on your bones before you join your group."

She sent Miguela to the kitchens for dish duty and put Max to work busing tables. "But you can help me as a waitress," she told Carina as she doled out the assignments. "You have the right look for it. All you have to do is take orders and bring out food, and if you smile, you'll get tips."

Miguela was horrified, but Carina thought it was fun to wait tables, and she didn't see how there could be anything wrong with earning tips for making people feel happy about being served by a nice waitress.

By the end of their first night, she'd made friends with the frazzled waitress (who called her a natural), the cook (a gentleman with a fat gut and a hearty laugh), and the bartender (a woman who reminded her of Sister Elizabeth and taught her how to pour three different kinds of mixed drinks). She was almost disappointed when the owner turned around the sign on the door that had read "open" to "closed," and the waitress, whose name was Rosa, announced that their shift was over.

"Dish duty is terrible," Miguela said resentfully to Carina as she toweled off the sink. "Why can't I wait tables?"

"Oh no, you don't want to be out there," Max said, coming in and untying his apron. Over the course of the evening, he'd dropped three plates. He'd have broken all three, but Carina saw him dropping the third and somehow managed to magically slow down the plate.

"Maybe we can try you out in the kitchen tomorrow," Rosa told Max cautiously. She beamed at Carina, though, and said: "But *you're* doing great out there." Then she brought them an enormous plate of stuffed blue spud skins and soft pretzel bites with a pot of melted cheese.

"We should see if Anthony wants to come with us tomorrow," Miguela said.

"Anthony?" Carina asked. "Who's he?"

Miguela rolled her eyes. "Our *roommate*. Don't you pay any attention to anything important? He seems like he needs money."

"When did he tell you his name?" Max asked, and Carina wanted to know the same thing. She was sure "Anthony" had barely said anything to any of them except to complain about how much the rooms at the hostel cost. But Miguela ignored the question and went to talk to Rosa about hiring a fourth person, and that evening she sat down on the lower bunk and had a whispered conversation with Anthony about it, too, while Max and Carina sat together at the table playing cards.

"He must be really shy," Max said to Carina, but apparently Anthony did need money. The next night he returned with them for work at four in the afternoon, and things went well again, except for Max burning the back of his arm so bad trying to take potato tots out of a fryer that the cook grounded him for half the evening.

"Poor baby," Carina said when she saw the burn.

"It was his fault," Miguela said. "He didn't pay attention when the cook told him how to do it. And he's lucky it's not that bad of a burn. It didn't even blister."

"It *was* his fault," Anthony, who was also on dish duty, said, almost at a normal-person volume. It was more than he'd said to Carina or Max since they'd met him in Mrs. Hiller's van, and Max did not look very pleased that Anthony had decided to speak up now only to support Miguela's critique.

"I was paying attention!" Max looked pitifully at Carina. "And it hurts bad."

"Oh, boo hoo," Miguela said nastily. "Why don't you

just kiss it and make it better already, Carina? That's what he wants."

Anthony laughed, but Carina bristled and felt compelled to lean in and kiss the back of Max's arm anyway, out of spite.

Max seemed pleasantly surprised. "Wow. That does feel better."

Rosa, who had just come around with a tray of sliders, said: "You're in luck, Max. The cook doesn't want you in the kitchen tomorrow, but the bartender thinks you're cute and says you can work with her the rest of the week." Then she frowned at Carina while the others dug into the sliders. "Aren't you hungry?"

"Carina's a vegetarian," Miguela said.

"Do you happen to have any sassafras beer?" Carina asked.

"No. But that stuff's all sugar, anyway," Rosa said. "I have bean patties. I'll go get some."

Max did better the next night behind the bar, though Carina did end up sliding a whole row of glasses telekinetically back to him after he accidentally sent them across the bar on some spilled water and nearly knocked them off. Once again, she wasn't sure how she'd done it, but he mouthed "awesome, thanks" to her, and the bartender didn't seem to notice.

That night, after closing down the pub, Rosa sat and told them stories about climbers that had died doing stupid things (like try to find the Guru) and encouraging them all to eat pretzel bites. She must have liked them a lot. She seemed almost teary as she took away their scraped plates the last night and came back with four envelopes of money. She told them to return if they ever needed work again, then she looked around like she was checking to see if anyone else was listening, leaned in, and gripped Carina's hand. "You're a good waitress," she said. "But you need to be more careful."

"With what?" Carina asked, agitated by the warning.

Rosa lifted the tips of her fingers toward the salt and pepper shakers. The shakers levitated briefly, then dropped back to the table. "With that."

Carina took in a quick breath. "You can do—"

"Don't say it out loud! You never know who you can trust these days, and the Southern Guard is everywhere."

"The Southern Guard?" Miguela asked. "But I thought it was the Red-Eyed Ones we needed to worry about."

"You need to worry about everyone," Rosa responded. "You don't want to get caught by the Red-Eyed Ones, but the Southern Guard could take you away in the middle of the day with a hundred people around. Those guys walk like they own the planet, taking our food and taxing us down the river. And they're on orders from the queen of South Kepler herself to arrest anyone with magic who doesn't report to be regis-tered." She shook her head. "The things they do with people who can—" She levitated the salt and pepper shakers again.

"Why?" Carina asked. "Doesn't the Cardinal Family of South Kepler have more magic than anyone else these days?"

"And they're the only Cardinal Family left, too," Miguela added. "Unless you count what's left of the Cardinal Family of the East, but they've lost almost all their magic."

"Yes, but the Cardinal Family of the South is always afraid someone new will one-up them," Rosa explained. "And the queen is a monster. Things were at least fair before the fall of the king."

"Oh. Was the king of South Kepler nicer?" Miguela said.

"Not really," Rosa said. "But I meant the king of North

Kepler. That was a good Cardinal Family. They never wanted a war with the Southerners or the Immortal Empire or anyone. Only wanted their folks left alone. And the Southerners were subtle about pushing the borders back, until …"

"Until what?" Carina prompted.

"They say it was the Red-Eyed Ones that did the Cardinal Family of the North in." Rosa lowered her voice even further. "But if you ask me, the queen of South Kepler is in thick with the Red-Eyed Ones." She patted Carina's shoulder. "That's why I'm telling you to be careful. It's not worth saving a plate if it's going to get you arrested and executed for treason."

Carina was anxious on their way back to the hostel, and Max suggested they check out the bookstore to get their minds off everything. Anthony generally seemed along for the ride, and Miguela loved books, so they agreed. Inside, they both disappeared fast, Miguela making a Kepler beetle line to the history section and Anthony towing his green backpack to the far end of the store. Max wanted to see if there were any books about the Immortal Empire, so Carina wandered by herself to the fiction section. She was reading the back cover of something raunchy Sister Elizabeth would have liked when someone tapped her shoulder.

"What, Miguela?" she asked, but when Miguela didn't answer, she put the book down and turned. Anthony was standing there, rocking back and forth on his heels while he held the straps of his backpack with both hands.

"Oh," Carina said. "It's you. What's up?"

"I need help," he said in a soft voice.

"With what?"

"Can you come with me?"

She followed him to a shelf of paranormal books by the back exit, where he stopped.

"Do you want to talk outside?" she asked, wondering if maybe Anthony had magic he was worried about, too.

He shook his head and pointed to a high shelf. "I'm trying to get the yellow book up there. I can't reach. You're tall."

Carina stepped up to the shelf. "Sure." The book was pretty far up. Even she had to stand on her toes. She stretched her arm to reach it. "Is this all you need?"

Anthony didn't answer. Carina felt something stab hard into her lower back. Her legs began to numb, and she fell, unable to catch herself as the rest of her body also numbed. From where she landed, she could see Anthony hold open the exit door for two men with red eyes. She tried to yell, but she could barely breathe.

"This her?" one of the men asked, while the other picked Carina up and hefted her over his shoulder. He gave Anthony a wad of cash.

Anthony counted the money. "This isn't enough. She's thermodynamic *and* telekinetic."

The man carrying Carina scoffed. "No one's thermodynamic in these parts."

"But I saw her do it!" Anthony said. "She can make things cold!"

"And if the girl gives us chills after the serum wears off, we'll pay you the extra money next time. We're not paying double now."

"But I *need* the money *now*!" Anthony said, sounding close to hysteria. "It's for my mom! We can't afford her surgery, and the doctor says she has to have it right away. She could die!"

"Shut up, or you won't have to worry about your mom,"

the man said cruelly.

Anthony's shoulders drooped. Carina couldn't see him as she was carried out of the store. She did hear him start to cry, though, and as the door shut, she thought she heard him say: "I'm sorry."

ROYAL DECREE NO. 849-16

By Royal Decree of King Cassius of the Southern Kingdom of Kepler, all citizens of South Kepler gifted with any magic shall register as such with the local governing body of the Crown and may thereafter be recruited for service in the Southern Guard, the Royal Guard, the Southern Civilian Corps, or another appropriate entity of the Crown.

Any citizen above the age of fourteen who is gifted with magic but fails to register shall be guilty of a felony crime, punishable by fines and/or up to ten years in prison. A child below the age of fourteen who is gifted with magic but not registered may be removed from the care of their legal parent or guardian and placed in the custody of the Crown.

CHAPTER SIXTEEN
THE GIRL WITH MAGIC

Foamy, rose-lavender scented bubbles swam through the small pool in Vivian's suite that her mother had called a tub. Vivian soaked for an hour while she sent her attendants out to purchase a copy of *Between the Moons*, a classic she'd always wanted to read. She traded her dirty jeans for a plush white robe and perused the room service menu. She ordered a tray of fancy candies, then stayed up late eating chocolate-dipped pearberries and reading. She woke the next morning in a luxurious bed under a cushy, buttery-soft duvet.

When her attendants came to retrieve her for the prayers, she pretended she was sleeping too hard to get up, but she was happy to allow in the man from the hotel who delivered breakfast—fluffy omelets with caramelized onions and sautéed mushrooms and fresh-squeezed juice.

She watched the sunrise through her floor-to-ceiling window view of Great Crater Lake. She didn't feel like dealing with Bast, so she ignored knocks on her door the rest of the morning.

At half past noon, Bast broke the locks telekinetically and stormed in.

Vivian was still in bed reading.

"What the hell are you doing?"

She didn't look up. "What does it look like I'm doing?"

The book flew out of her hand.

"I thought something happened!"

She slouched in bed. "Something did happen. The Gandhi Medical Centre won't see me. Give me back my book."

"Mom told me about the Centre." Bast yanked one of her pillows out from under her head telekinetically. "We have another plan. You can read in the coach."

She rolled over to another pillow. "I want to shop downtown. There's a place I like that sells the best shoes. They carry Prada-Gabbana."

Her new pillow flew off the bed as well.

"You're being childish. We don't have time to shop, and you wouldn't be strong enough for that anyway. I'm sending the attendants in to help you dress. We're leaving in an hour."

Vivian was tired of Bast ordering her around. "It will take at least two hours before I can go anywhere. My hair hasn't been washed in days."

The air around Vivian turned frigid. She pulled the duvet over her shoulders and thought that Bast needed to learn some manners. It was not kind to try to freeze your sister out of her very nice dignitary suite.

"I told you before: I'm *trying* to save your life."

"My life won't be worth as much with old shoes," Vivian said petulantly. She pulled the duvet over her head. "What new plan requires us to leave Gandhi?"

"The safe plan," Bast said. "You are not safe here. And we're going to find the Guru."

She pulled the duvet down again. "We're going to find … who?"

He snarled at her. "The Guru. I'm not going to sit around doing nothing while we wait for answers that might never come. What if no one has a cure? We need stronger magic. The Guru supposedly has it."

Vivian was extremely doubtful. "No one sane has ever found the Guru."

Bast tilted his chin up. "*I've* never tried to find him before, and I have reason to believe he exists. Get up. The Mountain of Peril is a long way from here."

She didn't know what to say. The Guru was a fairy tale. There was no way they were going to find him, no matter what reasons Bast had to believe they might. She felt almost as bad for him thinking it was possible as she did for herself knowing it wasn't.

Her brother folded his arms. "Are you going to make me resort to bribery? Will you get up if I agree to buy you a pair of shoes while you're getting ready?"

"You *personally*?" she asked suspiciously.

Bast made a "tsk" sound. "As if one of the attendants would have better taste."

Vivian considered that offer. Bast was certainly more polished than anyone else in their party. Even in a fight he never looked unkempt the way someone like Nate—who always looked like he needed a shower or a good night's sleep—could. And she *did* love new shoes.

She nodded.

The chill in the air lifted. "You better be ready when I get back," he warned. "And Nate and I are going to do the prayers with you tonight in the coach, so don't think you can get out of that either."

Vivian tugged the duvet up one more time. "I like three-inch heels," she told him.

"Yeah, yeah." She heard the door to the room shut.

Vivian left Gandhi with four new pairs of shoes that had probably cost more than the coach she was riding in. She liked the shoes, but she was frustrated with Bast anyway. She didn't want to spend her final days cooped up in a tiny, wheeled compartment.

News of the new plan had spread to the guards and attendants, and Vivian knew they thought it was crazy, too. She overheard her driver talking about it with an attendant.

"Where are we going again?" the attendant asked.

"Mountain of Peril in the Red Ridge Mountains," the driver answered. "They're trying to find the Guru."

Attraction was always red, brighter than rage, and with a steadier pulse. Vivian didn't need magic to know that's what the color of the connection between the driver and the attendant would have been. It aggravated her.

"That's a joke, right? The Guru is a legend."

"Yeah, and the number of people who've disappeared trying to find him isn't," the driver said without any detectable humor in his voice.

The attendant dropped her voice so low Vivian could barely hear her respond with: "What's going to happen after Queen Vivian dies?"

The driver hummed. "I suppose the crown will go to the next prince in line in a few years, but Queen Constance will take over again before then. You can bet she'll have someone's head for the security breach. That woman doesn't play games. It'll be like what happened after the king died, but worse. This is her daughter."

Then they hit a bump in the road, and the attendant said: "Quiet. She could be awake."

But she didn't want to hear the rest anyway. It was too depressing.

Vivian couldn't bring herself to actually think about dying, but as the days passed, she felt more and more fatigued. She was also nervous about how much magic she needed. Every other morning or so, Bast was siphoning magical energy from himself and Nate to her to keep the virus at bay. She didn't want to admit it to them, but the extra magic wasn't lasting as long, and she'd started noticing pain when she breathed too deeply.

The exhaustion made it hard for Vivian to stay awake in the coach, even if all she had to do was read and admire her shoes, and on top of everything, she kept waking up from dreams about her mother. In them, Mom tapped the upper half of an hourglass with her hard fingernails and said, "Live a little, Viv!" while the sand in the glass fell faster. Vivian had woken up screaming more than once just before the last grain of sand slipped through to the bottom.

She tried to think of ways to make her last days more valuable. Their new route passed right by Native Valley, so after dinner one night she asked Bast if they could see it.

He refused. "No. It's a long way to the Mountain of Peril. We are not detouring so that you can see a stupid valley."

"But it's one of the great wonders of Kepler," she said. "And I've never been there."

"There could still be Immortals following us. You can see it on the way back when you're not so vulnerable," Bast said, capably ignoring what she was sure was her most pathetic begging face. "It's not happening, Viv. Sorry."

Nate was sitting nearby, reading what looked like an extremely boring book comparing the demise of the Western Republic to the disappearance of magic in the Eastern Confederation. He peered over the cover, then quickly ducked back down.

Vivian leaned over to Nate and pushed his book away. "I could use backup," she said. Surely Nate would understand. She knew *he* hadn't been behind this plan to find the Guru.

Nate pulled his book away from her and stood. "We don't have time for side trips. You can see it on our way back," he said, and he walked away.

They always traveled late into the nights now and sometimes drove through to the next day. Vivian did get Bast to promise a stop at a hotel she'd heard good things about in Shadow of the Mountains, but the morning they were supposed to pass through, she slept through sunrise and woke up with her neck hurting. She began to stretch, then realized there was something wrong. Why hadn't she been woken for the prayers?

She sat up. The caravan wasn't moving. There were voices outside that sounded tense. She couldn't see anything from her window, so she stepped quietly out of her coach. There were several box trucks on the road, the motorized kind favored by less savory Keplerians and used to transport cargo. They had formed a blockade, and her caravan couldn't pass. Vivian spotted Nate on Pepper, riding warily near Bast, who was standing in the middle of the road, face-to-face with a man who was much broader shouldered than he was and probably twenty years older.

Or possibly two- or three-*hundred* and twenty, Vivian realized as she sneaked closer from behind the supply wagons and confirmed that the man's eyes were red. There were three more Immortals standing behind him, and Vivian could see at least four sets of red eyes watching from the trucks. They didn't look like Empire Immortals, but she'd have bet all her new shoes they were traffickers.

Had her caravan thinned recently? Vivian was ultra-aware all at once of how flimsy the coach she'd been traveling in was and how quickly she could count the number of guards on horseback. Eighteen. Including Nate.

Captain Thurlow was next to Bast, along with two of their guards. The captain and his soldiers were armed with broadswords. She thought maybe one of them was teleki-netic. The group of Immortals had crossbows, and the one in front was spinning a dagger.

"So, these are the Southern Royals," he was saying. "The bounty on your heads is extremely lucrative. Lord Godric is *very* interested in you."

Nate looked edgy, but Bast didn't seem to think they were at a disadvantage. "Lord Godric can come to South Kepler himself," he said. "Clear the road, or we'll clear you from it."

The Immortal man sneered. "You're outnumbered."

Alighieri had an opera company, a ballet, several theater groups, and two real movie theaters. Vivian had seen many shows that included dramatized confrontations like these between the Southern Guard and Immortals, sometimes Empire Immortals, sometimes bounty hunters. Those showdowns always took several minutes of banter before turning into a real fight.

Bast didn't see this as a showdown.

He made a disgusted noise and flipped his wrist. The four Immortals standing in front of him froze from the crowns of their heads down. The man in the front's mouth opened into an "o" as it happened, and he dropped his dagger. Bast picked it up telekinetically while a couple of the trucks revved and began rolling toward him.

But perhaps the training sessions had been paying off, because Nate had plenty of time to ride in front of Bast and telekinetically send the trucks veering to opposite sides of the road. One plowed into a field while the other crashed onto its side. Lack of power was for sure not Nate's problem.

The Immortals driving the other trucks must have taken that show of force seriously. At least one backed up and started driving the opposite direction. Nate followed on horseback. The other truck remained stopped, and six more Immortals appeared from behind. They, too, were armed with crossbows, and they weren't close enough to freeze.

Thankfully, Bast was talented with defensive telekinetic shields. Vivian could see the air shimmering in front of him as he blocked a volley of arrows from coming anywhere near him or the guards.

She was relieved. She did not anticipate anything that could throw Bast off his game now. They were safe enough, and Bast would be upset if he caught her out of the coach. She needed to trust him. She began to creep back.

Then something threw Bast off his game.

A girl climbed out of the back of the crashed truck—so they *were* traffickers—and ran straight into the line of fire between the Immortals and Bast. She must have been disoriented. She didn't look like she knew where she was going at all. She only caught on that she was in trouble when an arrow shot by her face.

"Get down!" Bast yelled as more arrows shot toward the girl.

She screamed and held her arms up around her face.

And three arrows *bounced off* the air around her.

Vivian's blood raced. That girl had created her own defensive telekinetic shield.

About ten percent of the Mortal population was telekinetic, but there were degrees of telekinetic skill, and most people didn't come close to the kind of magic Vivian and her brothers had. The Southern Kingdom kept tabs on their magicians, too. Anyone with any magic gift was supposed to be registered. That was how Vivian's family kept track of potential threats and managed valuable resources.

She should have known if there was someone living in this area who had any real magical power, and that girl had real power. The ability to manipulate everything around you to create a telekinetic shield was rare. Some Cardinals couldn't do it. Nate couldn't. Vivian could, but only if she concentrated very hard.

Even Bast, with all his talent, had to be conscious about it, and it seemed he was too distracted for that now. As he watched the girl run off the road and into the fields, the shield he'd been holding vanished. An arrow hit one of the guards standing by him.

"Bast!" Nate yelled, appearing on Pepper from behind the line of Immortals. Vivian had temporarily lost sight of Nate, but now he was galloping toward Bast and pointing to the side of the road near the crashed truck.

A man with red eyes and a bleeding gash on his forehead was standing there with a pistol. He aimed it at Bast, who was still looking in the opposite direction to where the girl had run.

He wasn't going to see it coming.

The Immortal cocked the gun, and what Vivian thought as she threw it out of his hand telekinetically was that if she'd used too much magic, at least it was better than cyanide.

Vivian was with her father again, on the white horses, looking at the beautiful bridge stretching out across the lake. He looked older than he had last time. There were gray hairs in his beard, and his face was thinner. The castle towered behind them.

"Can we ride around the castle?" she asked her father.

"I think I'd like that," he said.

They rode through the forest around the castle, and Vivian breathed in sweet pine and observed the outline of thick tree branches and healthy leaves bright against an impossibly blue sky. When they arrived back at the bridge, Vivian wanted to ride around the castle again, but King Herschel got off his horse. He seemed to be in a different mood today than he'd been before, and his melancholy felt heavy on Vivian, like impending darkness pressing in on her and rising up her throat.

"I don't want to cross the bridge yet," she told him.

He looked very sad.

CHAPTER SEVENTEEN
THE PIGGY AND THE PIE

Trotting behind her as Carina trudged through a heavily forested area was a wild piggy. It had been following for some time now while she navigated through who-knew-where to who-knew-what in the hopes that she would find who-knew-who to help her get back to Shadow of the Mountains. She had just escaped from a very bad situation, she was still very frightened, and she was otherwise completely alone. So, it was not insane that she was recounting her story to the pig.

"Reed's lucky Anthony went after me, not her," Carina told the piggy. "She'd have panicked. I bet she'd have passed out in the truck. Or wet herself and *then* passed out."

That second statement had been spiteful, and Carina felt bad about it right away. After all, a lot of otherwise strong-willed people would have panicked in a situation like the one Carina had been in. The back of the truck had been cold and dark, and it smelled like a cocktail of urine and vomit. The truck had moved right away, then stopped for what seemed like a long time, then moved again, then stopped again, all through the night. For hours, she couldn't move her legs or arms, or turn her head or even blink. Her insides seemed to be in working order, but her outsides refused to cooperate. Terror was the correct reaction to that.

Carina *had* been terrified, but every time she got close to real panic, a voice in her head that sounded like Sister Agda's said: "What do you think you're doing? How are you going to escape if you're too busy freaking out to notice when you get the chance?"

She'd forced herself to take deep, calming breaths and tried not to drive herself crazy worrying about what she would do when the serum wore off and the truck doors opened again. Sister Rachel had taught her to breathe like that, with the morning meditation sessions she'd always done before they started their lessons.

"Thank you, Sister *Rachel*." Carina looked down at her small-but-portly companion. "Too bad I don't have that survival guide she packed. I am going to find help, though. Eventually, I'll run into someone who can get me back to Shadow of the Mountains. Then I'll find Miguela and Max, and we can go find Max's uncle, or maybe we'll find the Guru, and someone can help us get to Cerulean, and everything will be all right."

The pig grunted.

"Sounds that unlikely to you, too, huh?"

But it hadn't been likely that she would get away from those Red-Eyed Ones, and that had happened. She wished she knew how. The whole thing was kind of blurry to her. The serum had worn off, and she'd been trying unsuccessfully to use telekinesis to open the truck doors when the truck crashed. Carina was flung sideways in the back of the truck.

She'd hit her head hard. It took some time for her to even realize the back door had busted open, and the morning sun was so bright that she could barely see after she'd climbed out.

If it hadn't been for all that, she might not have run straight into a crossfire between a bunch of soldiers and far more Red-Eyed Ones than she'd realized she was traveling with.

"At least I ran. I bet Reed would have been too scared to move."

The piggy stopped to mark a rock along the path.

Carina waited and thought, begrudgingly, that she should probably take back that last thing about Reed, too. The Sisters would not have approved of her dwelling on another girl's weaknesses to make herself feel better about her own failures. Women with real strength didn't need to judge each other that way.

"But sometimes you've just been *sold* and taken away from the only family you have, and you don't feel very strong," Carina said. And she did not feel strong. Not at all. She felt dumb for getting turned in by Anthony, dumber for not having realized she was running right into the middle of a fight, and dumbest for not knowing how she'd survived.

She *shouldn't* have survived. She'd noticed she was being shot at far too late to get out of the way. She'd screamed. She'd been sure she was going to die. But nothing hit her, and she had a second chance to run. So, she ran. It was a while before she realized no one was chasing her.

"And what the hell is that all about? I was important enough to buy, important enough to ship, but not important enough to chase? Who do those guys think they are?"

She started stomping through the forest. The trees here weren't like the tall Earth pines in the Red Ridge Mountains or the slender green apple and pearberry trees that had populated her family's orchard. These were short, bushy, cauliflower trees with plump leaves and a canopy of air creepers weaving a blanket of vines above her. It was dark, even in the middle of the day. She was furious enough to be moving fast, though, and the piggy had to trot faster to keep up with her. How was this kind of thing happening on Kepler? Carina knew she wasn't the first girl with magic those Red-Eyed Ones had taken. She might have been the first that had gotten away, though, and that made her spitting mad.

The piggy made a low, barking noise.

"You are so right. After we get to Cerulean and I learn how to use magic, I'm going to find the Resistance and join them."

The piggy squawked like it was laughing at her.

Which was fair. Because Carina had no idea if there was a Resistance. But if there wasn't, there should be. She should organize one. There had to be a Mortal Commitment against one human selling another human for any reason. Miguela would know it. Maybe she'd know if there was a Resistance. Carina would ask her. As soon as she saw her again.

Which was a thought she could not afford to cry about now. Instead, she thought about how hard she was going to work to learn magic—or at least to learn how *not* to use magic when she didn't want to—now that this had happened. If she'd had more skill, maybe she wouldn't have had to run. Maybe she could have stayed to help fight those Red-Eyed Ones. Then maybe she'd have a ride back to Shadow of the Mountains. As it was, she was alone (sort of), in the dark, with no map, no compass, no jacket, and no backpack. The potato field she'd just run into at the edge of the cauliflower forest was the most interesting thing she'd seen in two hours.

The freshly plowed potato field.

There had to be people within walking distance.

"You probably shouldn't come with me anymore," she said to the wild piggy. "Some people hunt pigs."

The piggy did not answer. It was busy digging up potatoes, facedown in the field and rear-up, curly tail waving vigorously with its efforts to procure dinner.

"You can only eat a few," Carina warned. "Or they might notice you here."

The piggy popped out of the dirt with a potato in its mouth, and Carina could have sworn it bobbed its head at her before trotting back the other way.

"And this is why I'm a vegetarian," she said while she watched it disappear.

She turned back to the field. She needed someone of her own species to talk to.

Carina followed plow lines to a barn, where she found a girl with pigtails milking a goat. When Carina asked the girl if either of her parents were home, the girl shook her head.

"But my auntie is here," she said. "Do you want to see her?"

Carina said yes, so the girl took her to an attractive house with blue siding, a white fence, and a delivery van with solar panels duct-taped over the windows parked outside.

Inside, Mrs. Hiller was sitting at a table covered by a crisp cloth in a sunny kitchen with floors that were tiled in a checkerboard pattern. She was wearing her multi-pocketed jacket and eating pie. "For Sam's sake," she said as she spotted Carina. "I knew I shouldn't have let that Red-Eyed freak on my van. What did he do to you?"

"Hi, Mrs. Hiller," Carina said. "It wasn't the Red-Eyed One from your van. It was the boy with the green backpack. He turned me in to some bounty hunters."

"The kid?"

Carina nodded. The pie smelled like it had come straight from the oven. Mrs. Hiller still smelled like dead fish. "Is this your house?"

"It's my sister's place. I visit whenever I come this way." Mrs. Hiller stood and came closer. "Your hair is matted with blood."

Carina reached to feel her head. She hadn't realized she'd been hurt that bad.

"How did that happen?" Mrs. Hiller demanded.

"Is the blood dry?" Carina asked, because the amount of blood that came from your head didn't necessarily determine the level of injury. Although, given what she was seeing now, she was a little concerned that she might have a concussion.

"Auntie, I don't think she's eaten in days," the girl said.

Carina had recently eaten *plenty* of pretzel bites. "I'm not *that* skinny."

Mrs. Hiller's mouth twisted in skepticism. "You better sit and have some pie anyway."

Carina tried to resume better manners. "No thanks, Mrs. Hiller. My sister doesn't know where I am. I'd appreciate a ride back to Shadow of the Mountains. I can pay when we get there."

Mrs. Hiller made a sound between a burp and a groan, pulled her jagged knife out of her jacket and pointed it at Carina, who had not realized that refusing pie was that kind of offense.

Then the little girl said "*move*" like Carina was very slow, and she realized she was standing in front of the counter where the rest of the pie was sitting in a glass dish.

She moved aside and watched with trepidation as Mrs. Hiller used her jagged knife to carve out an enormous piece of pie and set it on a plate. Then she wiped her knife on a dishtowel. "It's three hours back to Shadow of the Mountains and sixty dollars for the ride." She handed the plate to Carina. "But I'll only charge you thirty if you eat the pie before we leave."

And you simply don't refuse pie in that sort of circumstance. Carina ate while Mrs. Hiller cleaned blood out of her hair with a warm, wet cloth. Then Carina asked Mrs. Hiller for the recipe because it was good pie, and if she ever saw Sister Lindy again, she thought she might want to give it to her.

Four hours later, Carina was back at the youth hostel. Miguela wasn't there, but the clerk said: "The bossy girl? I think she's filing a police report."

Carina found Miguela and Max at the local police station, sitting on two old wooden chairs in a hallway. Miguela was staring down at the station's cracked floor tiles while Max scanned his surroundings vigilantly.

He saw Carina right away and jumped up before she could say anything.

"Oh, my God," he said, and an instant later he had swept her into the biggest hug she ever remembered anyone giving her. "Oh my God," he repeated, practically lifting her off her feet before he set her back down. "I thought I'd never see you again."

Miguela had her knees pulled up to her chest and had not yet moved from the wooden chair. Carina let go of Max and went to sit next to her sister.

She anticipated a second hug.

Instead, Miguela turned the other way and said: "Anthony told me what happened. He felt terrible. We looked everywhere, but the guys who took you were already gone. Do you know how hard it is to get help finding someone in this city? Runaways are a regular thing for them. They won't let you file a police report until the missing person has been gone for three days. It doesn't even matter if you *know* they've been kidnapped."

"I'm sorry, Miguela," Carina began. "They injected me with something, and then I was in a truck for a long time, and I can't explain how I got away."

Miguela didn't answer. She wiped tears hastily away from her face.

Carina tried to think of a way to make Miguela feel better. "We couldn't have expected Anthony to be dangerous ..." she started, and at that, Miguela jerked her head toward Carina.

"The Sisters were right." Her hair was coming out of its usual tight bun, and the whites of her eyes were spider-webbed with blood vessels. "They're always right! Every time you do magic, it's like sending a big flare into the air that says 'hey, look here, totally oblivious girl doing magic.' You are so careless!"

"But you liked Anthony, didn't you?" Carina asked, surprised at her sister's sudden anger. "You trusted him too, right?"

Miguela jumped up out of her seat. "It's not about whether I trusted him! The point is, you used magic, you got caught, and someone *kidnapped* you because of it!"

"But I'm okay now, and—"

"And you *never* think about the danger you put yourself in when you do stuff like that, do you?" Miguela continued.

"Or the danger you put *me* in! What was I supposed to do if you didn't come back!? You're the only person I have left! Did that even occur to you?"

"Of course, I think about you——"

"You weren't thinking when you were using magic to keep *him* from breaking half the plates in the pub!" Miguela pointed viciously at Max. "And where did they take you? Why did it take you so long to get back? You look terrible! You *smell* terrible!"

Carina looked down at her dirty clothes. She probably smelled worse than Mrs. Hiller.

Miguela shoved past Carina and stalked down the hall, leaving her behind with Max.

He sat down where Miguela had been and nudged Carina's shoulder. "She was really worried about you. You should have heard what she said to Anthony when he told her what he'd done. She was …" Max shook his head. "Let's just say I felt bad for the kid."

"She's right, though," Carina said. "This was all my fault. I wasn't careful enough."

"You can't be careful all the time," Max said. Then he let her stare at nothing for a while before he added, "Do you want to talk about what happened?"

"Maybe later," she said. Right now, what she wanted was to get back to the hostel, where there was a cheap bar of soap and a gross bunk waiting for her. She needed to clean up and sleep, and she didn't want Miguela standing outside by herself for long.

You never knew who you could trust in a place like this.

CHAPTER EIGHTEEN
THE BOOK OF MAGIC

Max thought they should stay another day in Shadow of the Mountains to rest. He said his uncle had been lost for a long time, Carina had recently gone through a lot of trauma, and it was unhealthy to pretend it hadn't happened and just move on. But Carina wanted to avoid more trauma, and she was worried about the possibility that someone else in town might have seen her do magic. So, the next day they took a bus out to the place where most of the climbers started their treks, and she and Max sat behind a group of hikers who were talking about the Guru.

"My cousin tried to find him," one of them said. "When he came back, he couldn't remember anything that had happened from when he left home to when he got down from the mountain. The natives there completely mess with your brain."

"It's not the natives," another said. "The Guru exists. I know someone who met him once. She had stomach cancer and he cured it, but he only appears to people he wants to appear to. No one else can see him."

"That's impossible," the first said. "Magic can't make people invisible. And there's no way some guy's been sitting on that mountain for hundreds of years, wiping people's brains when he doesn't like them and curing them when he does"

"Maybe he's Immortal."

"Immortals don't have magic."

Carina sank down in her seat next to Max. "He must have a lot of magic if he can use it to heal cancer and stop himself from aging," she whispered. "Maybe he really can help me if we find him."

Max was staring out the window. He slouched next to her. "Sorry. I wasn't paying attention. Don't you think you should try to sleep? You're pushing yourself hard."

"Doing what?" she complained. "Riding a bus?" But she was sleepy and leaning against Max's shoulder to nap was a cozy way to endure a two-hour ride into the mountains. She decided to take his advice for the moment and rest, though it would have been better if Miguela hadn't been sitting across from them, scowling at Max and peering around so suspiciously at everyone else that no one would sit by her. Carina guessed that it was going to take Miguela a while to get over what had happened yesterday.

It was a quiet day of hiking after they got back on the trail. Miguela was talking even less to Carina than she had been before, but today Max wasn't very chatty, either, and he didn't bother to stop and check out any amphibians. Carina was glad when they arrived at a clearing between two boulders and Miguela finally declared that she was tired and they should stop to rest.

They kept dinner light, and when they were done eating, Miguela set up the pop-up tent herself, climbed into it and zipped the door shut. She didn't say good night.

"She's not very happy with me," Carina said lamely to Max. They were sitting on one of the boulders, watching the dusk moon rise slowly. Carina pulled her jacket tighter around her shoulders and tucked her hands into her sleeves. They hadn't set a fire—it hadn't seemed like a good idea—and she was cold again.

Max was also huddled with his hands tucked into his jacket. "I'm happy with you."

Two days ago, Carina had felt like Max was the one thing standing between her and the Red-Eyed Ones. It had given her what she now thought was a false sense of security. She nodded at him but couldn't bring herself to smile.

He stood. "You need something to cheer you up."

She glanced at the zipped door of the tent. There wasn't much she could think of that would make her feel better right now. "Give it your best shot," she said drearily.

Max brought his backpack over, sat down again, and started digging through it. "I was going to wait until tomorrow, but I have a gift for you."

"You have a gift?" Carina *did* like gifts. "Why were you going to wait?"

"Because it's heavy and you were tired today, and I thought once I gave it to you, you'd refuse to let anyone else carry it." He pulled a thick book from his bag and handed it to her with a flourish.

She read the cover. "*The Book of Magic: Telekinetic Forms for Master Practitioners*, by Bosley Pinkerton."

"I know you're not a master practitioner," Max said apologetically, "and I think that book might be kind of outdated, but I thought maybe you could find something useful in it, and—"

Carina set the book down and dove at him with a hug, wrapping her arms tight around his neck. "Thank you, Max. It's perfect."

Max hugged back. "It was just something I thought you'd like."

She squeezed tighter.

"I keep thinking about you being kidnapped by a bunch of strangers, and how there wasn't anything I could do to help you," he continued. She felt him flatten his hand against her back. "I know your sister doesn't approve, but I think you need to learn how to use your magic. How else are you going to be able to protect yourself? Or her?"

Miguela didn't understand at all, but Max did. Carina felt something inside her that had been pulled tight loosen, and she sighed in his arms. He nuzzled her hair, and it occurred to her that maybe this was an embrace, not a hug, and that she'd never known the difference before.

"Don't you want to read your book?" Max asked, with what she thought might have been a touch of humor.

She leaned back so she could see his face. Despite his tone, he was looking quite affectionately at her.

"Thank you," she said again.

His eyes flashed down. To what? Her lips? A swarm of Kepler beetles invaded her stomach. But then he blinked fast, like he had seen something he hadn't expected, and let her go.

"You're welcome." He picked the book back up from where she'd put it aside and swiftly set it in her lap. "I'll get you a flashlight."

Miguela hated the book and demanded that they leave it behind, especially when she learned that Carina wanted to try some of the exercises in it.

"Don't you get it?" she cried. "The Red-Eyed Ones can *sense magic!* We're trying to get away from them. If you start practicing magic, we might as well start making fires when we stop. You'll be telling every Red-Eyed One in the area where we are!"

Carina was sure Miguela's logic was flawed.

"Don't *you* get it? I was defenseless against those bounty hunters. They shouldn't have bothered wasting their serum on me. I couldn't have done anything to them even if they hadn't injected me with it. And I do magic accidentally, Miguela! I'm not even sure I *know* all the times I'm doing magic. Ivan thought he saw me doing it in Mrs. Hiller's delivery van, and I didn't think I was doing *anything* there. Anthony told those bounty hunters I make people cold. I don't know *where* he got *that* from!"

"You don't have thermodynamic magic," Miguela scoffed. "Hardly anyone has that."

"But you *are* cold a lot," Max offered.

"See! I'm going to attract Red-Eyed Ones no matter what. I might as well learn how!"

Miguela didn't seem to have any more arguments. She marched ahead silently for a while. Max offered to help Carina in the evening after they stopped to rest, though.

"How?" Carina asked. "You don't have any magic yourself."

"A coach doesn't need the skill of the athlete," Max said. "He needs the right attitude."

"I guess it won't hurt if we're both trying to figure out the exercises," Carina said.

"That's the spirit, champ!" Max told her, and it was nice to have someone on her side.

A lot of the exercises in *The Book of Magic* assumed the practitioner could already do easy things, like lift bottles of beer across streams. Carina didn't think most of those exercises would help her and she wanted to start with *Chapter Two: Deep Focus Techniques*. Max, however, was intrigued by *Chapter Fourteen: Spatial Awareness*, and he was convinced they should start there.

"Trust me," he said. "I'm the coach, remember?"

Miguela, who was sitting on a thick, fallen tree trunk, watching, said: "Trust you? You suggested eating poisonous berries three times today."

"But not because I was trying to poison anyone," Max said. "I sincerely thought those were the good ones."

Carina was reading. "No one needs to eat any wild berries, poisonous or not. There's another village coming up tomorrow, remember? We have plenty of food until then." She flipped to the back of Chapter Fourteen. So far, she hadn't seen anything in the chapter she thought she could do. "Are you sure we shouldn't start with something simpler?"

Max took the book from her and dangled a wide strip of fabric in front of her face.

"What is that?" Carina asked.

"It's a blindfold," he said. "I got the idea from one of the exercises in the book, but this is how warriors always train with their masters. The teacher blindfolds the student to help them hone their other senses."

Carina was skeptical. "How am I supposed to move something I can't see?"

"You can't move something you *can* see," Miguela pointed out dryly. "This can't hurt."

Max smiled broadly at Miguela. "Exactly. Thank you, Miguela."

Carina's sister had agreed to assist Max, but only, she said, because she was afraid Carina and Max would try to do something really stupid with magic if she wasn't there. Now it looked like maybe Miguela was having second thoughts. But Carina decided they were both right and tried to take the blindfold from Max.

He held it out of her reach. "I'll do it for you. Wouldn't want you to cheat."

"I wouldn't cheat!" Carina said, offended.

"Yeah, right," Miguela said.

Max skipped around behind Carina and reached to situate the blindfold over her eyes. He tied the cloth snugly behind her head, then set his hands on her shoulders and said, "Ready?"

She tried to remember if maybe she'd eaten some of those poisonous berries. She didn't think the way his breath was tickling her neck should be making her light-headed. "Ready."

Max backed away, and there was a pause before he said: "Great. Now Miguela and I are going to take turns throwing rocks around you and——"

"You're going to take turns *throwing* stuff at me?"

"Sounds like fun, doesn't it, Care?" Miguela said, sarcasm dripping from her voice.

"No, no. We're not throwing rocks *at* you," Max said. The ground crunched nearby. "We're throwing them in front of you and behind you. Your goal is to figure out which."

Carina squinted at the light behind the blindfold. "I don't think I can do that, Max."

"You sure as hell won't be able to do it if you keep telling yourself that."

She didn't want to seem like a whiner. "Okay, okay. Positive energy and all. I'll see what I can do." She strained to sense what was in the air around her and waited while Max and Miguela positioned themselves to throw the rocks. She heard a rock land to her left.

"Could you tell if that went in front or behind you?" Max asked.

"I can tell it landed to my left," Carina said.

The ground crunched. She heard another rock land to her left.

"What about that one? In front or behind?"

"No idea."

More crunching. A rock landed to her right.

"Anything that time?"

Carina pulled the blindfold down. "I don't think telekinetic magic works this way, Max. I think you have to see what you're magicking."

"You don't know how this kind of magic works. Isn't that the point?"

"Yeah, but I don't want to waste time," she countered.

"I understand," Max said. "Let's try a different exercise instead. Put the blindfold back on, and this time, just take a few steps and see if you can sense anything at all."

"That's stupid," Miguela said. "She already told you she couldn't sense anything."

"It's not stupid! Telekinesis is a sixth sense. By taking away one of her senses, we're forcing her to hone all the other five. Including her telekinesis."

"Did you read that in the book?" Miguela asked.

"It's in Chapter Three," Max admitted.

Carina was willing to try the exercise, and Max/Pinkerton were partially right. After an hour of walking blindly in circles, she had a good memory of the clearing and all its most perilous obstacles. She thought she was getting much better at figuring out approximately how far she'd turned whenever she moved, too. Miguela had decided to go back to the tent ("because this is so boring, I'd rather be sleeping"). Max was still helping, though, and he was getting stealthier about moving around her. She could barely hear him walk anymore.

But she couldn't see anything with her mind.

"I'm tired, Max," she complained. "Can we stop?"

He answered after a pause: "Alright, one more try, and we'll stop. Where am I?"

She made a quarter turn to the left and started taking slow steps forward. "I think tomorrow we should try some of the exercises from Chapter Two." She stepped over a large branch she'd tripped on previously. "Is this the right way?"

"I can't tell you that. Just listen to the sound of my voice."

It sounded like she was going toward him. She took another cautious step. There were some large rocks she'd already stubbed her toes on a few times near here.

"Very good. You're doing great."

She took another step forward. "This way?" She took another two steps, and when he didn't answer, she stepped forward again. "Max? Is this the right direction?"

He laughed low, so she thought she must be close. She took one last aggressive step forward and felt him grab her arms as she nearly ran right into him. She stumbled back, but he held on to her. "Whoa, don't fall."

She pulled the blindfold away. He was standing so close she would bump into him if she breathed too deeply. It had gotten later than she realized. She could barely see him in the dark.

"Thanks for the help today," she said.

He tilted his head. "You don't have to thank me for that. I wanted to help. It's what friends are for." He was looking at her face, but not her eyes. "Honestly, it's practically a crime that those Sisters never let you make any friends. Lucky for me, though."

"How's that?" she asked as those damn Kepler beetles in her stomach woke up.

"Well, there's no way you wouldn't have a boyfriend."

She puffed out the breath of air she'd been holding. He was really, really close …

"You guys, it's dark. We should all—"

Carina shot back from Max like *he* was poisonous. Miguela had just returned to the clearing, and it was a good thing it *was* dark. Otherwise, Max would have known Carina was blushing beetroot red.

"If you want to work on Chapter Two tomorrow, we can," he said as they started walking back to the tent. His hand brushed hers. "But I kind of wanted to finish Chapter Fourteen."

Carina was going to be lucky if she could focus on *anything* in Chapter Fourteen if this is how practice was going to go tomorrow.

"What do you think?" he asked.

"I might be up for that," she said, a little breathlessly.

His hand brushed hers again, softly, before he took it.

"I hope so."

# CHAPTER NINETEEN
MEDIATION AND MEDITATION

Vivian was getting a very cold shoulder from Bast. While she'd hovered between life and death for the second time, her caravan had stopped in Shadow of the Mountains. Now they had new plans. They were still traveling to the Mountain of Peril to find the Guru, but they were also trying to find the girl who had produced the telekinetic shield. She had to have more magic than usual for a commoner, and Bast thought maybe if they could find the girl, they'd be able to harness the extra magic they needed to cure Vivian's virus. They hadn't been able to find the girl in Shadow of the Mountains, and now they were searching elsewhere.

But Nate had to tell Vivian all that because Bast was refusing to talk to her. He was barely even looking at her. He wouldn't eat with her. He wouldn't check on her. He wouldn't acknowledge her during the prayers. He was doing the magic transfers while she slept. And Nate was trying to compensate. Several times she'd woken to find him, not Bast, sitting with her in the coach reading.

A few days after Vivian's blackout, she woke to see Nate staring out the window.

"Are you okay?" she said.

"Yeah, sure," he said, but fake-happy was like a sweater that didn't fit right on Nate. "Do you need anything? Are you hungry?"

Her muscles ached, her head hurt, and she needed Nate to get out and send in Bast because having two people that tended hot in that little coach was making her feel like she was roasting in an oven. But she couldn't tell him that. She'd never been able to talk to Nate the way she could talk to Bast.

"Do you want to talk?" Nate asked.

Vivian felt the tips of her ears get hot.

He went on quickly before she could respond. "Sorry. I know you get along better with Bast, but since he's being … I thought …"

Vivian instantly felt guilty for making Nate feel like the second-best brother. "It's not your fault Bast's angry at me. He told me not to use magic."

"Yeah, and he can't fathom the possibility that you only did it because *he* was in trouble. He thinks he had that whole situation completely under control."

Vivian didn't answer. Nate was tapping his knuckles against the side of the coach and looking out the window while he talked.

"Bast doesn't understand that you can't stop trying to protect us. He only makes calculated decisions, you know? Not that you don't calculate. No one ever calls *you* a hothead. But in the moment, I think decisions are easier for you because you just do whatever you need to do to make sure we're okay."

He stopped for a breath, but Vivian couldn't come up

with what to say before he let out that breath in a big gush of air and looked straight at her.

"Maybe neither of you get it. You're *both* control maniacs. You're dying over—" Nate grimaced. "Er, maybe that isn't the right word, but you're really not happy that you're not in charge right now because you think you should be responsible for everything. And Bast is doing everything he can to be responsible for everything himself, and he's worse than you because *he's* trying to control fate. He can't *stand* the thought that someone *else* is going to decide what happens to you. Even if someone is *God*."

Nate sort of smiled at her.

"I think you're the only person Bast thought he could always trust to be there for him. He's angry at you because he thinks if you loved him the way he loves you, you'd know that he needs you, and you'd let him help you so that he can keep you. So, he'll come around. Eventually. He can't lose you."

The coach came to a stop while Vivian tried once more to figure out what to say.

Nate stood. "Geez, it's hot in here. Must be what happens when you stick two people that tend hot into one small space. Do you want to come outside?"

She shook her head dumbly.

"Okay. Poke your head out if you need something."

"Nate, wait." Vivian's tongue felt stuck in her mouth. She needed a few more seconds. This was all so strange. She couldn't ever remember Nate talking to her like this.

He stretched his neck to one side, then relaxed it. "Viv, I know you guys both think that if I'm up next, I'm toast. So maybe if you kick the bucket, I'll take Pepper and get the hell out of South Kepler. But if you're trying to control *my* fate, I think you should know that whatever happens, I'm not going to blame you. I have to figure out how to live my own life. If I don't, it's not your fault. Okay?"

Vivian blinked. In a certain light, Nate looked a little like their dad. Maybe even more so than Bast ever did.

"Okay?"

She nodded. "Okay."

He nodded back like that was settled and opened the door.

"Wait," she said again.

He turned back from the door one more time, and she realized she still didn't have anything to say. She just didn't want him to be in a rush to go.

She made up a question: "Have you had any luck finding the girl?"

He smirked. "I have wolves tracking her. I think even Bast thinks that's cool."

Vivian smiled at him. "It *is* cool, Nate. Your telepathy gift isn't very common. It's nice you finally have something useful to do with it."

He fixed his eyes on hers, and it made her realize that when Nate stopped for long enough, you could see the green and brown separated in his irises. But focusing on those little separations made the space behind her own eyes hurt, and she became annoyed that he was staring.

"What?"

He shook his head. "Nothing. Guess it's good to be useful."

Captain Thurlow stepped into Vivian's coach a few hours later. He was checking on her as regularly as Nate, but she paid more attention to how long it was between the captain's visits.

"Your brother's wolves showed back up." He didn't look

happy about it.

"That bothers you?" Vivian asked.

The captain shuddered. "They're *wolves*. They have huge teeth and jaws like traps, and Prince Nathanial scratches behind their ears like they're puppy dogs and feeds them scraps. From his *hands*. Prince Bastian keeps muttering stuff about fleas."

Vivian enjoyed laughing with Captain Thurlow about that, and it turned out the wolves had brought back good news about the girl. She was hiking with two other kids, and they were on an established trail that a lot of hikers took into the mountains. It ran parallel to the road Vivian's caravan was traveling. They were going to pass the girl, then stop in a village to wait for her to catch up.

"Then Prince Bastian and Prince Nathanial are going to intercept her and try to persuade her to help us," the captain said. "If necessary, they'll arrest her for unauthorized use of magic."

"But hopefully they won't have to do that," Vivian said.

"Hopefully," the captain agreed.

They arrived at the village late the next morning, and Vivian's caravan took over a small inn attached to a run-down tavern. She ate lunch alone in her room, anticipating an afternoon nap until an attendant brought her a note from Bast that said: "Nate and I are training on the patio behind the tavern this afternoon."

There was no such thing as an apology from Bast, so Vivian took the note as a peace offering. She went to the barren cemented patio behind the tavern, where all the tables and chairs were stacked in a corner. Three lonely paper lanterns, probably left over from an old party, were the only décor.

Bast was sitting cross-legged on a cushion. There were two empty cushions next to him.

"Where's Nate?" Vivian asked, and as Bast's face turned down, she realized she'd made a mistake. How did you manage to have two brothers without always making one feel like he was "second-best"?

Bast looked up, though, and she must have seemed suitably remorseful because his frown relaxed. "Late, probably. He should be here soon."

She stood there waiting awkwardly for him to do something.

"I'm told I'm being *unreasonably* difficult," he drawled eventually. "Personally, I think *you're* the one being unreasonably difficult. I'm not the one who's sick, though."

She sat down on the cushion closest to Bast. "Did Nate tell you that?"

Bast laughed dryly. "Yes. Would you believe I'm taking advice from him?"

"No." She groaned. "I think I had an actual conversation with him yesterday."

They heard footsteps, and Nate joined them huffing and puffing.

"You're late," Bast said.

"Sorry," Nate said. "Got turned around in the village."

"It only has five streets."

"And ten buildings," Vivian added slyly. Bast laughed for real, and her face broke into a smile at that.

Nate gave them a satisfied look. "So. We're back to Viv and Bast versus Nate, and all is right with the world, huh?" He plopped down onto the third cushion. "Well, I'm glad.

What are we doing today? Seems like a weird place for a training exercise."

"We're meditating," Bast said.

"You brought us all out here to *think?*"

"More like *not* to think. You need to learn to focus if you ever want to use your thermodynamics for anything other than blowing stuff up. Meditation will help you hone your ability to stay mindful when things get chaotic."

Nate kicked out his feet. "I already have an excellent sense of what my mind is being mindful of. How do you think I distinguish between what the animals are thinking and my thoughts when I talk to them?"

Bast considered that. "I *have* always suspected that your mental capacities must be similar to that of a lower-order mammal. How *do* you know which words are theirs and which are yours?"

Nate scratched behind his ear, and Vivian thought unwittingly of his wolves. "Animals don't think in words. They think in noises and pictures and stuff."

"Pictures of what?" she asked. It had never occurred to her before to ask Nate how his gift worked, but he had tried hard to help fix things with her and Bast, so she wanted to be nice to him right now. Even if he might have fleas.

Nate scratched again. "Basic stuff. What they're going to eat next. Where they're going to find it. Is that other animal a friend or enemy? If it's an enemy, should I run from it or fight it for territory? If it's a friend, should we play and can we share food? And enemy or not, there's always the very vital 'should we mate?' question, which tends to be tied directly to how attractive the other animal is, mostly from behind."

Vivian had caught giggles in there, and it became a straight-up attack when Bast demanded: "How are you supposed to control your thermodynamic abilities when furry creatures are constantly sending you pictures of furry butts they may or may not find attractive?"

"Stop." Vivian gasped. "We are not talking about pictures of furry butts."

"Oh, it's not just pictures," Nate said seriously. "Scent is critical."

"You did not go there," Bast said.

"Yes. I did," Nate said, and they were obviously enjoying watching her crack up too much because Bast went on with:

"Alright, then what we need to do is make sure you have the ability not to get distracted when we're being attacked, and your horse accidentally runs into another horse he finds attractive and thinks: 'damn, that horse has a fine-smelling rear-end.'"

"Pepper would never get distracted like that in a fight," Nate answered. "He has pride."

Bast grinned at Nate as Vivian tried desperately to breathe. "Too bad you can't do any of that with humans," Bast said.

Nate rolled his eyes. "Sure, Bast. Because it would *definitely* make my focus better if I could hear what all the animals *and* humans were thinking in a fight. Can we get to the meditation or whatever?"

Bast crossed his legs and put his hands on his knees. "Sit like this," he told Nate. "And don't fall asleep."

"Fine." Nate adjusted himself to look like Bast. "Like this?"

"You don't have to sit straight as an arrow."

"You're sitting like you have an arrow stuck straight up your ass. What's the right way?"

"Just sit straight enough that you can take in a breath that will fill your lungs, jerkwad." Bast looked at Vivian. "But *you* don't have to do it."

"No, this is restful," she said, sitting up like the boys. "I'll do it."

"Alright, we're all sitting like monks," Nate said. "Now what?"

Bast began to give Nate instructions, but Vivian had already started a deep breathing exercise, and their voices drifted away. She was thinking this was the most relaxed she'd felt since before the coronation when she saw something at the edge of the patio.

Or rather, someone.

King Herschel was standing there. She tried to stand, too, but she was stuck where she was. He looked as haggard and sick as he had the day he'd died. She didn't like it.

"Why are you here?" she asked.

"There's something you need to know," he said sternly. "The most likely way for you to survive the Immortality Virus isn't for you to use magic to kill it. It's for the virus to kill your magic. But if that happens, you will live as an Immortal. You will be unable to die naturally and doomed to some terrible end. And in the meanwhile, you will change. You'll become someone you don't want to be."

She was afraid. "That isn't true."

"Vivian, you know the Immortality Virus is what destroyed my magic, don't you?"

She didn't want to hear the rest. She looked away.

He lowered his voice. "I asked your mother for help at the end. She wasn't very good with love, but death ..."

Vivian didn't like this version of her father.

"I can't come back for you if you become an Immortal," he warned. Then he faded out as she heard someone shouting her name. She opened her eyes. She was lying on her side on the patio. Bast was shaking her. He pulled her up into a fierce hug as soon as he saw she was awake.

Vivian could not remember the last time Bast had hugged her—*really* hugged her—and he was shaking like he was freezing cold while he did it. She looked over his shoulder to where Nate was sitting back on his heels. Nate's face was grim.

"I didn't do magic," she said, and Bast made a noise like he might be trying not to cry and shook harder.

"We know," Nate said, reaching out to touch the back of Bast's arm. "You slumped over during the meditation. We thought you'd fallen asleep, but you stopped breathing and—"

He didn't go on. Vivian tried to return Bast's hug. He didn't seem to have noticed, but Nate was transferring warmth to him as he shook in her arms. When Bast was calm again, Nate dropped his hand surreptitiously, and Bast leaned away from her.

He sniffed and rubbed his eyes. "If you wanted out of the prayers that bad, you could have just *told* me. You can't *do* that again, okay?"

The boys wouldn't let her go back to her room alone after that, and they insisted on taking turns to keep watch over her all night. She faked like she was sleeping to make them feel better, but really, she was too afraid to go back to sleep. She was awake when Bast whispered to Nate: "We're running out of time. We need more magic. Now."

Nate said, "I know." Then he said, "What would you do with your time if you only had a few weeks left to live?"

And Bast said: "I'd spend it with Vivian."

EXCERPT FROM *THE BOOK OF MAGIC*

You may have heard that Keplerian magic is distributed unevenly, to a mere ten percent of the Mortal Kepler population. That is a myth! Magic is innate to all Mortals—and may be accessible to Immortals as well—if we are only willing to reach deep within ourselves to find it.

But of course, learning must always be a slow, deliberate process. One cannot expect to arise one morning capable of pushing a boulder up a hill! As with all skills, we must start where we are, pushing paper clips until we can move pebbles.

Do you want to become a master of telekinetic magic? Mastery requires active and diligent practice. You must never rest! Never allow what magical abilities you have to become rusty and dull as an unused knife. A master practitioner seeks always to build a way of life that revolves around magic.

Move something with your mind before you get out of bed and after you brush your teeth. Do you need a new pen? A green apple? A utensil from the drawer? Beckon it with your mind! Do not subscribe to mediocrity. Magic is within you!

CHAPTER TWENTY
THE COLD TENDENCY

Light from the dawn moon was barely visible when Carina woke up, grabbed her book, and tried to quietly unzip the door to the tent.

"Where are you going?" Miguela whispered.

Max was snoring soundly in the corner. Carina put her finger to her lips, squatted by Miguela, and started to think up a lie. Miguela preempted her efforts.

"Don't tell me you have to pee. You're going to practice, aren't you?"

That was exactly what Carina was doing. She'd appreciated Max's help, but she wasn't making any progress, and he was making it increasingly difficult to concentrate. There had now been at least four times when she'd thought he was going to kiss her and it hadn't quite happened. If she wanted to legitimately practice magic, she needed to do it alone.

"I want to try some easy exercises on my own."

Miguela stretched and yawned. "You mean you don't want Max to make you do things that are never going to work." She pushed her sleeping bag off her shoulder, snuggled down, and closed her eyes.

"You're not going to try to stop me?"

"Why bother? At least you're finally making a decision that doesn't involve *him*."

Carina resented that, but she wasn't in the mood for a fight. "Thanks," she said. "Maybe you could sleep in."

Miguela made a humming noise that didn't sound like total disapproval, so Carina padded softly out of the tent.

When she got to a clearing they'd practiced in the evening before, she sat down on a tree trunk and started reading out loud a section about "inner-eye-hand-coordination":

"'To improve dexterity, the practitioner must practice micro-magical motion as well as macro-magical motion. One simple exercise is to move a small object back and forth, side-to-side, and up and down in short increments, progressively increasing in size.'"

That sounded manageable. She set her book down, put a small rock on top of it, and tried to push the rock forward a little tiny bit. After ten minutes, she decided maybe she was in the wrong position, so she knelt by the log to get eye-level with the book and tried again.

Nothing.

She replaced the rock with a pebble and tried to move that instead. Half an hour later, she was ready to give up. She'd only seen the pebble move once, but it was a breezy morning, and it had happened when the wind lifted the book's cover. Which meant the *wind* was more capable of moving a rock than she was.

Super.

She folded her arms over the book, dropped her head down, and moaned at her own incompetence.

"I thought you said she had gifts."

She sat up immediately. She didn't recognize that voice. Or even that accent.

"She does," another voice said. "I saw her use them. So did Vivian."

That frightened Carina. Had the Red-Eyed Ones found her again?

"Who's there?" She looked around. She couldn't see anyone, but thanks to Max she was fairly certain the voices were coming from the opposite side of the clearing. She stepped cautiously over the log and picked up her book, hoping they hadn't found Miguela.

"I don't think she can do anything," the first voice said. It sounded irritated. "This was pointless. Let's go back. We're missing breakfast."

"She can do it." The second voice sounded lazy. "She was acting on instinct before."

"Who are you?" What *her* voice sounded was quite shrill. "Are you Red-Eyed Ones? I'm not alone. I have friends."

There was a pause before laughter traveled through the clearing.

"*Do* you?" Lazy asked. "Maybe we should try to meet them, too."

Bumps rose on Carina's skin. She shouldn't have told them she was with anyone. She'd put her sister in danger *again*.

"I don't think she's very smart," Irritated said. "She can't do anything."

"I told you," Lazy said. "She just needs the right incentive."

"Fine."

The Book of Magic flew out of Carina's hands and shot into the air until she couldn't see it anymore. They were telekinetic. That meant they weren't Red-Eyed Ones.

But they'd been spying on her.

"You better look up," Irritated said, and when Carina did, she saw her book falling straight back down. She yelped and held her arms protectively over her head, but the book didn't hit her. It ricocheted off an invisible something and landed—to her dismay—on a marshy spot of the clearing, nearby, open and facedown.

"Told you so," Lazy said. "But you didn't have to ruin her book."

"*You* said she needed incentive. What, did you want me to throw a rock at her? Anyway, you should be happy. You were right. Hey, what's your name?"

That last part was projected out to her. Irritated sounded more curious now, but Carina thought his method of initiating introductions was obnoxious. She marched toward her book and picked it up. The binding was ripped.

"It is *not* polite to sneak up on a girl and scare her into doing magic," she said as she started trying to wipe muck off her book.

They laughed again. She hated how they laughed. She heard them move through the trees, and soon two boys dressed in fancy-looking trousers and leather jackets stepped into the clearing.

They looked like they might be around her age. They both had gold-blond hair and smallish facial features framed with straight hairlines and angular jaws. She would have bet money neither of them had dimples, and she couldn't tell what color their eyes were, but they were both unpleasantly pale. *Vampires*, Carina thought, although the moment she did the boy on the left shifted out of the shadows, and she realized that he, at least, appeared to get out into the sun now and then. So probably not vampires.

"Tell us your name," the one on the right said. He had Lazy's voice, and he stood like he thought he was really something.

Carina was not impressed. "Are you bounty hunters? If you're looking for a girl with magic to capture and sell, you can get out of here."

Lazy didn't answer the question for so long that she became anxious.

She held her book protectively to herself. "*Are* you?"

The one on the left—he had to be Irritated—held out his hand, and her book went flying again, this time directly to him. "Relax. We're not bounty hunters." He started flipping through the book. "What *is* this thing? Is *this* what you're using to learn *magic*?"

"Let me see that." Lazy snatched the book and started flipping through it himself.

"If you're not Red-Eyed Ones, and you're not bounty hunters, then who are you?" They were dressed a lot nicer than any of the teenagers she'd seen since she'd left Novi Dupree. "Are you those Southerners the people talk about? The ... Southern Guardians or whatever?"

She was distraught when they both looked up from the book and started laughing even harder than before. Apparently, it was *hilarious* that she thought they were part of the Southern Guardians.

"You are not nice boys," she said grouchily.

"Sorry, sorry ..." That was Lazy. He elbowed the other boy, who Carina thought had to be his brother or cousin or something. "Stop. Stop! This isn't *nice*."

"I can't!" Irritated was bent over laughing. "She thinks we're the Southern Guardians!"

But they couldn't have been anything that official. They

were nothing more than posh, privileged, teenage bullies. "Give me my book back," she ordered. "Then go away!"

Irritated sobered up. "I take back what I said about you not being very smart." He glanced at Lazy, whose eyes were now narrowing at her. "You're downright *idiotic*."

Lazy's expression returned to neutral. "Ignore him. He's not that bright himself, and you obviously don't understand what's happening here. We *are* trying to be nice. But *we* are a *special* branch of the Southern Guard. We've caught you practicing magic, and no one who fits your description exists in the magical registry. Are you aware that we could arrest you for the unauthorized practice of magic?"

Carina's gut tightened. "Excuse me? You're arresting me? For defending myself accidentally with magic?"

"I said we *could* arrest you. We have a particular interest in you, and what we want is for you to come with us willingly."

She was not going anywhere *willingly* with Lazy and Irritated. She glanced regretfully at her book still in Lazy's hands, then turned to sprint the other way, but she didn't get far before a thick tree root rose from the ground unexpectedly. She tripped over it and landed hard, face forward. When she tried to get back up, she discovered she could not. She was pinned by some invisible force. She struggled against it, but all she could do was twist her head around to watch the boys walking closer to her.

"I hardly have any magic," she said as Irritated stooped down by her and Lazy stood back watching. "Please, let me go."

She could see Irritated's eyes now. They were a muddy, dull, greenish color, and he rolled them at her as he reached for her arm. "Calm down. If it turns out you hardly have any magic at all, we'll probably just register you and let you go.

But we have some questions first."

She could not calm down, though, because his fingers were right above her elbow, and they were unnaturally warm against her skin. And getting warmer. She tensed up all over. He let go instantly and backed away, yelling loudly. For a moment, she could move again. Then the invisible force was back, and Lazy was pulling her up by the arm instead.

"Well, *that* was a fun surprise for everyone, wasn't it?" he said. Lazy's fingers were too cold, and Carina was still tense and terrified. She whimpered involuntarily.

"Ice trick's not going to work with me, sunshine. I guarantee I'm colder than you'll ever be." He smiled sleazily. "Now, it's quite a distance back to the village, and we'd prefer to walk you there. But, if you insist, there are other options. It's your choice."

Carina thought about screaming—she'd considered it a few times already—but somehow, she didn't think Max and his gun would be able to do much against boys who could hold people down telekinetically. She didn't want Miguela to come running either. Who knew what would happen then? Maybe Lazy and Irritated would arrest Max and Miguela, too. Carina's best choice was to go with the boys and hope they would let her go right away when they figured out how little magic she had.

She gritted her teeth. "I'll walk."

"Good to know you can see reason," Lazy said, and he adjusted his hold, so his arm was around hers more like he was escorting her somewhere upscale. "Shall we inform your *friends*?"

"No," Carina said quickly.

"She burned my hand," Irritated complained. "I think it's going to blister."

"No, it's not. She didn't burn you at all."

"It feels like a burn."

"It's not."

"Then what the hell did she do?"

"She tends cold." Lazy started guiding her out of the clearing. "You're lucky she didn't freeze off your whole hand."

Carina tried to process that. Is *that* what it meant to have cold thermodynamic magic? That you could freeze things when you were afraid? Could she do that? Because she couldn't ever remember doing it before, but there *had* been that incident with the Red-Eyed One that had attacked her when she'd been running with Miguela from Novi Dupree. And before … when they were kids … and there was what Ivan had said, and Anthony …

But how was that possible? If she could make things cold, shouldn't she like the cold herself? Carina hated feeling cold. Also, if anyone was at risk of freezing right now, it was her. Lazy's hands were so cold she thought he might have a circulation problem.

"I can't believe she did that," Irritated said. "It hurts like a mother—"

"I hope it *does* blister," Carina muttered in response to his crude language, and Lazy snickered like they were in on a joke together and shifted closer to her.

"Don't mind his whining. I've done worse to him myself. That was solid defense, though. And not something you learn in a book written by a stage magician."

Carina didn't feel like conversing with Lazy, and she thought it was creepy that he wanted to be friendly now. He went on anyway.

"Bosley Pinkerton. The author of your book. That's who he was. A stage magician. And a fraud. Good with illusions and manipulation, but he didn't have any real magic gifts. He made a killing selling books to people who thought he did, though. Even told commoners they could learn if they *practiced* hard enough." Lazy snorted. "It didn't come out that he was a con artist until he died during one of his shows."

Carina didn't want to ask how Mr. Pinkerton had died, but Lazy continued like he knew that's exactly what she'd want to know next.

"Locked himself up in chains in an underwater tank and couldn't unlock himself fast enough. No one with any real telekinetic magic would have trouble with that. Worst-case scenario, you'd blow the walls out of the tank. Even you could have done it, and your telekinesis needs work." He nodded at the trail. "Don't trip. We're going downhill."

"I have *eyes*," Carina said as haughtily as possible, hoping he would understand from her tone just how much she hated him.

Lazy laughed low and short. "Right. My apologies, Your Grace."

They heard Irritated fall behind them and begin cussing.

Lazy stopped them to wait while Irritated got back up. "Be careful," he murmured to her. "Between you and me, we're freezing up the whole path."

"They're back with the girl," Captain Thurlow told Vivian. "She tends cold."

The boys had spent the evening spying on the mystery girl and her friends, and they'd left Vivian—reluctantly—in Captain Thurlow's care this morning so they could meet the girl at her campsite and introduce themselves.

"That way we'll all be fresh," Bast had said optimistically, and Nate, who was doubtful that the girl could have produced a telekinetic shield, said: "Are you worried about making an *impression* on her?"

But Bast had been sure first thing in the morning would be best, so when Vivian had woken up today, one of the female attendants was sitting by her bedside and Captain Thurlow was waiting outside her door. He did the morning prayers with her in her room, then he ate breakfast with her, and Vivian took longer than normal to finish her cup of tea because there was something about sitting with the captain that made her forget about other things.

Captain Thurlow had given her time with her attendants to properly dress after breakfast. Now she noticed his eyes traveling briefly from her eyes, down her body and up again. Both of Vivian's brothers had spent a lot of time over the last few days doing that to her, too, but whenever either of them did it, it felt like she was being scanned for signs of sudden death. When Captain Thurlow did it, his lips curled at the corners, and Vivian felt her cheeks pink up.

"Queen Vivian?"

"Sorry? What did you say?"

He pinched his mouth together like he was trying not to smile anymore and repeated: "She tends cold."

It was improbable enough that there would be a random girl out there that could produce a defensive telekinetic shield. That she would also have a rare thermodynamic ability and not be registered with the kingdom was next to impossible. Though it *would* explain the shield.

"Are you sure?"

"She injured Prince Nathanial," Captain Thurlow said.

"How?"

He raised an eyebrow. "Frostbite."

CHAPTER TWENTY-ONE
HOW NOT TO BE CHARMING

It took the better part of an hour for the two southern boys to walk Carina to a small village nearby, where they showed her into a humble tavern. At the outskirts of the village, Lazy whispered: "In case you were wondering, the people in this village know who we are. Let's not make a scene, okay?"

"Is this how you always make friends?" she asked, but Lazy only chuckled.

Now she was standing in the center of the tavern's poorly lit saloon. There were several round tables in the room, but all the chairs were turned upside down. The walls were covered with yellowed posters curling at the edges, and the bar at the back was stocked with only five squat bottles of liquor. The whole place smelled like stale beer.

Sister Raji would have died.

Lazy and Irritated were standing across from her, and there was an older girl between them. Her hair was golden like theirs, she had symmetrical facial features, and she was wearing jeans with Prada-Gabbana heels. Carina had only ever seen shoes like that on models in the magazines Sister Elizabeth smuggled into Novi Dupree. Also, the heels and jeans gave lines to the girl's figure that made Carina extremely jealous.

None of the three had said a word to Carina since she'd been brought to this place, and Lazy, Irritated, and Prada-Gabbana were staring at her like that alone could compel her to start rambling. But Carina felt she needed to regain some dignity, and she was determined to be careful about what she told them, so she was standing with her mouth clamped shut. If silence was their tactic, they'd have to try harder. Sister Agda herself had taught Carina how to do this. She'd been trained by the *best*.

The girl's lip twitched.

The skin on Carina's cheek twinged. She'd scratched it on something when she tripped back in the clearing and she'd only realized it hurt later. She was *not* going to touch it now. Sister Agda would never have done that. She'd have made it seem like she could stand here silent all day long even if she was gushing blood. Carina did not move.

Finally, Lazy stepped forward. He made Carina think of a cool breeze on a summer day when you were stuck cleaning out the barn. He was insultingly handsome, and his eyes were a clean, clear blue. Carina thought of Max's darker blue eyes and felt guilty for comparing.

Lazy flashed a disarming smile at her. He pointed to her cheek. "Does that hurt?"

She stood still as he came close enough for her to smell mint on his breath. She had not smelled mint before, though he'd been close enough she thought she would have noticed. He steadied her jaw with one hand and touched her cheek with the fingertips of his other. A light chill spread across her face, followed by a soft tugging sensation.

He smoothed the skin with his fingers. "There. All gone. And it's a good thing. You're far too pretty to walk around with gashes on your face."

Irritated crossed his arms and made a huffing noise, while Prada-Gabbana watched the interaction intently.

"Are you wondering if everyone with cold magic can do that?" Lazy asked. "The answer is no. Only people that tend quite cold can do it. I can do it." He put his hands in his pockets casually. "And I bet you can, too."

"Me?" Carina asked, feeling foolish for playing his game right after the word was out of her mouth.

"That cut on your cheek was much worse when it first happened. I'm glad I waited to fix it. But it would have been gone in a few hours anyway. You're a natural healer. You've probably always healed faster than anyone you know."

He went back to stand by Prada-Gabbana while Carina thought about that, feeling even more foolish because, for the second time in a few hours, Lazy had pieced something together for her that had never made sense before. The ankle she'd thought was broken after she fell out of that tree ... that burn Max had gotten that had already disappeared ...

Lazy looked extremely satisfied with himself as it all clicked for her. "We happen to be in the market for a healer. If you can prove that we can trust you, we can overlook the fact that you have far too much magic not to be registered with the kingdom."

"But I *don't* have a lot of magic," Carina said.

Lazy, Irritated, and Prada-Gabbana gave her identical "you don't actually believe that, do you?" looks, and it made Carina nervous, so she blurted out: "Who exactly are you?"

Irritated hit his forehead with his palm. "Haven't you figured out *yet*?"

But Prada-Gabbana spoke up for the first time. "Evidently, she has not." She looked evenly at Carina and said cordially: "I am Vivian, Queen of the Southern Kingdom of Kepler." She gestured to Lazy. "This is Prince Bastian." She pointed to Irritated. "And that is Prince Nathanial. Now, who are you?"

Carina gasped. "*You're* the queen of South Kepler?" That was impossible, wasn't it? The ruthless monster who arrested people with magic for no good reason was a teenage girl?

"You still don't seem to realize the situation you're in." Lazy's—Prince Bastian's?—voice had taken on a dangerous edge. "You are under our rule, and there is a decree requiring anyone with magic to come forward and register with the kingdom. You've committed a crime."

And she had the worst luck *ever*. How had she managed to get caught practicing magic by the *actual* royal family? She hoped Miguela and Max hadn't decided to come to the village to look for her. Maybe they were still asleep.

Prince Bastian smiled tightly at her. "But all we're asking is for you to tell us who you are and where you're from, and we can forget about the registry and move on to more important things. That's easy enough, isn't it?"

She considered that. What could she tell them that would make them let her go without putting Miguela in danger? She started slowly, attempted to craft a response that would be favorable for her. "I'm an orphan. I grew up in the mountains. I was ... isolated. I didn't know I had special magic or more magic than other people. I hardly know how to use it. I didn't know I was supposed to be registered." There was a lot she didn't know, she was now starting to realize, and it made her a little annoyed with Sister Rachel.

"*Where* in the mountains?" Prince Bastian asked.

Carina hesitated. Annoyed or not, she didn't want to get

the Sisters of Novi Dupree in trouble. "Near Great Crater Lake. By a very small village."

Prince Bastian laughed. "You're a terrible liar."

"It's the truth," she bluffed. "Hardly anyone lives there."

His expression soured, and he clenched his jaw tight. "Try *again*. And this time tell the truth. I'm *gifted* at knowing when people are lying."

She'd messed up. He had magic that somehow told him when people were lying. Of course, he did. He was the prince of South Kepler. A member of the Cardinal Family of the South. He had way more magic than anyone she'd ever met. Fear rose inside her, making all the warmth in her blood disappear as she stalled and tried to figure out what to say next.

Prince Bastian tipped his head up and around like he was looking at the walls of the tavern. The wood paneling was icing over. Carina noticed frost on the liquor bottles. "You cannot possibly be unaware of how rare your magic is," the prince commented.

Her thoughts were sluggish, now, though, and cold sweat was trickling down her back. "I never went to the village myself," she said faintly.

"Is she lying?" the queen asked.

Prince Bastian shook his head. "Not that time."

"How old are you?" the queen said to her.

"Sixteen," Carina said.

"Were you locked up? Was someone using you for your magic?"

Carina was scandalized into a more energized answer. As if Sister Agda would ever have *used* someone for magic. "No. They never *let* me do magic."

For a moment, the queen seemed sympathetic. "Is that why you ran away? It's hard to have talent you're not allowed to use. It was brave of you to run. You're not traveling alone, though, are you?"

"We've had spies watching you," Prince Bastian added. "Is the younger girl your sister? Does she have magic too?"

Carina's throat constricted at that question, which seemed inherently threatening, and it felt like her blood was freezing in her veins while her lungs burned. Prince Bastian's face had a mildly blue tint to it now. Was he trying to freeze her to death? Why had the Southern Royals been following her? How long had they been following her for? Would they hurt Miguela if she didn't cooperate? Even though Miguela didn't have magic?

"You're dressed like a commoner, but you won't tell us your name. You're lying to us about where you're from and you have magic almost like a Cardinal would have." Prince Bastian waved his arms around at the room. "You're turning this whole place into an icebox. *I'm* cold. We've *executed* people for less."

Tears were coming to Carina's eyes, but they froze on her face as they formed. She thought she could feel ice in her eyelashes.

"I supposed she could be from one of the Eastern clans," the queen mused. "Maybe even from the Cardinal Family of the East. There are rumors that there are still some Second Degree Cardinals left, even if the First Degrees have all died out."

"Are you from the East?" Prince Bastian demanded.

Carina tried to shake her head, but her neck was stiff.

"Do you *want* us to bring your sister back here?" Prince Bastian's blue eyes now looked like they, too, were covered by a layer of ice, and the only emotion she could detect anymore in his voice was rage. "Because we can. I bet she's looking for you anyway. We could send our guards out. Make the whole ordeal faster."

That was not what Carina wanted, but her vision was going black. Something bad was happening to her, these were bad people, and they were going to hurt Miguela.

"Don't you *care* about your sister? If you love her, can't you give us your *name?*"

Irritated spoke up stoically. "That's enough, Bast."

Carina was unsteady on her feet. She couldn't remember Irritated's actual name. She'd almost forgotten he was in the room.

Prince Bastian huffed. "*I'm* not doing anything. *She's* giving herself hypothermia."

Irritated made impassive eye contact with Carina for half a second. "Don't threaten her sister. It's making her too upset. She's going to hypothermia herself to death."

Prince Bastian sneered. "Hypothermia herself to death? Since when are *you* the sympathetic one? She hurt you, remember?"

"She's no good to us dead."

"Maybe she shouldn't be so selfish."

Carina couldn't feel her feet anymore. Or her knees. Or her hands. She thought she heard the queen say: "He's right, Bast," but Carina wasn't sure because she was very warm all at once and falling over. Before she landed, everything went dark.

Vivian looked at the girl, now lying in a heap on a floor covered with so much grime that Vivian's shoes were sticking with every step. The girl's recently healed cheek was planted in that sludge. Her face was colorless.

Nate crouched down by her, then looked reproachfully at Bast. "She's barely breathing."

Bast must not have felt any remorse. "She's the one who tried to freeze herself to death."

"Because you were *terrifying* her and threatening her sister."

"She was uncooperative. She could be a threat."

Nate stuck his thumb toward the girl. "*This* girl? I thought you *liked* her!"

"I thought you didn't." Bast countered.

"You're such an ass."

Vivian shivered, and an odd memory flashed through her mind. The boys had both brought wounded animals into the castle when they were little, and the family had known Bast was a healer from the time he was four years old, when he brought a bunny with a broken leg to their dad and asked for the family physician.

"For God's sake, Bastian, kill it, so it doesn't suffer," she remembered her dad saying.

Bast's face had paled like he'd been sentenced to death himself. Then his eyes had hardened. "It doesn't have to suffer," he'd said, and the air in the room became frigid.

The bunny had shivered pathetically, and Nate had yelled at Bast to stop torturing it.

"I'm not torturing it," Bast had answered. "I'm saving it."

Then their dad said "hell" while Bast held the creature tight and Nate started to cry. King Herschel had reached to take the animal from Bast, but miraculously, the poor thing's leg straightened and the pain in its eyes faded.

Bast had handed the bunny to Nate immediately after. "Make it warm again," he'd said, and that bunny had lived with the boys for *years*.

Vivian thought about how scared the girl had looked before she'd passed out. Her eyes had been far more panicked than the bunny's. Vivian rubbed the bumps on her arm and wondered if it was the girl making the room cold now or Bast.

"We should get her off the ground," Nate said.

Bast made an annoyed grunt.

"Do you think she can still do the death freeze defense thing while she's passed out?"

"Pick her up telekinetically if you want to be safe." Bast glowered. "But you'll have to be careful since she's out like that. You could dislocate her shoulder or, you know, break her neck or something if you move her from the wrong points. I'd leave her there."

Vivian hummed agreement. There wasn't any good reason to move the girl. But Nate apparently disagreed. He grimaced, then bent over and pried the girl physically from the sticky floor. Her limbs dangled, and her head hung back loose behind his arm. He slid a chair to himself telekinetically and set her in it, but she flopped to the side, and Nate had to catch her shoulders to keep her from falling. He tried to prop her up straight, and when she was balanced, he stepped back with his hands out like she was a block tower that might tumble over.

"Tie her in," Bast suggested.

Vivian surveyed the girl's appearance. She was wearing plain jeans, muddy hiking boots, and a yellow T-shirt. Her long, skinny arms and legs looked like they should have been awkward to move, but she had lush eyelashes that fluttered restlessly, and it didn't even look like she needed mascara to get them to flare out at the corners like that.

Nate plucked a long hair from his jacket. "I bet her sinks are always clogged."

"Probably," Vivian agreed. She could never have tolerated those long tangles.

"What are we going to do now?" Nate asked.

The question made Vivian feel extra tired. Bast slid another chair over telekinetically to her. Vivian sat down gratefully while he returned his attention to the girl.

"We can't trust her," Bast said. "We should bring the sister in. For incentive."

Nate rubbed his forehead. "Isn't the bigger problem *her* not trusting *us*?"

"I can't help that. The first thing you did was destroy her book."

"That book was garbage, and you know it! And I am not the one who scared her into a thermodynamic defense reaction!"

Bast looked thoughtful about that. "Not the second time. But we probably *should* make this decision based on who she's less afraid of now."

"*What* decision?" Nate asked suspiciously.

"The decision about which of us should try to talk to her alone." Bast gazed innocently at Nate. "You're the obvious choice. You saw that ugly pug of a boy she's dating."

Nate wrinkled his nose. "You think that guy we saw yesterday was her boyfriend?"

The girl moaned quietly and said something that sounded like "Mickey Gall." That was a terrible name. Vivian felt extra bad for the girl if it was her boyfriend's name.

Bast continued. "I know, right? If she's willing to date *that* guy, she must have a bleeding heart. All *you* have to do is be more dashing than him—"

Nate looked startled. "Wait, what? Why would I want to do that?"

"Because if you can get her to like you, she might want to help Viv." Bast kicked out his legs and slouched down in his chair. "I can siphon magic from her to Viv even if she isn't willing, but she'll have to want to do it to help as a healer."

"Some awful seduction act isn't going to get her to want to help Vivian!" Nate sounded higher-pitched than normal. He turned to her. "You tell him, Viv. This is a rotten idea."

Vivian didn't think there was a chance the girl would help them no matter what now. So Bast's plan was as good as any, and if they were going the romance route, Nate *was* the best choice. Vivian couldn't remember any girl Bast had ever expressed interest in other than this one, and things had clearly gone badly with that.

Nate, however, had had girlfriends. Plural. He might even have one now. A girl with curvy hips and auburn hair had been hanging around the stables before the coronation. Vivian didn't know her, but she knew Franklin had read Nate the riot act for some incident involving her. It was beyond Vivian why any girl would want to date Nate. Still …

"Viv," Nate begged. "Please."

Maybe some girls liked a fixer-upper. "No, Bast is right."

Nate stared at her, his mouth agape.

"I'll tie her into the chair," Bast offered. "Then you can make a thing of rescuing her from me again."

"How are we related?" Nate asked weakly.

"I don't understand that either," Bast said.

CHAPTER TWENTY-TWO
HOW NOT TO BE DASHING

Normally Carina didn't get headaches, but when she came to, it felt like someone was trying to pierce knitting needles through her eyes to the back of her brain. She was still in the tavern, sitting in a chair she hadn't been in before. The queen and her brothers had left, but she discovered quickly—and to her dismay—that her hands were tied behind the back of the chair and her feet tied in front.

The knots were tight. She wasn't skilled enough to untie them telekinetically. Was there anything she could do with thermodynamic magic? She knew almost nothing about how that worked, but all the times she remembered being especially cold recently, she'd also been especially angry.

And she was *very* angry right now. Could she make herself angrier and somehow make the ropes cold enough to freeze off? What could she focus on that would make her feel furious? The fact that she'd been forced to flee from Novi Dupree? Being sold out by a little boy to Red-Eyed bounty hunters? Getting arrested—or rather being taken "voluntarily" against her will—by a trio of arrogant jerks (AKA the Cardinal Family of South Kepler)? If this is what all the Cardinal Families were like, Carina didn't feel too bad that the other three were basically extinct.

The ropes began to chill.

"That is not in your best interest."

Carina jerked her head around.

The Irritated Prince. He'd been watching her struggle from behind. Now he walked in front of her, looking at her like she was a Kepler beetle that annoyed him.

She thought his hair looked greasy.

"You tend cold," he said very slowly, like he was explaining something to a four-year-old. "That means you can make those ropes stiff and hard to untie, but you can't get rid of them. Not that way."

Carina narrowed her eyes but decided not to give him the satisfaction of a response.

He didn't give her the satisfaction of a decent reaction.

"But I can help you. If you want," he said mildly.

She was instantly suspicious. She vaguely remembered Irritated telling Prince Bastian not to do whatever he'd done to try to kill her, but she didn't exactly think Irritated deserved a prize for that. She did not have a good first impression of him.

He disappeared from her sight again.

She waited for him to do or say something.

He didn't.

"If you're going to help me, could you get on with it?" she said after a good minute had passed.

"Hold your ox beasts," he said from behind her. "I'm thinking about how to do this. The last encounter we had didn't end well for me."

He paused again.

"Guess I better try it by hand, but if you freeze my fingers off while I'm untying the rope, that's not going to be good for either of us. So, don't freak out. That's when your thermodynamics go out of whack, and unexpected things happen. It won't be helpful if you pass out again, either."

"My thermodynamics—" she felt strange putting "my" before that very big word out loud for the first time "—didn't cause me to pass out."

He must have taken that answer as assent because she felt him start working at the rope. "Oh, yes, they did. You went into thermodynamic panic. All Bast did was scare you." Irritated tugged on the rope. His hands were still overly warm, but at least this time it wasn't shocking. "God, he really tied this tight. Honestly, I'm impressed. With *you*, not the knot, and not in a good way. For someone who's terrible at magic, you're totally screwing with Bast. I think maybe he did something with magic to make these ropes stick so hard. If your hair wasn't everywhere, I'd burn them off, but—"

She couldn't help the squeak she made at the thought of him using *fire* to undo the knot.

"Chill. No! Wait, *don't* chill! I'm not going to do that. It's too dangerous. Geez … you don't know anything about us, do you? There's nowhere to hide a body around here. What do you think it would look like for some story to come out that the Southern Royals had kidnapped and killed some pathetic girl?"

Carina thought about purposely attempting to freeze his stupid fingers off, but he hadn't been rough trying to get the ropes untied, and since he apparently had hot thermodynamics, she didn't want to give him a reason to defend himself with fire. Although, for now, he was carrying on a conversation by himself, and that didn't make him seem too threatening.

"What's up with you, by the way?" he asked. "How come you barely know anything about your gifts? Don't you know how uncommon it is to be both telekinetic and thermodynamic?"

His voice was suddenly low and right in her ear. "In all seriousness, Ice Girl, you might want to find someone who can tell you something about the world. Locked away in the mountains and never allowed to do magic? I would *not* want to be you, and I don't want to be me most of the time, so that's saying something."

The rope finally loosened. She pulled her hands in front of her again and rubbed her sore wrists while he stepped back around so she could see him.

"I could be that person. We need more magic. You obviously need someone to teach you *everything*." He twisted the rope. "You should think about it. We don't make these kinds of offers every day. You'd be smart to accept. You only have to tell us the truth about who you are, so that we know you're not a spy for the Immortals or a northern rebel or something."

Carina scowled. "I'd rather jump in a lake."

"Maybe we'll *throw* you in a lake if you don't cooperate. We could make *that* look anonymous." He smiled nastily. "I'm trying to give you an *opportunity* here."

Carina continued scowling, and he started to pace in front of her.

"Think hard about it. What could you possibly have to lose?" She felt a strange pressure in her head. It rapidly increased to spikes of pain. Panic rushed in again, and she felt like every blood vessel in her brain was threatening to burst.

"What are you doing?" she cried.

The pain dissolved. He put his hands under his armpits and shivered. "Nothing anyone would believe I can do." He looked critically at her. "You shouldn't have felt that. What did *you* do? I mean, other than drop the temperature in this room ten degrees."

"I didn't do anything. Maybe you're just not as impressive as you think," she said with as much bravado as possible. Until then, Irritated had only annoyed her. Now she *was* a little afraid of him. But *only* a little, she told herself.

He snorted. "You wouldn't be the first person to think that."

She wanted to hide while his eyes panned down over her, pausing at what she could only assume were weaknesses he was assessing, then scanning back up until he met her eyes again.

"I thought Bast was crazy to chase you, but you know what? Now I think he and Viv are both underestimating you. They think all you need is the right incentive. I think you're stubborn as hell." He gave her a sheepish smile. "Guess we got off on the wrong foot, huh?"

"Being attacked, threatened, tied up, and interrogated isn't my idea of the right foot," she said sarcastically.

"Yeah, I suppose it wouldn't be anyone's." He stretched out his hand, and the ropes around her feet untied themselves.

Now *Carina* was irritated. "It took you forever to untie the ones on my hands!"

"That was for show. In case you were the type that would swoon over being rescued."

That was insulting. Was he kidding? He thought she'd *swoon*? Over *him*?

"I get it. You're not the type. *I* didn't expect you to be anyway."

She didn't have time for this. She looked around the room for the doors. There was one to the side that must have led to the inn. There was one behind Irritated that she knew led outdoors.

He looked along with her. "Wouldn't bother. The side door's locked. As for the other … I could probably take you down on my own. But even if you get lucky and make it by me, Bast is standing right outside. You know. The guy who *didn't* bother thinking about the whole 'where are we going to put the body' if we kill her problem?"

Carina folded her arms. "I can't believe you think *I'm* the one who doesn't know anything. Do you have *any* friends?"

"Man, you have no idea how to address royalty, do you?"

She didn't like his accent. It was too formal for the casual way he scoffed at people. The other two made it sound better. "Look, Prince Whoever-You-Are, as far as I can tell, all you are is a royal pain, and if you think—"

"Prince Nathanial," he said. "And you are ….?"

"*Forgive* me, Prince Nathanial," Carina said, honeying up his name so much she hoped it would make him feel sick. "My apologies for failing to address you properly. Let me try again. *Your Highness*, if you would be so kind as to step aside, I would like to leave."

He smiled back in a way that made her feel quite sick herself. "Sorry, *sweetheart*, but I can't do that. If my method of persuasion fails, Bast gets another turn. And he's in a bad mood."

"What do you people want from me that you can't just leave me alone?" she said shrilly.

Prince Nathanial dropped the smile. "Alright. I don't like you, but I also don't want to end up with blood on my hands because of you, and you don't know anything, so I think you need to understand that we don't let people with serious unreported magic go. We haven't in decades. Getting caught by *us* with magic like *yours* is like asking to be arrested. Or worse."

Carina's stomach turned. "So those rumors about the Southern Guarders or whatever making people with magic disappear are true? Are your prisons full of people who got turned in for using magic?"

"Southern *Guard*. And no. Our *dungeons* are full of people that got turned in. Prisons are for regular people who might get a fair trial."

"You have *dungeons*? Isn't that against the Mortal Commitments or something?"

He didn't answer.

"What happens to people who end up in the dungeons?"

Prince Nathanial toed the disgusting floor. "Every now and then they're released. But mostly? The Royal Court finds a reason to convict them of something—murder, treason, tax evasion—and usually, that means execution. Bast wasn't making that up."

Carina moved back so fast she tripped on the chair she'd been tied in and nearly fell.

"God, and people say I'm a mess," Prince Nathanial commented. "You're a walking disaster. Can't move a little rock. Can't untie a rope. Barely capable of walking. You don't have to panic. Like I've been saying, we don't *want* to put you in the dungeons for your magic. What we want is your help, and we can return the favor."

Carina steadied herself and tried to look less afraid. "I'd probably be ten times better at magic than you if I'd had anyone to teach me anything."

"Maybe if you'd ever left your mountain to train with a

real master, you'd be almost half as good, but you obviously never did," he retorted.

"I couldn't! If the Red-Eyed Ones hadn't sensed me, I could have been arrested by your people!"

He made a funny face. "Wait, what?"

She started to repeat herself. "If the Red-Eyed Ones hadn't sensed—"

"The *Red-Eyed* Ones? You mean the Immortals, right? You think they can sense, what, you? Your magic? How?"

Carina was starting to hate how this guy made her feel like she was stuck in a bad dream where she wasn't prepared for something important. "I don't know. Sister Agda always said they would just know if—"

He cut her off. "Did she also tell you that if you had to get out of bed at night to go to the bathroom, the bogie man would get you?"

"All the way from the outhouse?"

His eyes widened. "Oh my God, you did grow up in the middle of nowhere." He swished his hand to the side. "The Immortals can't detect magic like that. They're not zombies with magic-sensing radar or monsters who can sniff magic in your blood."

"But Sister Agda—"

"But nothing." Prince Nathanial looked like he might pity her, and Carina's sick feeling worsened. "She lied to you. The Immortals are just humans with a nasty virus and zero empathy. They're not the special ones. *We* are."

"Why would the Sisters lie to me?" Carina asked, more to herself than to him.

He answered anyway. "I don't know. But if I were them, I'd assume you'd be dumb and end up caught by the Southern Guard. And you proved your Sisters right. You got caught practicing magic, and not by *any* members of the Southern Guard, either. You let yourself get seen by *Bast.*"

"They lied to protect me from *you*," she said slowly.

"Probably."

Carina needed *out* of the room with the horrible prince who had only stopped his horrible brother from killing her because they were on the road and there was nowhere good to hide a body. She thought about trying to fight him. Or charge him or something. If she knocked him down, she might be able to get to the door before he could do anything with magic to hurt her. Did she have any hope of getting past Prince Bastian?

Prince Nathanial was examining his fingernails. "Do you want to reconsider your willingness to work with us? There would be ... benefits."

"I don't want your benefits," she said, spitting out the words.

"Fine." He shrugged like he'd given up, walked to the door, and put his hand on the doorknob. Then he stopped, and for whatever reason, he turned back around. "I can't say it was a pleasure to meet you, whoever-you-are, but most people I spend this long talking to call me Nate. So, when I see you again, maybe you could tell me your name. When you see Bast again, though, try to greet him formally. He's not going to be happy with you."

And with that final comment, Prince Nathanial left the room. Carina sank down onto the chair. She wondered if she'd just made a huge, huge mistake.

"How did it go?" Bast asked as Nate came out of the tavern and sat down next to them on the bench where Vivian and Bast had been waiting.

"She hates us. She'll never agree to help."

Bast stood up. "We haven't tried good old-fashioned torture, yet."

"Sit down, Bast," Vivian said. "We are not torturing her to get her help."

He slashed his hand through the air. "Forget her help. She has too much magic. I say we treat her like an enemy of the state."

"We're *not* torturing her," Vivian repeated. She stood up.

"What are we going to do? Let her go?" Bast asked incredulously.

Vivian walked toward the door. "I'm going to talk to her."

"Alone?" Bast said. "But she could be dangerous."

"Viv," Nate said. "I don't think you should—"

"I'm the one who needs her help," Vivian snapped.

"Fine," Bast said, "but—"

"No *buts*, Bast," Vivian said, and she opened the door to the tavern.

CHAPTER TWENTY-THREE
HOW TO TEACH A LESSON

The queen was not the person Carina expected to walk in next. Prince Bastian was behind his sister, though, and as soon as he saw Carina, one of the other chairs flew at her. She held both hands out and shrieked, and the chair bounced off something invisible in front of her.

The queen turned back to Prince Bastian. "I want to talk to her *alone*," she said like she was quite annoyed, then she closed the door hard behind her, shutting him out. She walked to the chair Prince Bastian had flung, set it upright near one of the tables, and sat down.

"Good block," she said to Carina. She sounded sincere, but Carina found that she was more afraid of the queen than she had been of either of the princes.

"You have a natural talent for magical shields. It goes with tending cold. Bast knows that. He's just angry, and he wanted to scare you."

"He did," Carina said.

"I know," the queen said.

"Are you here to threaten me or bribe me?"

"Yes, but I don't think I'm going to do either." The queen paused. "Yet." She rested her elbow on the table. Her face was drawn, and there were lines at the edges. The queen probably had to use her gifts all the time. Magic really took it out of you, Carina supposed.

"I get tired using magic, too," she said. "I can only do so much at once."

"You get tired using your gifts?"

Carina felt like she'd said something wrong. "Doesn't everyone?"

"No." Queen Vivian's brow knit together. "They don't. I was never like this before …" Her eyes shifted slightly, and she didn't say before *what*. "This isn't how I normally am, and Bast never gets tired. I suppose I've seen Nate down after a bad practice session, but he expends *so* much energy with unnecessary movement."

Carina became conscious of her own fidgeting and tried to stop.

"Hmm … maybe …" The queen sat up. "How do you call on your magic? If you want to move something telekinetically?"

"I don't know," Carina said, surprised into answering. "I'm not very good. I try to focus on what I want moving where I want it to move, I guess. And, sometimes, if I concentrate hard enough, it does. But mostly things only move when I'm not expecting it. I really don't have all the magic you think I have."

The queen took a shiny metal pin with a sparkly green stone at the end out of her hair and set it on the table. "You mean if you wanted to move that hairpin you would focus hard and try to visualize it moving?"

"Yes."

"And if you put all your energy into it the pin moves?"

Carina blushed. "Only sometimes."

"Hold out your hand."

Carina couldn't think of a reason not to, so she did. The pin floated up from the table and traveled directly into her hand.

"I didn't do that," Carina said.

Queen Vivian looked amused. "I know. I did."

"But you didn't lift a finger. You didn't even *try*."

The queen's mouth twisted into a wry smile. "I tried. Probably tried too much for Bast's liking. I just didn't try the way you would have."

"What did you do to make it move?" Carina asked, wanting badly to understand.

"I didn't focus on making it move at all. I only focused on my energy reaching out to it." The queen nodded at the pin again, and it lifted from Carina's hand. "See how it did that? That's because I just sent my energy out to it. And now …" The pin started floating back across the room. "All I have to do is bring my energy back to me to retrieve the pin."

"Like fishing," Carina said, and the queen seemed confused as she put the pin back in her hair. "You sent a line out to catch it, and then you reeled it back in."

The queen pursed her lips. "Not the analogy I would have used, but sort of. The important part is that I wasn't focused on the pin. I was focused on myself and my own energy: how fast I'm moving, with how much force. How much momentum I have. I can't change the nature of the object I'm trying to move or how *it* naturally behaves. But if I change myself, I change what the object has to react to, and it does something different than before." She smiled. "*That* was a good analogy."

An image of Sister Rachel dashed through Carina's mind. "That wasn't an analogy."

The queen's smile dissolved. "It doesn't matter. We need to get down to business. My brothers don't think there's anything we can do to get you to cooperate with us. Have they told you what we need your help with?"

Carina shook her head. "No."

"Good." The queen's smile returned. "We should go on a first name basis. You may call me Vivian, and, when you feel comfortable telling me your name, I'll call you by your first name. Okay?"

Again, Carina couldn't think of a reason to say no. "Okay."

"Wonderful," Vivian said. "Now, you have a lot of magic. We need a lot of magic, and we're willing to bargain with you to get it. If you help us, we can help you. Or we can help anyone you want if that's what you'd prefer. You and your sister are orphans, right? And you've been living in some remote village?" She changed her facial expression to pity. "That must be a difficult life."

Carina had the bad feeling that the queen was now trying to reel *her* in like a fish, and she didn't like that this girl, who knew nothing about her, was judging her life based on the fact that she was an orphan who'd grown up in the mountains. Sister Agda had been strict, and Novi Dupree wasn't luxurious, but Carina and Miguela had been warm, fed, and mostly educated.

"Think about it," Vivian went on. "I'm the queen of South Kepler, and what we need you to do is important. You would be rewarded. Have you ever been to Alighieri? It's beautiful. We could find places there for you and your sister. You'd be safe. We'd find you somewhere nice. You could have separate rooms. Have you ever had that before?"

Vivian was practically an angel compared to either of the princes. Carina couldn't detect any of the slimy film that had been there when Prince Nathanial mentioned benefits or when Prince Bastian healed that cut.

"I could teach you how to use your gifts. You've never had a proper magic teacher, have you? Why don't you try the tip I gave you?"

Carina wondered if the desperation she felt to learn magic was that obvious. She needed not to look like she wanted to learn so badly.

"Oh, what's the harm?" Vivian asked. "Worst-case scenario it won't work. Best case, you can protect yourself better against my brothers. I hear they used telekinesis to stop you from running in the woods. That's easy to counter if you can adjust your own telekinetic energy. All you have to do is shift your energy a little, and they won't be able to hang on to you that way."

Carina's resolve wavered. "What should I move?"

Vivian pointed to the bottles of liquor on the bar shelves. "How about one of those?"

"Those are a lot bigger than a pin."

"I saw you create a defensive telekinetic shield that stopped three arrows. If you can do that, you can move one bottle." She nodded toward the bar. "Go on. Try like I told you. Imagine your energy connecting and bringing one of those bottles to you. Find your magic and just ... extend yourself."

Carina looked at the bottles skeptically. They were different shapes, but they were all larger than a bottle of sassafras. And where was she supposed to *find* her magic?

"Try to think of something that makes you feel like you

want to run because you're happy or excited," Vivian advised. "That's the kind of energy you need to tap into. And don't worry if it's hard for you to locate right now. People who tend cold are always naturally better at stopping things first."

Carina thought about things that made her feel energized. Like Max giving her that book (he hadn't known Bosley Pinkerton was a fraud) or the bottle of sassafras finally lifting from the windowsill of the shack back at Novi Dupree.

"Good," Vivian said softly. "Your own energy isn't something you should have to think hard about. Don't try to figure out where you stop and it begins. It's a part of you, and it's always there. Move it like you'd move one of your hands. All you have to do is reach out."

Carina tried to relax. Maybe she didn't need to work so hard. She extended her arm and instead of imagining any of the bottles coming to her, she imagined energy from her fingers extending out to the bottle in the middle.

And as easy as that, she knew she had a grip. The bottle lifted from the shelf.

"Whoa," she breathed.

"You've got it," Vivian said. "Now bring it back."

Carina imagined drawing the bottle back to her, and it dropped back onto the shelf.

"No, no. You're trying to make the bottle move again. Don't bother with that. Bring your *own* energy back."

Carina tried again. The bottle lifted back up.

"Pull your energy back. Telekinetic energy is magnetic. The bottle *wants* to follow."

Miguela would have thought the queen was dragonbat crazy. Carina followed her instructions anyway. She thought about pulling her own energy back, and sure enough, the bottle came with it. In fact, it flew right into her hand.

"It worked." She turned the bottle around to look at it like maybe it was rigged.

"Of course, it did," Vivian said confidently.

"But it was so easy your way. Like you didn't need to *think* to make it happen." Carina tried to pick up the bottle again and move it back. She felt clumsier this time.

"Same concept. But remember, you tend cold, so it's always going to be easier for you to do things to contain your energy or keep it close. You'll be able to bring things to you from further away than you can move things out, and you'll have more force pulling something to you than pushing it away. But you can build up your telekinetic abilities the same way you build muscle memory and strength. With the right exercises."

Carina floated the bottle back and forth. "This is so cool."

Vivian appeared to be having a good time watching. There seemed to be a little more color on her than there had been before. "It's a shame you've had to struggle so much with it. Telekinesis shows early for most people. In our family, we start learning it before we learn to read. We're Cardinals, of course, but still … you're good. We could have had fun training. I bet if I'd taught you, we could have destroyed Bast and Nate together in a fight."

That prospect sounded fun to Carina, too, but Vivian looked unhappy.

"Not right now, though," she said. "That's not an option unless—"

Carina nearly lost her grip on the bottle. She'd almost forgotten she was here against her will. She set the bottle back down and faced the queen. "I don't know if I can help. I've heard you hurt people with magic. Why should I be different?"

"I don't hurt people with magic," the queen said. "What are you talking about?"

"But you arrest people just for having it. Prince Nathanial told me so, and Prince Bastian said I could be executed for … being me and not telling you, I guess? Because that's what you do with people that have magic but aren't registered or whatever? It doesn't seem fair. Why would you ever punish someone for having a quality they're born with and can't help?"

"We don't want to execute *you*. That's not our intention at all. We only need to make sure you're not with a group of rebels or something. And we don't punish people for being born with magic. We only require everyone with magic to come forward, and then we put them to work in the best way possible for the kingdom." The lines on Vivian's face deepened as she frowned. "The registry is about resource management."

"That's not what I've heard," Carina said.

Vivian's eyes flashed. "It's how it is."

"Then nothing bad happens to people who get brought in for having magic?"

Vivian had a scowl like the one Carina had seen on both her brothers' faces now. "Most of the time, those who don't come forward are hiding something. They are traitors."

Carina took a deep breath. She thought Vivian would have been a good teacher, and really, that was all she wanted. If she could overlook the things she'd heard about the Southern Royals, she could learn magic, keep Miguela safe, and probably find a ride for Max to the Mountain of Peril, too.

"How do I know I can trust you?" she asked Vivian.

"How do I know you're not a spy?" Vivian retorted.

Carina felt her face flush. "You're the one who found me.

And *you're executing* people who haven't done anything wrong just because you're afraid of them. For things I bet you can't even prove."

"*I'm* not executing anyone!"

"You're the queen."

"I've only been the queen for a few weeks. My *mother* has control of everything."

"Then you should change things. And if you think it's okay not to try to change things in your position, why would I want to stay and help you? Why would I tell you anything? What would make me think you would protect *me* if you're letting other people get hurt?"

It had started to feel hot in the room, and it occurred to Carina that Queen Vivian had a thermodynamic tendency, too. There was an alarming flare in her eyes as she responded: "How dare you question my integrity like that. I am the *queen,* and I am offering to *help you.*"

"I thought you wanted to be on a first name basis," Carina said cautiously.

"We could have been," Vivian said.

Carina extended her magic to the chair Queen Vivian was sitting on. "We're not." She snapped the chair out from under the girl and sprinted for the door.

Prince Nathanial and Prince Bastian were sitting on opposite sides of a bench outside. They both stood, but Carina managed to pull the bench toward her telekinetically, ramming it into their knees from behind and making them both fall.

"Find your help somewhere else," she said. Then she ran.

My decision to apply for the Immortality Program was as much a mistake for me as it was for anyone else, but some suffer from the Immortality Virus more than others.

Anna Dupree ended her Immortal life last week, at the age of three-thousand, nine-hundred and two Earth Years. Our remaining colleagues gathered at Novi Dupree Sanctuary and held a quiet funeral for Anna, mostly for Lizzy Dupree's sake.

I slept with Lizzy that night. Her eyes were red the whole time. I thought she needed a distraction. She was pliant in my arms, melting into me as she cried tears that she thought sprang from deep grief. But they were tears of rage. I knew because I'd felt the same thing, a few weeks after I'd awoken in the hospital from my Immortality Injection. My fury then had bloomed from a handwritten letter, tucked into a quilt that smelled like Stella.

The letter has long-since turned to dust, and I was never willing to take a digital image of it. I didn't need to. I still know every word:

I turned back at the last minute. Not because I didn't want to be with you, but because I didn't think you would go through with it. You had so much in your life, and the needle was so final. I thought I knew you—knew that you could never do it. I stopped the nurse with the needle almost grazing my skin.

They won't let me reapply for the program, Myles. My heart is broken, as I know yours will be when you read this. I don't expect your forgiveness, and I know I may never see you again. But however long it takes, I hope you one day read this letter and know that I will love you longer than forever.

She had no idea how long forever could be.

~Myles Alexander Kayes

249

CHAPTER TWENTY-FOUR
THE THREE WOLVES

Carina had knocked over the village water tower. She hadn't meant to do it. She hadn't meant to cause most of the destruction she'd just caused. But Prince Nathanial had yelled, "Don't let her go!" after she ran from the tavern. Then he got up and chased her.

With his *guards*.

Luckily, Carina was fast. She could outrun the guards, and she was managing to slow them down throwing things back telekinetically. She was clumsy, though, and Prince Nathanial could both outrun and outmagic her. So, thanks to her lack of ability—and what must have been general recklessness on his part—the village was in chaos behind them. People shouted as carts crashed into walls and trash cans rolled. They probably smashed a dozen potted plants between them. At some point, a whole barrel of river sardines came flying her way, and she returned the favor by chucking an entire sack of Kepler long grains back. Prince Nathanial made a gratifying "oof" noise when it hit him.

At the edge of town, he was still running after her, and that was when Carina saw the water tower. She didn't consciously decide to rip it telekinetically from the ground. She couldn't have. She hadn't expected to be able to do something like that. Maybe telekinetic energy was fueled by adrenaline, though, because she'd slammed the tower down between herself and the prince with what felt like no effort at all before she could think.

The water splashed out spectacularly. She thought about freezing it, so he'd fall. But she was livid, and her cold ability seemed to know it. The water didn't just freeze. It burst up in huge, frozen spikes. She was as stunned as Prince Nathanial looked as he fell and slid right into one.

After that, Carina dashed into the woods. Apparently, the water tower had been enough of a deterrent, because it didn't seem like Prince Nathanial followed. But that didn't mean the princes weren't going to track her down later. She wasn't sure why only Prince Nathanial had chased her in the first place. Prince Bastian had seemed more talented.

Still, whatever their plan was, Carina knew she needed to get back to Miguela and Max right away. Then they were going to have to ditch any non-essential supplies and get out of the area as fast as possible. They couldn't take an obvious route because the queen and her brothers had been following her. She was wondering just *how* on Kepler they'd managed to track her when she came face-to-face with something that gave her a clue:

Three wolves.

Each with a strip of red fabric tied around a front leg.

They didn't look friendly.

Normally, Carina thought of herself as an animal person. She was good at repairing broken wings, getting baby monk squirrels to eat, and taking thorns out of the paws of stray dogs. She had never realized before that her affinity for animals extended mostly to the cute ones.

Growling wolves did not fall into that category.

Also, which of the princes kept *wolves* to sic on innocent girls?

Carina tried to stay calm. Animals responded to human reactions. If the wolves thought she was aggressive, they might attack. "Are you one of the prince's wolves?" she asked in as soothing a voice as she could manage given the stressful day she'd had.

Not that she expected them to respond.

But maybe they were special, magic wolves. The one in the middle took a step forward and grunted through its snout like it understood. It was bigger than the ones on the sides and had more gray hair. The others were skinnier with shiny black coats.

Carina continued cautiously. "If you are, you can go away now. I spoke with the prince. He told me to tell you he doesn't need me anymore."

"Carina? Is that you?"

She hoped the wolves couldn't sense her distress at that. Miguela had the worst timing.

"Can you hear me? Where are you?"

Miguela's tone was the opposite of the tone Carina had been going for with the wolves. The big gray wolf took a second predatory step toward Carina.

"Carina? Are you there!?"

"I'm here," she said, trying to make her voice loud enough for Miguela to hear but still flat. "Stay where you are."

"What? Why?"

It would have been nice if just this once Miguela could

have followed instructions. She didn't listen to Carina, though. Instead, it sounded like she started running. "No! I'll be right there. I think I see you!" she called. The relief in Miguela's voice was premature. Carina flinched as her sister came into view. She stood still and held out a hand, hoping Miguela would understand to stop.

Thankfully, she did.

"What's wrong?"

Carina took a long breath and subtly nodded toward the wolves. "I have company. You need to stay calm."

Miguela's face turned to ash. "Are those wolves *wild?*"

"Worse," Carina said. "I think they're trained, and they are reacting to us, so try to relax and don't make eye contact with them."

Miguela nodded silently and stood like a statue while the wolves snarled and Carina tried to figure out what to do. Unfortunately, she hadn't figured out anything before she heard Max.

"Miguela, could you slow down? Where did you go?"

"Oh no," Miguela whispered. "He's such a moron."

Carina called out as evenly as she could: "Max, Miguela is here. She just found me. Stay where you are. Don't come any closer. We have a situation."

"Can't you tell them to go away?" Miguela suggested softly. "Sister Raji always said animals liked you."

"No, I can't *tell them to go away*. I don't speak *wolf*."

"Should we run then? Do you think they're fast?"

Carina thought they would be faster than Prince Nathanial, but she didn't have a chance to answer because Max showed up just then. He saw the wolves, came to a halting stop, and, to her horror, reached for his gun.

"Stay back, girls. Those wolves are *huge*," he said, and for once, even though Carina thought what Max had just said was completely stupid, Miguela didn't make any smart remarks.

The wolves turned their attention to him. The one in the middle growled and bared his teeth. It didn't sound like he liked Max.

"And they are not friendly," he added.

Miguela covered her mouth like she was trying not to make a noise, but for Carina, everything had tipped sideways.

"Don't shoot them," she said to Max.

"It's okay." His voice was low. "Stay exactly where you are. The others will probably run as soon as I get the big one."

"What if you *miss*?" Miguela asked.

"What if he *doesn't*?" Carina said.

The wolves were uneasy. The skinny black ones were looking sideways at the one in the middle like they were waiting for it to tell them what to do, and the one in the middle had his back hunched like he knew he was facing a real threat now.

Carina felt *bad* for them. "Don't shoot, Max. They haven't done anything. They have the wrong owner. That's all."

Max pointed his gun at the gray wolf. "They're wild. They don't have an owner."

But she was *sure* the only reason those wolves were here was that one of the princes had sent them for her, and the princes hadn't seemed to want her dead, so she doubted the wolves were on orders to kill her.

"No. They do. Look at the red cloth around their front legs. I don't think they're a real threat. I think if we walk away calmly, they'll go, too." She made cautious eye contact with the wolf in the center. "You will, won't you? If we go away, will you go away, too?"

The wolf tilted its head at her.

Miguela squeaked. "Are you *sure* you don't speak wolf?"

Max still had his gun trained on the wolf. "It's antagonized. I'm sorry, Carina. We can't take risks."

He did something with the gun that made a soft clicking noise. Carina felt the hairs on the back of her own neck rise. A bird flew overhead, one of the younger wolves to the side barked at it, and Max fired his gun.

Carina had already done something to extend her telekinetic energy out around the animals, though. It was like the water tower. She didn't even know what she'd done. She only heard herself yell "No!" while Max dropped his gun and cried out, and the wolves scattered, unharmed.

Max grabbed his leg.

Carina ran to him. "Max, are you okay?"

He was bent over, holding the side of his leg. His face had turned white. She had no idea how, but she was sure she'd done this. She'd wanted to protect the wolves from him, and she had, but somehow, she'd made the bullet bounce back at him. Now he was shot.

She'd hurt him. Badly.

Pointless apologies came pouring from her lips. "I'm sorry, Max!"

He looked at her like he didn't even recognize her, then abruptly looked away. She half-expected him to keel over any minute. The Red-Eyed Ones he'd shot had died fast. But Max didn't *look* like he was dying. He only looked angry.

"Are you okay?" she asked again frantically. "Did it hit you? I'm *so* sorry. I didn't mean for the bullet to ricochet. I was afraid you were going to kill those wolves." She tried to pull his hand away from his leg, but it was clamped down tight.

"Let me see it. Is it bleeding a lot? I'm so sorry. I was so scared." She tried to move his hand again, and this time he jerked it out of her reach. This allowed her to see that the bullet had grazed the side of his thigh, tearing the fabric and leaving a raw line of skin.

It was bleeding a little.

She breathed out. "That's barely a scratch." She examined the wound and recalled Prince Bastian telling her she could heal things. "I might be able to …

Max spun away from her.

"Did *you* do that?" His voice sounded harsh like she'd never heard it before.

She looked briefly toward Miguela, who was frozen in place.

"I … yeah. I think I did."

Max's shoulders were tight, and Carina could see his jaw clenching from behind.

"You *reversed* that bullet and sent it back at me? On *purpose*?"

Miguela shot him a fast and nasty look as Carina took in the question. She stood up. "No! I was only trying to shield the wolves. You were going to kill them. I didn't realize the bullet would bounce back … I didn't even know what I was doing."

Miguela's eyes darted back to Carina. "You used magic you didn't understand, and someone got hurt," she observed.

For a moment, Carina regretted not taking up Queen Vivian on her offer. At least then she'd have been with someone hostile who *wanted* her to learn magic. She immediately took that thought back, though. Miguela was right.

"I'm really, really sorry, Max," she tried again. "I had no idea that would happen. I would never hurt you on purpose."

Another bird chirped nearby, but neither Max nor Miguela spoke. Carina wondered if this was going to be the end of her friendship with Max, and she felt almost as frightened as she'd felt when Prince Bastian had threatened Miguela earlier.

Max breathed out and ran his hands roughly through his hair. Then, to Carina's relief, he turned back to her, and he was hugging her before she could process that it was even happening.

"It's okay. I know you weren't trying to hurt me. You just scared me." He put his hand on the back of her head and pulled her into his shoulder like he needed her close to make sure everything was fine. "I've been scared all morning."

Carina couldn't ever remember wanting to be hugged as much as she did now, so she let herself melt into Max, and she ignored the way Miguela huffed as he kissed her hair lightly. Her sister was being immature about this. He was obviously only doing it because he was so relieved. It's not like it was romantic. Or like every nerve in her body was reacting.

Max backed away just enough that she could see his face. His eyes were shiny, and this close she could see spikes of indigo in his irises next to lighter shades of blue. "Where have you *been*? Miguela said you got up early to practice, but when you didn't come back, we were worried. We searched everywhere."

Carina wanted to tell him everything. But she'd been up since before dawn, it had not been an easy morning, and she'd been so sure a minute ago that she'd done something she could never take back. If she'd really hurt someone, she didn't think she could have forgiven herself. Her lips quivered.

"Hey, don't cry!" Max pulled her right back into that hug. "Just tell us what happened."

Over his shoulder, Carina could see Miguela standing sullenly with her hands in her jeans pockets, but Miguela had always hated magic and Carina thought she could tolerate that if she knew they were all safe and sound.

Which they were not.

She pulled away from Max. "We have to go back to the campsite and get our things."

"Sure." He sounded happy again. "Are you hungry? You've been gone for hours."

Lunch was not Carina's priority right now. "No, we have to go. I got caught. Not by the Red-Eyed Ones. By the Southern Royals. They arrested me for using magic."

Miguela's sullen face turned to shock. "You got picked up by the Southern Guard?"

Carina shook her head. "No. I got picked up by the Southern *Royals*. The two princes and the queen. They've been tracking us. They want me to do something for them, but they're not good people and I only barely managed to escape—"

Miguela and Max were looking at her like she was crazy.

She wrung her hands. "I'm not lying! I don't know what they want, and they didn't want to let me go." She realized something. "The wolves. I bet they've already made it back."

"You ran into the *queen*?" Max said. "Of South Kepler?"

"Yes," Carina said. "And we have to get out of here. Now. I'll explain later."

Miguela's eyes were enormous. "Guela," Carina said, reverting to a nickname she hadn't used for her sister in years. "I'm not lying."

Miguela rubbed her eyes like she was trying to wake up from a bad dream.

"Please," Carina begged. "You have to trust me."

Her sister stuck her hands in her pockets again. "I believe you."

CHAPTER TWENTY-FIVE
THE LOYALTY LINE

Vivian couldn't find her cyanide. She'd checked the pockets of her jeans, her makeup bag, and the drawstring sacks her new shoes had come in. Then she'd asked Captain Thurlow to take her back to the coach, so she could look there.

She told him she'd lost an earring.

"What does it look like?" he asked, while she searched the cracks alongside the bench cushion. "Maybe I can help."

"It's hard to describe." She ran her hand along the cushion a third time. She was agitated, and when the jewelry pouch with the cyanide did not materialize, she sank to the floor of the coach.

Captain Thurlow said: "Queen Vivian," but she had started to cry. Hard.

She covered her face with her hands. She hadn't cried like this since her father's death. It was humiliating. There were teardrops falling onto her jeans, and her mascara was seeping into the fabric like watercolor paint. She tried to wipe the tears away, but more kept coming. From where she was sitting, she could see that the captain kept his shoes polished.

"Go away," she told him.

He shut the door to the coach, but she could still see his shoes.

"Go," she said, and when he *still* didn't she said: "I'm *ordering* you to *leave!*"

Vivian guessed that Captain Thurlow had never disobeyed a command from a superior in his whole life. He did not seem like the type who would disobey a direct order from the queen.

He sat down with her. He had to bend his knees up to sit like that. It didn't look very captainly.

She wiped snot from her nose with her sleeve. It wasn't very queenly. "I told you to go."

He stood, and she thought forlornly that he *was* going to leave. Then he sat back down and handed her a box of tissues that had been sitting on one of the benches.

"I heard about the girl," he said.

Everyone had heard about the girl. She'd wrecked half the village running away, and Nate had wrecked the other half chasing her before he lost her. He'd returned with a black eye, a twisted ankle, and a bad attitude.

Bast had been too worried about Vivian—who had fallen hard after the girl magicked her chair away—to chase the girl himself, and now he was annoyed with Nate. "He had twenty guards, and she was on *foot.* He's supposed to be one of *us,*" he'd said. But Vivian thought Bast was embarrassed about how angry he'd let the girl make him, because he was with Nate now anyway, healing his injuries.

He'd been gentle with Vivian about her part in the debacle, too, even after Vivian admitted she'd demonstrated magic for the girl. "I guess she wasn't impressed by any of us, huh?" he'd said, and that was it.

Vivian couldn't ever remember feeling more hurt by a stranger, though. She hadn't had her hopes up for anything, but when the girl finally managed to pick up that bottle, her whole face had transformed. Right then, Vivian experienced something new: the gratification of seeing someone else succeed because of help she'd given them. It made being rejected after even worse. Vivian was enraged, hurt, and very disappointed.

There was a mountain of tissues accumulating in her lap.

The captain spoke up. "There are still three letters that haven't come back." That made her sob harder. "And Prince Bastian is sure the Guru is more than a legend."

Vivian threw another tissue down beside her. "He's delusional. And there aren't three letters left. There's one. My mother got the other two herself."

The captain's face remained neutral. "You didn't tell the princes."

More tears rolled down her face. "How would that help?"

He leaned his head against the bench silently.

"Do you think it's wrong not to tell them?"

"I have two older sisters and one younger brother." He tapped the side of her shoe with the side of his. "Everyone keeps secrets from their family sometimes, Queen Vivian."

The floor of the coach was getting uncomfortable. Vivian didn't think she would mind knowing more about the captain's family. She sniffed again. "Could you call me Vivian?"

"The queen of South Kepler wants me to call her by her first name." He looked at her a little devilishly. "Do you even remember *my* first name?"

This time her sniff was more indignant. "Yes, I remember

your first name! It's ..." She wasn't completely sure, though. She thought it was Brendon. Or Brian. Or possibly Breton.

He snickered. "It's Brandon. And if you want me to call you by your first name, the condition is you have to call me by mine."

She wasn't crying anymore. Maybe it was stupid, but she was wondering if the caravan had to move on first thing tomorrow morning. If not, she'd like to have breakfast with Brandon again. Also, she was wondering if he'd let her ride with him tomorrow. Because somehow things didn't seem so bad with him smirking at her.

He shifted like he was getting up and crouched on the balls of his feet in front of her. He had a tiny birthmark on his face near his jaw and the hint of laugh lines at the corners of his eyes. He took the box of tissues from her lap and reached over her shoulder to set it back on the bench. She had the funniest feeling that he'd done it that way purposely to invade her space.

"So, do we have a deal, Vivian?"

For her, that one question lowered a veil between them that had never come down between her and anyone else. It felt ... fine.

"We have a deal, Brandon."

He took her hand and helped her stand, and there was already so little space between them that it seemed like the only *appropriate* thing to do was to lean in the rest of the way. He must have felt the same because when she rested her head against his shoulder, he slid his arm around her. She exhaled once, and they heard Bast's voice from outside the coach:

"Viv? You in there?"

Brandon looked at the door like it had done something wrong. "I can't call you Vivian in front of your brothers."

"No, of course not," she agreed. "You'll have to call me Viv in front of them, or they won't know we're friends."

He made good use of those laugh lines.

Someone had turned the empty patio behind the inn into a nice place for dinner that evening, but Nate was late again. Vivian and Bast were halfway through the meal before he finally stormed onto the patio and dropped into his chair at their table.

He did not say "hi." He scowled at the meat on his plate and said: "What is *this*?"

"Meatloaf," Bast answered. He swirled a chunk in thick gravy. "And mashed potatoes."

Nate glared at the offensive entree. "I don't *eat* meatloaf."

Vivian took another bite. It wasn't gourmet, but it was good. The mashed potatoes, too.

Bast swallowed. "I take it your meeting with the wolves went badly?"

Nate flared his nostrils like an animal and flicked his fingers. His plate slid to the center of the table. "They didn't come back."

Bast cut up another piece of meatloaf. "Wow. You're having a bad day. Your pets are gone. You scared some poor girl into giving you frostbite this morning. Then she rejected your romantic advances, and this afternoon you let her give you a black eye—"

"I didn't *let* her do it." Nate snarled. "She *hurled* a sack of grain at me. She couldn't lift a *pebble* this morning. And you should have seen what she did with the water tower."

"Fine. You were defeated by a sack of grain and some water—"

"*No.* She yanked the whole tower from *concrete*, heaved it at me, made the water explode, and turned it all into scary, super sharp ice picks." Nate made hand motions to illustrate, then stared wrathfully at his uneaten plate of meatloaf. "I'm lucky I'm still alive."

Vivian tried to keep a straight face. She was weirdly proud of the girl.

Bast smiled dreamily. "I *knew* she was like me."

"Yeah. Guess that explains why I like her so much." Nate put his head down in his arms on the table where his plate had been. "I don't understand why my wolves didn't come back."

"Which rejection hurts more?" Bast asked. "The wolves or the girl?"

Nate grunted. "The wolves. Because I thought *they* liked me." He picked his head up and looked at Bast. "What's your plan to capture her, by the way? I've been thinking next time we should consider telling her *why* we need help. Maybe if she knows how sick Viv is—"

"No," Vivian said quickly. "We're not going after her. She's not interested in helping. And she thinks I'm … she doesn't think highly of me, either."

"She has to be with a rebel group," Nate said. "They've filled her head with all kinds of stories. Did you know they don't have indoor toilets where she lived?" He tipped his chair back and craned his neck toward the inn. "What kind of place doesn't have indoor toilets? And what do you think they're having for dessert?"

Vivian hadn't been thinking of dessert, but Brandon walked out onto the patio then. Maybe he'd go for a walk with her after dinner. He seemed a little nervous coming their way. She thought she might have to initiate the first-name thing in front of her brothers, and she was about to say "Hi,

Brandon," when he caught her eye and barely shook his head.

Bast leaned back. "What's going on, Captain? Immortals?"

Brandon stood in front of the table. "No, sir. Two scouts came back this afternoon with other news. One reported bad storms moving in from the east. The valleys are flooding, and our route is blocked ahead by mudslides."

"Perfect," Nate said, putting his head back down. "Exactly what we needed to hear."

Bast frowned. "Are there alternative routes?"

"Yes, sir," Brandon answered. "We can head back west toward Great Crater Lake and take the ferry across. There's a safer route into the mountains from there. It will add a week to our trip, but our route could be blocked longer if we stay."

"Fine. We'll take the alternative route. What's the other report?"

"Lord Franklin was apprehended—"

Nate sat up straight. "What do you mean *Franklin* was *apprehended?*"

"Caught, sir," Brandon said. "There's a warrant out for his arrest."

Nate shot out of his seat. "A *warrant?*"

The warrant was news for Vivian as well, but Nate was clearly distraught. She tugged on his sleeve to try to get him to sit. "Calm down, Nate. I'm sure there's been a mistake."

"No mistake," Bast said. "Mom issued the warrant. There's evidence that Franklin was conspiring to bring in those Immortal assassins that tried to kill you at the coronation."

Vivian felt the temperature of the air around them go up as Nate whirled toward Bast. "What *evidence* does Mom have?"

"I don't know. They searched his quarters in the castle—"

"They did *what?*"

"Someone tried to *kill* Viv," Bast said practically.

"Alighieri's security was breached. *Everyone's* quarters were searched."

"That's *ox* shit. Franklin would *never* hurt one of us. He's completely loyal to the crown. All he's done for years is try to help me and—" Nate's face paled. "This is because of me."

"You're not that special," Bast scoffed. "Hasn't Franklin taught you anything?"

Nate gave Bast a hard look. "Franklin's taught me *everything.* He's the only person in this family who *gives* a damn about me. Constance can't stand me, and she *knows* Franklin's the only person who will protect me if …"

Bast stood up. Now there was something deadly in his tone. "Do you realize what you're saying? You're accusing our mother of fabricating evidence and falsely accusing someone of conspiracy to assassinate our sister. That would be *treason*, Nate."

"That's how Mom works, *Bast.* She's a heartless bitch who doesn't think twice about getting rid of anyone who stands in her way. The only reason you don't know it is that *you're* the one person *she* cares about, and that's only because she thinks you're *just like her.*"

The temperature in the air dropped instantly, and for a moment Vivian thought Bast was going to freeze Nate like an Immortal. But for once, Nate seemed to have the upper hand. Flames sprang up all around them on the patio, and the air became hot again. Nate leaned in and pointed his finger into Bast's chest. "Why didn't you tell me there was a warrant out for Franklin's arrest? Why is the captain reporting directly to you?"

"Relax." Bast pushed Nate's hand away. "I told him to report to me. I didn't think you cared about that kind of minutia."

The flames rose. "A *warrant* being issued for *Franklin's arrest* is not minutia."

Sweat was dripping down Bast's neck. "I said *cool* it, Nate. Maybe I didn't think you could be objective about Franklin."

One of the old paper lanterns caught a spark and lit up. Smoke began to rise.

"*I* am next in line," Nate spat. "Not you. And *you* do not get to decide whether I should be in on the briefings. I *outrank* you."

Bast blinked like he didn't recognize Nate.

Nate faced Brandon, who glanced anxiously at Vivian.

"Nate," she said. "Captain Thurlow didn't—"

"I know," Nate said shortly. He took a shaky breath in and another out, then did it again. The second time, the flames died down. He took a third breath. "Captain, I am the next person in the line of succession. In Queen Vivian's absence, you report to me. Do you understand?"

Brandon wasted no time nodding. "Yes, sir."

Nate nodded back and rubbed his hands on his trousers. "Okay. Good. I would like to receive any report from the scouts, be briefed on all correspondence, and be involved in any major decisions, along with Prince Bastian. Can you make that happen?"

"Yes, sir," Brandon answered promptly.

Nate's hands were shaking, but his voice was mostly steady. "Thank you, Captain. Now, do we ... know where Franklin is being held?"

"I'm sorry, sir. Lord Franklin *was* apprehended, but he escaped arrest."

Nate's shoulders relaxed. "Oh." He wiped sweat off his own forehead. "Sure, he did." He glanced up at the charred paper lantern then looked back at Brandon. "Captain, how's your swordsmanship? I could use some practice while we're on the road if someone will lend me a sword. Mine is back at the castle, but that's how I usually take my mind off things."

Brandon's face relaxed, too, and right then, Vivian saw something unexpected materialize between Brandon and Nate. It was a deep blue connection, wrapped with gold and so evident she didn't need to actively use magic to see it. It was like the connections she remembered between her father and his closest guards. A loyalty line. She'd never seen one of those between Mom and anyone. Nate was not the person she thought she'd ever see inspire one.

"I'll practice with you, Your Highness," Brandon said. "I'm sure we can find an extra sword."

Bast sat back down noisily. "*His Highness* is a paranoid drama queen."

Nate glared, reached into his pocket, pulled out a small pouch, and tossed it to Bast.

Vivian's insides lurched.

"What the hell is this?" Bast asked.

"Cyanide," Nate said. "I found it in Vivian's coach when you were refusing to talk to her. Ask her who gave it to her."

Bast looked blankly at the pouch, then met her eyes. She couldn't bring herself to tell him the truth out loud.

He pocketed the cyanide.

Then he threw up all over the patio.

CHAPTER TWENTY-SIX
THE WAGON RIDE

Miguela thought they should ditch their plans and go straight to the Eastern Ridge Trail. Also, she still didn't want Carina practicing magic.

"I don't care if the Red-Eyed Ones can't sense it. It gets you in trouble no matter what," she said, tapping her foot impatiently as Carina attempted to magic a baby rattycat out of a tree. "And how did you hear that thing mewing up there?"

"I think there's a second one, too," Carina said, petting the rattycat she'd just rescued. "And we can't go to the Eastern Ridge Trail. Max needs to find his uncle." She tried to hand the rattycat over to him.

He held his hands away. "That is a rat." He scrunched up his nose. "A weirdly fluffy rat with very pointy, catlike ears, but definitely a rat. I am not touching it."

Carina had thought she and Max were okay after what happened with the wolves, but the more she told him about the Southern Royals, the more distance he put between them as they walked. She handed the little guy to Miguela instead.

"It's not a rat. It's a rattycat. Look at its paws. It can't help that it has a skinny bald tail and a pointy face."

"Are you sure?" Max was looking at the animal like it might bite.

"Haven't you ever seen a rattycat?" Miguela asked, petting the rattycat's head while it purred happily in her hands.

"I've seen rats, and I've seen cats." He watched the rattycat warily. "I don't like either."

Carina was offended, but she had pushed them all hard the last few days, insisting that they walk late into the night after her encounter with the Southern Royals, then making them walk most of the day yesterday, too. This morning they were all crabby. Even she was yawning when they came to a road an hour or so after she'd rescued the rattycats.

Max got out his map, took one lazy step into the road, and a horse-drawn wagon came barreling toward them from around the bend. He backed up fast while the wagon hurtled by.

"That guy was really in a hurry," he said, stretching out "hurry" with a yawn of his own.

They all looked down the road… and the wagon barreled back into view.

"Oh, oh," Max said. "We better hide."

"No, wait," Miguela said.

"*Wait?* There are people *chasing* Carina."

"Just *wait,*" Miguela repeated while the wagon stopped, and a man hopped out. "I think we know him. I think I recognize his *wagon.*"

Max reached for his gun, but Carina had seen what Miguela had seen. She put her hand on his wrist. "No. Miguela's right."

"Do you think he recognized us?" Miguela asked under

her breath.

It wasn't possible. He'd been going way too fast to recognize a few kids on the side of the road. Especially two girls he hadn't seen in years.

The man approached them. "You kids heading into the mountains?"

"Yeah," Max said defensively. "What of it?"

The man had a thin-lipped smile that stretched across his face like he was almost amused. "Haven't you noticed the skies? There are storms up ahead and mudslides. No one's going up the mountains anytime soon."

"Mudslides? We're not afraid of dirt."

Miguela clucked her tongue while the man laughed. "If you don't know how dangerous the mudslides in these mountains can be, you shouldn't be climbing alone, young man. Where were you going?"

Max set his jaw and pointed in the direction from which the man had originally come. "None of your business, but that way."

The man folded his arms. He was intimidatingly muscular. "Maybe you're not too bright, but *that* is the way of miserable demise." He lowered his voice. "Do you have any idea how horrible it would be to die suffocating in mud?"

"Do *you?*" Max asked, but he was losing his standoff with the man, who seemed to think that retort was funny.

"Why don't you kids come with me? If you want to get to the peaks, your best bet now is to go back around Great Crater Lake and take a ferry across. I can get you as far as the falls."

"That will delay us forever," Max complained.

"Better delayed than dead, son," the man said, not unkindly.

They followed him to his wagon, Max grumbling about lost time the whole way. But Miguela reached for Carina's hand, and Carina knew exactly what she was thinking. The man might not recognize them, but there was no way they'd mistaken him. She couldn't remember if his hair had been so gray the first time they'd met, but the scar across his face wasn't something she could ever have forgotten.

Miguela's curiosity about the man seemed to have overcome her exhaustion. She asked if she could sit up front with him in the wagon, and the man said yes with a spark in his eyes that made his scar seem friendlier. So Miguela sat in front, while Carina and Max climbed into the back. As they headed out of the mountains, Carina filled Max in on how they knew the man.

Max thought the man must have been following them and was suspicious of his motives.

"But he saved us when we were kids," she said.

Max hummed like he was still apprehensive.

The wagon was smaller than Carina remembered, and it was full of supplies it looked like the man had packed hastily. She started trying to straighten things out telekinetically, mostly so there would be more room to stretch and sleep. It was harder for her to make things rotate than it was to make them come straight to her, but she thought she was getting better.

Max watched her practice. "That's incredible. I can't believe that girl was able to teach you so much so fast." He groaned. "I can't believe the book was a scam."

"I liked it anyway," Carina said. There was an empty bottle rolling back and forth across the wagon. She magicked it to her and sniffed inside. Whatever had been in there had been a lot stronger than sassafras. She concentrated on trying to chill the glass. Nothing happened.

"I don't understand how you can lean cold, either." Max was sitting with his arms around his knees. She'd gotten into the wagon first, and there had been room for him to sit next to her. He'd chosen to sit on the opposite side.

"Tend cold," she corrected.

"Sorry."

She rolled the bottle under her hand.

Max tipped his head back. "I thought it would be cool if you could float a spoon through the air. Freezing stuff and making bullets bounce off wolves was not on my radar."

It had not been on her "radar" that he might not like her as much if she could do more than float a spoon.

"Carina. Look at the bottle."

It had frosted over.

He pulled his knees in tighter and shivered.

Carina hadn't been sure if she'd been doing things right with Max before. She wished she could take a time-out and ask Sister Elizabeth about it. She'd thought he liked her. Now she wasn't sure. Had she been taking everything wrong?

Max laughed. "I'm such a dope. You're completely beyond me. I bet both those guys have crushes on you. And they're actual princes. With magic superpowers." He held out his hands and wriggled his fingers.

The frost on the bottle turned to sweat while Carina tried to puzzle out what he was saying. "But I like you," she said slowly. When he didn't answer, she was sure she'd said something wrong. She closed her eyes. Maybe she would feel better about everything after she'd gotten some sleep. "And I didn't want either of those guys to kiss me," she confessed.

A moment later, Max touched her hand. She opened her eyes. He was right in front of her. "I've wanted to kiss you since I met you. I've been waiting for the perfect moment, but your sister is always around, or you're being kidnapped by someone, and ..." He hesitated before going on. "Sometimes I'm scared."

"Of me freezing you?" she asked sadly.

"Of me messing things up with you."

Carina waited while he looked anxiously at her. Did he really want to kiss her? Was he waiting for some kind of cue? She thought she'd indicated what she wanted. Was he still waiting for perfect? If he was waiting for that, it was never going to happen.

"Do you want to kiss me now?" she finally asked, just to make sure.

He nodded again.

So, she leaned forward, shut her eyes, and kissed him before she could think enough about it to take it back. She tried to make it firm, but hopefully not forceful, and she knew she'd surprised him because for the first second or so he tried to say something that sounded like "whoaumokay" rather than kissing back.

Then, thankfully, he stopped trying to talk. When his lips pressed back into hers, she was extremely relieved. The kiss stopped, and he said, "Can we try that again?" and all she had to do that time to get him to kiss her was nod once. It was much better that way. He put his hand behind her neck and extended the kiss for a long time, and it was nice, even if it did involve some awkward things (like how her teeth kept accidentally hitting his) and some things she didn't normally associate with nice (like how he was getting slobber all over her face).

Overall, though, Carina thought kissing was fun. Max was enthusiastic, she became enjoyably light-headed, and they spent a lot of time devoted to the discovery of kissing before she called it off and said they needed sleep. Max agreed and seemed happy pulling her down with him on a blanket they spread out in the wagon. He fell right asleep with his arm wrapped around her, and that, Carina guessed, must be what cuddling was supposed to be like, although she wasn't as content as he seemed to be. His arm was heavy, and she had to shift around a lot to get comfortable.

Also, even though she was the one who had suggested sleep, she thought she might be feeling kind of buzzed (a term she had previously associated primarily with Sister Raji after a few beers). She wanted to talk to Max, and she was a little annoyed that he'd fallen asleep so easily when she hadn't. He'd kissed her neck before he dozed off, too, and that felt more intimate than the rest of the kissing had. So now she was worried that he'd want to kiss more when they woke up. What if her breath was bad by then? What if *his* breath was bad? And how was she supposed to fall asleep with him snoring in her ear?

Still, she did feel very safe curled up in that wagon with Max. She finally drifted off, and if either of them had bad breath when they woke up later, that didn't deter him from kissing her again or her from liking it. "I don't care how cold you tend," he told her between kisses. "I'd be crazy about you either way."

She told him how much she appreciated that with more kissing.

She thought he got it.

They spent several days in the wagon, and although Miguela joined Carina and Max in the back to sleep a few times, she mostly rode up front. This gave Carina and Max time to explore their new favorite hobby without Miguela watching, but she seemed to know something was happening anyway. The morning of the fourth day, Carina opened her eyes to find Miguela watching her. Miguela didn't look pleased.

"Are you sleeping with him?" she asked.

Carina had been snuggled up with Max. She unwrapped herself slowly from him and scooted closer to Miguela. "Well, I *was.*"

"I meant are you having sex."

Carina did not like the words "having sex" coming from her sister's mouth.

"You shouldn't be," Miguela continued. "If you are, you should stop. And if you're not, you shouldn't start. He's bad for you."

Max continued to snore like he was sleeping soundly.

"No, he's not," Carina said. "I like him, and he likes me. And we're not … *having sex* … but if we were, it wouldn't be any of your business."

Miguela growled like she was one of those wolves they'd met. Max only snored louder.

Carina changed the subject. "Have you found anything out about our driver yet?" The man was clearly in a rush to get somewhere. He'd only made two stops to sleep since he'd picked them up, and both times he'd gone right to sleep. Also, since she had mostly been busy with Max, Miguela was the only one who'd really talked to the man.

"Who, Leo?"

"His name is Leo?" Carina had expected something rougher. Like Jack. Or Bear Claw.

"I told you that two days ago," Miguela said. "He's nice. He tells funny stories. He was in the Southern Guard years ago, but he left after some fight. That's how he got his scar. I don't think he likes them much anymore."

"Do you think he recognizes us yet?"

"Maybe. I think he knows a lot about a lot."

Max made a noise like he was inhaling mud. Miguela made a noise like she was gagging in response.

"I don't understand," Carina said. "How can you trust a stranger who might have been following us and admits he was part of the Southern Guard, but not Max?"

"Because Max is lying about things, and Leo isn't," Miguela said firmly. "And we know Leo from before."

"Why do you hate everything that makes me happy?" Carina complained.

"I only hate two things that make you happy: magic and Max." Miguela counted them off on her fingers. "And I'm being perfectly rational about both. I hate magic because it's dangerous and we can't trust it, and I hate Max for the same reasons."

"Max is not *dangerous*," Carina hissed.

"He has a *gun*. You had to stop him from shooting something a few days ago!"

"*You* wanted him to shoot those wolves!"

"I was scared. I wasn't thinking straight. And that's the whole point. When people are scared, they do dumb things, and if you have a gun when you're scared, you might do something dumb that you can't take back."

"You're jealous," Carina said, ignoring Miguela's point.

The wagon stopped. Max sat up fast like he'd been startled awake. "What's going on?"

The doors to the back of the wagon opened, and Leo

appeared. "This is your stop. Great Crater Lake Falls. From here, you just follow the shore west. It'll be a good walk to get to the ports, but there's a cheap public ferry that'll take you across the lake." His scar stretched to the side as he peered in at them. "Did you organize all my stuff? Some of that was heavy."

Carina blushed as she climbed out of the wagon. "Sorry. It seemed cluttered."

Leo looked shrewdly at her, and she expected him to tell her how foolish she was for getting caught practicing magic. Instead, he said: "It was a good idea for a telekinetic dexterity exercise. Try it with objects that are further away if you want a challenge."

"Thanks." Carina put on her backpack. "And thanks for the ride. You, uh, drive fast."

"No problem." Leo climbed back into the driver's seat. "But do me a favor. When you see Agda again, don't tell her I was the one who gave you the ride. That woman will have my ass for not sending you straight to Cerulean."

And that was the second time the man with the purple scar drove away from Carina while she was in too much shock to say goodbye, though at least this time Miguela looked just as shocked.

"Guess he recognized you," Max said as the wagon faded out of sight.

"Guess so," Carina said.

CHAPTER TWENTY-SEVEN
COMMONER FOR A DAY

Things were quiet as Vivian's caravan moved on. The boys had gone back to eating meals with her and doing the prayers in the coach. Brandon and Nate had started sparring in the evenings. She liked watching, and sometimes Bast sat with her, providing light commentary about how barbaric the practice was. Since their last evening in the mountains, neither Bast nor Nate had brought up the cyanide, the letters, the girl, or Franklin.

She wanted to know how the boys had worked things out. She'd never seen Bast so physically upset or Nate so furious. The vomiting seemed to go on forever, too, with Bast's skin turning bluer and bluer, until Nate finally asked her to leave.

"Please, Vivian," he'd said as he crouched by Bast on the patio. "You can't fix this."

So, Brandon took her to her room, and she cried herself to sleep, even though Brandon was right there and wouldn't leave her alone. When she woke up the next morning, he was gone, and Bast and Nate were slouched side-by-side in chairs at the foot of her bed.

She supposed they were all in denial now, but she wasn't about to correct it. Instead, she made a list of things she wanted to do on the long way around to the Mountain of Peril.

Such as see Native Valley.

Bast refused. "I told you we don't have time for side trips," he said. But she had expected that, and she'd prepared a backup request. To which he said: "Why on Kepler would you want to spend an afternoon dressed down like a commoner?"

"I want to be normal for a day."

Bast gagged like he'd swallowed something bitter. "Normal people get terrible service at crowded restaurants where they eat disgustingly greasy food. They use public restrooms with questionable cleanliness. They wear cheap clothing that itches and doesn't fit right. They have unintelligible conversations."

"I want to try it," Vivian said stubbornly.

Bast sighed a long-suffering sigh. "Fine. We'll stop at the next village for lunch, and you can eat and dress like a pauper."

"We can shop too if you want," she offered.

Bast flicked a speck of dust from his shirt. "Normal people don't shop where I shop."

She, Bast, and Nate borrowed clothes from the attendants, and Vivian was excited about their excursion as they mounted horses and set off apart from the caravan for the afternoon, even though her borrowed clothes didn't fit quite right and did feel a bit scratchy.

As they got closer to the next village marked on their map, she started to feel like something was wrong. The roads leading into the village were too quiet, even for an area that wasn't very heavily populated, and the signs they saw were out of repair. They started to see a few dark houses, then some closed shops, but there weren't any people around.

By the time they got to the center of the village, it was clear the place was abandoned. Vivian felt nervous as they trod quietly through the downtown square. Bast got off his horse and strolled toward a glass storefront. There were dresses on busts inside the window. He peered inside. "They didn't clear out their inventory before they left. And those styles aren't that old."

The next store's windows were shattered.

"Maybe they were attacked by Immortals," Vivian said.

"But we haven't seen bodies," Bast said. "Maybe the Guard found out there was going to be an attack and ordered an evacuation."

"Then how come no one came back?" Nate asked. "And why is this place still on the map if no one lives here anymore?"

Vivian didn't feel like *they* should be here anymore. She didn't want to say it, but the place had the scent of death hanging on it, even if there weren't any bodies.

Bast got back on his horse. "The next village isn't too far away. Let's just go."

The next village was not abandoned. They left their horses by a small but crowded diner and went inside. There was a young man standing at a lectern by the door, watching a game of toggleball on a television mounted in the corner. A wobbly antenna made of crumpled up foil had been rigged to receive what Vivian assumed were very long-distance signals from New Paris or Cerulean, where toggleball was supposedly still extremely popular. She was disturbed. Didn't anyone know the Second Mortal Commitment? What a waste of energy.

Also, what were they supposed to do now?

"Do we seat ourselves?" she whispered to Bast.

"I don't know," he whispered back. "I've never done this before."

Nate shouldered past them both and said: "Table for three please."

"Fifteen-minute wait," the man said without looking away from the game. "Name?"

Vivian shared a panicked glance with Bast. She hadn't realized they were going to need a name for this. They could not tell the server they were the Wellington family.

"Davis," Nate said promptly. Vivian breathed out in relief. Davis was their mother's family name, and it was much more common than Wellington in the South.

"We'll call you when the table's ready," the man said, gesturing vaguely toward a bench that looked like it was on its last legs. But Nate went and sat, so Vivian followed.

Bast stood in front of them and refused to sit. He did not bother lowering his voice to say: "I knew this would be hell. Explain to me again why we're doing it?" He nodded at Nate. "And how do you know how to do this stuff?"

Nate was watching the toggleball game. "Franklin takes me places sometimes. And we're doing this because Viv wants to eat at a greasy diner. Deal with it."

Bast said something unkind under his breath, and they waited twenty-five minutes before the man pulled out three floppy, stained menus and told them to follow him. He seated them at a table with a wet top near the back. Bast dried his spot with the back of his sleeve, while Vivian began looking over the menu.

She didn't have time to finish reading the dining options,

however, before their waitress arrived. The waitress didn't look very old, she had rosy cheeks with unfortunate acne, and her apron was tied too tight. She pulled a flip pad out of a pocket at her waist, clicked a pen, and said: "Water yr want?"

Vivian didn't understand the question. Bast squinted at the girl.

"Uh, we could use more time," Nate said.

The waitress looked up from her pad. "You have an accent. Where are you from?"

Nate put his menu down. "Capital."

"That's a capital accent? Wow. It's so fancy." She stood looking at him for several more seconds before it seemed to dawn on her that she was still working. Then she flashed a smile. "How about drinks? We import soda from the best brewery."

"Sure," Nate said. So, they ordered drinks, and the waitress sashayed away with a hip swagger that Vivian was sure she reserved solely for guys with capital accents.

"Did that just happen?" Bast asked.

Nate said nothing, but when the waitress came back, he turned up his accent to order the tomato bisque soup and grilled cheese. The waitress seemed to narrowly avoid swooning before she said to Bast: "And what'll you have, dear?"

He gave her the coldest stare he could give someone without frosting their nose and dryly ordered a chicken salad.

"Don't mind him," Nate said. "He's charming when he's not on a diet."

This made the waitress giggle, and Vivian could only barely choke out that she wanted a burger after that. The waitress didn't seem to mind. She just took the moment as an opportunity to go for an upsell and asked if Vivian wanted to try the sweet potato fries, which came layered with cheese and a garlic aioli sauce but cost an extra dollar.

Vivian said: "Yes, please."

Nate grinned at her and slurped his soda with a straw as the waitress left.

"Do you know how bad that stuff is for you?" Bast said. "You might as well hook yourself up to a sugar drip." He had ordered unsweetened iced tea.

Nate continued to slurp. "Who cares? This sassafras beer is amazing. Why don't we have this brewery on call at the castle?"

Vivian thought they should put the whole diner on the catering list. Her burger was juicy, her cherry cider was tart, and her sweet potato fries were perfectly greasy. Bast refused to try them, but Nate stole several and declared loudly that they were "the best thing he'd ever eaten." When the waitress brought out a second order—on the house—he told her she'd read his mind. She blushed like he'd complimented her smile.

"We just passed through the town to the south," he said to the waitress, apparently taking her demeanor as an opportunity to milk her for information. "We were going to stop for lunch there—" Vivian kicked him under the table "—but it's completely dead. Do you know what happened?"

Bast shut his eyes and mouthed something Vivian thought might be a prayer, but the waitress nodded with big saucer eyes.

"It *is* dead. No one was willing to go back."

"Really?" Nate asked curiously. "What happened?"

The waitress leaned inappropriately close to him and whispered: "Red-Eyed Ones."

"You mean Immortals?" Bast said.

The waitress offered Bast a sideways glance without moving from her position near Nate. "I mean Red-Eyed

Ones. They were looking for something. Or someone. The whole town was ransacked. Lots of people were taken away. Some were killed. And they were organized like it was a hired job."

Bast scrutinized the waitress. "*Hired* job? Hired by *whom*?"

"The royal family. Probably the queen herself. You won't find many loyalists up here. Those people—" She shook her head.

The air around them chilled.

"Oh, we've heard things, but we didn't realize it had gotten that bad," Nate said hastily. "Are you sure? Why would the royal family do that?"

"Who knows?" the waitress said. "They're cracking down though, especially on the magic registry, and the taxes are criminal. Some people think it's because the family's afraid they're losing control. Others think they're losing their magic. There's a rumor that's what happened to the Cardinals of the North before the attack. And now there's the new queen … Victoria or something. She's only eighteen years old. That's how old I am." The waitress looked directly at Vivian. "You look about my age, too. Can you imagine one of *us* as the queen? It's ridiculous, and Queen Constance is probably training the poor girl to be a monster."

"Maybe they're not that close," Vivian said weakly while Nate started pushing food around on his plate and Bast set down his fork.

"My mom says the green apple doesn't fall far from the tree. But we've heard rumors that something happened to the new queen. She might be dead."

Vivian wondered what the girl was seeing on their faces. Maybe indigestion.

"I almost feel bad for her if she's not. They say she's

never had any friends. And a whole kingdom's a lot to put on one girl. I wouldn't want to be her. What can I get you for dessert?"

Vivian never wanted to be a commoner again.

She'd always assumed it was obvious she was nothing like her mother. It had never occurred to her that people outside the castle might think otherwise. Were people worried about her being queen? Did people truly feel that way about her family?

It wasn't fair. Vivian knew her mother had a reputation and that her father had done some unpopular things. But South Kepler was fighting a *war*. Not all the choices Vivian's family had made over the years were pretty. Everything was for the greater good, though. They simply couldn't be weak-willed, especially when they were the only Cardinal Family left. They had to be firm. Their magic was all that was keeping the Immortal Empire in check.

She got into an argument with Nate about it on their way back to the caravan. "Have people *forgotten* what happened to the other Cardinal families and *their* people?" she ranted. "The whole East is infested with Immortals. The North would be too if we hadn't taken control of the border. The West doesn't even *exist*! *Our* people in the South are safe because of us!"

"Except for the innocent people who are dead because of us," Nate said.

Bast shot him a warning look while Vivian's blood boiled over that comment.

"That is a *very* limited group. It is—" she struggled for the right word "—*regrettable* that we sometimes have to do things that harm a small minority of the population. But that is our *job* as the Cardinals. To do what we have to do to protect the greater kingdom."

Nate didn't respond. Vivian knew from the look Bast gave her that *he* at least was with her, but this was something they all needed to be united on. She pushed the issue with Nate.

"Well, don't you agree with me?"

"No," he said. "I don't."

Vivian could feel sweat on her brow. "What do you mean, *no?*"

He replied like a stubborn, insubordinate fool. "I mean no. I don't think it's ever right to do something you know is going to hurt someone innocent."

"This isn't about *right.* It's about *justified.* Don't you think it's justified sometimes?" When he didn't answer that after a long pause, she stopped, stood in front of him, and said: "I'm *ordering* you to answer, Nate."

He looked stonily at her, but when she refused to move, he finally heaved out a breath and said: "Fine. I think it's justified sometimes if sometimes means almost never."

After that, Vivian was so angry she couldn't speak. This was exactly Nate's problem. He was too impulsive with his actions and too slow with his thoughts.

Vivian was trying not to dwell on what might happen to her if they couldn't cure the virus, but the Guru didn't seem any more real as they moved on, her nightmares weren't getting better, and she felt worse every day. Furthermore, there was the loyalty line between Nate and Brandon to consider. Connections weren't necessarily predictive, but Nate was next in line to rule South Kepler, and she wasn't seeing loyalty lines between herself or Bast and anyone else.

Nate didn't have time to be naïve anymore.

Vivian refused to speak to Nate for the next couple days. He tried to speak to her, but she made a point not to eat with him and refused to let him do the prayers with her and Bast. When they stopped a couple of hours after breakfast one day, and there was a knock on her coach door, she didn't even look up before she said: "If you're not ready to admit you were wrong, you should go away, Nate."

The door opened anyway. It was Bast.

He climbed in and sat down on the bench across from her. "Sorry. Not Nate. And I'm offended, by the way. Why do you always take fights with Nate so bad? You don't do that with me."

Vivian was lying on her back with her knees bent. The summer heat was making the coach extra stuffy, even with the curtain shading her from the sun. Bast's presence was more than welcome. Which made her wonder why Bast always thought she liked Nate more than she liked him. How obvious could she get about having a favorite brother without actually saying it out loud?

"You fight with me. I never fight with you. And Nate's different because he doesn't know *any*thing about being a Cardinal."

"Ahh." Bast folded his hands over his stomach. "Then he's right that you're basically pissed off at him for being him."

Vivian stared at the ceiling of the coach.

"Nate flirts with small-town waitresses by gushing over the house fries. You can't expect him to be on the same level you are."

"The fries were good," Vivian said. "And if his objective was more, he achieved it."

Bast stretched his legs out. "If it was anything else, he was a complete failure. The fries were gross. I could smell garlic all the way across the table. He could have killed that waitress with his breath. But he has been helping me plan another stop. He's been unexpectedly useful."

"We're not stopping at another village, right?" Vivian said.

Her brother delayed answering, choosing to notice a tiny scuff on the toe of his boot instead. He polished it off with his thumb.

"Come on, Bast. Tell me where we're going. I can't handle another day like that." She turned on her side and let her cheek rest on a pillow.

He reached over to pat her head. "Aww. You're tired. We're almost there, though. How much would you pay me to get up and open that curtain for you, so you can look out and see where we are?"

"I am capable of opening the curtain myself," Vivian grumbled. She sat up, slid to the coach window, and pulled the curtains open.

They were not where she thought they'd be.

"Bast, is this—?"

He tightened his mouth like he was trying not to smile while she launched forward to hug him.

"Well, you said you wanted to see Native Valley," he said. "And you are the queen."

CHAPTER TWENTY-EIGHT
NATIVE VALLEY

Native Valley was the only place where the aboriginal Keplerians were easily visible to the human eye. The valley was like a giant bowl carved into the planet and sheltered by forests that rose to the west and mountains to the east and south. It hosted its own unique ecosystem, fueled in part by the aboriginals, who all had thermodynamic and aerodynamic magic.

Vivian wanted to appreciate the awesomeness of it all, but Brandon was walking next to her as they headed to the first lookout point.

"Brandon, have you ever been here?" she asked, trying not to be too loud since her brothers were walking just ahead of them.

His arm brushed hers. "No, Vivian. Have you?"

She was pleased to know their deal was still on. "No."

"I thought the royal family visited all the important sites."

"Sometimes when kids with magic gifts come here, strange things happen," Vivian explained. "There have been cases where a child's magic has completely disappeared, or they've lost the ability to speak. By the time we were old enough, my father was too sick to take us."

"And we've been busy with a war," Bast added. He looked back from her to Brandon, and his face morphed into a deep scowl. Nate tugged him forward with an apologetic glance at her. Brandon seemed amused, but he didn't say anything.

They reached the lookout point soon. It was a deck with a rail and a sign that said: "Native Valley: Home to the Kepler Aboriginal Species."

Nate leaned over the rail. "I can't see anything."

"That's because you're dumb," Bast said. "Look closer. The aboriginals constantly change how the light reflects off them. That's why we didn't even know there was an intelligent form of life on Kepler for so long. Normally, you have to catch them at just the right angle to see them, but here there are so many, they can't use the light to hide."

Nate stared out at the valley. "I still don't see anything."

Vivian didn't see anything either, except a pretty valley with faint glimmers of color that seemed to fly in the breeze.

"Don't focus so hard. Try to relax and see with your peripheral vision."

Nate flinched. "I can't do it. They're making too much noise."

Bast looked at Nate like he'd grown an extra ear. "What are you talking about? The aboriginals are silent, and even if they talked, we'd be too far away to hear."

"Or maybe you can't hear them because *you're* dumb," Nate said. "*Listen closer.*"

Vivian resisted scolding them for acting like kids and instead walked toward Brandon, who was standing at the other end of the deck, holding a cardboard box to his face.

"Can you see anything?" she asked.

He removed the box from his eyes. "It's amazing. But this viewfinder helps. It tricks your brain into looking beyond what you would normally see." He handed it to her. "Here. Try it."

She took it from him and looked through it.

"Can you see anything yet?"

"No." She pulled the box away from her eyes. "And I can't hear anything either."

Brandon grinned. "Prince Nathanial's making that up to mess with Prince Bastian. The natives hardly make any noise. Supposedly they communicate entirely telepathically with each other." He pointed to the box. "May I?"

She handed it back to him. He stepped around her and put it to her eyes again. "Hold it like this." She held the box, and their fingers overlapped briefly before his hands dropped away.

"Now find one spot in the valley to focus on. Then just walk back and try to keep looking at that one spot."

"I'll run into something!"

He put his hands on her arms. "It'll only be me."

The thought of running into him was at least as nerve-wracking as the thought of running into something else. She didn't tell him that, of course, but he seemed to figure it out. She took baby steps until he said, "this is never going to work" and pulled her straight back into him.

"There. Now you don't have to worry."

She giggled like Nate's waitress—she couldn't help it— and it took two more tries with Brandon's aid before the aboriginal community shimmered into her vision. It looked like a crystal city, with fuzzy, colorful streaks whizzing between crystal spires like someone was painting in the sky. "Whoa." She tilted the viewer up and down to try to see everything while she leaned against Brandon. "I've never seen anything so gorgeous."

She felt him hum. "Me neither."

"Viv! Nate and I want to see the next lookout point," Bast called.

She winced at the reminder that her brothers were still right there, and quickly put space between her and Brandon.

Bast looked impatiently at her, but Nate looked apologetic again. "Bast, how about you and I go on without Viv?" he suggested. "Captain Thurlow can stay with her. She'll get tired at our pace."

"We can slow down," Bast offered, but Nate elbowed him and coughed like he was trying to send a message.

"It's no problem, sir," Brandon said. "If Viv—" He flushed. "If the queen doesn't mind."

Vivian looked hard at Bast. "I *really* don't mind."

Nate was now trying to pull an innocent look, while something dawned on Bast's face.

"Very well, Captain," Bast said slowly. "Nate and I will circle the valley, and you'll accompany the queen as far as she'd like to go."

Vivian thought maybe she would forgive Nate for being Nate.

Brandon's father had been in the Guard, and his grandfather had too, and they'd lived in Alighieri for generations. No one in his family had any gifts, but they'd always thought his grandmother might tend hot because of how fast she could whip up a pot of tea.

He told Vivian that and a dozen more stories about his family while they walked leisurely together, and he let Vivian borrow the viewer box at every lookout point. They made it to four points before she was too tired to go further. When Bast and Nate came back around, she and Brandon were sitting on a blanket in a spot where they could look down on the valley together. They'd just finished a late picnic lunch, and Vivian was getting sleepy.

Bast saw her yawn. "We have plans for tonight, too. Maybe you should take a nap, so you'll be rested later." He made a face, but Nate nudged him with his elbow and Bast continued grimly: "If Captain Thurlow doesn't mind, perhaps we could impose on him again to stay with you while you rest."

The idea of being left to snuggle with Brandon sounded lovely, but Bast's willingness to help Vivian with her romance made her recall how sick she was. She stood up before she could sort out her motivations for why.

"That's okay. I'm used to napping in the coach." She smiled as nicely as she could at Brandon and hoped he wouldn't take this too badly. "Thanks for walking with me today."

He seemed mildly disappointed, but his facial expression was nothing compared to the twin looks Vivian got from Bast and Nate, who obviously thought she was crazy for deciding not to take advantage of unsupervised alone-time with the captain.

She did not explain herself to them. She napped soundly in the coach, though, and when she was woken a few hours later by an attendant, she did feel rested. Also, there was something going on. The attendant had a garment bag, and in it, there was a long, silky emerald-colored gown. Apparently, the princes wanted her to dress up. The attendant offered to help her and suggested a hairstyle that took an entire hour to complete.

When Vivian stepped out of the coach a while later, she

felt exactly like a queen, and she was greeted by her brothers both dressed in formal royal attire and looking like they were keeping a terrible secret.

"What did you do?" she asked suspiciously.

They shared pleased glances, and Vivian almost asked who they were and what they had done with her brothers. Then she heard music playing.

"Did someone spike my juice at lunch?"

"*No.*" Bast bowed. "Your Highness, may we escort you to your coronation ball?"

"My … what?"

"Your coronation ball," Nate said. He'd bowed too, but now he was smiling up at her like a lunatic. "You should have had one, but we never got to do it because … you know … near-death experience."

Bast grunted. "Because we were *otherwise occupied.* But it's time to celebrate now."

They led her to a sparsely wooded area nearby that had been transformed to look like a fairy queen's ballroom. There were lanterns strung between trees and a surprisingly well-controlled bonfire. The tables were adorned with ice sculptures. Two of the guards had guitars, and the group they were traveling with wasn't large, but everyone was dressed up.

Bast flourished his hand out. "Ta-da! Coronation ball!"

Vivian stood still. "But, I don't have a speech," was all she could say. Also, if she tried to say anything else, she thought she might cry. The boys laughed at her, though, and she thought maybe she'd given them the reaction they wanted.

"How did you do this?" she asked when she'd pulled herself together.

Bast plucked a speck of dust from his sleeve, preening with pride, and she noticed the light from the lanterns brightening his eyes. "Nate handled the food, and I did every-thing else."

"They made all your favorites," Nate said eagerly. "That crispy roast duck you think is so good with the drippings that go all over the sweet mash, and blue peas soaked in sauce—"

"And rolls," Vivian said, spotting a mountain of bread.

"And rolls," Nate confirmed. "Covered in butter."

Vivian didn't think she'd ever seen her brothers so excited. Bast could hardly keep from beaming at her. He grabbed Nate by the arm. "And when we're done eating—" They started hopping around in ridiculous, gleeful circles.

"Dancing!" Nate finished for him.

Sometimes Vivian didn't think her brothers were related. Then they did something like this, and they had to be broth-ers, and she hoped they were hers.

It was a fantastic party. The mood was festive, the air was warm, and the guards and attendants seemed to have been in on the surprise. Everyone applauded when Bast gave a toast "to the new queen!" and Captain Thurlow caught her eye and looked like he was admiring her dress.

After dinner, Bast and Nate took turns spinning Vivian around to the music until she was sure she'd pass out if she didn't sit. Then she watched them goof around while the rest of their party kept up the dancing, and the dusk moon started rising.

"You are going to dance more, aren't you?" Bast asked at a lull in the music.

"Sure," Vivian said, but she wasn't in a rush. She'd been perfectly happy watching all the loveliness, and she felt like she was in a very pleasant daze.

"You can't just dance with us, though," Nate said.

"Who else would I dance with?"

Nate shared a wicked grin with Bast. "Gee … I'm not sure." He was exaggerating the tone of his voice. "Bast, can you think of anyone Viv might want to dance with other than us?"

"I'm not sure either, Nate," Bast said with light glistening in his eyes. "We're the most dashing men here."

"Men," Vivian scoffed.

Bast sat down by her and put his arm around her shoulder. "We're wounded, Viv."

Nate crouched in front of her. "Terribly. But you do have other options. Like maybe …" He tilted his head subtly toward Brandon, who was chatting with his second-in-command.

She blushed. "Aren't you worried that he's a guard? He works for us."

"You think you can find a prince you're not related to instead?" Bast said.

"But isn't he too old for me?"

"Nope," Nate said. "I asked. He's only twenty-two."

Bast waved his hand in the air like age was no obstacle to love. "That difference is negligible. And we know you like him. Did you get in a fight with him already?"

She looked at her shoes. They were sparkly silver things that fit just right, and she did want to dance more. "No. I do like him. But I'm not sure it's fair to him, when I might …"

The boys sobered up.

"Isn't that all the more reason to go for it?" Nate asked after a while. "What if this *is* all the time you have? Don't you want to know what it's like to … you know?"

"To what?" Vivian asked forlornly. "Get rejected by some guy I like? Break his heart with my tragic early expiration?"

Bast gave her a light shove. "He meant to *kiss* someone."

Nate messed with a cuff on his sleeve that was

buttoned wrong.

"That wasn't exactly what I was thinking. But yeah, if you've never kissed someone, definitely that first."

"How did *you* ever get anywhere beyond kissing with anyone?" Bast demanded while Vivian tried hard *not* to imagine how that might have happened.

"I'm a prince who can talk to horses and puppy dogs," Nate told Bast. "You don't need to know the logistics, do you?" He turned to her. "You've kissed someone before, right, Viv? I understand if Bast hasn't, but you …"

"Yes, I have kissed someone!" Vivian said indignantly, thinking of a boy she'd ordered to kiss her after church when she was seven.

"Right," Nate said doubtfully. "Well. I bet you haven't done it the way you want to when you look at the captain."

Brandon looked their way right then. Bast and Nate waved merrily, and Vivian was so embarrassed he could probably see her face turn red from across the fairy ballroom.

"Why didn't I have sisters instead?" she moaned.

"Sisters wouldn't have been nearly as much fun," Bast said.

"Ooooh, look, he's coming over," Nate said.

Brandon must have been extremely courageous. When he got close enough to talk, he smiled and said, "Do you want to dance, Vivian?"

"Does she look like she's eighty?" Bast asked, pushing her up when she failed to answer. "Of course, she wants to dance!"

So, she danced with Brandon for a few songs. He told her a little shyly that she looked beautiful. Then she wanted to spend the rest of the evening finding out what it was like to kiss someone the way she wanted to kiss Brandon.

He obliged.

Bast was in a good mood the next morning. "They have private ferries at the ports at Great Crater Lake, and when we get off we'll be right down the road from New America," he told her. "No one has lived there since before the Cardinal Split, but All Saints' Cathedral is there. We have to see it. It's the oldest church ever built on Kepler, and it's where the All Saints' Rebellion happened. Our family led that, you know, and the Royal Church basically started because of it."

Nate was excited about New America, too. "I've been reading about pre-Cardinal history. The android nannies were programmed to be idealistic, so the first Kepler Mortals were the same. Do you know Earth was three times the size of Kepler, but only 1% of the land was undeveloped? That's why we work so hard to preserve Kepler's natural resources."

Vivian said, "hmm," because she was watching Brandon approach. When he got to her, he leaned down to kiss her lightly—on the mouth, right in front of everyone—and said, "Morning, Viv."

Her damned brothers burst into laughter.

"We need to head out," Brandon said. "Our scouts still think we're being trailed, and one of our best told me she thinks it might be Empire Immortals this time. Want to ride with me today, Vivian?"

"If we're being followed by Empire Immortals, she'd be safer in the coach," Bast warned.

"But she wants to ride with Brandon," Vivian said. "And she's the queen, so she will."

"And that, Captain, is the benefit of *dating* the queen," Nate said.

The queen was happy.

EXCERPT FROM *MEA CULPA: EARTH'S INTERGALACTIC MESS UP*

It may be that the temptation of immortal life will always be too strong for ordinary precaution. In the beginning, scientists foolishly believed that red eyes were the only negative consequence to the Immortality Virus, and we Earthlings were so excited about it that numerous programs sprang up to take advantage of the massive increase in human lifespan. Immortal cities were planned, a version of the Immortality Virus was tested on pets, and spaceships were redesigned to accommodate Immortal astronauts. Those programs were sending enthusiastic Immortals out into the galaxy decades before anyone knew better.

The damage the Immortality Virus does to its victims' ability to empathize didn't become obvious on Earth until patterns of cruel, selfish, reckless behavior began to emerge in the first Immortals, long after their hundredth birthdays. The Immortality Programs were immediately shut down. Immortals were restricted to Immortal cities with high-security borders. Scientists worked to develop treatments to reverse the damage, while lawsuits claiming billions of dollars in damages were filed against the manufacturers of the virus.

The Immortal Ships were called back to Earth as well, but it was too late. Most refused to return. In a desperate attempt to correct our intergalactic mistake, the Nanny Ships were developed. Designed to be nimble arks of mortal Earth life and armed with android "nannies" programmed to raise humans born from cryogenically frozen embryos on other planets, the Nanny Ships launched hundreds of years after the Immortal Ships but landed on their destination planets hundreds of years sooner.

The hope was that the Mortal humans born from those ships could be raised to protect alien planets from the Immortals bound for them. Fifteen planets were chosen for human colonization, and the Nanny Ships eventually reached twelve of those planets. Immortal Ships made it to two of the planets the Nanny Ships never reached and ten of the planets the Nanny Ships did reach. Of the ten planets where Mortal humans and Immortal humans coexist, there are only three on which Mortal humans are still in power. On two of those planets, that victory is attributable to an alliance between Mortal humans and an intelligent alien species.

The planet Kepler is the only exception. There, the development of extrasensory capabilities in humans or "magic" as the Mortals like to call it—is the factor that tips the scales. The Kepler Mortals are also uniquely committed to a set of moral standards, which they call the Kepler Declaration of Mortal Commitments. However, as of our last communication with Kepler, magic on Kepler was declining, and the Immortals were on the rise. It remains to be seen whether the Keplerian Mortals can hold their ground. If not, further intervention may be required.

CHAPTER TWENTY-NINE
MIGUELA SPEAKS OUT

The ferry rides across Great Crater Lake were overnight ordeals. For five hundred dollars, Carina, Miguela, and Max could rent a private sleeper cabin for the trip. A hundred and twelve dollars a person would buy them bunks in first-class. For eighty each, they could have seats that reclined in coach.

But it was still going to be a hike to the Mountain of Peril after they crossed the lake, and Miguela was now controlling their money, so they bought second-class tickets for twenty-five dollars apiece. That gave them access to all three of the ferry's lower levels, where hard benches were nailed down in rows or they could fight for a limited supply of dirty mats to sleep on wherever they could find space.

"Those mats have to be crawling with bugs," Carina said, watching as a man with a greasy beard hefted three away from the pile. "No way am I sleeping on one of those. Our wool blankets are fine."

"Our wool blankets are filthy," Miguela pointed out.

"Yeah, but we know where that filth came from," Carina said.

Still, their clothes were crusty, their backpacks were grimy, and those wool blankets were at such a high level of gross that Sister Lindy probably would have voted to burn them. Carina attempted to rub a streak of dirt off her sleeve and succeeded only in smearing it.

"Maybe we can find a place to do laundry in one of the next towns," she suggested.

"I checked out the map this morning," Max said. "We're going to pass through New America not long after we get off the ferry. Let's find a laundromat there."

Miguela gave Carina a *look*. Carina cringed. New America was ancient, and it was considered a historically preserved site. You could visit as a tourist, but no one lived there.

"We can't do laundry in New America," Miguela said.

Max was offended. Carina could tell from the way his eyes glassed up and his lips pursed out. She hooked her arm around his. "He's a biologist, Miguela. Not a geographer."

His face relaxed immediately as a wide smile brightened it, and he leaned her way to kiss her cheek with a loud smacking sound. Carina stiffened briefly—there were a lot of people on the ferry and it made her uncomfortable for Max to do something like that in public—but she forced herself to loosen up when he said quietly: "Thanks, Care."

Miguela made a frustrated noise so loud it drew the attention Carina hadn't wanted. "Are you two going to make out the whole time we're on this thing?" she asked spitefully.

Carina flushed. "That's not your—"

"We might," Max said. "Why?"

"Then I'm going down a level to sleep," Miguela announced. "Do not follow me. I'm seasick already. If I catch

Carina with her face glued to yours, I might vomit."

Carina and Max found a dark corner no one else was occupying, spread their dirty-but-probably-insect-free blankets together on the ground, and Max pulled her close to him and said: "As long as we know there's no way your sister's going to show up, I think we should make out as much as we want."

"Do we have to refer to it as 'making out?'" Carina asked. "When you say it that way, I feel like I'm doing something wrong."

He caressed her jaw, drawing her face toward him. "You're not doing anything wrong," he assured her. But she thought it was a good thing Miguela had decided to claim another level of the ferry as her own. She would never have approved of the way Max's hands had started to travel while they kissed.

Miguela was in a foul mood the next morning when they disembarked. Her hair was frizzy and matted in the back, and her shirt was extra wrinkly. Laundry was for sure a priority.

"I hate public ferries," she complained as they began their hike again toward the Mountain of Peril. "I was sick all night, the bathrooms were sludge pits, and I saw at least ten Red-Eyed Ones. I couldn't sleep at all. We need to be careful."

"I didn't see anyone with red eyes," Carina said. She glanced sideways at Max, who sent a goofy smile back. Neither of them had slept much either, but *their* ferry ride had been perfectly pleasant—dirty blankets and all.

Miguela held her backpack straps with two hands and scowled down at the cracked pavement they were walking. Technically, they were in the North now, but roads that would have been maintained by the Northern Kingdom were now under Southern rule. Repaving must not have been a priority for Queen Vivian.

"I didn't see anyone with red eyes either," Max said. "Is that the only way you can tell if someone's Immortal?"

Carina thought Max was refreshingly willing to think outside of his own limited knowledge. Her sister obviously thought his brain was limited. Miguela shot laser eyes at Max. "Yes. Unless *you* know some other way?"

He shrugged. "No. If you saw Immortals on the boat, though, we should all stay alert."

Miguela didn't respond, and when a group of riders on horseback passed shortly after, she tensed like she was getting ready to run. "Were those Red-Eyed Ones?" she asked.

"Relax, Miguela. They were Mortals," Carina assured her, but Miguela only responded by demanding to know if she'd done magic on the ferry.

When Miguela didn't believe the "no" Carina shot back defensively, Max stood up for her. "She didn't. No floating and no freezing." He waved his hands through the air, then pantomimed a shiver.

"I have a bad feeling about this anyway," Miguela said. "I *know* I saw Red-Eyed Ones on the ferry, and Carina does magic accidentally sometimes. They could be following us."

Max sidestepped toward Miguela and nudged her elbow. "You don't need to worry so much." He patted the gun at his hip. "I still have this. And Carina is getting better at magic. I bet she's not doing it accidentally nearly as much as she used to."

Miguela jabbed her elbow sharply at him. "Carina knows nothing about magic." Her voice crackled with anger. "And you don't know anything about anything."

Carina was relieved when they arrived at a wall of cobbled rocks that marked New America's outermost border later that day and Miguela seemed to perk up. Her eyes darted curiously from one abandoned building to the next as they walked a tourist's route through the town.

Max was also intrigued. "Guess I'm a lot better with a microscope than I am with a map," he said as he stopped to examine a spring-green grassnewt clinging vertically to an ancient lamppost. "I wish I had some way to collect a few of these as samples to study."

"A whole city of ancient ruins, and you notice the grass-newts," Miguela commented.

"I'm looking at other things, too," Max said. "Have you guys seen how the buildings get more rudimentary as we get closer to the center of town? Look at that—" He gestured toward an ugly square building with concrete walls. At some point the walls had been painted, perhaps in colorful murals, but the paint had mostly faded and worn off by now. A wood sign in front read: "Bank of New America."

"The stores we passed near the city walls were all bricked," Max continued. "These are made of materials that wouldn't require as much labor. But check out the sewer grates. They're the same everywhere."

Miguela crouched down to examine a grate but did not deign to reply to Max. When she stood up, she turned in a full circle, like she was sweeping the area for the phantom Red-Eyed Ones she thought were chasing them.

Carina sighed. They hadn't seen *anyone* for the last hour or so. New America wasn't a popular tourist destination. Most of the people on the ferry had probably taken the road north from the port toward the lakes.

She carried on the conversation with Max herself, trying

to recall what she'd learned in Sister Rachel's history lessons about early Keplerian architecture. "The first Mortals were working from Earth blueprints, right? They must have improved as they developed. But sewers would have been a priority to keep people from getting sick."

"Whoa. That's not rudimentary," Max said, his eyes widening as they came upon an enormous church with a beautiful stone-bricked facade, tall double doors, spires that stretched up to the sky in sharp points, and a dome with a steeple rising above everything. Max pointed to a row of concrete angels standing and demons crouched between the front spires. "Those are incredible. What religion do you think they were practicing here?"

Religion was one subject Sister Rachel had never spent much time on with Carina and Miguela. "Rachel's a Southerner," Sister Raji had explained once. "But she's Immortal Jewish, not Universal Orthodox like the Damn Royal Church of South Kepler thinks everyone should be. It's a sore subject for her. You can be arrested in South Kepler for being Immortal Jewish, even if you're a Mortal, and if that happens, they turn you over to the Immortal Empire. Rachel was forced to flee after one of her colleagues reported her."

Carina thought Max might secretly be fleeing South Kepler himself—that would explain some things—so she was nervous about offending him. "Everything in New America predates the Cardinal Split, so maybe Universalism?" she said cautiously.

Miguela stared at the church and muscles protruded in her cheeks as she clenched her jaw. "It's All Saints' Cathedral." She tilted her nose into the air and looked down from there at Carina. "First church ever built on Kepler? Place where all the android nannies were sealed after the All Saints' Massacre?

Do you pay attention in any of the history lessons?"

Max frowned. "Sealed? You mean they were buried here? Is there a cemetery behind this thing?"

Miguela looked at him like he was an idiot. "Clearly you didn't pay attention to any of your history lessons either. No. The nannies were sealed in the crypts below the cathedral after their programming malfunctioned and they killed a little girl with a gun. Don't you know the story of All Saints' Massacre?"

Max turned slowly toward Miguela, crossed his arms like hers were now crossed, and steadied his eyes on her. "Maybe I haven't paid enough attention to Kepler history," he said with a somber note to his voice. "They *killed* a kid?"

Carina eyed the cathedral again as the story came back to her, and she noticed that the stairs were tarnished and the lower layers of stone on the facade were blackened.

"There's a reason Mortals don't use guns," Miguela said. "The nannies had extreme programming, and when religious leaders started to emerge amongst the Mortals, the nannies took it as a threat and tried to eliminate the leaders. With guns. From Earth."

Max examined the church again. "Wait ... so those little holes are from a gun fight?"

Miguela delayed her response as Carina noticed the holes sprinkled all over the church and a shattered stain-glassed window.

"Yeah," Miguela finally said. "You're probably standing right where Isolde Wellington died. She was younger than I am. And her mother ..."

Carina recalled the rest of the story now. "Oh, and that's when Mortals started thinking of the Wellingtons as an especially powerful genetic line, right? The burn marks everywhere are because Isolde's mother literally exploded or something."

"She caused an explosion," Miguela said flatly. "It destroyed all the nannies there and killed a lot of innocent Mortals. Then all the functioning nannies that hadn't been there were rounded up and sealed in the crypts below All Saints' Cathedral with the ones that were destroyed in the explosion. It's all very creepy, and I'm really uncomfortable, and there could still be Red-Eyed Ones following us. Can we go? I don't like this place."

Carina opened her mouth to say "sure," but Max interrupted. "All the nannies are still down there? We have to go inside."

"We *can't*," Miguela said. "The doors are *locked*."

Max pulled on the doors again. "No. I want to see the crypts," he said stubbornly. "And I don't think the doors *are* locked. They're just heavy, and they haven't been opened in a while." He let go of the doors. "I bet Carina can do it with magic."

"I don't know if I can," Carina said. "They look heavy."

Miguela shook her head several times. "No. Carina. You *can't*. This is a bad idea. Please, let's go."

"It's a great idea. Come on, Carina," Max encouraged. "All you have to do is slide them out. I'll pull too if you promise not to knock me out accidentally with your mind."

Miguela glowered at him. "Did you *hear* what you just said? Carina has powerful magic that she *doesn't know how to use!* We have no idea what she could do if she tries something that's too much for her!"

"It's not that dangerous," Max said. "What's the worst that could happen? She freezes the doors?"

"What if she freezes *everything*? Some people can kill with cold."

Max laughed. "Carina's not going to freeze us to death."

"What if she does?"

"Then we'll have no idea it happened."

"But—"

Carina rolled her eyes. It was unlikely that she was going to freeze something to death. Anyway, the sun was scorching hot today. Even she felt a little sweaty. "I'm not *that* strong, Miguela. If the doors are locked, I probably won't be able to do anything with them. If not, maybe we'll be able to see inside."

"Carina, no—"

Carina ignored Miguela and thought about reaching out to the doors with her own energy like she did when she wanted to move something smaller. She tried to pull back on the handles, but they wouldn't budge.

"Wait, were you doing it?" Max asked. He braced against the doors like he was ready for them to burst open. "Try again. I'll pull at the same time."

"*Stop*," Miguela pleaded as Carina nodded at Max and attempted to get a grip on the doors once more.

"Ready?" Max asked.

Carina took a deep breath, and then let it all out at once as Max suddenly fell back from the door. She was going to run over to him, until Miguela said the thing that made everything change:

"I have magic, too."

Carina pivoted toward her sister. "You have what?"

Miguela bit her lip and Carina's backpack flew away from them.

Carina's mind whirled. Miguela had magic. Miguela was *telekinetic.*

"How long have you been able to do that for?"

"Forever." A breeze blew a loose curl from Miguela's bun, and she tried to tuck it back behind her ear while she continued staring at the ground.

Carina looked at the backpack now sitting several meters away. Max was standing up and dusting himself off. Had that been Miguela? She hadn't even moved her hand.

"Do you have to try at all?"

"Not really," Miguela said to the dirt.

Something burned in Carina's chest. "Why ... why didn't you tell me? All this time you've been ... what ... a natural magical savant? And you didn't want me to learn anything?"

Miguela looked up again. There were tears in her eyes. "It's *dangerous*. I don't want you to be able to do something *dangerous*."

Carina didn't really care. *Her* whole body was shaking. "What's *dangerous* is having a skill you don't know how to use. You should have helped me. I've been kidnapped *twice*. And when those royals threatened to go after you, I was *afraid*. I thought if they found you, they would hurt you, but if we both knew magic, we could have fought them—"

"*No!* We couldn't! You don't understand!" Miguela's face was now flushed, but she was clenching her arms so tightly to herself that the skin at her elbows had turned white.

"*What* don't I understand?" Carina shouted back. "This isn't a hobby to me, Miguela! And it doesn't matter if you think it's dangerous! If we can both do it, then we both need to know how to do it well because—"

"*I killed them!*" Miguela screamed, and a cloud of dust burst up around her.

And *that* made everything in Carina freeze over again. "What are you talking about?"

Tears streamed down Miguela's face. "When the Red-Eyed

Ones were there. In the barn. When we were little. *I* killed them. That man with the sword. He was going to hurt Mom, and Eugene was crying, and Dad was too far away, and I …"

She paused to hastily wipe her eyes.

"It wasn't just telekinesis. I can make things hot. Really hot. That explosion … that was *me*. I didn't even know I had that much magic, and I couldn't control it. Then I passed out, and when I woke up, everyone was dead." Miguela's next words were preceded by a heartbroken sob. "*I killed them.* I killed our family."

All the anger had dissolved from Carina, but she didn't know what to say. "You were *seven*. We were being *attacked*. You're not responsible for what happened," she tried, feeling as though what she was saying was woefully inadequate. How had her sister been holding all that pain?

Miguela backed a few steps away, wiping tears from her cheeks with her thumbs. "Yes, I am. It was *my* magic that caused the explosion. Mom, Dad, and Eugene *died*. Magic is *dangerous,* Carina, and I don't care if you hate me for not wanting you to use it. I don't ever want you to do something you'll regret forever because I know what that's like and it's not good."

Whatever had happened wasn't Miguela's fault. Carina was *sure* of it. And this had to be why Miguela had taken everything so much worse than she had. Her wounds weren't clean. But she was so so so wrong about anything being her fault. Nothing about what had happened the night the Red-Eyed Ones had attacked their family was Miguela's fault.

"But … your magic wasn't the reason—" she began, unsure of how to explain any of that to a sister who had lived with what had to be overwhelming guilt for years.

Miguela's face fell. Then it tightened again as she clenched her fists. "I know. You still don't care what I think. You still think magic is fine. I'm only your little sister who doesn't know anything. But one day, you're going to find out you *don't* know everything yourself. And when that happens? *I'm* not going to care how *you* feel."

"Miguela—"

"No!" Miguela yelled, her face a mix of disgust and hurt. "I'm done talking about this. If you won't listen to me, I don't want to hear what you have to say."

"Miguela!" Carina shouted as her sister stalked away after that, disappearing around a corner before Carina knew what else she should do.

"Care?" Max said quietly. "I'd like to hug you. But—" he pulled his sleeves over his hands. "—you look a little cold."

Carina felt her cheek and realized that her tears were freezing. "Miguela's right," she said. "I don't know what I'm doing."

CHAPTER THIRTY
ALL SAINTS' CATHEDRAL

"Can you turn it off?" Max asked.

Carina laughed humorlessly. "No idea."

Something inside her was quaking with fear, and she wasn't even sure she could label what she was afraid of. That things had just changed between her and Miguela for the worse? That Miguela was right about magic? That Miguela would never be okay? No matter what Carina said or did?

"Do you think you can get so cold you freeze yourself solid?"

Her teeth were chattering too much for her to answer. She looked helplessly at Max. He looked helplessly at her.

"Maybe we should walk," she suggested.

"Right! You can't end up frozen stiff if you're moving." He reached for her arm but pulled back like he'd thought better of it first. "Uh, let's walk around the church."

Carina's joints were stiff as she followed him. There was a side door to the church that they hadn't been able to see from the front. Max walked up to it. "Come on, you need a distraction. Maybe we can open this one."

"I don't feel like using magic right now, Max," Carina said.

He waved his hands in the air. "No! I know! You don't have to. Just help me push it."

Carina went unenthusiastically to help. "Do you think Miguela will be okay?"

"I don't know her like you do. But this explains some things, right?" Max said reasonably. He pointed to a rail on the door. "You hold there." He put his hands on the other side. "When I say three, push."

She held the rail. "I wish she would have told me. Why do you think she didn't?"

"I don't know, but she cares about you a lot. You should see her when she's worried about you. Ready to try the door? One, two—"

Carina didn't feel like going inside now, but she followed instructions, and on three, the door swung open like it hadn't even been locked and she and Max fell into the church.

Max scurried away from her.

She stood up and dusted herself off. "Sorry. Did I hurt you?"

Max was feeling up and down his body. After what seemed like a thorough assessment, he smiled. "Ice free." He rubbed his forehead. "Phew! I was worried that if I accidentally touched you, you might literally turn me to ice. But you're just kind of chilly."

"Glad to hear it," Carina said sarcastically. She wandered into the church. They had come in somewhere near the front in a hallway that opened to a larger cathedral. She went slow, waiting for her eyes to adjust to the dark, but the dome was stained glass, and there were several long, narrow windows along the side of the church that let in natural light. Soon

Carina could see pews and what she thought might be an archaic altar.

Max walked down an aisle between the pews staring with his neck stretched back at the vaulted ceilings. "This is really impressive. Do you think the Mortals that built it used magic?"

"I don't think they had magic back then." Thinking of magic made Carina think more about Miguela. No trail of ice had followed her into the church, but now she had to rub her hands together to stay warm.

"Look at those." Max pointed to some frescos painted on the church walls. A few were of angels and demons, like the statues outside, but there was a whole set telling a mythological story of the universe. A committee meeting of gods in heaven looked down over an inky expanse. An especially colorful god with a lot of jewelry rose above the rest and created a planet of blue, white, and green. Naked people hung out on a boat with weird animals, and the colorful god threw ships of humans into the stars.

"None of the animals look right," Carina said. "Except for the horses."

"And the dogs." Max nodded at a pair of dogs sitting by the naked people. "Because that panel shows Earth animals, not Kepler animals. But you'd need my kind of background in biology to know. Where do you think those crypts are?"

He turned back up the aisle and headed toward the altar, running his finger through a layer of dust on the pews as he went. She wanted to tell him not to do that, and she didn't know why. He climbed up into a raised pulpit that she hadn't noticed before. For some reason, it didn't feel okay that he'd done that.

"Get down from there, Max."

"Why? Who's going to know I'm here?" He looked out

over the church. "Do you see a door or anything?"

Carina wanted to look for Miguela, not a bunch of ancient tombs. She started walking to the side door. Max clambered down the pulpit and bounded toward her. "You're not mad at me, are you?"

She was in a bad mood, but she couldn't think of a reason she should be mad at him.

"I just want to leave," she said.

And then the heavy doors at the back of the church creaked.

She and Max looked at the doors together.

"Do you think that's Miguela out there?" Max asked nervously.

"She was the one who said no magic," Carina said. "And I don't think she could have opened that with her hands."

"Maybe it wasn't as stuck as we thought. Or it's the wind."

There had been no breeze outside before. Carina tried to work up the nerve to take another step toward the side door. Then it opened, someone took a few steps in, and a cold, lazy voice echoed through the church from that direction.

"I guess you just can't stay out of trouble, can you?" it said.

She heard louder steps after that, followed by a more grating voice. "What am I doing wrong *now*? Where's the light switch? God, why don't these places ever install solar panels?" Firelight flashed through the room, and both Prince Bastian and Prince Nathanial came into view at once. "Hey, Bast—" Prince Nathanial started, and then he saw her and Max. "Oh damn," he said. "And here I thought today was going to be a good day."

"Okay, maybe we should all learn how to do a proper greeting," Max said. "I'll start. I'm Max, and I'm—"

Carina telekinetically shoved a stack of books that had been sitting in a corner toward the two princes and grabbed

Max's hand. "We're not doing introductions." She pulled him to the back of the church toward the doors they hadn't been able to open. She was frantic now, and adrenaline was pumping through her body. Maybe if she tried again …

A burst of fire swept over their heads.

Max yelled and dove to the ground. Carina scrambled for cover behind one of the pews and peeked up just in time to see another ball of flames whoosh toward her. She tucked her head down. The pew behind her became a spectacular wall of fire.

"Nate! This is *All Saints' Cathedral*!" Prince Bastian yelped. "What are you doing?"

"I'm pinning them in," Prince Nathanial said as Carina ran toward Max, who was cowering behind a pew on the other side of the aisle. She didn't make it before the aisle went up in flames like someone had poured lamp oil on it and lit a match.

Prince Bastian looked almost as horrified as Carina felt. "Don't use *fire*, you idiot! You'll destroy the whole place!"

"This is controlled fire," Prince Nathanial said, and the pew two rows in front of Carina lit up, too. She was boxed in on three sides. She ran for the other end of the pew but didn't make it before a wall of fire sprang up there. There was no smoke, but Carina could feel the heat from all four sides.

"Carina?" Max shouted. "Are you okay? I can't see you!"

She crouched back down. "Go, Max! I'll find you later!"

"Like *hell* am I leaving you with these psychos!"

The psycho that could produce *fire* strode through it down the aisle and stopped at her pew. "It's Carina? For some reason, I was thinking you would be an Amanda or, like, a Felicity."

She moved toward the opposite end of the pew again and

reached experimentally toward the fire. If he could touch it, maybe she could. She could not. She yanked her hand back.

"Yep. It's *hot*," Prince Nathanial said from his end. He was leaning on the edge of the pew now like he was far superior to her and she entertained him. "And I can walk through it because I control it. But if you try that, you'll end up burned to a crisp."

He'd said "hot" like she was a child that needed to learn how not to touch an iron. She looked at the fire again and had an idea. She might not be able to touch it without getting burned, but she'd unintentionally iced over everything around her only half an hour ago. She held out her hand and willed the fire to cool.

Nothing happened. Prince Nathanial laughed, and Prince Bastian appeared at the other end of the pew. He looked past Carina to his brother. "I cannot believe you set the pews in All Saints' Cathedral on fire," he snarled. Then he looked back at her. "And you *ruined* those books. Those were *sacred texts*."

"I can't decide which of you I hate more," Carina said, but she targeted a row of vases behind Prince Bastian that looked ornamental, and with one great effort she heaved them all at him telekinetically.

Prince Bastian saw them coming, but only in time to hurl them back in the other direction. The vases smashed against the wall.

Prince Nathanial laughed harder. "Bast! What were you thinking? Those were *sacred*!"

Prince Bastian gave Carina a look that might have been furious or awed, and said, "You've been practicing."

She *had* been practicing, but she was still blocked in by the two princes. She looked around for something else to throw. She'd done okay with those vases. There were thick books in pocket shelves on the back of all the pews. She picked one up. Prince Nathanial was still laughing. She thought of trying to use telekinesis again, but he wasn't that far away, and she didn't think she had that much magical control. She threw the book as hard as she could at him instead with her arm.

It hit him in the face.

He yelled, and the fire he'd been standing in died down. She didn't think she was going to get another chance, so she charged forward, hoping that with enough force, maybe she could push right by him.

He grabbed her arm and spun her wildly back toward him.

"What is your problem!?" he shouted.

"Let me *go*!" she shouted back, kicking at him and struggling to get out of his grip. There were going to be bruises on her arm.

"*Make* me. And good luck. This time you can't surprise me with your stupid ice trick."

"You are an extremely rude person." She could feel herself getting cold again. She hoped it would hurt if she froze him. He only glared intensely at her, and suddenly the place where he was gripping her arm was scorching hot.

Carina cried out, but she thought maybe she'd won that round because all at once he cried out, too, and shoved her away hard.

"Oh, for heaven's sake, Nate!" Prince Bastian yelled, and Carina realized he'd occupied himself putting out pew fires instead of helping Prince Nathanial. "Did you let her win?"

"No!" Prince Nathanial yelled. "I didn't *let* her win! I'm *not* the one that *likes* her!"

Carina looked for Max, but before she could figure out where he'd gone, Prince Nathanial flung her down past the pews. She landed painfully near the back doors but managed to throw another vase at Prince Nathanial as he stalked toward her.

He blocked it. It shattered on the ground. She tried to scramble up again, but her ankle had twisted, and all she could do was scoot. She'd hardly gotten anywhere before he was hovering over her. He put his hand up, and a sword flew to him from a nearby statue of a guardian angel. How had she failed to notice that when she'd been looking for something to throw at him?

He held the sword above her. "You are *such* a pain in the ass." The sword lit on fire. "Why can't you just hold still?"

The floor around Carina completely froze over. She heard Max yell for her again. She heard Prince Bastian yell at Prince Nathanial again (presumably because the sword was sacred). She *hated* Prince Nathanial, and she thought he might be about to kill her. But she didn't have much time to consider the latter because several things happened rapidly then:

First, Queen Vivian—who Carina had not seen come in—screamed: "Nate! No!"

Second, Max—who Carina had not seen stand up—yelled: "You bastard!"

Third, Prince Nathanial dropped the sword. He seemed a little stunned as blood spurted from his shoulder.

The queen screamed louder and ran toward them. Prince Bastian did the same, without the scream. Max, however, had also run toward Carina, and he was holding his gun out. He grabbed her arm and pulled her up. "Come on, we have to go."

Prince Bastian spared a moment to look at them. "What are you doing with a *gun?*" he asked, but his mouth fell open and his eyes widened as Max pointed the gun at *him*.

"Don't try anything," Max ordered. "Or I'll shoot you too. Just let us walk out."

Queen Vivian looked up at Carina. "We're Mortals!" she shrieked. "We don't carry *guns*! And we certainly don't shoot other Mortals with them!"

"What is *wrong* with you people?" Max said. "How is a gun worse than a fiery sword?"

"It was just a threat!" Queen Vivian yelled. "He was only—"

Prince Bastian interrupted her. "He's not a Mortal."

"What are you talking about?" Queen Vivian asked frantically, looking at Prince Nathanial again as if to check for signs of immortality on her brother.

But Prince Bastian looked directly at Carina. "He is *not* a Mortal," he repeated.

Max tensed next to her. "Shut up," he said sharply.

"Look at his eyes," Prince Bastian said. "*Now.*"

"Care—" Max said.

She didn't want to, but she turned anyway to look Max in the eye. There was just enough light for her to see what color they were.

Red.

"I thought your eyes were blue," she said dumbly.

"I can explain," he said.

"I don't think you need to explain." She yanked herself away from him and hobbled toward the door on her own. The sunlight hit her hard as she exited the church. She didn't see Miguela. She didn't see anyone. Max came out behind her.

"Please, Carina. I would never hurt you—"

His eyes were even brighter red in the sunlight.

"I need to find my sister," she said.

"I'll come with you," he said. "I'll protect you."

She looked at the gun, held limply at his side, and thought about the wolves and the blood gushing out of Prince

Nathanial's arm and the other Red-Eyed Ones Max had killed. She thought of the Red-Eyed Ones that had attacked her family and the ones that had thrown her in that truck. She thought of the stories Max had told her about himself and all the things he should have known that he didn't.

She thought of how Max had been at Novi Dupree the same day the other Red-Eyed Ones had found them ...

Miguela had said they couldn't trust him.

"Don't get any closer," Carina said. "We're done."

E. DUPREE PERSONAL LOG #498635

Raji *drinks* while she drives the cart and thinks nothing of it because there is no Mortal Commitment against drinking and driving. A few millennia should be enough to make you forget things like traffic accidents and DUIs, but Anna bailed me out three times before I was twenty-five. She probably wrote several poems about it; I know she wrote at least one novel, back when she was going through her dark, writer days.

I was afraid for Anna all the time during that phase of her life—the things she knew about subjects such as exsanguination and postmortem art—but I didn't truly understand darkness until after she left me. The day before she killed herself, she spent the whole afternoon in a hammock, sipping spring water and soaking in the warmth of the Kepler sun.

"It's so much better than the Earth sun, isn't it, Lizzy?" she said to me, and I grumbled back that it could be warmer in the winter, because I was going through a quiet-dissatisfaction-with-everything phase, and I thought she was fine.

Then she asked me "how I did it."

I'll never forget.

"How do you stay so joyful when you're so irritated with the world in so many ways?" were her exact words. So, I told her. I can't be content. It's impossible for me. My mind won't do it. If nothing could get better, I would be so bored.

At that, she looked out away from me—maybe at something she didn't think could get much better—and then she looked back at me and almost smiled. She said, "I hope you never get bored, Lizzy."

Those were her last words to me.

I am not bored right now. Raji just took a mountain curve so fast I thought she'd lose control of the cart. When she isn't trashed on lager, she's a careful driver. Painfully slow, even. But I suppose she's in a hurry now. I support her in the rush, at least. The girls are some of my favorite Mortals yet, and I don't mind interfering in cases like this.

Myles would have a heart attack.

No. He wouldn't. Myles is too healthy for that, and his heart is too strong. It's nearly impenetrable, in fact. I would know.

Raji curses in an odd mix of Indian and Russian that would have offended both populations on Earth. I'm not good with languages, and I don't understand much of what she adds to the cursing, except that I catch Agda's name in there a few times.

I've asked her if she wants me to drive, but she says if I drive, we'll never catch up.

Maybe I'll shut my eyes for a while.

CHAPTER THIRTY-ONE
MAGICAL FATIGUE

All the color was draining from Nate's face and pooling in a puddle of blood by his shoulder. Vivian had told him at least six times he was going to be fine. Bast could heal this. This was not going to kill Nate.

Except Bast was taking his sweet time about it.

"How do you think that guy hid that from her?" he asked absently. He was kneeling by Nate and still looking toward the door from which the girl and the monster who'd shot Nate had left. "His eyes were bright red."

Nate groaned pathetically.

"Focus, Bast!" Vivian commanded. "Nate's hurt!"

Bast turned his head back and narrowed his eyes. "Viv, how many times do I have to tell you? You can't do magic! Stop transferring energy to him!"

Vivian hadn't realized she'd been doing that. She'd thought she was only clutching Nate's arm because she was so upset. Nate tried to pull away from her. She let go. He moaned.

"Don't be such a baby, Nate," Bast admonished. "It didn't

hit anything important."

Nate grimaced. "It hurts like a fu—"

Bast prodded at the wound, and Nate howled.

"What are you doing?" Vivian asked.

"Trying to find the bullet." Bast pushed Nate sideways and Nate's second howl echoed through the cathedral. "Hey, this is great luck," he said cheerfully with Nate's blood all over his hands. "The bullet went out the other side. This would have hurt much worse if I'd had to yank it out first."

"Could you just fix it, you jackass?" Nate said.

Vivian watched nervously, and Brandon touched her hand. She'd nearly forgotten he was even there. This was the first time she could ever remember having someone else around to support her during a family emergency.

"Where do you think he learned to talk like that?" Brandon whispered to her as Nate's torn flesh started knitting back together and Nate used his words to tell them it hurt. "He's worse than any of the Guard."

She wasn't sure where her brother had learned that from. She was sure she hated the Immortal who'd done this to Nate and sure this was taking too long. Bast should have been able to heal a bullet wound in minutes. Then they could have gone after the Immortal with the gun and made sure he would never shoot anyone again. Instead, they sat there on the hard stone floor of All Saints' Cathedral forever before Bast finally sat back.

"You're done." He wiped his hands on Nate's shirt. "It's going to be sore, and you lost a lot of blood, so you should take it easy for a few days."

"Thanks," Nate said begrudgingly. He sat up, and Vivian flew forward to hug him.

Then she remembered what had caused this in the first

place. New America was supposed to have been a pleasant stop on their way to the Mountain of Peril. Vivian, Brandon, Bast, and Nate had sent the rest of the caravan on a detour route because Bast said horses and coaches could do damage to historic sites. She'd strolled with Brandon right through town while Bast and Nate darted ahead under the pretense that they both just couldn't wait to see everything.

Really, she thought it was just that neither of them wanted to watch her and Brandon acting gooey sweet together, and Vivian didn't mind admitting that things with that were rising to a level of cute that was totally unprofessional for a queen. Brandon spent more time looking at her as they walked than he did looking at New America itself, and she ordered him to stop and kiss her every few blocks.

As one does when one is a queen.

Which all meant that Vivian was in a lovely, dazed state of mind when she walked into All Saints' Cathedral, and it came to an abrupt halt when she saw Nate standing by that girl with a sword over her head. She watched in complete horror as he set it on *fire* and an angry frost spun out around the girl on the floor. Then the girl's breath puffed into the air like she was breathing out the last warmth she had inside, and another connection materialized for Vivian.

A red line between Nate and the girl.

Vivian pulled back from him. "What were you doing with that sword!?"

Nate let her go and examined the new scar on his shoulder. "I was neutralizing the girl."

"It looked like you were going to hurt her."

"Good." Nate's face darkened momentarily, then he glanced back at Vivian and seemed to realize that had not been the right response. "I wasn't going to, though."

"Who cares if you were?" Bast asked. He had lain back on the floor like he was exhausted. "She's obviously a threat."

"We don't know that," Vivian said. "Was she obviously trying to hurt either of you? It seemed like she just wanted to get away."

"With her Immortal boyfriend." Bast sat up on his elbows. "I bet she's being tricked by a whole group of Immortals training her to be some kind of super weapon."

Nate laughed. "Carina's not *that* powerful."

"*Carina* was beating you."

"She was not!"

"Is that her name?" Vivian asked. "Carina?" It was strange how putting a name to a face changed how you felt about someone. She thought again about that red line.

"Are you okay?" Brandon asked her.

"Yeah," she answered, realizing uncomfortably that she'd practically forgotten Brandon was even there again. She wasn't okay, though. She wasn't okay because her family was not okay. The loyalty line between Nate and Brandon had been frightening enough in its own way, and that was a positive connection. Seeing a red connection like that between Nate and anyone was terrifying. That was not the red of attraction. That was the red of rage. It was a mortal enemy line. Nate did not need a mortal enemy.

"We should work on your defense," Bast was saying to Nate. "If that girl gets any stronger, she'll be able to take you out."

"She is not going to take me out," Nate said spitefully.

"Maybe if you never see her again," Bast said.

Nate only grunted in response.

Vivian couldn't decide if she should tell Nate about the mortal enemy line. She told Bast instead, the next time they were alone in the coach.

"So, what?" Bast said.

"So, I can't decide if he should know, and I think you should help him more with his magic."

"Why?"

"Because if he runs into the girl again and they fight, he might lose."

Bast had been sitting relaxed across from her. At that, he straightened up, leaned forward over his knees, and raised a suspicious eyebrow. "And the *real* reason is …?"

That first statement hadn't been a full lie. It was more like a half-lie. Because she *was* concerned that Nate would lose if he ran into Carina again and they got in a fight, but what Vivian was really worried about was that Nate was about to inherit a whole hell of a lot of problems that he wasn't equipped to handle. He needed better magic for more than just a fight with a single girl.

"Out with it, Viv."

She caved. "There's a loyalty line, too. Between him and Brandon. Like the ones I used to be able to see between Dad and his favorite royal guards."

Bast froze and the air in the coach chilled. "Are those lines predictive?"

"No," she admitted.

He immediately relaxed again. "Then this conversation is closed. Stop worrying about the lines. And stop trying to protect Nate from everything."

Bast was in denial. She'd also asked him a few times recently how often he was siphoning magical energy from himself and Nate to her—because she thought he might be doing extra transfers when she was asleep—but he would never give her a straight answer. She didn't like it. He was doing too much. She decided not to tell him when she noticed it was getting even harder for her to take deep breaths. She didn't want him doing more.

Anyway, mostly she just wanted the time she spent with him right now to be happy time. When they were next alone, she skipped talking about connections or magic and asked if there was anything he wanted to put on her agenda as queen regarding the Royal Church. And as it turned out, Vivian's brother had more than passion for the Royal Church of South Kepler.

He had plans.

"I'm not saying the Church has done anything wrong," he told her. "But our messaging is out-of-date, and we're losing our connection to the community. The Church should be in touch with the spiritual needs of the people."

There was this thing Bast did when he was truly engaged in a discussion where he would catch himself getting excited and it would almost seem like he was surprised himself that he could feel that way. When it happened, he would stop mid-thought, lean back, and look down at his lap. Then the corners of his mouth would lift, one at a time, before he shifted his gaze shyly back up, and for a second or so, the only thing in his eyes would be light.

He did exactly that after he told her about an idea he'd had to make the prayers more accessible for disabled people and the elderly. Then he added: "because prayer should be for everyone," and it happened right as a shot of sunshine flashed through the window.

Vivian thought that if Bast ever fell in love with someone, that truly happy-shy-pleased look was the only move he would need to make the girl all his. But for now, she wanted to savor it with him. Before she lost him to someone. Or before he lost her to something. She took advantage of how calm he seemed right then to confess that she wasn't sure the Guru was real.

"He is," Bast said confidently. "A friend of mine met him once."

This was interesting to Vivian on multiple levels. "What friend?"

"Just a friend. He has an interest in the Church. You wouldn't know him. I met him at a festival one summer, but he left Alighieri. We keep in touch via correspondence."

She probed a bit, but Bast remained nonchalant. Still, she was glad to know he had a reason to think the Guru was real. She'd thought they were chasing a fantasy.

As it turned out, Nate asked Bast for help with magic on his own behalf.

"Not because I'm afraid of Icy," he told them. "But I *am* afraid of her Immortal."

Which meant he was in denial, too. Because he was definitely afraid of Icy, a name he'd adopted for Carina after Vivian told him the other things he was calling the girl were unacceptable. She had decided not to tell him about the mortal enemy line; she didn't want it to become a self-fulfilling prophecy.

Anyway, he was incapable of relaxing these days. When Nate sat with Vivian in the coach, he was nearly always tapping something or fidgeting, and mostly all they could do was read together. He sometimes teased her about Brandon, though, which was fun and gave Vivian the opportunity to ask Nate about the girl he'd been dating before the coronation.

Her name was Aubrey, and she'd broken up with him.

"But it was for the best," Nate said. "Pepper didn't like her." Apparently horse approval mattered in Nate's dating life.

In any case, Bast agreed to help Nate with magic, and he brought a dagger to the training session Nate requested.

"You have to be kidding," Nate said, crossing his arms *quite* defensively.

"Nope," Bast said. "You need to learn how to create a shield." He pointed at Nate's shoulder. "If you could have done it before, maybe you wouldn't have been shot. Fear is a good motivator."

"That was a bullet," Nate said. "I didn't have time for fear. No one could have protected themselves from it. I bet even you couldn't have done it. Viv couldn't have."

Vivian had never seen Bast stop anything as fast as a bullet, but Nate was right that she could never have done it herself. Tending hot meant being naturally good at injecting energy into a situation. She could easily set off major explosions. She was also strong enough—when she wasn't sick—to create a defensive telekinetic shield. But one that would stop bullets? No. Bast had a major advantage over her and Nate with that. He was naturally good at slowing things down.

"You were the one who wanted to learn," Bast said, twirling the dagger. "Don't you want to be able to compete with *Carina?*"

Vivian thought she could see steam coming out of Nate's ears.

"Fine. Throw the damn dagger at me."

Bast smirked but seemed to think better of using the dagger for his first throw. He set it down and picked up a couple of rocks from the ground instead. "We'll practice with these. I'll throw a rock at you, and you block it. And if you get better, we'll switch to the dagger."

"Why is learning defensive magic so much worse than offensive magic?" Nate asked, but they began, and Nate gamely batted away rocks Bast threw at him until Bast got irritated.

"You're redirecting, not blocking," Bast said.

"They're coming slow enough that all I have to do is change their direction to keep them from hitting me," Nate responded. "Isn't that good enough?"

Bast tossed one of the rocks up into the air and made it bounce from an invisible shield around his hand on the way down. "No. Your goal with a defensive shield isn't to change the direction of the movement. It's to stop the movement cold. It should be like the rocks hit an invisible wall."

"Yeah, okay, let's try again," Nate said, and they went on unsuccessfully for an extremely frustrating hour.

"We're in the mountains," Vivian said when both boys were upset with the lack of progress. "The air is thin. Maybe it's making Nate too tired to do this."

"Or maybe I just suck," Nate said.

"It's probably that one," Bast said, but she'd noticed that he was getting a little careless with the rocks, too.

Vivian curled her knees toward her chest. "It's my fault, isn't it? I'm draining all of us."

Her brothers both avoided eye contact.

"I'm not wrong, am I?" she continued. "You two shouldn't be tired. You're giving me too much magic. What if we get attacked by Immortals?"

Bast sighed. "We're almost at the Mountain of Peril. No one's going to want to follow us up. All we have to do is get there and find the Guru."

"What if he can't help?" Vivian asked. "What happens then?"

Bast bent down and grabbed her hand. "Then we'll figure out something else."

Vivian looked at Nate staring at the ground a few steps away.

"Hey!" Bast moved to block her view of Nate. "Ignore him. He's just moody because he's so bad at shields. Right, Nate?"

"Yeah, it's going to be fine," Nate said flatly. But on the way back to the caravan, Vivian heard Bast mutter to Nate: "Say it like you believe it next time."

Brandon showed up to keep her company later that night.

"Did they send you here to make it better?" she asked morosely.

"They didn't have to," Brandon said. "Nate almost took off my head in a match a few minutes ago. He has no idea how lethal he is when he's pissed at himself."

Vivian sat up feeling alarmed, but Brandon only seemed to take that as an opportunity to slip his arm around her back as he sat. He pulled her close for a kiss that did not seem at all bothered with the possibility that her brother was going to slice him in two with a sword.

"Why are you loyal to him?" she asked.

Brandon's eyebrows knit together. "I'm loyal to *you*."

This was not what the connection between Nate and Brandon told her.

"What if you find out there's something you don't like about me?" she pressed.

"Oh, do you have a deep, dark, dirty secret that I should

know?" he said, smirking like that was impossible.

"I could," she said petulantly.

"Let's make it a game, then," he said. "I'll tell you my secrets, you tell me yours, and we'll compete to see who can make the other person not like them first." As consideration for the bargain, he offered an extended kiss, then sealed it with: "And there's no way you'll win."

So, they traded secrets, and Brandon's worst was that he didn't think he could *ever* be loyal to Vivian's mother. He prefaced that with: "Do you think I could kiss you one more time before I tell you this? Because you may decide to execute me for treason after."

She saw no reason for such drastic punishment. She benevolently rewarded him for his honesty with more kissing. Then she told him about the vision she'd had of her dad, and how he'd said the only way for her to survive the Immortality Virus was to become Immortal.

"Do you think that's true?" she said. She was enclosed in Brandon's arms and leaning back against his chest in the coach, and from that position, she felt braver than normal. "Because I don't want to be Immortal, but I also don't want to … you know."

Brandon kissed the back of her head. "I don't know. But if so, I think you'll know, and you'll make the right choice— whatever that is—whenever you have to make it."

He must have sensed the dip in her mood. "Do you want my last secret?" he said.

"Yes," she said.

He twisted around so he could do the thing where he kissed her before he told her something that he thought might ruin everything between them. She liked how he did that; it always made her feel like it was meant to make her want more.

"I volunteered to lead the new queen's security detail," he told her. "Most of the older captains didn't want to do it because of how dangerous everyone thought the job would be."

"So why did you volunteer?" she asked.

He kissed her several more times. "Because I'd always thought Princess Vivian was prettier than any girl I'd ever seen. I wanted a chance to meet her."

It was a good secret.

CHAPTER THIRTY-TWO
THE UNEXPECTED ALLY

Carina was experiencing the worst heartbreak of her life.

It was not over Max.

He had wanted to stay, but Carina threatened to freeze him to death, and she must have looked like she could do it, because he left. Then she found a nook behind the church, flattened herself into the shadows, and held her breath until the Southern Royals left, too. The whole time, she prayed to any god that would listen—something divine *had* to be associated with this church—that Miguela wouldn't show back up right when the Southerns came out.

She didn't.

But all Carina found when she circled the church later was Miguela's backpack.

Carina ignored a dull pain in her stomach that told her this was very, very bad and dug their guidebook out. She tore a page off, wrote a note in the margins, and set it under a rock next to Miguela's backpack on the church stairs. Then she went out to search New America for her sister, telling herself and the pain in her stomach that Miguela had been really, really angry and maybe she'd just taken a super long walk.

At first, this mental strategy worked for Carina. New America wasn't a very large place, and with Max gone, Carina felt like she was thinking more clearly. As she walked, she rehearsed the profuse apology she owed her sister. She walked every road twice, then returned to the church.

No Miguela.

After the third time around, Carina sat down on the church steps and hugged her knees. Maybe Miguela had come back already but hadn't seen the backpack. Carina waited two more hours on the steps before she decided to head out a fourth time. She nearly fell down the church steps getting up. It was summer, but the steps were covered in ice.

Four hours later, Carina had looked inside every old building and down every crumbling well. She'd searched behind abandoned posts and crawled into an ancient drainage ditch. Miguela wasn't in New America.

She was gone.

Carina returned to the church. She missed Max briefly before she remembered that he was a Red-Eyed One. For all she knew, *he* had found Miguela first. Maybe he'd taken her to wherever Red-Eyed Ones came from. Maybe he'd had friends following them this whole time. She wondered what he'd planned to do with her and Miguela when they got to the Mountain of Peril. Was he going to turn them over to someone?

She should never have trusted Max. They should have gone straight to the Eastern Ridge Trail. She should have been more careful with magic. Carina wished she and Miguela were both back at Novi Dupree, where her biggest problem was boredom. She tried to ask herself what Sister Agda would do, but Sister Agda wouldn't have gotten herself in this wretched situation. Carina stayed on the church steps between her backpack and Miguela's all night, wrapped in both their wool blankets and shivering until morning. Then she got up and searched New America several more times.

After three terrible, hopeless nights on those church steps, she gave up. Miguela was gone, and there was no one here who was going to help Carina find her.

She'd never felt more alone than she did as she left New America, leaving Miguela's backpack behind with several notes tucked inside. Maybe Carina would somehow find Miguela on her way to the Eastern Ridge Trail. If she didn't, maybe she would find help in Cerulean. That's what the Sisters had said. That's what she had to believe.

It was hard to walk alone. With Miguela and Max-acting-like-a-Mortal this had been an adventure. On her own—and without knowing if she'd lost the only family she had left—it was all Carina could do to make herself take one step after another.

This route wasn't well traveled, either. So far, she'd only been passed by three wagons, one woman on horseback, and two old men on bicycles. Carina had marked her new route on her map and estimated that if she walked fast all day, she might reach the nearest town by night. But it was hard to walk fast feeling so down.

She was starting to think she simply couldn't keep going when an old, orange, gas-powered pickup truck blew a cloud of dirt in her face while passing her. The brakes screeched, and the truck stopped hard before it was out of sight. It backed up. The driver rolled down the window.

A woman who looked almost exactly like Sister Agda was behind the wheel.

"Get in," she commanded.

And a Sister Agda look-alike in a truck was better than nothing, so Carina walked to the other side of the truck, opened the door, and climbed in.

The woman started the truck up again, and for the better part of an hour, Carina sat numbly with her as they drove on. After that, Carina decided her driver was the real Sister Agda. She looked ten years younger wearing blue jeans and a gray sweater, but it was her. No one else could have kept that silence up for so long.

"I didn't know you had a truck," was what Carina said when she started talking. Not that many Mortals did. It was much more common to own a wagon or cart or even a solar-powered delivery van. As far as Carina knew, there were only even a few small shops on Kepler that made trucks.

Sister Agda's face barely twitched. "There's a lot you don't know."

Like where her sister was, Carina thought. "Miguela's not with me. She was, then I made her angry. Really angry. She walked away. I thought she'd come back, but she didn't. It's been days. *Days.*"

Sister Agda held the steering wheel with two hands and looked forward.

"And I know it's my fault. All of this. Miguela wanted to do what you told us to do. Then we ran into Max—I *hate* Max—and he was going to the Mountain of Peril to find his uncle." Carina gritted her teeth. "He probably doesn't even *have* an uncle, and I thought maybe I'd find the *Guru.* There's probably no Guru either."

She pinched the bridge of her nose hard. Sister Agda

wasn't the kind of person you showed this kind of emotion in front of. Carina let go of her nose after a wave of potential sobs passed. Then she looked down into her lap.

"I'm sorry, Sister Agda. Miguela is gone. I don't know where she is. I'm afraid she's hurt or lost or something worse. Whatever happened is all because of me, and even if she *is* okay, I'll never forgive myself because I put her in danger. And … I need help."

Sister Agda moaned softly, then smacked her hands so hard on the steering wheel that the truck swerved. "I can't believe he *ran into* you two on the road and let you go on like that! What an imbecile!"

Carina jumped in her seat at Sister Agda's sudden wrath and tried to piece things together. "Who? Are … are you talking about Leo? The guy with the long scar? But he told us … wait … did you talk to him?"

Sister Agda smacked the steering wheel again, made a pained growling noise, and then cussed the way Sister Elizabeth could. She looked sideways. "Trust me, Carina. You're not the only woman in the universe who's ever fallen for a man who turned out later to be a complete loser."

"Max is a Red-Eyed One," Carina said dryly.

Sister Agda laughed. "That's pretty bad."

"What am I going to do? How am I going to find Miguela?" Carina looked suspiciously at Sister Agda. "How did you find me?"

Sister Agda smiled wryly. "Let's start with this isn't all your fault. You're sixteen. You're not supposed to be getting everything right. I'm forty-six—"

Carina gasped.

"It's not *that* old."

Carina clamped her mouth shut. She could never tell

Sister Agda she'd assumed the eagle-eyed object of her night-mares was at least sixty. The jeans really helped.

Sister Agda went on: "I should have known better than to try to restrict you from learning magic. You're … honestly, a lot like I was at your age, but we didn't have anyone who could teach you properly. None of us have thermodynamic abilities—"

"You knew I tended cold?" Carina interrupted.

"Thermodynamic abilities are hard to miss if you know anything about them. If it had only been you, I could have taught you some rudimentary telekinesis, but the hot tendency needs to be controlled so carefully. It's lucky for Miguela she *wasn't* by herself. We always thought she was only ever a few steps from a meltdown. She needed you to keep her calm. Still, maybe if we hadn't kept so much from you—"

Sister Agda shook her head several times and then looked sideways at Carina once more. "Look, I'm not saying you didn't make mistakes or that you shouldn't learn from them, but what's happened isn't all your fault. It's at least as much mine." She made a sour face. "And *his*."

Carina felt like Sister Agda had lifted a crushing weight from her chest. Then she thought about how they still didn't know where Miguela was, and the weight dropped right back down. It didn't matter whose fault it was. Her sister was still gone. Maybe forever. She choked back tears.

Sister Agda jerked the truck to the side of the road and turned off the engine. They sat for a long time while Carina fought down immense, overwhelming pain inside. Then Sister Agda suddenly slid over on the bench seat and pulled Carina into a hard hug. She had bony shoulders, and she smelled like a strange mix of sassafras root and smoke, but she didn't let go, and Carina cried.

Sister Agda drove even faster than Leo. It was past night-fall when they arrived at a small sledding lodge and checked in for the night. Sister Agda said they needed to eat, so they went to the lounge, sat at a low table, and asked for the late-night menu. There was one bartender handling the whole place and only three other patrons: a man eating alone and a middle-aged couple sharing a bottle of wine.

Sister Agda ordered mac and cheese for them both. The local version was laced with roasted hare, but she ordered plain mac and cheese for Carina, who hadn't expected Sister Agda to know she was a vegetarian. Carina couldn't eat, though. She was too upset.

"They have something they're calling Summer Berry Ginger Ale," Sister Agda said doubtfully. "Do you think you could drink that? You need to get something into your system."

Carina speared a noodle mutely, stuck it in her mouth, and tried to chew. It felt rubbery. She could barely swallow.

Sister Agda threw the drink menu down with vigor. "It wouldn't have been as good as the stuff we make anyway."

There was a stubby candle on the table. Carina stared at it. Since Miguela tended hot, would she be able to defend herself with fire if she needed to? Or would she be too afraid?

"But you must be in bad shape if you don't even want to try the beer."

The candle flickered. "I tried the sassafras," Carina admitted, looking back up. "Twice. Sort of."

Frown lines appeared on Sister Agda's face.

"I'm sorry," Carina added guiltily.

The lines smoothed over. "The thermodynamic tendencies are fueled by energy. Processed sugar messes with people who have them," Sister Agda said. "And there's something you need to know."

What Carina needed to know was where her sister was. She was far too exhausted to think about everything else. She pushed macaroni around on her plate.

Sister Agda twisted her napkin in her hands, then picked up the drink menu again. She flipped it over to read the back and Carina could practically hear her thinking she needed something stronger for this. She set the menu down shortly after like she was even more disgusted, and then she said: "Do you know what a Second Degree Cardinal is?"

While Carina tried to remember what that term meant, Sister Agda called the bartender over and asked for two hot drinks. Sister Agda ordered hers with whiskey before she went on to explain. "It's a member of a Cardinal Family who isn't in the direct line of succession but is still close enough to have two native magic abilities." She glanced furtively around the room. The man sitting alone was engrossed in a book. The couple was engrossed in each other. She lowered her voice. "I'm a Second Degree Cardinal. Of the East. My mother was a First Degree Cardinal."

That did *not* match up with Sister Rachel's history lessons. "I thought there weren't any First Degree Cardinals left in the East anymore," Carina said.

Sister Agda shushed her. "Keep it down. We're probably safe here, but it isn't public knowledge that the family still has that kind of magic. We spread rumors that it's vanished because the First Degrees prefer to exercise more subtle influence. I'm trusting you with a very important secret."

Carina wondered what she could possibly have done to earn Sister Agda's trust in this situation.

"I won't tell anyone," she promised.

"Good," Sister Agda said firmly. "Now. The reason I'm telling you is that it's something you and I have in common." Her eyes lifted to the other side of the room. Carina turned to follow her gaze. Four Red-Eyed Ones had just come in.

"Shit. I thought I'd lost them," Sister Agda said. The keys to the truck had been sitting on the table, but they floated into Carina's hands. "Carina, I want you to go through the bar kitchen, get out a back exit, find the truck, and go," she whispered.

"But I can't drive!" Carina protested quietly.

"It's not that hard. The pedal on the right makes the car go. The pedal on the left is the brake. Put the key in the place where I had it, press the brake, and turn the key. Then put the truck in drive, and—"

She stood up. Carina stood next to her. The middle-aged couple in the far corner of the room had been drinking too much to notice the new company sauntering lazily into the lounge. The bartender had disappeared. The man with the book was now watching them. His eyes were red.

Sister Agda grabbed Carina's wrist hard and stepped in front of her. She talked through her teeth: "When I say run, you're going to run. Got that?"

Carina shook her head frantically. "No, I don't. I don't know how to put a truck in drive. And I'm not leaving you. I can help."

"There's a map in the glove box," Sister Agda continued, backing Carina toward the bar. "You'll figure out the truck. Go straight to the Mountain of Peril. Word has gotten out about you, so don't stop until you get there, then find shelter. I'll find you later."

"What!? Why would I go there? I need to find Miguela."

"Miguela is there."

"*Miguela* is there?! How do you know?"

"I'm a Second Degree Cardinal," Sister Agda hissed, squeezing Carina's wrist even harder. "I have two gifts. Telekinesis and a telesthesia gift that allows me to sense where people I care about are located in relation to me. How do you think I found *you*?"

"Why didn't you tell me that?" Carina hissed back. "We should never have stopped if you knew where Miguela was!"

"Exactly why I *didn't* tell you. You needed rest in case something like *this* happened."

The Red-Eyed Ones stopped at their table. The largest of the four, a woman with slick hair and a sick smile looked past Sister Agda to Carina. "So, *you're* her," she said.

A man with a shaved head next to her sneered. "And being protected by Raider Agda herself."

Sister Agda let go of Carina's wrist. "Run."

Carina didn't know what to do.

Sister Agda rolled up her sleeves. She had the look on her face that had always made Carina terrified of her. "*Run*," she ordered again, and the chair Carina had been sitting in flew up and slammed into the man with the shaved head. "I've got this."

CHAPTER THIRTY-THREE
THE MOUNTAIN OF PERIL

Vivian didn't like the Mountain of Peril, and she wished they'd never reached it. Every time she thought about why they were here, she got woozy. The place gave her a bad feeling.

She wasn't the only person in a dismal mood. Bast and Nate were fighting. Just before they'd reached the mountain, a scout had brought news that Franklin was in custody and being taken to the capital to stand trial.

At the time, Vivian had been with the boys in her coach, listening as Bast tried to explain again to Nate how to create a defensive telekinetic shield.

The scout's report brought the conversation to a stop. Nate jumped up, leaned out the door, and whistled for his horse.

"What are you doing?" Bast asked.

"Going to find Franklin," Nate said.

Bast pulled Nate back physically and slammed the door to the coach shut. "You can't."

Nate struggled to get away from Bast. "But this is a mistake! Franklin will never get a fair trial! He'll be executed!"

"Stop it," Bast ordered. "You can't go."

"Why the hell not?" Nate yelled.

Bast drew his hand down over his face, and Vivian suddenly got it.

"Because if you do, I'll die," she explained. "Bast doesn't have enough magical energy left to keep me alive on his own."

Nate seemed to deflate, his shoulders sinking and his head drooping. "You can let go of me," he told Bast. "I didn't realize you were that tired. Of course, I'll stay."

There was a tiny hamlet too small to be a village an hour's ride away from the Mountain of Peril. They stopped for the night but left in a rush before the morning prayers because another scout returned to inform them that a group of Empire Immortals was traveling between New America and the mountains.

Brandon suggested they split up and send a decoy group up the Mountain of Peril while Vivian and the boys switched course and headed north instead. Vivian thought it was a good idea, but Brandon brought it up in front of her brothers and Bast saw red. It was a good thing Brandon was her boyfriend, or Bast might have barked treason for the suggestion alone. As it was, he gripped Brandon's shoulder, scowled, and said, "We did not come this far to give up."

Nate had to act fast to reverse frost spreading to Brandon's neck after Bast let go.

"Sorry," Brandon muttered, rotating his shoulder as Bast left them.

"For what?" Nate muttered back. "He's *our* cold ass

brother. But the decoy's a smart plan. If there are Empire Immortals after us, we should at least force them to divide up. I'll talk to Bast about splitting the group into a few smaller parties while we check out the Mountain of Peril."

"That's a good compromise," Brandon said.

Vivian thought the loyalty line might be one of her favorite connections to see. That deep blue was such a solid tone, and with the gold wrapping around it, the line was sturdy like good rope.

"Thanks for helping Brandon, Nate," she added.

Nate gave her hair a playful, telekinetic toss. "As if everything I do is for you. Thurlow's the only one around here who can give me a good fight with a broadsword. Can't let an injured shoulder ruin that."

The Mountain of Peril was marked by wooden signs warning people to stay away, but there were paths that seemed to have been frequented often enough to be more than just bunny trails. And clearly, the mountain was frequented by humans, because Vivian and the boys ran across more than one makeshift grave stele, indicating that someone had lost their life there.

Vivian stopped at a grave stele that was decorated with red boot laces. They'd been hiking for two hours, and she couldn't catch her breath. It was the third time she'd needed to stop in twenty minutes. Brandon—who Bast had grudgingly allowed to join them on the climb—stopped next to her.

"This is too much for you," he said. "We still have a long way to the top. You should let us carry you."

It was only the four of them climbing. Bast had some idea that the Guru found people at the top of the mountain only and that he wouldn't show up if they overwhelmed him with a big party. They had, in fact, sent most of the rest of the caravan out as decoys to distract the Empire Immortals. It was almost hard to believe the Empire had decided to come after them directly. All this time, Vivian had thought her mother was the primary threat. She tried harder to catch a breath of cold mountain air.

"Vivian? Hey? Are you okay?"

"Carrying me isn't an option," she gasped. "My brothers can't do it. They're too tired."

"I didn't mean with magic," Brandon said. "And I could easily do it. Physically."

She thought about it. One strange thing about the Mountain of Peril is that it didn't seem especially perilous. In fact, she'd started to wonder if there was anything extraordinary about it at all. The only peril she could detect was in her trying to climb a mountain when she had real-life enemies trailing her and was too sick to have stepped out of her coach anyway. The Guru seemed more like a legend with every step she took.

Still … things seemed strange to her today. For some reason, she wanted to get to the top of the mountain using her own legs, even if it was difficult.

"No," she said.

"Hey, guys," Brandon called, "Vivian needs to rest."

Bast turned around, looked her up and down, and then stormed back angrily. His eyes were cloudier than they should have been. "We need to do the transfers every hour," he said to Nate, who walked to her without a word.

Vivian drew back. "No. I don't want more magic from anyone."

Nate sighed and reached quickly for her arm. Bast had

been facilitating all the magic transfers before, but he thought she needed more warm energy as they ascended the mountain and the air became colder. It was uncomfortable with just Nate transferring magic. Without Bast's involvement, the energy that flowed to Vivian from Nate felt oddly chaotic. When he let go, she did feel better, but Nate's eyes were dimmer than they should have been.

Brandon put his arm around her shoulder. "Think maybe you two could lighten up a little? The death march attitude isn't helping your sister."

"Sure, Captain," Bast said icily. He had a cruel expression on his face that reminded Vivian of their mother. "Hey, Nate, want to kid around? How about we make jokes about the cyanide Mom gave Vivian?"

Vivian felt ill.

"Or about the letter we got back from New Paris Medical School yesterday." He barked out a laugh. "They said they might be able to come up with a treatment plan in a few months. If we give them the right funding."

Nate made a disgusted noise and glared at Bast. "Why do you have to be such a turd? I thought we agreed not to tell her that."

Bast crossed his arms. "Oh, I'm the turd? You're the one who wants to leave to go save your treasonous mentor."

At that, Nate said something that sounded like "fudge off" to Bast and started trudging up the mountain again.

Bast went after him. "Hey, maybe they got the wrong guy," he taunted. "Maybe Franklin's safe and sound in some hideout in the North, polishing his swords and planning his next attack on the Crown. Of course, it would be hard to mistake someone else for Franklin. It's not like just anyone could pull off that giant scar on his face."

"Stop it, Bast," Vivian said.

He met her eyes with a hard stare, and she looked for something there that would prove he wasn't frozen solid inside. He turned before she could find anything.

"Sorry," Brandon whispered to her.

"It's okay," Vivian whispered back, feeling more unnerved than she hoped she sounded. "It's just sibling bickering."

Vivian had to slow down her pace significantly as they went higher. Brandon offered to carry her twice more, but she refused even as her lungs burned and her legs began to tingle. Nate and Brandon started walking side-by-side with her, while Bast stormed forward, adamant that the Guru would find them when they got to the top. More than once, Vivian saw Nate glance at Brandon over her head, which was weird not only because she'd never really internalized that Nate was taller than her but also because it almost seemed to tip the power balance between him and Bast.

"We could go back down and head to New Paris," Nate said to her at some point, too quietly for Bast to hear. "So what if they're Northerners? They've done all kinds of research on the Immortality Virus. The doctors at the medical school might be able to do something to delay the onset of the virus longer without magic."

Vivian thought the crisp mountain air might be good for Nate. He seemed calmer than he'd been at the bottom of the mountain, and he'd taken it in stride as Bast continued to make childish digs at him.

"I agree," Brandon said. "And it would get you off this mountain. We could head back to that little hamlet right away. We could be sitting by a fireplace, drinking hot cocoa together a few hours from now."

"Yeah. Maybe even in a private room. With one of those enormous bathtubs that could fit, like, two people," Nate said. "You know, if you get creative about it."

Brandon started coughing, and it took Vivian at least three more steps before she understood what Nate was implying, and really, all of those things, including the tub, sounded enticing to her now that she was freezing near the top of a mountain.

She watched Bast walking ahead with his hands in his jacket pockets and his shoulders hunched together around his neck. He'd put a lot of space between him and her, probably because he didn't want to make her colder. But when she looked at him, she knew it didn't matter how appealing a private room in a mountain lodge sounded. It didn't matter if she ended up needing Brandon to carry her the rest of the way. There was no way she could tell Bast she wanted to go back down now. They at least had to get to the top of the mountain.

Unfortunately, the higher they went, the worse things got for Bast. By the time they reached the peak, his skin was almost transparent and the blue lines sticking up underneath made it seem like he genuinely had ice hardening in his veins. Vivian wanted to hug him. Even if she couldn't make him warm like she would have been able to do when her own magic was stronger, she thought he might need the human contact.

Since she couldn't help Bast, she sat with her face tucked into Brandon's shoulder and chatted idly with him and Nate while they waited for the Guru to appear.

And waited.

And waited some more.

After an hour, Nate asked Brandon to stay with Vivian while he talked alone to Bast. So, she and Brandon huddled together, and Vivian wondered if Brandon ever looked at anything other than her while they were together. He'd missed most of Native Valley, and at least half of New America. Now he was letting her distract him from an amazing view of the Red Ridge Mountains.

"You must think I'm pretty," she teased while they sat together.

"I don't think much at all when I'm with you," he admitted. "Mostly I just feel."

"All good things?" she asked.

"All the best things," he said.

When the boys returned, Bast was sniffling, and he'd stuffed his hands under his arms. He stood away from her and Brandon, looking like he needed a thicker coat, while Nate came over and asked Brandon if they could have some privacy.

Brandon kissed her forehead. "I'll check out what's on the other side and meet you later, Vivian," he said.

"I feel all the best things when I'm with you, too," she said. Then he headed down the other side of the mountain alone.

Nate sat where Brandon had been. "Come on, Bast," he called. "You're going to turn into a human ice cube standing by yourself over there."

"I'll make Vivian cold," Bast grumbled through chattering teeth.

"You'll make me sad if you stay so far away," she said, so he reluctantly sat down with them, and Vivian tried to be stealthy about tucking her hands under her legs because it actually did get that much colder with him there.

"What now?" she asked, trying to keep her tone light.

Bast scowled at the view, and Nate took a deep breath. "Bast thinks if we stay on the mountain long enough, the Guru will show up—"

Vivian stopped him. "No. There's no Guru. There's nothing on this mountain but a lot of places where it would be easy to fall." She put one hand on Nate's arm and one on Bast's. "We need to get realistic about what's happening."

"There *is* a Guru," Bast said, clenching his fists like an ornery child. He leaned over Vivian to speak directly to Nate. "We *have* to keep looking."

Nate leaned over her as well. "I *agree*. The Guru might exist, and we should keep looking. But *we* don't need to be the ones doing it. You're getting too cold. And Vivian's right. We're transferring a tremendous amount of magic to her doing things like this. We should be thinking about conserving that energy. We need to go back down and send some guards up to scour the place—"

"I *told* you," Bast said. "It can't be the guards. It has to be *us*. The Guru finds you, not the other way around, and he only appears to people who really need help. You're giving up."

"I am not giving up at all," Nate said. "And stop making this so difficult. We are not out of options. We could reach out to the two labs that never got back with us and fund New Paris Medical School's research." He nudged Vivian's shoulder with his own. "And in the meanwhile, we'll get you somewhere safe and off the road where you can rest, and—"

Bast stood up. "You're a quitter," he said to Nate.

"It's okay," Vivian tried to tell him.

"How is this *okay*? Nate wants us to go to a … a luxury cottage or something. Where we can all just sit and … and …"

"And make sure Vivian is as comfortable as possible

while we explore other options," Nate said carefully.

"There *are* no other options!" Bast yelled. "New Paris Medical School only wants our money, and Mom got letters back from the other two labs weeks and weeks ago!"

"You knew that?" Vivian asked.

He rubbed his temples with his fingers. "Mom's a good liar, but she's not that good."

Nate bit his lip. "Then we'll issue a decree asking anyone with healing magic to come forward. We'll put out a reward." He grimaced. "We could try to make it big enough to attract Icy. Or maybe we'll find someone more amenable to helping us."

"We won't find someone," Bast said tiredly. "That kind of magic is incredibly rare."

Vivian looked out over the mountains, which seemed to go on forever and ever. She didn't hate the Mountain of Peril as much from the top as she'd hated it on her way up. This wasn't the tallest mountain in the area, but everything she could see from here was awesome. It was like the things she'd seen in her dreams: so beautiful it was almost unreal.

"Do you guys ever think about what else is out there?" she said. "I mean, in the places where humans went besides Kepler? Do you think there's anything more amazing than this?"

Bast sniffed again, while Nate looked over the mountains with her.

"If there is, it must be really frickin' amazing," he said softly.

Bast was now rubbing tears away, and he sounded stuffed up answering: "That's the whole point of an infinite creator, isn't it? Something more amazing is *always* possible." He made a noise like he was trying not to let them hear him cry. "We're too limited as Mortals to see everything, though, so we're just supposed to have *faith* that we're living in the *right* possible." He wiped his nose with his sleeve. "But sometimes I don't believe in anything. And I think we're basically all alone."

Vivian had had moments when she was afraid of dying, moments when she was afraid of being an Immortal, and moments when she felt that everything was all too much. If Bast had lost hope, maybe all that fear should have come back to her now. She watched him wipe his nose again. He looked absolutely forlorn by himself on top of the damn mountain.

So maybe she could feel afraid for herself again later. Right now, the only thing she could feel was pain for Bast.

Nate helped her stand, but she didn't think either of them knew what to do to help their brother. They all stood there on top of the mountain, trying not to look at each other, for the longest time.

Then Bast's eyes rose, he started blinking rapidly, and a gravelly voice interrupted them from behind Vivian.

"I understand you've been looking for me. Is this a bad time?"

CHAPTER THIRTY-FOUR
THE SECOND STRAIN VIRUS

Carina ran past the bartender cowering behind the bar, then through a flap to a brightly lit kitchen, where a young man was washing dishes at a sink.

"Who are you?" he said, and she said, "Red-Eyes, get out!" and barreled past him to a door marked "EMERGENCY EXIT." Alarms started screaming as soon as she opened it, and she dashed around the lodge to Sister Agda's truck.

She went to the passenger's side first, realized she couldn't drive from there, and had to scramble over to the driver's side. She couldn't see well, she had never learned to drive, and she couldn't remember Sister Agda's rushed instructions. She was looking frantically for a place to put the key when the Red-Eyed man with the shaved head came sprinting out from behind the lodge. Sister Agda was following him.

It was sheer luck that Carina finally found a place for the key right then. She jammed it in and turned. Nothing happened. She recalled something about needing to put her foot on the brake, so she did and tried turning the key again.

The truck's headlights flashed on, and the engine rumbled to life. She hit the pedal on the right, and the engine revved but the car didn't move. "Come on, truck, move!" she screamed at the steering wheel.

"Put it in drive!" Sister Agda shouted, but this was not something Carina knew how to do, and it took her long enough to figure out that the Red-Eyed man was directly in front of her before the truck jerked forward. It nearly hit the man, who dodged out of the way at the last second and landed at Sister Agda's feet.

Sister Agda laughed loudly, picked up a tree branch, thwacked the guy on the back of the head, and waved Carina on. "*Go!*" she yelled, and enough bad things had already happened to Carina after times when she'd failed to follow Sister Agda's instructions. She stepped on the pedal again, and the truck lurched down the road.

Now Carina was driving badly with a lot on her mind. Like why was Miguela at the Mountain of Peril? Why had that man called Sister Agda "Raider?" Why didn't the Cardinal Family of the East want people to know they had magic?

Also, what had Leo done to make Sister Agda hate him? Because Carina would far rather have been driving a wagon with fast horses down a dark road than a hunk of metal she could barely control. She wondered if it would be better to die crashing the truck into a tree or rolling it off the side of the mountain, and that wasn't her only problem. Shortly after leaving the lodge, something caught her eye in the mirror hanging down from the truck's roof. She nearly ran the truck off the road looking back.

A whole *pack* of Red-Eyed Ones was chasing her.

Who on Kepler did they think she *was*?

A line of bullets sprayed through the back window, blowing it out completely. The hanging mirror shattered next. Terrific. They had guns. Carina shrieked, swore, decided Miguela had been completely right about guns, and stomped the pedal to the floor.

She was now going faster than Sister Agda had been going. She was going faster than *anyone* should be going around a mountain, and she was afraid to slow down. She drove terrified around four more mountains before she hit a fork in the road and had to stop to find the map Sister Agda said was in some compartment. She nearly skidded off the side of the road braking, and she may or may not have used magic to save herself right then. She wasn't sure. It had been a difficult day.

She thought of stopping for rest, but what if the Red-Eyed Ones caught back up? Anyway, how was she supposed to sleep when she had so much on her mind? She decided to keep driving, and several nerve-wracking hours later, the dawn moon had come up and set, the sun had risen, and Carina had somehow made it to the Mountain of Peril, where a big wooden sign said: "MOUNTAIN OF PERIL. DANGER. MORTAL PERIL AHEAD."

"Awesome," Carina said after she had parked the truck in plain sight by the side of the road. "Because I'm not in enough peril already." She grabbed her backpack from the passenger seat, stole a full canteen she found in the back of the truck, and hiked past the sign.

Miguela was up there somewhere.

By afternoon, Carina was muttering to herself about what lies that sign had told. There was no mortal peril on this mountain. There wasn't anything interesting on this mountain, unless the Red-Eyed Ones chasing her had seen the truck and decided to follow her up. But Carina took some comfort knowing that if they were on the mountain, too, finding her wasn't going to be easy. The mountain was huge, and there were no marked trails. There were a lot of steep paths that seemed like great places to tumble down and crack your head, though, and it was taking all of Carina's energy just to make sure that didn't happen to her.

She had no idea how she was going to find Miguela.

A blue-tailed bunny rabbit was hopping alongside her, but even it wasn't living up to expectations. Carina had recently chatted with three wolves and a wild piggy. Honestly, she was disappointed when she said: "I'm looking for someone, are you looking for someone, too?" and the stupid bunny didn't answer. Then she tripped over a branch and ripped a hole in her jeans falling, while the bunny hopped gracefully over the branch. Carina felt many very unjust and undeserved things about that bunny as she watched it disappear into a cluster of thick-skinned trees that had grown up around several giant moss-covered boulders.

She was unsteady getting up, and she tried to remember the last time she'd eaten anything other than a few noodles of mac and cheese. She set her backpack on the ground, unzipped the pack, and dug around for something edible. She came up with three granola bars and Sister Agda's canteen, which she was about to open when she noticed one of the moss-covered boulders *move*.

She lowered the canteen and cautiously climbed over the same branch the blue bunny had cleared, focusing hard on the part of the boulder that had just moved. If she tilted her head just right, she could almost imagine those boulders forming the shape of a house that had grown up out of the mountain. She took another step forward.

The boulder moved again. Or rather, a flap about the size of a door swung out toward her.

She got closer, something in her vision shimmered, and the flap she was looking at became an actual door—a wooden one—marking the entrance to a small house, cobbled together from stone. It had a single window, ivy was crawling up its sides, and its roof was thatched over with brush.

Then *Max* stepped out of the door.

His face was paler than before, and there were lines under his deceptively indigo-colored eyes. He looked right at her and said "Carina?" and she wondered if she might be hallucinating. The house that had materialized certainly fell into the category of things she might be making up in her head right now. She didn't think she would have hallucinated her ex-boyfriend, who she was still very angry at, though.

She gripped the canteen tight. "Where's Miguela? Are you going to kill me?"

He was wearing the strange clothing he'd been wearing when he first met her. Sister Elizabeth would have been disappointed in her. Carina should have known that fabric was synthetic. What Mortal wore synthetic fabric?

He scuffed his stupid rubbery shoe in the dirt. "No. I'm not that kind of Immortal. You should come inside with me. This is my, uh, well he's not exactly, but I guess it doesn't matter. This is my uncle's place."

She stood still. "You are a Red-Eyed One and a liar. Why should I go with you?"

For a second, he didn't answer, and she thought he was going to try his pathetic puppy dog look on her. If he did, she would try her cold tendency on him. Instead, he rubbed his forehead and met her glare straight-on. "Look, I'll admit that I lied to you about a few things, and yes, my eyes do turn red under certain very rare circumstances, like when I'm terrified that my girlfriend is going to be killed by a bully prince who has a sword that's on fire. But I am not a Red-Eyed One. Not like the kind you're thinking of."

Max's hair curled up at an ugly angle on one side. It hadn't bothered her before.

"Wait here. I'll be right back." He disappeared into the house. Carina unscrewed the top of Sister Agda's canteen and tried to decide if she should run. But she'd been running from everything recently, and right now she needed at least water to try to clear her head.

She took a sip.

Sassafras.

Carina pulled the canteen from her lips. Then Miguela came out of the house, and Carina dropped the canteen entirely and ran for her sister, who immediately started talking while Carina hugged her to make sure she was real.

"How did you get here?" Miguela cried. "I was so worried. I think there are Red-Eyed Ones following us. They have a serum that makes it so you can't use magic. I thought they'd gotten you." She pointed to the canteen in a puddle of beer on the ground. "Was that sassafras?"

Carina had never noticed before that hugging Miguela made her feel warm. "*You* were worried? What are you doing with Max? I'm so sorry, Miguela. You were right about him. You were right about magic. You were right about *everything.*"

Miguela made a pained face and glanced back at Max, who was standing in the doorway of the house, watching them. "I wasn't completely right. He helped me get away from the Red-Eyed Ones. If it hadn't been for him ..."

Carina looked at Max over Miguela's shoulder. "You didn't tell her *you're* a Red-Eyed One? You're *still* a liar. What do you want with us?"

"He's not a Red-Eyed One," Miguela interrupted.

"I've seen his eyes turn red, Miguela."

"So have I. He's not a Red-Eyed One."

"Then what is he?"

"I'm a Second Strain Immortal," Max said. "I was born on Earth. We have an improved version of the Immortality Virus there. I'm not like the First Strain Immortals. I don't have the empathy problems the Red-Eyed Ones have here. Second Strains don't sustain the brain damage First Strains do—"

"I still think your brain is damaged," Miguela said, but she didn't say it nasty like she would have spoken to him before. She said it like she was teasing him now.

Max rolled his eyes and half-smiled at her. "Ha, ha, Miguela."

Carina did not like this development. "No," she said to Max. "You do not get to act like you and my sister are friends. Why aren't your eyes red all the time? Why didn't I see them before?"

Max swallowed and sobered up fast. "With this version of the Immortality Virus, it only happens when I'm extremely stressed. It's not that big of a deal. On Earth, a lot of Second Strains wear colored contact lenses to make sure no one sees their eyes turn, and it's allowed because no one's afraid of us." He paused and that sheepish smile she'd liked before appeared. "Do you, uh, know what contacts are? I've studied a lot, but little things like that are hard to remember."

That sheepish smile wasn't especially cute right now. Nothing about Max was especially cute right now. In fact,

Carina had the sense that she was looking at Max for the very first time. "You're from *Earth*? How old are you?"

Max's smile dissolved and Miguela filled in the answer for him:

"He's seven-hundred thirty-six years old. In Earth years. Which is like five-hundred and fifty-three Kepler years. Your boyfriend is five-hundred and fifty-three years older than you."

"Ex-boyfriend," Carina said feebly.

"Sure," Miguela said. "But wait until you meet his 'uncle.' That guy is three-thousand one-hundred and fifty Kepler years old. He came here on the *nanny ships.*"

There were a lot of things that didn't make sense about that, but all Carina could think to ask was: "Does he look like a teenager, too?"

Max flushed. "No ... Myles doesn't ... it's ... I didn't lie about being a scientist. Or about my amphibian research. It's one part—one, uh, small part—of a thousand-year study I proposed for Kepler when I applied for this expedition. I'm with the Academy for Intergalactic Expedition and Observation. Our mission is to observe human migration and integration on other planets. We're supposed to have partners, but mine ditched me at the drop-off before this one, so I had to come alone and look for the other Second Strain Immortals, which is why I was at Novi Dupree—"

"Your age, Max," Miguela said while Carina's head reeled with information. "Explain to her why you don't look your age."

Max scratched his head. "Yeah, right. That's a good idea. We take these age-inhibitor injections, because the Academy's research says a mentor-mentee relationship is best for your survival if you have to depend on other Second Strains to orient you to the new planet. You stop taking them as soon as you land, but since I'm Immortal, my body will only age until—"

He stopped suddenly, winced, and looked past Carina. She turned. A man with smooth, freckled skin, shaggy brown hair, and eyes the lightest shade of gray Carina had ever seen was standing behind her.

He was not alone. Queen Vivian and the two princes were with him. They looked … bad.

"I *told* you to keep your mouth shut," the man said brusquely to Max. He ran his hands—which were unnaturally unwrinkled—through his hair, tugged on it, and looked tiredly between Carina, Max, Miguela, and the Southern Royals.

"Oh, look. It's *Carina* and the Immortal she still hasn't broken up with," Prince Bastian said instead of "hello."

"And who shot me," Prince Nathanial added. Then he seemed to notice Miguela. "Also, there's some other girl. Are you Icy's sister?"

To Carina's horror, Miguela *blushed* and said "hi" just before a noise like a horn blowing began sounding continuously from the house. Queen Vivian collapsed on her feet. The princes caught her between them. The shaggy-haired man plodded past Carina, Miguela, and Max to the door, opened it, and did not bother holding it for any of them. Miguela caught it instead and held it open for the Southern Royals, who went in slowly while the horns continued to blare.

Carina went to the door, too, and put her hand on Miguela's arm. "We should get out of here. We need to find Sister Agda."

"Is that the queen? What's wrong with her?" Miguela asked, nodding at Queen Vivian.

"Yeah. I don't know what's wrong with her," Carina said,

and she was going to repeat her suggestion that they leave, but Miguela had already let go of the door to follow the Southern Royals. Carina reluctantly followed her stubborn sister and ignored Max following her.

The house was larger inside than it looked from the outside. It was mostly open space, and it was cozy. Wood rafters stretched across the ceiling like the rafters of the barn at Novi Dupree. The floor was tiled with cracked orange Keplercotta. The walls were lined with overstuffed book-shelves. One of the back corners of the house was serving as a kitchen nook with appliances so dingy they would have made Sister Lindy shudder. A round table was stacked too high with papers for anyone to possibly eat at it.

A narrow bed with a faded quilt was situated in the other back corner. There was a large-but-thin circular rag rug in the center of the house, where a single broken-down sofa, two chairs, and a wooden coffee table were arranged. And that is where the man and the Southern Royals had gone.

The man picked up a small remote from the coffee table. He pressed several buttons, and the alarms finally stopped. Prince Bastian stood looking disbelievingly at him, while Prince Nathanial helped Queen Vivian onto the sofa.

"But we need help," Prince Bastian was saying.

"Obviously," the man said. "But I didn't promise help."

"You're the *Guru*. You're supposed to have magic."

The man grimaced and pressed more buttons on the remote. Two of the bookshelves across from the sofa rotated to reveal a wall of television monitors, each showing video footage of the mountain. That was not cozy. That was extremely high-tech. Carina had a memory of seeing some-thing similar once, but she didn't know where. There were people moving on some of the screens. Red-Eyed Ones.

Probably the ones that had been following her.

"Hell." The man threw the remote back down and walked swiftly to his bed. He retrieved a large duffel bag from underneath and nodded at Max. "Kozlov, get your pack."

"What is going on?" Prince Bastian demanded while the man proceeded to walk around the room, rapidly collecting things to throw in his duffel.

The man grabbed a gun with a long barrel hanging above a second door at the back of the house and swung it over his shoulder.

"What is going on is that thanks to all of you, my mountain is under attack. If it were Mortals, I could scare them off. But Immortals are never as impressed with my tricks."

"Your *tricks*?" Prince Bastian repeated. "What does that mean? We need your help. Queen Vivian is infected with the Immortality Virus."

The man went back to his bed and whisked up the old quilt. "I owe a favor to someone you know. If I could help you, I would. But I don't have a cure for the virus. No one does."

"We need *magic*, not a cure."

The man opened the top drawer of a dresser by his bed, took out a smaller gun, and tucked it into his waistband. "Look, I'm sorry, kid. Kozlov and I are Immortals. We're different from the Immortals climbing up my mountain, but we don't have any magic. Whatever you're here for, you're probably not going to get it."

A POEM FROM *THE COLLECTED WORKS OF ANNA DUPREE*

That days extended would be fair,
Golden sunshine not in haste;
Yet one year is one dark hour,
An eon a minute of waste.

This grand bargain of time,
Inescapable, for all are Mortal,
Calls on breath only to seek
To live. One second—

CHAPTER THIRTY-FIVE
FIREWORKS

Vivian's vision was clearer now than it had been since her coronation. She'd been infected with the Immortality Virus. There was no cure. Her body was rejecting the virus, and it was draining her of life and magic. If she survived, it would not be because she'd defeated the virus. It would be because she'd learned to live with it forever. As an Immortal.

She should have been dead weeks ago.

Now that she knew that, she knew she'd done everything wrong with the time she never should have had. She'd been completely preoccupied with herself. She'd thought she needed to learn to be less controlling. She'd thought she needed to learn to savor life. She'd let her brothers worry, watch, and take care of her because she'd thought she only needed to make it from one day to the next. She'd never thought she'd run out of time to worry about them.

She'd been so *selfish*.

Why hadn't it occurred to her that this wasn't about her at all? Bast was turning the Guru's rug into a blanket of frost.

Nate had sunk down next to her on the sofa. Their faces were blank and pale. Why hadn't she spent time helping Bast learn to let her go? Why hadn't she spent time helping Nate adjust to his new role?

"This can't be right," Bast said hoarsely. "You … you found us. There has to be something you can do."

The Guru had colorless, emotionless eyes that made Vivian extra certain that being an Immortal was not an option for her. "There is *nothing*. If I could do something, I would. I *always* do whatever I can for you desperate Mortals, and the favor I owe is significant. That's why I even bothered bringing you here. I thought I'd have a chance to explain, but now the best I can do is not inject you with the memory loss serum I usually give the hikers who come to make trouble and aren't scared away by one of my decoys." He zipped his duffel bag, went to the front door, and frowned at Carina's Immortal. "Get the lead out of it, Kozlov."

Carina stepped forward. She and her sister had faded into the background for Vivian, standing to the side near the door and watching everything. The sister's eyes were more piercing than Carina's, she was shorter by at least a foot, and she wasn't nearly as spindly, but pity looked the same on both girls. It was in the way their mouths hung with their lips barely parted and their heads angled slightly to the left. Vivian hated pity.

"You can't help them. You can't do any magic. There are a bunch of Red-Eyed Ones on their way here, and you're just going to take your guns and *abandon* us?" Carina said.

Vivian's heart sank. She'd screwed this up even more than she'd realized. If she and her brothers hadn't been so drained, they could have handled the Immortals that had finally found them again. Now they were *all* going to be easy targets. A perfect prize for a group of assassins. She wondered where

Brandon was now and hoped he hadn't been killed by them. Maybe he would get away. The Guru had refused to let them wait for Brandon to return, and Bast had refused to allow Vivian to waste the chance for a meeting with him.

The Guru harrumphed. "Kozlov and I have to rely on measly *guns* if we run into those wretched First Strains. *You* are hardly defenseless."

Carina's Immortal had hefted a large backpack up over his shoulders and was holding the straps with both hands. "Can't they come with us?"

The Guru clenched his fists, unclenched them, and pulled a gun he'd just tucked into his waistband back out. He pointed it directly at Carina. "Our mission is observation, not interference. We are leaving now. Alone. That's an order. Or I'll shoot her."

Immortal Boyfriend hesitated. "Wouldn't shooting her be interference?"

The Guru cocked the gun.

Immortal Boyfriend was more stubborn than Vivian would have guessed. He stood his ground. "I've seen Carina stop bullets."

The Guru pointed the gun at Carina's sister. "Are you willing to gamble on that?"

"Just *go*, Max," Carina said.

The boy squeezed his eyes shut and turned his face away. "Sorry, Carina," he said, and he went out the door.

The Guru kept his gun pointed as he backed out the door, too. "They'll probably be here in a couple of minutes. You might consider working out a temporary alliance to deal with them," he said, rather cryptically, Vivian thought. Then he looked directly at her. There was red swimming up in the gray in his eyes. "My deepest regrets, Your Highness," he said, and he left, too. The door shut behind him with a bang.

Carina's sister went to the monitors. "There are at least thirty of them. They're organized. I don't think they're bounty hunters."

"They're not," Bast said. "Those are Empire Immortals. I never thought they'd try to follow us up here."

The girl seemed to notice the frost on the floor around Bast. "What's wrong with your sister?"

He stared at her, then glanced at Carina. "You two should get out of here. This isn't about you. Those Immortals are after us."

The girls looked at each other, and a connection flashed between them. It was thick orange with a white core, the kind of familial bond that made Vivian think they would do just about anything for each other. She wondered if Bast and Nate had a connection anything like that and it felt urgent for her to know, so she pulled on magic she hadn't used in weeks and looked between her brothers. Their connection was a thin orange line, twisted through with green, blue, and red, all braided and gnarled together. Like the line itself was saying, "It's complicated."

It made her heart hurt. Her vision spun with all the colors. A second later she heard Bast saying her name, and she felt cool magic rushing through her veins. She opened her eyes. She was lying on the couch. Her brothers were crouched in front of her. Nate looked upset. Bast looked panicked. He was clutching her wrist.

"*Stop,*" she told him, struggling to sit up. "No more healing."

He tightened his grip.

She attempted to pry his fingers away. "*You* need your magic."

He shook his head like an obstinate little boy while Nate looked the other way. She remembered thinking Nate would make an easy next target, but Bast was the one who seemed broken now.

"Prince Bastian?"

Carina was standing behind Vivian's brothers, and her sister was next to her. "I don't know how to help, but we both have magic. If you can tell us what to do—"

Bast closed his eyes for a moment, then started laughing as if he might cry. "You want to help *now*? We needed your help weeks ago."

"I didn't know your sister was sick." Carina took a tiny step closer. "If you need more magic ..."

Bast didn't answer, and when Carina took a second, larger step closer, Nate lashed out telekinetically. She crashed into the bookshelves across the room. Vivian thought she heard something go *crunch*.

"*Stay back*," Nate said harshly.

The other girl turned like she intended to go to Carina, but they were all out of time. The front door blew open like someone had taken it out with an explosive first. A large chunk of the door flew in and knocked the girl to the ground.

"Miguela!" Carina yelled. She picked herself up from the floor, but as she did a crowd of Immortals appeared in the open doorway.

Nate stood up and moved forward like maybe putting himself between them and her and Bast would make a difference. It wouldn't. Those were indeed Empire Immortals: they were wearing black military garb and the Empress's insignia: an H shaped with two swords pointing in opposite directions and adjoined by an infinity loop. It was a lame insignia. As far as Vivian knew, the Empress's Immortals hardly ever fought with swords. The Immortal Empire was the only place on Kepler that had access to a significant stockpile of semiautomatic weapons. Nate didn't stand a chance against them.

Bast's grip became painful, and Vivian knew what he was thinking. This was it. Even Bast didn't have enough magical energy left to fight off Immortals with assault rifles. Vivian realized with distress that her mother probably *hadn't* had anything to do with the assassination attempt, and, more importantly, that if she hadn't drawn her own death out so long, the Immortal Empire couldn't have taken out her and her brothers all at once. Her mother had been *right*. She should have killed herself with the cyanide. This was a terrible way for Empress Hildebrand and Lord Godric to win. The last Cardinal family standing should have gone out in battle. Not cornered without magic on the top of some godforsaken mountain.

"Please don't try to help, Viv," Bast whispered. "I'd rather …" But he trailed off, and instead of finishing that thought he leaned forward and kissed her cheek. "Please," he repeated before he let go of her reluctantly and went slowly to stand by Nate as one of the Immortals stepped into the house and started laughing.

The boys both crossed their arms and Vivian winced at their bravado.

"Ahh … so *these* are the princes of South Kepler," the Immortal said. "I've heard about you two. Are you going to freeze me to death? Or burn me alive?"

"Is that what you want?" Bast said. "Because we could do either."

The Immortal laughed again. "If you were going to, you already would have. Guess it's true. The Southern Royals are out of magic."

He was right. Vivian thought Bast might have enough energy to freeze three or four of them. She wasn't sure about Nate, who could have had more energy than Bast now but had never been as skilled to begin with. Neither of them would be able to produce a shield.

"And the girls are here, too. Like the poor Mortals wanted to make this convenient," a woman said. "Nice of them to confirm the Empress's theory."

The man that had been laughing stopped and looked disdainfully from Carina standing by the bookshelf to the other girl—Vivian thought Carina had called her Miguela—pushing herself up from where she'd been crumpled on the ground.

"How pathetic," the man said. "This is going to be like a bad VR game."

Vivian had no time to process any of that. The Immortal pointed the rifle at Carina and fired without another word.

Carina's sister screamed. A line of bullets ricocheted off Carina, and the rat-a-tat-tat-tat-tat caused a fear reaction in Vivian that made her entire body quiver uncontrollably.

Her eyes focused on Bast as the echo reverberated in her ears. She didn't understand why at first. He was standing silently. The man had been shooting at Carina, not Bast. But Vivian watched in horror as he twisted his elbow up to examine his own arm. His jacket was torn. He touched exposed skin, then lifted his own fingers. Bright red blood dripped from his fingertips.

Vivian couldn't ever remember seeing Bast bleed. He was supposed to be like Mom. He was supposed to be untouchable. He was supposed to be the one person in the room shielding himself naturally from bullets sprayed out by a semiautomatic weapon.

"Bast!" Nate yelped, turning to grab Bast's arm and check things out himself.

"Surface wound," Bast said, as both boys stared dumbly at the wound.

And Vivian knew this was where it all had to end.

The man who had fired the first shots had apparently been thrown enough by the ridiculously strong defensive shield Carina made to pause momentarily. He opened his mouth to shout something. That was enough for Vivian. She could accept her own imminent demise, but she would *not* accept the demise of her brothers. No one else was going to touch them.

She stood up. Maybe Bast, who had done everything he could to keep her alive, was too tired now to save himself. Maybe Nate would never have had the talent. It didn't matter. Vivian had started out with more magic and skill than either of them.

She drew all that she had left together. The connections between everyone in the room brightened. Magic surged through her, and she understood why it was so at odds with the Immortality Virus. She had spent the last several weeks slowing down, little by little, as the Immortality Virus gained on her. Magic had kept her heart pumping, her blood flowing, her brain firing electrical charges through her nervous system despite the destructive virus inside her. It had fought the Immortality Virus hard on her behalf, and now she was channeling all that magic toward a different, single purpose. The Empire was going to have to try another way to destroy the last Cardinal line because Vivian was about to incinerate the Immortals threatening her brothers.

The Immortal with the gun aimed at Carina again. Then something Vivian hadn't counted on at all happened.

A hard scream cut through the room, followed by a burst of energy so strong and so hot that Vivian felt it before she saw anything. It was heat in its pure form.

Coming from Carina's sister.

The girl tended hot. Very hot. And she had absolutely no ability to control it whatsoever. Vivian wasn't sure why it hadn't occurred to her that there might be someone else in the room with someone to protect. She almost couldn't believe she'd missed it. That poor girl. She didn't know how to direct the heat. It was going to kill anything in its way in a second or so, and *everything* was in its way. Including the girl's own sister, if she couldn't shield herself. Probably Nate, too, if he wasn't strong enough to manipulate it.

Definitely Bast.

Vivian's plans changed. She connected to the energy without thinking because that was the only choice. The girl was powerful, but Vivian was precise. Bright energy exploded around them in a burst of fire so hot it glowed white before it became a beautiful blue-purple-red-orange. It was breath-taking—all that magic all at once. Like a firework, Vivian thought, as she used the last of her strength to make that energy flow smoothly around both her brothers.

They'd turned toward her, so she had a perfect view of them together in that final moment. She'd always thought her brothers looked a lot alike. Their facial features were so similarly delicate in a way that would have annoyed them both so much to know. Their hair was exactly the same color. They were both still too slender for her to think of them as men. Though maybe she'd never have been able to think of her little brothers as men.

What would things have been like if she'd lived past today? Would they have been friends with each other, or would some quarrel have driven them all apart? Would Bast have joined the Church as a clergy member? Would Nate have joined the Guard? Would either of them have fallen in love with someone? Would they have tolerated whoever she married? (Would that have been Brandon?) Would they all have lived long, happy lives?

At least they would have a chance.

As for her … the Immortality Virus was now the only thing left in her body, and it was going to take her.

They knew what she'd done. Shock washed both their faces, and she wished she could apologize. But there wasn't time because she'd only been able to protect them from the energy explosion. The whole house was on fire now. It was going to collapse around them any second.

She needed her brothers to run.

A burning rafter fell and crashed into the Guru's kitchen table. She willed them to move. They weren't far from the door. They'd have to climb over some dead Immortals, but they could make it.

Nate's face hardened, and she thought he understood what he had to do. Bast, however, only looked more scared and uncertain than he'd probably ever been. She wished it didn't have to be the last way she'd see him. She didn't have the strength to yell. She tried to smile a little, to give him some reason to run, and to her immense relief, Bast gave her one last look, turned and ran for the door.

She crumbled to the floor, unable to hold herself up anymore, and Nate, who she supposed must be tragically impulsive and idiotic after all, ran toward her. Out of the corner of her eye, Vivian saw Carina running her way as well. Of course. Carina's sister was lying on the floor nearby.

That mortal enemy line appeared again, and it was all such

a shame. There was a deep purple streak shooting through that line, and the red was such a beautiful, vibrant shade for a color of so much violence.

Vivian used the connection to find Nate one more time. It looked like he was trying to outrun a fiery storm of ash, clay, wood, and stone.

CHAPTER THIRTY-SIX
THE REUNION

Carina's world had become terribly, awfully, excruciatingly sluggish. Charred walls were crumbling around her. Ash was falling in her hair. The house was collapsing above her, and her legs were not moving her fast enough. She dove toward Miguela, making it in time to pull her sister flopping like a rag doll into her arms.

The queen was lying not too far away. A minute ago, she'd been alive. *Alive* alive. The way everyone should hope to live. It was a complete change from how ragged she'd looked lying passed out on the couch with the two princes kneeling by her. She'd risen to her feet like she was *strong, glowing* with energy—her cheeks rosy, her posture steady, and her face pure with determination—as a multicolored halo of energy exploded around Miguela.

While Carina was barely understanding what the heat of that energy explosion was doing swimming by her own shoulders, the queen was parting the explosion actively around her brothers like she was some kind of fire goddess. They survived while the Immortals at the door blackened to ash.

And now Queen Vivian was a waif crumpled on the floor.

Carina saw Prince Nathanial running, too, but if he was trying to get to his sister, he wasn't going to make it. No one was going to make it, despite Queen Vivian's sacrifice. Except Prince Bastian, who'd fled when he had the chance.

Carina wondered vaguely whether the rest of them would wake up in some kind of afterlife together. She tucked Miguela under her as a rafter careened toward them. She put one arm in the air and threw everything she had into a last-ditch effort at blocking that rafter from crushing her and her sister while the roof caved in on them.

And the rafter didn't hit her and Miguela. *Nothing* hit them. The house disintegrated while Carina sat with Miguela in a perfect bubble of safety, watching a shower of debris fall around them.

It was surreal. More surreal than Sister Agda picking Carina up in a truck on the side of the road or Max turning out to be an Immortal she couldn't trust. More unbelievable than Mrs. Hiller making her eat pie or Ivan saying thank you for a blanket or a wolf acting like it understood what she was saying. But this was still easier for Carina to understand than what had happened just a few minutes before. Seeing her own sister—the person she loved most in the entire universe—explode into a ball of human fire—feeling that she, too, was connected to the fire as it merely flowed around her: pure magical energy…

That was going to take some time to work through.

When all the noise stopped, and all the dust began to clear, Carina finally let her arm down, and she sat, shocked, in the middle of a house that was flattened and smoldering in a circle of rubble around her. Miguela was unconscious and feverishly hot, but she was breathing, and Carina couldn't see any visible injuries on her sister. She hugged her.

"Nice shield," a weak voice said.

Carina pulled Miguela around with her. The bubble had apparently protected the queen, too, and she was conscious, though her face was gray, and she was wheezing for breath. Carina wished there had been something she could have done for the queen. Her heart had ached with grief for the girl and her brothers earlier, and neither of the princes were even here now. Prince Bastian was long gone, and Prince Nathanial had been inside the house, but the whole place was leveled except for where she, Miguela, and Vivian were now. Carina couldn't see him anywhere, and he couldn't have survived that.

"You're … very talented," the queen said.

It was hard to see the queen as anything but a girl in a lot of trouble this way, but Carina knew what the queen had looked like directing Miguela's magic around the princes. She wondered what kind of power that must have required.

"I've never seen magic as strong as yours," she said.

The queen moved her head in a barely perceptible nod. "You should have seen me when I wasn't two minutes from dying." She struggled to take a deep breath. "But … I am."

She coughed, and splotches of blood appeared on her lips. Carina breathed in sharply at the sight, and the queen noticed her noticing.

"Immortality Virus," she said. "Nasty way to go when it catches up with you, and people like us aren't usually compatible with it. Bast was using magic to help me fight it."

"You should have told me," Carina said. "I would have helped. Even if I didn't like you, I'd have helped. I'll help now if you tell me what to do."

The queen tried to swallow. "You can't. Healing magic is

fueled by emotional energy. Has to come from the right place. Guilt is never enough."

Carina didn't think there was enough time to explain to the queen that guilt wouldn't have had anything to do with it, and she wasn't sure the queen could have understood anyway. She tried to wipe some of the blood from Queen Vivian's mouth, and the other girl just watched.

"Are you sure? I could try."

"*No.* Please. I … don't want to be Immortal," the queen said. "I don't want to be a monster. Though some people already think I am one." She coughed hard again, and when she was done she asked pitifully, "Do you think I'm a monster?"

More blood bubbled up from her lips.

"I don't think you're a monster." Carina adjusted Miguela in her arms and reached out to push a stray lock of hair from Queen Vivian's cheek. Her skin was warm to the touch as though the queen had a fever as well. Carina would have liked to help soothe away the heat. The other girl sighed like she felt relief as Carina stroked her cheek gently.

"Bast was right. Your sister tends hot, like me … and Nate, but you … you're cold like him. You're a natural healer." She nodded toward Miguela. "You should … try to help her. Not me. It's too late for me, and I don't want … but your sister …"

A few months ago, Carina wouldn't have thought of herself as cold at all. Now, as she sat with Miguela unconscious in her arms, next to a dying girl Carina thought she might have liked under some better circumstances, she hardly felt anything but frozen inside. What was she going to do now? After the queen was dead … where was she going to go?

"I don't know … exactly what he does …" Vivian

gestured weakly toward Miguela again. "But healing magic …
it's the right emotions with her. It won't hurt her. And you're
… powerful. You should try."

Carina hugged Miguela. Even if she had healing abilities,
she didn't know how to use them to help her sister.

"Where … where are they?"

Carina knew the queen was talking about her brothers, but
Prince Bastian still hadn't returned, and there was still no sign
of life coming from anyone lying in the rubble around them.

"They're not … monsters … either."

Carina nodded blankly.

"You don't believe me." Vivian's eyes were watering.
"Because you think … bad things … about my family. Which
… sort of makes sense … because you *must* be … but my
brothers were only trying to protect me. We're not … like the
Immortals. Immortals don't love anyone. They both loved
me. They're going to be … angry at me. They'll think I didn't
love them enough. Especially Bast."

Vivian's eyes were glazing over, and her face was getting
grayer. Carina wished again that she had known earlier that the
queen was dying. That would have changed so many things.

"I'm sorry," she whispered.

"Don't be. Even Bast couldn't do it, and he tried everything." The queen looked at Miguela again. "But for your
sister. She only needs a little help."

Carina looked down at Miguela. She was ashen, too, and
her breathing was shallow.

"She has … the same connection to you … as Bast had
… to me," Vivian said. "She needs you. Things move too fast
inside her. She can't contain them when she gets like this. Try
like you did with me. You don't have to heal anything. Just
soothe her. That's all."

Carina thought Vivian wasn't making much sense anymore, but the girl seemed desperate, so Carina smoothed her fingers over Miguela's forehead, hoping that Miguela would feel something that would bring her back from wherever she'd gone.

Miguela's breathing seemed to even out a bit.

Carina glanced at Vivian. "Was that me?"

Vivian smiled the tiniest smile ever. "I would have liked teaching you. You're a good student. Your sister used too much magic. When you do it, you go into hypothermia. When she does it, it's like overheating. But there's nothing else wrong with her. Just keep doing what you're doing. Stay with her until she stabilizes, and she'll be okay."

"Thank you." Carina ran her fingers over Miguela's forehead again, and Miguela seemed to relax more in her arms. "I think I would have liked learning from you." She considered that. "I *have* liked learning from you."

Vivian's eyes lost their focus. She closed them, and Carina thought that might have been the last for her. Then the queen revived suddenly and lifted her head, looking up like she'd seen something in the distance. Carina looked with her. She didn't see anything.

"It's him," the queen said softly. "He came back." Her graying lips turned up again. "I didn't think he would. I thought … because the other times I was never awake after … maybe I'd messed things up for good this time."

"Who came back?" Carina asked.

Vivian ignored her and continued peering into the distance.

"Who's coming, Queen Vivian?" Carina tried again, smoothing her fingers over Vivian's face one more time. At that, Vivian reached abruptly for her hand. She grasped it tight and made eye contact with Carina.

"Please. Tell Bast there was nothing else he could do. And if he needs to know it … I always loved him most. And Nate … the connection … it might not tell the future. Give him a second chance. Not to be friends. But … he can't have more enemies. Promise me."

Carina didn't have the heart to tell her Prince Bastian had fled and Prince Nathanial had already perished, so she squeezed Vivian's hand and said, "I promise."

Vivian's eyelids closed shut. "Eighteen years and almost five weeks. It was … a longer sentence than I thought I'd have."

She breathed out and her grip on Carina's hand went slack. Carina's own throat tightened. She set the queen's hands over her body gently and held Miguela to her closer. Her sister's breathing was steadier now, but she was still unconscious. "Miguela," she whispered. "Please come back."

It wasn't safe here. She didn't know where Max and his uncle had gone, or whether there were any Immortals left alive anywhere nearby. Prince Nathanial had thrown her back hard enough earlier that Carina thought she might have cracked a few ribs herself. And she was tired. So tired. Tired of running and tired of being afraid and tired of not understanding anything.

She looked around and tried to see whatever it was Queen Vivian thought she'd seen. There was nothing out there, though, and somehow that was even more terrifying than if there had been more Immortals coming for them. Carina hoped Sister Agda was looking for her and Miguela, but for now, they were up here on this mountain, all by themselves, and probably in a lot of danger, and …

"There she is! There they *both* are!"

A rush of noise seemed to come out of nowhere along

with the sound of a man yelling, and Carina thought she heard horses.

Why was someone always coming for her? Why was her world so terrifying? And what was she going to do? She was sitting next to the dead queen with her unconscious sister in her lap. There was a slew of fallen Immortals around her, and somewhere in the ruins at least one of the princes was dead. She didn't want to join him.

"Are you sure it's both of them?"

Carina was afraid, but she wasn't going to have gotten her sister back only to let something happen to her again. With a surge of adrenaline, she lifted a tornado of debris into the air and held it around her and Miguela, ready to pummel whoever was there.

"It IS her!" a voice shouted, and then there were a lot of voices, saying things like: "We've found them!" and "It *is* them!" and "Look at that!"

Then finally, someone yelled: "Everybody back off! She doesn't know who we are!"

Carina held the debris, and when everything quieted, she let it back down around her slowly and discovered that she was being watched very curiously by a group of soldiers in uniforms she didn't recognize. They were on horses, but one of the soldiers in the front dismounted and gestured for the rest to do the same. He was dressed a little different from the others, so maybe he was a different rank.

He walked carefully toward her, bowed respectfully, and then said, "Princess."

"Princess?" Carina said. "Vivian was the *queen*. And she's …" She looked at Queen Vivian's dead body. "She's passed away."

The soldier's eyes shined. He seemed friendly. And

Mortal. Though you never knew these things for sure.

"Are you Carina Garcia from Novi Dupree in the Red Ridge Mountains?" he asked.

"Yes," she answered. "How do you know that? What do you want from me?"

He smiled. "We've been looking for you for months. Ever since we got word there was a possibility you were alive. Your father will be beside himself."

"My *father*?"

"King Reginald," the soldier said. "Of North Kepler. We're the Northern Militia, Princess Carina, and it is our honor to escort you and Princess Miguela home."

EPILOGUE
THE PRINCES OF SOUTH KEPLER

Prince Bastian's lungs burned from breathing in too much cold air, his eyes stung from the wet tears freezing below his eyelids, and numbness was spreading from his toes up past his knees. He tripped on something and fell headlong on an unmarked trail, where he lay for several minutes, hating the chill in his blood and praying to a God that hated him that he would somehow manage to die.

Bast.

It was dusk, the shadows crossing over were swallowing him whole, and there was nothing here for him. Nothing but incompetent, sinful, reckless, magicless humans. Kepler was a hell crafted for his own personal misery. There was not a soul he could trust. Not a soul who would want him alive, except for their own selfish needs.

The kingdom, of course, was doomed without him. But why shouldn't he let the kingdom suffer? What had South Kepler done for him? What had anyone done for him?

The dampness of the ground was seeping up through

his clothes. Maybe he really could allow himself to freeze to death. Maybe if he just let his subconscious take over ... lulling him to sleep with memories of times when he hadn't been so alone.

Vivian. *Why* had she done it? *Why* hadn't she let him die with her? Didn't she know everyone else had already left him? Didn't she know that without her, death was a better option?

Bast. Get up.

Though he hadn't thought so when she'd needed him at the very last, had he? Stupid Nate had run to his death, probably with some moronic idea that he could save Vivian—doing what? If anyone could have produced the defensive shield Vivian needed right then, it would have been *him*, not Nate—and in the meanwhile, Bast had run for his own life. Chosen himself over everyone. Not his brother, his blood. Not his sister, the only one he loved.

Get up. Now.

He closed his eyes, allowed a layer of frost to cover him, and waited. Surely this was what he deserved? What reason could God possibly have had to allow him to make such a terrible call? There was no way this was God's will. He was the one who had run. He was the one who had saved himself. If this had been God's doing, then God would have notified him by now. Some *reason* for his survival would have made itself apparent ...

"Prince Bastian?"

Someone was running toward him.

"Your Highness? Your Highness! Prince Bastian!"

Someone had reached him. Was kneeling by him. Had rolled him over onto his side. Was pulling him up. Was looking at his face like Bast himself was the harbinger of the apocalypse.

"What happened? Where's Vivian? Where's Nate?"

Bast. Don't do this.

The   someone   shook   him   by   the   shoulders.
"Where's Vivian?!"

And all at once, the frost cleared from Bast's eyes as he realized what had happened and who was really at fault. The face of the man in front of him was twisted into a disgusting expression of false grief. The coward who had used his sister was asking him over and over where she was.

Where *was* she? She was dead on a mountain with a cadre of Immortals who had somehow found them despite the decoys *this* man said they should send out and the unlikely route this man had led them on, tracking a myth that no one believed in.

"Prince Bastian. Where. Is. Queen. Vivian?"

Bast brushed the man's hands roughly away.

"Thurlow," he said coldly. "Don't touch me. And don't pretend you don't know."

"Know *what?*" the sniveling traitor said.

Bast ...

"Queen Vivian is dead."

Nate woke up coughing in the dark. This is not what he thought death would be like. All his sources said death should involve white lights and choirs of angels, or, if, as he suspected, God didn't like him enough to want him in heaven, then it would involve fire, brimstone, and hopefully an absurd amount of alcohol. A pit of fiery drunken despair. Not a mouthful of dirty phlegm and the realization that if this was not heaven and not hell, then he was still alive, and, probably, buried under that creepy old Immortal's house.

Eww. That meant he was not alone. As he recalled, Icy had been hurtling in approximately the same direction he'd been before the whole frickin' house had collapsed, and she was annoyingly good, but she wasn't a Cardinal, so chances are she didn't have quite the magic necessary to prevent a house from crushing her and her apparently *incredibly* powerful sister. Which meant they were both dead somewhere near where he was, along with Vivian.

Viv.

Oh, God.

Vivian was dead.

She'd been the only member of his immediate family who actually liked him—even if she obviously cared more about Bast—and she was dead. His sister was dead.

Shit. Bast was going to be a wreck. He was going to blame himself. He was going to blame Vivian. He was going to blame *everyone*. He'd probably even come up with a reason to blame Nate, once he figured out Nate wasn't dead. Especially when he realized that Nate not being dead meant that Bast was also not the new heir to the throne.

In fact, Nate's survival was going to be quite the nasty shock for Bast. There was no way Bast would believe that Nate could have produced a defensive telekinetic shield at a moment when *he*, the smart one, had been too weak to do it himself.

Yeah. That story wasn't going to fly. Nate was going to have to come up with some other way to explain his non-death to Bast. Which made it a good thing that Nate was such a damn good liar.

Nate was used to being underestimated, and he sort of liked it that way. Fewer expectations. Less judgment. Better chance that Bast wouldn't decide to kill him one day. But Bast would never think Nate was equipped to be the new king, and Nate really needed Bast on his side because now …

Oh.

Oh, ox shit.

That was …

That was bad.

Nate was next in line to be king of South Kepler.

Maybe this was hell. Maybe if he wanted to die, he could just … like … not try to get himself out from underneath this shell of a house. He wasn't sure how long it had been since the explosion had happened. Might have been a while ago, based on how stiff and weak he felt. Minutes? Possibly hours? It wouldn't be that hard to just stay here and die of dehydration or something.

Nate lay for a second or so considering the possibility.

But nah. He didn't really have the attention span to wait long enough to die.

"Nate? Nate?!"

That settled it. He was going to have to haul his ass out of this place, say goodbye to Vivian, find Pepper, and hit the road. They could figure out what to do about the whole "king" thing later.

"Nate!!! Stop playing around. We have to go."

Nate had to cough several times to clear his throat. "Hang on, Franklin," he said when he could finally talk again. "I'm coming."

TO BE CONTINUED.

THE KEPLER DECLARATION OF MORTAL COMMITMENTS

We, the Mortal humans of the planet of Kepler, in order to pursue a more perfect and harmonious world, do hereby commit:

1. To respect life above all.
2. To be stewards of Kepler's land and resources.
3. To safeguard the aboriginal Keplerians.
4. To facilitate conflict peaceably when possible.
5. To shun the use of weapons of extreme violence, including firearms.
6. To uphold the sovereignty of nations.
7. To seek the highest standard of living for all humans on Kepler.
8. To prohibit slavery and trafficking of any human or aboriginal Keplerian.
9. To use and develop technology responsibly and purposefully.
10. To value every human as equal to another.

THERE'S MORE TO LEARN AT THE LIBRARY!
THE JULES VERNE PUBLIC LIBRARY OF MORTAL KEPLER
HTTPS://MORTALHERITANCE.COM/LIBRARY

ACKNOWLEDGEMENTS

This book was never meant to be nearly four-hundred pages of anything serious. It was meant to be two-hundred and fifty pages of experimental fun. See, I'd been telling myself stories forever, but for years, I was never able to get any of those stories down on paper in any truly finished form. When I did finally manage to finish a story, it wasn't even mine. It was fanfiction. Based on a cartoon.

P.S. Fanfiction is amazing.

However, I don't have any creative credentials beyond the School of Fanfiction. Arguably, I have the opposite: a law degree from Harvard, which is not a place where one learns to be as flawed and vulnerable as one needs to write a novel. You know what happens when you start out your novel trying to write a perfect first chapter? You never finish the book.

So, this was supposed to be a low-stakes project about characters who would make me happy, living in a world that would fascinate me, doing things I think are hilarious, romantic, and brave. My goal was to finish it. That's pretty much it.

I think maybe there's some magic in writing that way, though. If you got this far, I hope you saw it yourself. For me, at least, there was a lot of joy in this project. It made the characters breathe for me, and now a project I thought was going to be "just for fun," has a whole world of its own. Crazy how that happens.

In any case, the other thing I need to acknowledge is that while I am not, and may never be, a traditionally published author, I still had a lot of help getting this thing out. Turns out that when you self-publish fiction under your own publishing house, you get to take on far more than just the writing. There's also finding beta readers, ARC readers, reviewers, editors, cover designers, and more.

If I listed everyone who encouraged me to get this book written, this section would be longer than any of the chapters in the book. I had friends, family, church family (hi Kirkwood!), and neighbors (mostly from the amazing Rockford Commons Book Club) chug through some—and sometimes even *all*—of this book in very early stages. Then later I had amazing supporters who read *Sassafras and the Queen* and encouraged me to find a way to give the series wings. If you were one of those people, thank you so much.

Special thanks to Alsu Kemp, for being the first reader in my target audience to encourage me to keep writing this. Jane Jesser, Neill Blake, Carol Vasher, and Tina Howell: thank you, thank you, thank you for being the readers who got through the manuscript fast and spent significant time providing feedback. That made a huge difference. And Crystal Lovell, you are the only person I would trust to give me objective feedback about what I would have liked in my own book if I hadn't written it. So, thank you for getting through that slow stretch and giving me encouraging (honest) feedback!

That memory Carina has of her mom totally being a ninja warrior with a garden rake instead of a sword was made possible by Sirona and Dante from the Kingdom of Meridies. Sirona and Dante lead sword practicing lessons in the park for the Society for Creative Anachronism. They graciously allowed me to attend a few meetings, where they helped me figure out how swords work and choreographed that scene for me. Sirona and Dante, you two are awesome.

To Alicia Hollenbeck: you are the best critique partner ever. This book would have been choppy, confusing, and boring without you, and I don't know what I would have done without someone to go through this indie publishing journey with me.

To Steven James, who critiqued my first fifty pages back in 2017 at a stellar Novel Writing Intensive workshop: before your workshop, I thought of my writing as a somewhat embarrassing hobby that I probably wasn't much good at anyway. You saw me as a writer, and it was the coolest reveal I'd ever experienced. I don't think there is a way to explain why and how much that mattered. (But if you are reading this book and you are also a writer, you need to attend Steven James and Robert Dugoni's Novel Writing Intensive. www.novelwritingintensive.com)

To my parents, Brenda and Tom Vasher: I don't know how many hours you guys spent reading and re-reading everything, listening to me talk about my characters and plot, brainstorming with me, and then later encouraging me to get this thing out to the public, but I know those hours were way beyond the call of duty. I love you guys like crazy. Thank you for believing in me.

To my husband, Malcolm: I'm sorry for ditching the chapter I made you listen to fifty times. You should probably get a medal for that, amongst other things related to this book. You made this whole thing possible. But since there is no such medal, would my eternal love and affection do instead?

I designed the illustrations inside the book, as well as Carina's sassafras icon and Vivian's crown icon, using Affinity Designer, Rise of Kingdom font made by vladimirnikolic, and free vectors designed by Freepik. The earth, reference book, bishop, and knight icons were designed by Freepik.

Jenny at Seedings Design (www.seedlingsonline.com) designed my cover and title pages. She took wisps of ideas from my head and somehow made an awesome cover out of those. Her portfolio is amazing, and she is in demand for a reason.

Graham at A Fading Street Publishing Services (www.fadingstreet.com) was my copy editor. He was efficient and easy to work with, and he tolerated many more parentheses than he was comfortable with. I highly recommend him!

Finally, every time I had decided I should throw my computer out the window and give up, I got a favorite or an online review from someone who'd seen my fanfiction. I crave those like Carina craves sassafras. It's what keeps me going. So, if you found me here because you know me from fanfiction.net, you are incredibly dear to me. Thank you.

~Sandra L. Vasher

SANDRA L. VASHER

THE IMMORTAL MISTAKES BOOKS

STELLA ROSE GOLD FOR ETERNITY
LIZZY DUPREE AND THE THOUSAND-YEAR CRUSH
MILA HILDEBRAND IS FOREVER NOT YOURS

ABOUT THE AUTHOR

Sandra L. Vasher is an indie writer, recovering lawyer, dreamer, consultant, blogger, serial entrepreneur, and mommy of very spoiled dog. She enjoys long drives in fall weather, do-it-yourself projects, animated movies and cartoons, fanfiction, red wine, traveling everywhere, and baking sweet and savory treats. She can often be found trying not to hunch over her computer at her favorite coffee shops in Raleigh, North Carolina. Follow her online at sandyvasher.com.